THE AUTISM WAR

T0058198

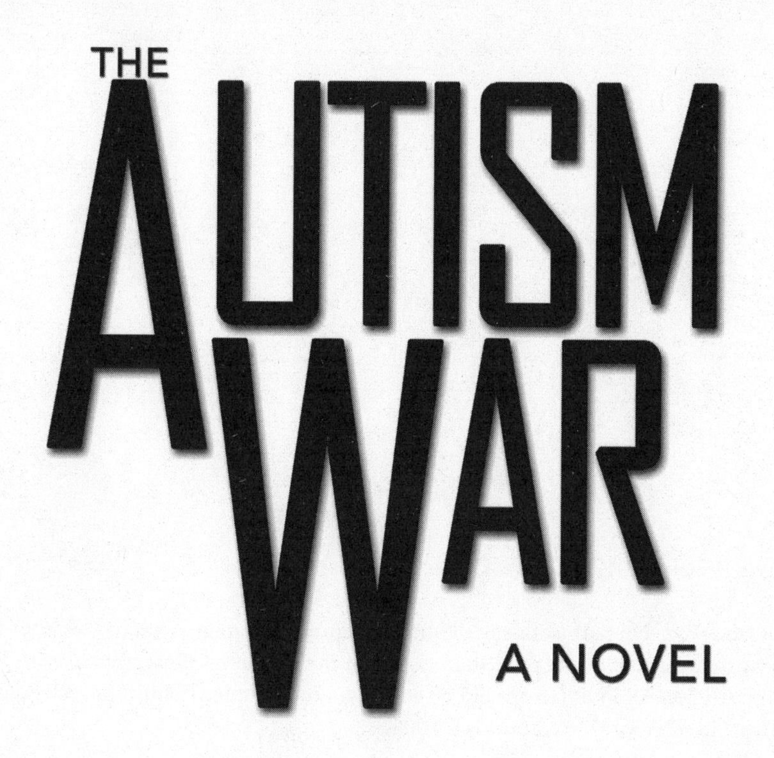

LOUIS CONTE

Skyhorse Publishing

Copyright © 2014, 2017 by Louis Conte

All rights reserved. No part of this book may be reproduced in any manner without the express written consent of the publisher, except in the case of brief excerpts in critical reviews or articles. All inquiries should be addressed to Skyhorse Publishing, 307 West 36th Street, 11th Floor, New York, NY 10018.

Skyhorse Publishing books may be purchased in bulk at special discounts for sales promotion, corporate gifts, fund-raising, or educational purposes. Special editions can also be created to specifications. For details, contact the Special Sales Department, Skyhorse Publishing, 307 West 36th Street, 11th Floor, New York, NY 10018 or info@skyhorsepublishing.com.

Skyhorse® and Skyhorse Publishing® are registered trademarks of Skyhorse Publishing, Inc.®, a Delaware corporation.

Visit our website at www.skyhorsepublishing.com.

10 9 8 7 6 5 4 3 2 1

Library of Congress Cataloging-in-Publication Data is available on file.

Cover design by Erin Seaward-Hiatt

Print ISBN: 978-1-5107-1786-2
Ebook ISBN: 978-1-62873-928-2

Printed in the United States of America

With love for Andrea, Thomas, Sam, and Louie

Dramatis Personae

Zviad Kokochashvili—Scientist who defected from the Soviet Union
Anya Kokochashvili—Zviad's wife
Timothy Lonnegan—Police chief, Winston-on-Hudson Police Department
Anthony Colletti—Detective, Winston-on-Hudson Police Department, father of a boy with autism
Glen Forceski—Detective, Colletti's partner, Winston-on-Hudson Police Department, father of a boy with autism
Robert Randazzo—Police officer, Winston-on-Hudson Police Department
Veronica Fournier—Mother of two boys with autism
Anne Colletti—Anthony Colletti's wife
Akinori Saito—Sensei in the art of jujitsu
Dr. Robert Bangston—Director of the Division of Vaccine Injury Compensation
Dr. Phillip Snyder—Vaccine industry spokesman
Dr. Jennifer Kesslinger—Director of the Centers for Disease Control
E. Gordon Calthorpe—Public relations director for The Rollins Group
Lance Reed—Freelance English journalist
Russell Sampson—United States senator
Diana Sampson—Russell Sampson's wife
Parker Smithson—United States senator

Carl Mantkewicz—Chief special master of the National Vaccine Injury Compensation Program
Laura Melendez—Attorney, mother of a child with autism
Herb Newman—Attorney, father of a child with autism
Jack McLeod—Autism activist, father of a child with autism
Maria Contessa-Guevera—Research scholar, attorney, mother of a child with autism
Dr. Bryce Ramsey—English gastroenterologist
Wilson Garrison—Attorney
Herman Tyler—Civil rights attorney and college professor
Susan Miller—Law student with a brother with autism
Sara Donovan—Investigative journalist at SNN
Seth Millman—Senior news producer at SNN
Dr. Randall Cook—SNN medical correspondent
Clyde King—Investigative journalist for the *Era of Autism*
Dr. Ronald Washington—Pediatrician
Raphael Molea—Detective
Angie Riley—Detective
John Morris—Detective (retired)
Eddie Camacho—Supervising probation officer
Dr. Yuri Leonodovich—Retired Russian public health minister

Few men are willing to brave the disapproval of their peers, the censure of their colleagues, the wrath of their society. Moral courage is a rarer commodity than bravery in battle or great intelligence. Yet it is the one essential, vital quality for those who seek to change a world that yields most painfully to change.

—Robert F. Kennedy

THE AUTISM WAR

PROLOGUE

ISTANBUL, TURKEY, 1986

"Anya, tell Georgi to come inside."

Zvi Kokochashvili and his wife, Anya, entered the Hagia Sofia through the main entrance. Although at the height of Istanbul's tourist season, the ancient Byzantine church was empty, dark, and imposing.

Anya walked back out into the sunlight and pulled her five-year-old son inside. "There is nothing to be afraid of Georgi," she said in Georgian. But Anya, ever protective of her son, was lying. There was much to fear.

"Talk to him in English. Georgi must learn English." Zvi's hazel eyes darted around the vast expanse. A brilliant scientist, he was well known in research circles for his ability to analyze complicated data and see patterns when no one else could. Although Zvi was not a risk taker, he was now taking an enormous gamble.

The family stood together, nervously half-looking at the paintings on the ceiling and the magnificent tile frescoes on the floor. Zvi felt trapped in the cathedral. Was he also trapped by the KGB?

"Where is he?" Anya asked urgently.

"He will come. We must not be afraid."

But they were, with the fear that people fleeing oppression feel that others do not understand. Zviad Kokochashvili was risking his life and the lives of his family to get away from Soviet oppression. To get away from the bioweapons research. To get away from the escorts who accompanied him to international conferences. To get away from the army of unknown editors who censored his articles. To get away from the army of apparatchiks who directed him to study what the state wanted studied. To get away from the State that had ravaged his homeland for the "greater good."

The American emerged from the shadows of an alcove. "Welcome to the Church of Holy Wisdom, Dr. Kokochashvili. I am Mr. Vincent." The tall man wore a gray suit and a comforting smile. "I trust that the trip through the Kaçkars was scenic?"

"It was beautiful. The mountains were beautiful, almost as pretty as Sakartvelebi is."

"I have your new papers. It is all here, you, your wife, and your son. Your flight is set."

"You don't look like, eh, what's the name? James Bond." Zvi forced a smile.

"He was English. I'm from New Jersey . . . We know that you were not followed. We have a car." Vincent leaned into Zvi and whispered, "How are your wife and son doing?"

"They are terrified. And my wife knows that she will never see her family or our home again."

"Many people came to America knowing that as well. It is difficult, but years from now you will see that you have brought your family to freedom."

"I am not sure that I really understand freedom. I have never known it."

The group left the church and walked down to the street. A car pulled up and everyone got in. The Black Sea sparkled in the distance.

It took many years before Zviad Kokochashvili understood that the Americans had lied to him.

His family now lived in a lovely suburb of Atlanta, and his son and daughters who were born in America were happy, young Americans. Georgi was studying to become a doctor. Zvi had a job at the FDA monitoring safety trials on new drugs. His wife could now study literature without it having to be Soviet literature. The family was free to travel without anyone looking over their shoulders or checking their papers.

They had everything that they could ever want, but Zvi had come to learn that America was not really free. It wasn't that the government was omnipresent as in the old Soviet Union. The real truth about what had happened to America was much more insidious. Americans did not see what Zvi saw because they were busy being Americans. And it filled him with regret.

CHAPTER 1

WINSTON-ON-HUDSON, JANUARY 2011

Detectives Tony Colletti and Glen Forceski were trying to stay warm in their unmarked car. It was just past dawn and the men were watching the home of a businessman named Bryan Bell, waiting for him to stroll out of his condo. Once Bell got to his BMW, they would arrest him and take him to Winston Town Court where his bail would be set at exactly the amount of money that he owed on all of his traffic infractions.

"Lights on in the kitchen," Tony said while downing a little coffee.

"Go figure this guy," Forceski responded. "He pulls down six figures in a nice Pine Plains office and he refuses to pay his speeding tickets."

"Looks like we will be playing cuff the yuppie in a few minutes," Tony said.

The two officers had worked together for years. Colletti was a dark-haired man of medium build with penetrating, dark eyes. He didn't really exude "cop," but he had trained for years in the martial arts, and could be intimidating if he had to. He had a well-earned reputation for being a dogged investigator with expert interviewing skills. Chief Lonnegan always said that Colletti could get people to talk just by looking at them in the eye.

Forceski, tall, ruddy with blond hair, could be downright scary—the bad cop to Colletti's good cop. Even if criminals knew the old formula, the old formula still worked. While Winston was not a tough town, it had its share of problems. Those in town who lived on the edge of the law knew these two men and that you shouldn't make a scene if they came to bring you in.

The radio clicked—it was Sergeant Chavez. "Tony, guess what?"

"What?"

"The chief is bringing Dazz in for an ass-tightening."

Tony chuckled. "If anyone needs one, it's Randazzo."

"Freakin' guy," said Forceski still looking at the condo.

"We're waiting out in the cold for public enemy number one. How goes the rest of the empire?"

"All quiet on the western front," said Chavez clicking off.

Tony turned to Forceski, suddenly serious. "Glen, guess what? The chief's granddaughter just got an autism diagnosis. Keep it to yourself."

Forceski shook his head. "What are we at? Eight kids with the diagnosis?"

"I think ten. But who's counting." Tony shook his head. "I saw the kid at the picnic. It was obvious six months ago. She couldn't talk. Couldn't look you in the eye. Then I saw her flapping her hands by the kiddies' pool watching the water fall."

Forceski looked away from the condo. "I don't know what we are going to do, Tony. My guy is fourteen and just about my size. My wife can barely deal with him now."

"The car lights just went on," Tony said. "The guy can afford a remote car starter but won't pay his tickets. Let's get ready to do the deed."

Chief Timothy Lonnegan looked out his office window at the ice floes, bobbing in the Hudson River. It was the third week of frigid weather, and the burly chief was already sick of winter. So was everyone else. There was a foot of snow on the ground, and more was on the way tomorrow. Just keeping the roads clear was beginning to be a problem. And when you live in an affluent suburb of New York City, people expect the roads to be cleared. If they are not, they call the police and complain.

That is the way it is in deep, dark suburbia.

Lonnegan tugged at his walrus moustache, then walked out of his office and barked at his desk sergeant. "Chavez, how we doing?"

"Nothing major. Fender-bender on Route 9. Colletti and Forceski are sitting on that warrant. You're gonna go old school on Randazzo, aren't you?"

"You got a problem with that?"

"No sir."

Lonnegan glanced at the daybook. "Call him in."

The chief had worked his way up the ranks in what used to be a blue-collar town. He was in year twenty-eight and planned to retire soon and travel with his wife for a while.

Lonnegan was a mixture of old-school beat cop, professional police administrator, and local politician. The Winston-on-Hudson Town Board was like a reality television show full of dysfunctional egomaniacs who argued over everything but still got re-elected. No one handled them better than Chief Lonnegan.

But this time, the problem came from his shop. The problem was the good-looking and charming young officer, Bobby Randazzo. He was a "legacy hire"—retired Captain Vinny Randazzo's kid. The chief now deeply regretted hiring him. Randazzo decided it was his divine right to have sex with the town supervisor's twenty-year-old daughter. Colletti told him to break off the relationship. And Randazzo had, but only for a while. But now word had come to him from a board member that Dazzling Bobby Randazzo was at it again.

It was time for an old-fashioned ass-tightening. What was the kid thinking? Lonnegan asked himself. A good job and a pretty wife with a child on the way. But that wasn't good enough. Lonnegan wondered how Randazzo would handle adversities in life. What if he suddenly had a child with special needs like so many of his other officers had? Winston-on-Hudson PD had seventy-six sworn officers. Nine of them had children who had autism.

And now, it was ten.

The chief had just heard the bad news about his third granddaughter. His beautiful, red-haired, Emily Anne.

Lonnegan found himself walking through the lockup and staring at the empty cells.

John Fournier walked in a circle, flapping his hands and saying "Whooo . . . whooo." When his mother tried to redirect John to another behavior, he started punching himself in the head, then banging his head against the wall, leaving holes in the Sheetrock.

John had severe autism and was really having a tough time lately.

Veronica Fournier was at her wit's end. She had been up with her sixteen-year-old son for most of the night.

Veronica's husband was away on business, and her oldest son was away in college. She was alone, frustrated, and exhausted. Veronica had once been a legal assistant at a well-established Castleton County law firm, but her career had to take a backseat to raising her children. Veronica now worked when she could and tried to do her best for her sons with autism.

The bus that was supposed to take John and his younger brother Evan to their special school program didn't show. The school had closed when a pipe broke in the cold, flooding the building. The boys would be home today and Veronica would not have any help.

John was now back in his room, replaying the same scenes of a Harry Potter DVD over and over again. He had eaten some cornflakes for breakfast, and he seemed less agitated. Evan was in his room playing with his puzzles.

Veronica went downstairs to call the new psychiatrist in town for a prescription for something, anything that could help John. The receptionist put her on hold.

Chavez hailed Bobby Randazzo on the radio. "Randazzo, report to headquarters. The chief wants you."

"Copy that."

"Now what?" Randazzo thought to himself. The older guys were always busting his nuts. Every time he turned his head, he noticed Colletti, the chief, or Chavez shaking their heads at him. Maybe he should go back to college and try something else.

Veronica Fournier couldn't help it. She was so exhausted that she fell asleep on the couch while on hold with the psychiatrist's office.

A few minutes later, John came down the stairs and went into the kitchen. He opened the pantry and took out some cornflakes. He noticed that the house keys were sitting on the counter by the back door. He took the keys and opened the top lock.

The Fourniers had internally keyed locks on all the doors because John was a wanderer. Like many children with autism, John would simply walk out of his home and wander away. His parents had no idea that he had figured out which key to use.

John loved being outside. Being in the woods calmed him down and he loved the old town reservoir where his dad would take him and his brothers swimming.

Wearing nothing more than pajamas and sneakers, John quietly walked out his back door across the snow-covered lawn and into the woods toward the reservoir.

CHAPTER 2

Randazzo walked into headquarters and waved to Chavez to buzz him in. "What's up?"

"You got me," said Chavez with an odd smile. "Chief, Randazzo's here."

"Send him down."

"It's lecture time." Randazzo thought to himself as the chief ushered him in and closed the door.

Randazzo stood at attention in his usual lackadaisical way. "Sir, you wanted to see me?"

Randazzo never saw it coming. The chief landed a right hook into his jaw. Randazzo staggered and fell to the floor holding the side of his face. "What the . . ."

"Sit up! You listening now?"

"What . . . what the . . ."

"Hey, Randazzo, you don't shit where you eat!"

"Huh?"

"Don't give me that," Lonnegan said through his clenched teeth. "You know exactly what I am talking about. Colletti talked to you, but you didn't listen. So now I talked to you."

As Bryan Bell strolled down his walkway to his car in his driveway, he saw Colletti and Forceski walking toward him. He knew who they were and didn't think anything unusual about their presence. He put his briefcase on the roof of his car as he opened his car door.

"Hey, guys. PBA donation time?"

Colletti offered his right hand. "How'd you guess?"

"My checkbook is in my briefcase," he said. As Bell reached out to shake Colletti's hand the cop's left hand popped a handcuff on him. Bell was turned around and cuffed, hands behind his back, before he knew what happened. "Hey? Hey!"

"You gotta pay some fines in court, Mr. Bell." Tony said.

"Don't worry," said Forceski, "I got your briefcase."

They placed the stunned man in the patrol car's backseat, "We didn't want to arrest you in front of your family," Tony said smiling. "You'll be out quick enough. But you're supposed to pay your tickets in this town."

"Sure. Okay. But why the cuffs?"

"You blew off a court appearance. Judge Lange got the red ass. You got a warrant," said Forceski. "You're lucky that we didn't take you in front of your family."

"But I have a client coming. I do have a real job, you know."

Chavez heard the commotion down in the chief's office and tried not to laugh out loud.

Then the call came in. A woman was so upset she could hardly get the words out. "My son John escaped . . . he escaped . . . he wanders . . ."

"Please slow down. Tell me your name."

"Fournier. My son John has autism. He can't talk. Can't communicate. He wanders. He walked out of the house. I was exhausted."

Chavez popped open the Kid Find drawer. He had the address and phone number on the computer screen. "Is it Johnny or Evan?" he asked.

"It's Johnny. He left out the back door. I can see tracks in the snow heading toward the woods."

Chavez hit the call button, "Chief, we got a kid with autism wandering out into Wampus Park. I'm deploying units."

"Copy that. Coming now."

This was a situation that Winston police understood well. The department had a program, Kid Find, in place to deal with this kind of situation.

The chief grabbed his jacket and turned to Randazzo. "Get up! You're driving me. Let's go."

Randazzo followed, still rubbing his jaw.

Colletti and Forceski were rolling back into town when the call came in. Forceski hit the lights and sirens and began accelerating. "Shouldn't you drop me off first?" said Bell from the backseat.

"Shut up," Tony said. "Glen, I know the Fournier family pretty well. They have two. Johnny is the wanderer. Last summer he went swimming at the old reservoir. His father got to him before he got in too deep. Damn near drowned."

"If that's what he's doing, then we could be looking at an ice rescue." He called headquarters. "Chavez, get the fire department out to the reservoir. We could be looking at a kid under the ice."

"Copy that," said Chavez over the radio. "I don't know if the highway department plowed the access road."

"That's why firemen wear boots, Chavez," Forceski said loudly. "Tell them to get there!"

The car flew around the ice-covered suburban streets. Brian Bell was getting nervous. "Hey guys. I am still back here. Be careful will ya?!"

They pulled up in front of the Fournier residence. Forceski popped the trunk. "Damn it! No rope."

Veronica Fournier came running out, crying hysterically, and pointing toward the woods in the back of the house. "We're going," said Colletti. Both men ran through the deep snow. Their jackets, ties, and dress shoes were for court and not a winter rescue.

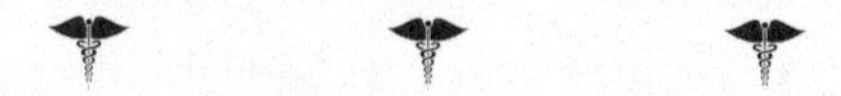

John never really felt the cold. What confused him was that the water in the lake seemed to be covered in snow. He looked for the trees he knew so well. Even without leaves, he knew the tree line and he followed it out to where there should be water. John looked up at the brilliant blue sky and felt the calm that being in the woods gave him.

Then the ice gave way, and John fell under the water. He gasped and swallowed freezing water as he sank, watching the blue sky disappear.

Tony and Glen slogged through the deep snow as best they could. Sweating and freezing, they picked up a trail of sorts that made the going a little easier. Suddenly they came to a clearing at the edge of the reservoir.

There were footprints leaving the shoreline and an opening in the ice, fifty feet from the shore.

"Shit. Tony, we have to go in."

"You can't do that. The heart thing rules you out. I gotta do this. Get a tree branch, something long that I can grab onto after I come up."

"When you hit the water, keep your head out so you don't gasp and suck down freezing water. You have to let your body sort of adapt. Otherwise, I'll have to go in after you, and then I'll be really pissed."

Tony removed his jacket and shoes. The temperature was in the low twenties, so the water would be just above freezing. This was going to be awful. As he got closer to the opening in the ice, he went down on his belly and pushed himself farther onto the lake.

The cold water hit like an explosion. Tony gasped and yelled out. Every instinct in his body told him to get out, but he willed himself to stay in the freezing water. He turned to see Forceski sliding toward him pushing a long tree branch. He was bleeding from a cut on his forehead.

"What the hell happened to you?"

"Caught a tree branch in the head. Don't worry about it. How are you?"

"Freezing! The water is deep. I can't feel the bottom."

Forceski got the branch as close to the opening as he dared. Three people in freezing water would only make everything worse. "Talk to me, Tony. How you gonna play this?"

"I have to go under."

"No, you don't. I hear sirens. Help is coming."

Tony pushed himself under the ice. More shock hit him. He wasn't sure that he could move his arms and legs. He felt so heavy—not slow—but a weird sort of heaviness.

The water was clear enough to see bubbles silently running along the ceiling of the ice. Tony looked down. Nothing. Where was the kid? He needed air. He gasped as he hit the surface. The air made him feel even colder.

Tony surfaced. "Ah! This sucks! I can't see the kid yet."

"Tony! Get out. You tried. Come on!"

"No way, Bro." Tony went back under the ice. A slight current to his left was taking bubbles under the ice. He followed the bubbles and looked down.

Nothing.

It was getting eerily dark away from the hole in the ice. Tony looked down again and saw a hand swaying slowly in the current. It was the kid! He grabbed the arm and pulled the boy toward him. Johnny's eyes were open but lifeless. Tony turned and tried to locate the opening in the ice. He lost the opening! Fighting dread and panic, Tony turned himself around pulling the boy with him. Then he saw the opening and swam as hard as he could. He burst through the surface gasping.

"Gl-Glen! I g-got him!"

"Thank God!" Then to Glen's horror, Colletti disappeared back under the water.

"Tony!"

Suddenly the boy heaved up out of the water and landed sprawling out on the ice. Colletti surfaced behind him and pushed the boy away from the opening with the last of his strength. Forceski grabbed the boy's shirt and pulled him slowly toward him. "We got you, Johnny. We're taking you home."

They made slow progress toward the shore. Forceski realized he was following the trail of his own blood.

"Gl-Glen. How does he look?" Colletti held onto the edge of the ice.

"He's not breathing. Now *you* get the heck out of the water."

The only problem was Tony couldn't really move. All he could do was hang on the edge of the ice. He could move his arms, but they had no strength in them. He couldn't pull himself up.

The chief and Randazzo appeared out of nowhere. Forceski was getting the boy closer to Randazzo. The chief was behind him, also on his belly.

Glen looked back and saw Tony still in the water. "Tony, get out!"

"G-Get the k-kid off the ice."

"Glen!" the chief called out, "He can't move. We're going to have to go get him."

Now Forceski was really pissed off. "Sorry Johnny. I'm going to have to move you out of here now," He slid the boy forcefully across the ice toward Randazzo.

Randazzo dragged the boy back to shore. The chief laid him on a blanket and began CPR. Johnny Fournier was blue and didn't have a pulse. Lonnegan worked compressions furiously. He was beginning to feel desperate. And he had a man in the water who wasn't doing well either.

Forceski was sliding toward Tony when he heard a cracking noise and froze. Colletti clung to the edge of the ice. "Tony, how are you doing?"

"Gl-Glen, I've been submerged in freezing water for ten minutes. How d-do you think I am doing?"

Forceski smiled. Colletti was still acting like Colletti even though he couldn't seem to move. Then he saw Randazzo sliding toward him. "Dazz, I'm hearing ice cracking here."

"Move back, Detective. I'm lighter. We might need you to pull us both out of here. Where *is* the damn fire department?"

"Dazz, you'd better move. I don't want him sliding under again."

Randazzo slid on his belly toward Colletti. The good news was that he seemed to have enough rope.

On shore, things were not going well. The CPR compressions were not working. Forceski moved in. "Let me work him a while, Chief."

"What the heck happened to your head?"

"Caught a branch. I wasn't ready for a wilderness experience today."

Sirens from the fire department and EMT vehicles could be heard in the distance. "Thank God," the chief said.

Randazzo finally got to Colletti, who was shivering, blue, and exhausted. "Hey, Detective."

"Hey, Dazz, you know the chief w-wanted to talk to you."

"Yeah, we had a great meeting . . . I'm sliding this rope around you."

"You're g-going to h-have to. I can't move my arms."

"No problem." Randazzo had to put his hands in the water. He was already freezing. He couldn't imagine what Colletti was going through.

He was about to find out.

The ice cracked and Randazzo plunged face first into the water. The cold was stunning, and he flailed and swallowed water in a panic. Then he saw Colletti sinking to the bottom.

Forceski and the chief heard the ice crack and saw Randazzo's backside and legs slide into the water. A huge opening now appeared with chunks of ice floating around Randazzo.

"I'm pulling. You work the kid," the chief said.

Randazzo reached down and grabbed Colletti's shirt collar. He burst through the surface screaming, "Help! Help! Ahhh! Shit! This is c-cold!"

Colletti hit the surface. "G-Good thing you got me."

"Pull the rope! I can't let go of Colletti!" Randazzo screamed.

Colletti was trying to say something but Randazzo couldn't make sense of it. "Detective, what is it?"

"You're choking me!"

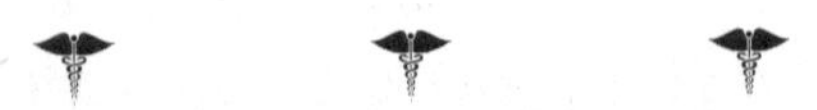

The EMTs and firemen administered first aid to the men. Randazzo could walk, but Colletti had to be carried. Both men were loaded in the ambulances that arrived after John Fournier had been taken away. Colletti asked the chief if the boy was doing better.

"I don't know, Tony. I'll let you know. Right now, go get warm."

The ambulance door closed. Although he was conscious, Tony was lost in the fog of hypothermia.

The chief looked in on Randazzo who was bundled up on a stretcher, drinking coffee.

"You did good today."

"Thank you, sir."

The chief got back to headquarters just before Forceski. Chavez stood up. "Sir, we have Wilson and Ramirez delivering Bell to court. I pulled Henry and Wanda in to secure the reservoir site. We got coffee. What the heck happened to you?"

Chavez meant Forceski who had just walked in, freshly adorned with stitches on his forehead and dried blood on his shirt.

"Don't worry about it. How's Tony?"

"They're warming him up at North Castleton Hospital."

"I think I should head over."

"Go," the chief said. "I'll catch up with you." He turned to Chavez. "Press?"

"Yeah, Angie says that News 13, CBS, and NBC locals are descending upon us as we speak."

"That figures. Remind everyone of the media relations protocols. I talk. No one else. Schwartz call yet?"

"The town supervisor is on his way over, Chief," Chavez said, and then paused.

"What's wrong?" the chief asked.

"The kid died. They called three minutes ago."

The chief turned and walked down the hall to his office. He quietly shut the door and went to the window. The ice in the Hudson now seemed even colder to him.

CHAPTER 3

Tony Colletti sat in his bed at North Castleton Hospital looking out the window into the darkness. The television was on, but he wasn't watching it. Johnny Fournier had died. Despite everything he had done, the kid died.

Chief Lonnegan had told the press about the morning's events and how his heroic officers did everything they could. "This has been one of the worst days of my career," the chief said. "We now need to support the Fournier family."

But the truth was that the Fourniers had very few friends in town. They were nice people, but their sons' autism had left the family isolated. When Tony started the Kid Find Program, he went to the Fournier home and talked to Mrs. Fournier at length. She almost refused to let Tony in the house until he told her that he had a son with autism too.

As Tony talked to other families he heard stories that left him shaking his head. For a small town, there were a surprising number of children with autism. What was eerie was that there were no autistic adults, just children and adolescents.

Some of the kids were charming and surprisingly endearing. They were impaired, but their family lives didn't match the media descriptions of autism. There were no *"Rain Man"* kids. Some kids had some skills and talents, but most were completely dependent on their families.

They needed constant, one on one supervision. It was clear that the children were impacted socially, but many had really good connections to their parents and siblings. They were loved.

But it was behaviors that defined autism. Some kids were self-abusive; some spent hours doing odd, repetitive behaviors; some obsessed over objects, turning lights on and off, staring at ceiling fans, and replaying DVDs and videos over and over again.

Tony enjoyed meeting the families and took pride in the Kid Find Program. The chief said that this is what professional policing is about, being proactive and solving problems in the community. Tony was a natural to lead the program because he could always get people to talk. He was famous in Castleton County police circles for his work on the Stracuzza homicide case. Tony got Joey Stracuzza to confess to the murder of his girlfriend, and then Stracuzza actually thanked him for taking the time to listen.

But right now, Tony didn't feel like a hero. Despite the program he had started, a kid had died. He knew it wasn't his fault, but he had never felt such bitterness. What if this had happened to Anthony, Jr.?

Anne had just left. She was seething when she arrived, her dark eyes cutting right through him. "Still think that you're twenty-three, don't you? You had to go in the freezing water. You have kids too, you know." But as they talked, she began to warm up to him and her Sicilian anger receded.

"Anne, if Anthony was in that lake, you'd want the cops doing what I did. It's what we do. You know that."

His wife kept holding his hand and shaking her head. As he told her what happened, she kept shaking her head. "You're a rock head, you know that? But I love you."

When you're freezing to death, you want a warm Sicilian woman with you. But Anne was home now to get the kids to bed. His daughter Sophie called him three times to make sure he was all right.

Tony kept seeing Johnny Fournier's eyes, open and peaceful. He thought about the family. It must be the worst night of their lives. Tony remembered his conversation with Veronica Fournier last spring. Once she started talking, she couldn't stop. And she mentioned something that he had also heard from other parents. "Johnny was a beautiful child, happy. Then everything changed after the vaccines."

Tony did not know what to do with that. But he heard it over and over. "I think it was the vaccines." Something didn't add up. The parents who talked about this seemed reasonable. Many were reporting similar observations.

Anthony Colletti, Jr., had also been a happy and healthy boy. Then one morning, he awoke with a terrible scream. He had a fever, horrible diarrhea, and an awful rash.

And Anthony had gone for some shots the day before . . .

Anthony was never right again. The happy, gorgeous boy with his wife's eyes was gone. The next months were a blur of doctor's visits, neurological tests, meetings with early intervention people, and finally a visit by a psychologist who announced that Anthony was "clearly autistic."

Anne called Tony at work with the devastating news that their lives would never be the same.

Tony found himself asking "Why did this happen to my son?" He was grieving the loss of his child, but his child was still alive. "How will he live after I am gone? Who will take care of Anthony?"

Tony withdrew and was depressed for weeks until one night after dinner, Anne exploded. "If you are going to sit there with your head in your hands for another night, then get the heck out! We have to start doing things for Anthony. I have too much on my plate, and I have to keep the rest of this place together. I can't drag you along too!"

Tony stormed out and walked around the block. Finally, he got into his car and drove twenty miles to the martial arts dojo in Yonkers where he had trained for twenty years. The dojo was always a place where he let go of negativity and got refocused.

He got there just as the class was starting. "Welcome back, my friend," said the sensei, Akinori Saito. Colletti bowed to the gray-haired jujitsu master, whose eyes immediately focused on Tony. "I have missed you. I was getting worried. Go put your ghi on."

The class began with the customary respects of bowing to the sensei, bowing to classmates, and then bowing to the small group visiting the class that night. Then came stretching, calisthenics, *kata* exercise forms, and, finally, sparring.

As always, Colletti found that releasing himself to the art of jujitsu brought him focus and peace. It was the act of "emptying your cup" as Sensei Saito would always say. The ancient art worked its magic, and Tony began relaxing, executing techniques, throwing his classmates, being thrown and hitting the mats.

And getting back up.

As the meditation period was ending, Saito made a simple statement: "Life is about change. Resisting change only leads to sorrow. Accept reality as it is and be of service to others."

Tony came home three hours later. Anne was reading a book in bed. "Okay," he said, "what do we have to do?"

The Collettis immersed themselves in the enormous amount of work needed to begin dealing with an autistic child. There were dozens of meetings with therapists and the case manager. Setting up and getting Anthony to therapy appointments was a full-time job. All sorts of professional people began working in the Colletti's home: speech therapists, physical therapists, and behavioral therapists. Little Anthony spent hours working harder than any young boy should have to work just to speak a few words or correctly use a spoon. Applied behavioral analysis therapy helped Anthony focus but it also frustrated him, producing some horrible meltdowns. There were times when Tony came home to find Anne crying.

It was that hard.

One night in bed, Anne held Tony and said, "I just wish that he could be free. Free to play. To imagine being a superhero. To be a boy."

"I know."

"He's becoming more affectionate, though. I am getting some hugs from him again."

Anne kissed Tony's cheek. "A hug from him is better than hitting the lottery. You know he loves you."

Anne began to attend support meetings where parents discussed therapies and interventions. Tony avoided those, but he did talk to the other police officers whose children also had autism. One of them was Glen, "the Polish Hammer" Forceski. The two men, who immediately bonded over their sons' situations, noticed how many other Winston children had the condition. And some of those kids were "wanderers" who often quietly left their homes and roamed away causing their families to call the police in a panic. That was when Tony got the idea for Kid Find.

The program caught on, and soon a file drawer at the station house front desk was full of case folders on Winston's wanderers. The department developed training about children with autism wandering and shared the information with cops from other departments. The innovative program received positive local media attention and an Autism Friendly Community Award from Autism America. The chief, the town manager, Colletti, and Forceski had their pictures taken with the lovely actress, Kate Darby, Autism America's celebrity spokesperson.

Copies of the photograph were put up all over headquarters. Chavez—always a prankster—started a rumor that Forceski was having an affair with the actress.

But today's events only emphasized how tough the lives of the affected families really were. Veronica Fournier dropped her guard for a few minutes because she was exhausted. And now her son was dead.

To make matters worse, District Attorney Jeanette Borelli had called a press conference to announce that she would seek criminal charges against Mrs. Fournier. Child Protection workers took Johnny's brother into protective custody when word had leaked out that there were holes in the walls of Johnny's room. Forceski told Tony that the chief was furious at Borelli, and that the walls at headquarters literally shook from their telephone screaming match.

Tony lay in the hospital bed thinking "It could have been Anthony in that frozen lake. It could have been Anne who now needed an attorney and who was planning a funeral." Then he drifted into a fitful sleep.

Tony was back in the frozen woods under the deep blue sky, in a crowd of people who were walking through the deep snow. Everyone moved in one direction with their heads down away from the frozen lake that they had all just crossed.

Something told him to turn around and walk back toward the lake. Hundreds of children and their parents were now crossing. All of them had blank looks on their faces. No one would look him in the eye. He tried to say something to them. What was it? The words wouldn't come out.

Tony walked out onto the ice and saw the blue sky turning dark purple. He noticed that certain children just stopped as if frozen in place. He tried to yell, "Get off the ice!" But the words still wouldn't come out. The children were frozen in place.

And then it began to happen.

One by one, the children plunged through the ice, their desperate eyes looking at him. Something was pulling them down. Some horrible, faceless force pulled them under the ice. Tony ran to them, but they were gone, and the ice had refrozen as if they had never been there. The other adults continued walking, heads down into the darkness of the woods.

Tony turned and saw Anthony. He ran toward him screaming, "No!" But like all the others, the ice erupted and pulled his son under, then refroze. Anthony was trapped underneath.

Sobbing, Tony fell and pounded the ice. He wanted his son back. He wanted the other parents to help, but they just kept marching, heads down. He rose and pulled his gun. He was going to shoot through the ice to get to Anthony. Then he saw what was happening on the other side of the lake. Thousands and thousands of children were lining up.

Tony awoke to see a nurse standing over him. "Mr. Colletti, are you okay? Are you okay?"

Tony sat up. "I was having a bad dream."

"Well, you had some day from what I saw. Let me take your blood pressure. The sun will be up soon. Did you fill out your breakfast slip?" The nurse slipped the blood pressure cuff around his arm and pumped. "Your numbers look good. The doctor is going to release you in the morning. Oh, one other thing—we offer all of our patients the annual flu shot. It's flu season. Interested?"

CHAPTER 4

The director of the Division of Vaccine Injury compensation, Dr. Robert Bangston, sat alone with his head in his hands in his dimly lit office in the Health and Human Services Building in Washington, DC. Every few minutes, he flipped through the case folder on his desk, read some of it, and then went back to holding his head in his hands.

Darkness always surrounded Bangston. His staff called his office "The Tomb." He had been a good looking man in his youth, but, he had become haggard and worn over the years. Bangston now felt as though he was suffocating.

The lawyers from the United States Department of Justice had decided to settle one of the first cases in the Omnibus Autism Proceedings. They felt that they would lose the case if it went to a hearing. It was devastating.

The United States was about to concede that vaccines could cause autism.

"Your people should have caught the Kellerman report!" Department of Justice Attorney Terrence Stone shouted. "Don't run up to Secretary Chamberlin pointing the finger at us. Your people review these stinking cases."

"We can't concede an autism test case," Bangston said. "The anti-vaxers will have a field day with this."

"Oh? Is it better to let Whittaker go to hearing? Then the petitioners roll Kellerman up there, and he testifies in exquisite detail that the kid developed autism from the vaccines. You do know that Kellerman was supposed to be a witness for us on the other test cases? Come on Bob, he'd be testifying against himself! Lose this one case and we lose 'em all."

"Terry, what do I say to the Secretary? 'Every now and then vaccines *do cause* autism. Sorry about that.' Think she'll be happy?"

"Robert, this isn't about making her happy. Look, we got bushwhacked. We have to do a lot of creative writing and, crap, we'll see if we can contain this. It is what it is."

The unstated purpose of creating the Omnibus Autism Proceedings in the National Vaccine Injury Compensation Program, the NVICP, was to end the vaccine-autism issue once and for all. But the Whittaker case was a disaster for the program that Bangston had been running since the program began. The nation's vaccine program—the cornerstone of American public health policy—was now in jeopardy. The NVICP was created in 1986 to maintain the vaccine supply, protect vaccine manufacturers from liability, and compensate the injured. If the program went down, he would be held responsible.

Bangston called the Secretary of Health and Human Services. She seemed to take it well but she was known for being nice to people before firing them. "Robert, get to Jennifer and start planning to deal with public relations. There has to be a plan—stat!"

Bangston still had his job—for now.

Dr. Jennifer Kesslinger, the director of the Centers for Disease Control and Prevention, was apoplectic when Bangston phoned. "You do understand that we have made dozens of statements that there is no link between autism and vaccines? That vaccination is absolutely the cornerstone of everything we do—everything!"

Bangston explained the catch-22 to her. It only made her angrier. "You mean the father of this autistic kid is a doctor! Oh come on! Does the guy have any loyalty? And who is this Kellerman guy? You tell him he's done in this town! You tell him!"

"You can't threaten a witness in a federal proceeding . . ."

"These aren't federal proceedings! These are *our* proceedings! This is *our* program—*our* game—*our* rules. Damn it, Robert, we got beat on our own field."

"We need a containment plan."

"Well, yeah, you're telling me?" She was smoking again. Bangston could tell by her voice. It was a closely held secret that Kesslinger—one of the nation's leading health authorities—smoked like a chimney. She could drink a room full of sailors under the table too. "It can't be government, Robert. It has to be done outside. Figure it out. There are lots of resources from the private sector. Take it from there."

And so Bangston made another call.

Dr. Phillip Snyder was playing golf at the Cambridge Beaches Resort in Bermuda. A middle-aged man with graying hair, he was spokesman for the pharmaceutical industry after he made millions on a vaccine he developed. Snyder was not born to wealth and felt a great sense of loyalty to the industry that had made him affluent and respected. For Snyder, respect was everything.

Snyder had great influence on the prestigious federal Advisory Council on Immunization Protocols, the ACIP. A few years ago the "anti-vaccine people" publicly embarrassed him when he didn't abstain from a vote approving a vaccine he had developed. An autism blog declared him unethical and ran a short film starring a Muppet-like toad called *Snyder the Pharma Toad.*

But all that seemed miles away. Snyder was playing golf and enjoying a stunning view of the Atlantic Ocean. Officially, he was attending the annual conference of the North American Foundation for Infectious Diseases. His team of another doctor and two executives were having a glorious time, courtesy of Xerxes Pharmaceuticals. Snyder was about to putt on the eleventh when his cell phone rang. It was Bangston. "Phil, we have a big problem! Get off the golf course, and call me from your hotel room in twenty minutes."

Twenty minutes later Dr. Snyder got the news and threw his wineglass against the wall of his executive suite. "How the hell could this happen? Are the DOJ people out of their minds?! Don't they know what the anti-vax crowd will do with this?"

"I told them. They say that they had no choice." Bangston told Snyder the rest of the saga. Snyder was stunned.

"Is the family going to talk?"

"I think so."

"I say we settle only if they agree to remain silent. Didn't something like that happen with the Nebraska family?"

"You mean the Kansas family."

"But they were from Nebraska, weren't they?"

"Yes, Phil. That's why we call them the *Kansas family* . . . look, what do we do? We need a plan. Jennifer wants it done outside the government."

"That guttersnipe wants to make sure that she has a landing pad after she leaves CDC. What a piece of work. She and the rest of those epaulet-wearing idiots can't solve a problem to save their lives. She still bitching about Hans Jurgenson?"

"She should be," said Bangston, pulling back his graying hair with his free hand. "That drunken Viking is like a villain from a James Bond movie. He got a research assistant pregnant so Kesslinger threw him out of Emory."

Snyder chuckled. "He produces studies with numbers that we like, Bob. It's really that simple. Look, I'll make the call. My people will come up with a plan. It's what they do. How're you doing?"

"I hate this job. I hate this place. I'm sick of sitting on cans of gasoline while everyone around me smokes cigars."

"You're our man, Bob. Come on now, you're our man." With that, Snyder hung up the phone and walked out onto his balcony. The sun was setting across the bay. He was about to enjoy a lovely evening in the company of admiring peers. At tonight's dinner he would receive the Jacob Fletcher Award for all that he had done to promote vaccination. For all that he had done for the greater good.

And so he went back to the telephone. In a dark, oak paneled office in London, E. Gordon Calthorpe answered the phone and exhaled a stream of cigarette smoke.

"Hello, Phillip."

"Gordon, we have a problem."

"Of course, you do, Phillip. Why else would you call me?"

CHAPTER 5

Russell Sampson, the US Representative from New York's Ninth Congressional District, paced around his office in the House Office Building in Washington, DC. Sampson was tall, with a chiseled jaw and an athletic build. Female reporters called him strapping. The Republicans called him their "Dream Candidate." Because he was.

And now he was waiting on a phone call from the governor of New York. Maybe, just maybe, Sampson was going to be appointed New York's junior senator.

The phone rang. "Sampson here."

"You know I bet you are standing there in your uniform, you good-looking bastard," said Lou Miller.

"Actually, I'm wearing the red tie you got me for Christmas, Governor. How are you?"

"I'm in Albany, Russell. You know what that means." Both men laughed and had a quick conversation about New York politics. Both agreed that it had been a good month in Albany; not one assembly member or state senator had been arrested. Of course, the month wasn't over. "How's your wife feeling? Everything good with your new baby?"

"Yes, Diana and Jordan are both doing great. Thanks for asking."

"Hey, how many kids do you have now? Seven? Eight?"

"Just four. The girls and now Jordan."

"Diana just can't keep her hands off you, can she? Everyone says you're gorgeous. My wife says you're gorgeous. In fact, everyone wants to make babies with you."

"Well, thank you, Governor."

"Your wife is gorgeous. Your kids are gorgeous." Lou Miller could go on like this. It was part of his charm. Mercifully, he moved on to the purpose of the call. "So, listen, I have a bunch of people telling me that Dean Markos from out on the Island would be a good senator."

"He would be, Lou. He is a good man and . . ."

"Yes, he is, but he isn't the *best* man. I'm talking to the best man right now. Yeah, you're young, and, yeah, the old guard will grumble. But a governor rarely gets to make this kind of decision. Most of the decisions are ones I'd rather not make. So, on this one I'm doing what I want. Do you accept my appointing you to the United States Senate?"

Sampson got up from his chair and swallowed hard. "Yes, Governor, I do."

"Good! You'll be great, although my rabbi is going to ask why I didn't pick a Jew." Sampson laughed. "Seriously, do you know how difficult it is to be a Jewish Republican in New York? Don't ever ask me how I ended up here. I couldn't explain it. I mean, I'm not gorgeous or anything, like you. Okay, my office will call your assistant about scheduling. Good day . . . Mr. Senator."

Russell Sampson was a good and honest man from middle-class Catholic stock, who believed in national service. His father was a former Marine, so after graduating from Fordham University, Sampson joined the Marines too. He flew jets in the Gulf War and rose through the ranks. When he left the military, he got a law degree, and went to work for the Dutchess County district attorney. The local Republicans recognized talent when they saw it and begged him to run for the Democrat-dominated New York State Assembly. To everyone's amazement, he easily defeated the Democratic incumbent. As a Republican, Sampson couldn't do too much, but it didn't matter. His primary job became being Russell Sampson. He was constantly seen at veterans' functions with his blonde, blue-eyed wife, Diana, and their growing family.

Although conservative in just about every way, Sampson resonated with the diverse people in his district. In a stroke of innate political genius, he took to the streets of the failing Hudson River Valley city of Newburgh in 2003 and talked to young gang members. Charisma is charisma, and the young men related to Sampson. They listened to his talks about commitment to community and family. The local police reported that gang violence decreased.

Sampson's appearance on a talk show made him famous for one particular comment. "Mr. Sampson," asked the host, "do you really believe that you can get these gang members to change by just talking to them?"

His answer made headlines: "Only if I listen to them first."

One year later, Sampson was elected to the House of Representatives. And now he was going to the United States Senate.

CHAPTER 6

E. Gordon Calthorpe entered his oak-paneled office and lit a cigarette. His assistant, Donna Willoughby, said, "The callers are lining up, sir."

"Excellent. They are behaving exactly as I expected." Calthorpe said, exhaling smoke from his nose as though he were a dragon.

Calthorpe was a senior partner in the Rollins Group, the world's premier private public relations firm. The Rollins Group was vital to the world's elite, yet most ordinary people didn't even know the company existed. Because of its power and influence, Rollins could do things that no other public relations firm could. As Calthorpe liked to say, "We shape truth. We create reality."

Calthorpe relished the power and the influence that the firm had. It created financial opportunities that went well beyond the public relations world. And that only fueled more power and more influence, particularly with Rollins's media allies. When the interests of the elite were challenged, Calthorpe and his people were called upon to "adjust" the situation. Often, the people targeted did not realize that they had been targeted until a negative news story came out about that person's business or character.

This was just the beginning. Eventually, someone in government—and it didn't matter who—would see the gain in going after the targeted person. It was all just a matter of altering the terrain in the way that Rollins wanted. As Calthorpe would say, "It's time to release the dogs." Eventually, the dogs did what dogs do. Altering the terrain simply made it easier.

This did mean, of course, that you sometimes had to lie down with some bad dogs.

Although Calthorpe began his career as a gifted barrister, he was bored by practicing law and wanted the power to impact the world beyond the courtrooms of England. He always convinced juries that his clients were right, but it was the public that he wanted to mold. Why not create a world where your client's interests were so well protected that no one dare challenge them? Rollins Group was a perfect fit. Calthorpe and Rollins made millions. And they were about to make millions more. His gray reptilian eyes calmly focused on the telephone in anticipation of the conference call.

"George Patel for party A on the line," said an Indian-accented voice over the phone.

"Good to hear you again, George. How are you?"

"Very well, Gordon. Very well."

"Wilson Egley for party B."

"Hello, Wilson. How is Manhattan today?"

"Freezing."

"Heinz Obermayer for party C."

"Hello, Heinz."

"Deborah Johnson for party D, Mr. Calthorpe."

"How is your father, Deborah? Last I heard, he was unwell."

"Still with us."

"Juan Romero-Santiago for party . . . party E."

"Buenos dias, Juan," Calthorpe said, breathing out more smoke through his teeth. "Very well then, we are assembled. Everyone here understands the reason for this gathering. You have received the documents retaining our services. Rollins shall endeavor to be of great service to you. This matter will receive our utmost attention and, as you certainly know, we never fail to protect our clients. Donna, please inform the gathering of the situation."

Willoughby rose to her feet as though addressing people who were actually in the room. "We learned two days ago that the US Vaccine

Injury Compensation Program is going to settle one of the test cases in what they are calling the Omnibus Autism Proceedings. We expect that this family will eventually choose to speak out and . . ."

Johnson interrupted, "Is the US government actually going to admit that a vaccine caused autism? If so, why?"

"Because," said Willoughby, "the child's father is a Harvard-trained physician, the mother is an attorney, and the doctor who submitted an expert report on behalf of the family explains in exquisite detail how the vaccinations led directly to the autism outcome. Further, this same expert was also slated to be a witness for the respondent, who happens to be the Secretary of Health and Human Services."

"In other words," Calthorpe said, "the matter has to be settled—taking the case to a hearing would be a disaster. It would have established bad precedent."

The phone lines were silent until Patel spoke up, "My friends, this is a disaster. I can tell you that my clients will be very concerned. There will be a massive impact on the financials in this market."

Romero-Santiago spoke next. "We all understand that this marketplace is totally unique. Our clients all enjoy a level of product liability protection that is . . ."

"Quite correct, my friend," Calthorpe said. "You have almost achieved complete protection from American civil law. That is now threatened. Right now there are a handful of cases moving through the American courts that may eventually result in real exposure outside of the compensation program."

"This is a disaster for the entire industry," said Obermayer. "With so many other drugs going off patent, vaccines have become critical protected income that we all have become dependent on."

"Same here," said Egley. "This market is vital to our interests as well. This is very bad news. Isn't there some way to convince this family to remain silent?"

"You do understand your countrymen, don't you?" said Calthorpe. "These people will talk. We know already that Clyde King plans to release the story on the bloody *Pulsipher Post.*"

"Can we keep the networks from getting this?" asked Johnson.

"Part of the strategy will be to insert corks in those bottles," Calthorpe said,

"Word of this issue—vaccines and autism – really took off with the use of the Internet," Egley said. "Can we do anything about these annoying bloggers?"

"One can't control the Internet, but we can get our side out on it as well. Tit for tat," Calthorpe said.

"We just need to keep the press from getting specifics!" said Egley.

"Actually," said Calthorpe, "that is quite right. Spot on. Vague language should be used. We want a lot of gray here."

Obermayer pressed for details. "What exactly will you do?"

"We shall implement a plan that renders this case a footnote in the history of your industry. We shall restore trust in your vaccines and protect your market."

"We need to do something," said Johnson. "One of these cases will eventually get up to the Supreme Court. We all know how that could end. There are upward of 700,000 American children with this disorder. Our industry could well find ourselves held responsible for the largest mass poisoning in history."

Patel interjected, "This is a disaster from a world health perspective. We can't have people in the Third World believing that vaccines cause autism *and* having American courts saying that. We must do something."

Calthorpe relished their panic. They were eating out of his hands. "My friends, please be comforted by our capabilities to shape public perception. *This is what we do.* We are making plans. We already have significant resources in this arena, particularly here in the UK. We just have to ramp it all up and build some more opportunities to prepare the battlefield in the US. We have already dispensed advice to the Americans. We just need commitments from all of you. Agreed?"

"What will it cost?" said Johnson.

"Whatever it needs to," said Calthorpe calmly. "But it will be well worth the cost, don't you agree?"

"I do," said Patel.

"One question," said Romero-Santiago. "Is it true?"

"Is what true?" asked Willoughby.

"Did the vaccinations cause the child's autism?"

"That is beyond the scope of our discussion, my friend," said Calthorpe. "Are you in agreement?"

"Yes, I am."

Calthorpe and Willoughby smiled as more affirmative comments came over the line. Calthorpe glibly explained that some resources would be needed and would be requested through various channels. It was part of the plan. They didn't need to know the details. "Now remember my friends, this conversation never really happened."

The others voiced their approval and the call ended.

Calthorpe rose from his chair and lit another cigarette. "Donna, get that little fiend, Lance Reed, on the phone."

Willoughby's face showed disgust. "Do we have to use him?"

"I am afraid so, Donna."

"But sir, I loathe him. He is repulsive."

"Indeed he is, Donna. Indeed he is . . ."

And so the new offensive began.

CHAPTER 7

It was autumn of 1986, and Zvi Kokochashvili was in his third day of meetings with federal government agents in an office building just outside Washington, DC. Zvi told them everything that he could about the Soviet Union's bioweapons program and his other research. He and his family were still adjusting to their new country and the security presence that surrounded them. The Americans promised him more independence soon but the security was for protection. While the bad old days of the Cold War were winding down, the Soviet Union was still capable of assassination.

Zvi sensed that the Americans were good people who recognized the stress his family was under. The good news was that his son loved the six-foot tall African American agent who guarded the family. Georgi called him "Mean Joe" because he looked like the Pittsburgh Steelers' star. But nothing could be done for Anya, who missed her family and cried every night.

On the afternoon of the third day, an official named Vicky Glazer from the Centers for Disease Control and Prevention came in to chat. She wore a white uniform with epaulets on the shoulders. "Are you from the army?" Zvi wanted to know.

"No," said Glazer. "Why do you ask?"

"Because you are wearing a uniform. Do scientists here always wear uniforms?"

"Well, like we always say, the CDC is at war with disease, Dr. Kokochashvili."

"I see," said Zvi sipping coffee. "Do you think that smallpox cares that you wear a uniform?"

Glazer opened her briefcase. "It's just a tradition in our service."

Zvi watched the woman place a series of folders on the desk. "What would you like to discuss?"

"Some background on your published research." As Zvi suspected, the conversation went right into the weapons research and how that influenced his published papers. They spoke for hours. Then, Glazer asked about his foray into DPT vaccine research.

"We received word of problems from the army," Zvi began. "Some soldiers suffered neurological illnesses following DPT administration. Soldiers have superior officers who get, how you say here in America, pissed off, when soldiers are too sick to fight."

"Really? How sick?"

"Most of the soldiers were fine, but we had a group who had very bad reactions. A subset of the soldiers suffered paralysis. The men in this group all had severe damage to their nervous system, myelin damage. They suffered horrible seizures. Some lost the ability to speak. They became shells of who they were. The generals called them ghosts."

"Ghosts?"

"The ones I evaluated were, well, haunting. They suffered convulsions and could hardly speak anymore. They became shells of who they were. It is disturbing to see young men affected like this. So, yes, ghosts was descriptive."

"Then this led to the research on the younger populations?"

"Exactly. The generals wanted to know what the effect would be on future soldiers. The Soviet Union views young males as soldiers or future soldiers. So we commenced a review of the effects of the DPT on children. We looked at a large group of children who were vaccinated. They tended to be from families connected to the party and the military.

Then we looked at a large group from other families who were not vaccinated. Seizures and encephalopathy outcomes were significantly above the non-vaccinated group."

Glazer sat stunned. "Did you ever determine what in the vaccine was causing the encephalopathy?"

"We found many toxic ingredients and simply judged the product unsafe. There was ethyl mercury, aluminum hydrochloride, pertussis toxin. Ultimately, the health minister decided that no vaccines in the Soviet Union would be allowed to have the mercury product—it was called thimerosal—because the evidence of its toxicity was so obvious. It was not a hard decision. Many children died from infantile spasms. Some were left unable to walk or talk. They ended up in wheelchairs. The ambulatory children suffered psychiatric issues that we had never seen before. They did the same things over and over again. How do you say?"

"They had repetitive behaviors, like obsessive-compulsive behaviors?" asked Glazer nervously.

"Exactly. They also lost whatever speech they had. It became difficult to manage these children. I am told that many were institutionalized. Many were also like the ghosts." Glazer looked at Zvi with great intensity. "It is what we found."

Zvi could not know why Glazer seemed so concerned about his study, which he viewed at the time as being a minor work. He did not understand that 1986 would be a crucial year in the history of the vaccine program in the United States. Congress was considering passage of a new law, the National Childhood Vaccine Injury Act. Pharmaceutical interests were telling Congress that they were getting out of the vaccine market due to lawsuits. Vaccine safety groups led by Dissatisfied Parents Together, or DPT, were gaining influence in Washington. The families reported injuries that Zvi would have recognized from his own research. Children died or were left incapacitated with severe developmental delays and seizure disorders. Some of the children also developed odd behaviors.

And there were whispers that some of these children had what was then a rare condition that psychiatrists called autism.

Autism was not the biggest concern to these families. Most of the children suffered from devastating seizures from which many died. Just keeping these children alive was a struggle. If a child also had a weird behavioral disorder, it wasn't the first priority.

Zvi did not know that the vaccine research he had done could confirm the claims of vaccine safety advocates. His paper, gathering dust in Moscow, could cost pharma millions and derail plans to expand the US vaccine program.

Zvi knew none of this. He was just glad to be free of the Soviet Union. He wanted his children to grow up as free Americans. Within a year, he began a series of government jobs under his new name, Victor Petrov. His cover, that he was a Christian fleeing religious persecution in Kurdistan, worked perfectly.

But as the years passed, Zvi began to see why Glazer was concerned about his DPT paper. As he was shuffled around through different research projects in the CDC and FDA, he recognized that America had a problem; government agencies had become silent partners with the industry they were supposed to regulate. Zvi met administrator after administrator who made sure that everybody on the team played by the unstated rules. Problems with drug trials always ended with the administrator explaining that the company involved needed a break. If an administrator "went by the book," pressure from pharmaceutical lobbyists on Congress usually resulted. And Zvi noticed that most of the administrators ended up working for the companies they used to regulate.

The pattern was obvious: the regulations existed only on paper. Real oversight was thwarted. In the end, the companies got what they wanted and whined all the way to the bank about burdensome government regulations.

Zvi heard about what went on in vaccine research from other FDA employees. With the passage of the National Childhood Vaccine Injury Act, regulation became even more of a hostage to industry. The pharmaceutical companies rarely did meaningful safety testing.

Vaccines were tested for safety against other vaccines, not placebos. Follow-up periods of the subjects were inadequate. More vaccines were being added to the schedule and administered in combination with other vaccines, but safety trials were not addressing this. What happened if you gave an infant nine vaccines in one visit? No one really knew.

In 1989, Zvi offered his services to American and British researchers working on a lengthy study about the DPT vaccine called The National Childhood Encephalopathy Study. His offer was not accepted.

As the years passed, Zvi came to understand that the odd behaviors he saw in the vaccine-injured children in Russia were the behaviors now called autism. He realized it after he met his next-door neighbor's son. Over the years, he saw more children with autism. It was everywhere. And Zvi Kokochashvili knew the cause.

He just didn't know what he could do about it.

CHAPTER 8

John Fournier's death was portrayed as a tragedy immediately after the drowning. Then the district attorney portrayed Veronica Fournier as being a neglectful parent. A headline in the local paper read "Mom Naps While Son Drowns—DA." Child endangerment charges were quickly filed, which angered the town's police chief, Tony, and Forceski because the DA hadn't listened to their explanations about what this family had been through. The DA even commented in the article that Winston police "weren't objective due to their personal experiences with autism." The comment sent the chief into a rage, and he tossed two of the DA's investigators out of headquarters.

The next day a reporter called Tony to ask whether he believed Laura Fournier was guilty of neglect. "The Fourniers made sure that Johnny was enrolled in the wandering program. Does that sound like a neglectful parent to you?"

The DA telephoned Lonnegan to complain that "Colletti was undermining the case." The conversation ended in a series of expletives. The chief called Tony in.

"You got a problem with the rule 'bout who talks to the press?"

"No sir, I don't. My bad. I accept full responsibility."

"Yeah. Well, don't do it again . . . The DA can pound sand."

Once the charges were filed, the Department of Social Services filed a petition to remove Evan, the Fourniers' other child with autism, from his parents. Castleton County CPS removed Evan to the Roosevelt Children's Home. It was a huge mistake. Evan was unlike any child CPS had ever seen before. They couldn't control him. Evan had a meltdown and banged his head against the walls. When the workers tried to stop him, the behavior got worse. Evan bit one of the workers who tried to restrain him. The case managers then determined that the usual options of group homes and foster families would be unable to deal with him. When Evan climbed out a bedroom window and fled the facility's grounds, a psychiatrist ordered medications that turn normal adolescents into zombies, but they made Evan even more difficult.

Controlling Evan Fournier was beyond the capabilities of one of the wealthiest counties in America. They simply didn't have programs for children with severe autism. Administrators reluctantly came to the conclusion that Evan Fournier should be returned to his family. The county would offer the Fourniers services and assistance. When the DA learned of the plan, she demanded to know why the county hadn't done this for the family before. Bureaucrats pointed fingers at each other.

Tony Colletti sat on the bench in the hallway next to the oak doors of the Castleton County Family Court. He didn't want to be there. Evan's Law Guardian, Laura Melendez, had subpoenaed Tony to appear. Melendez was one of the best in the business and understood autism because her son had autism. The attractive redhead was loaded for bear when she saw Tony sitting on the bench. "Hey, you're the cop who went in the lake, right? Thanks for answering the subpoena."

"Yeah, I'm the one. Cops are supposed to answer subpoenas. You're Melendez?" She nodded. "What's gonna happen? I don't get family court stuff."

"No one does. And this case is a . . . ."

"A complete disaster, counselor."

"Don't leave. Sit right there." Melendez darted into the courtroom. The county attorneys were already sitting at the table to the right. "Hey, Darcy, what are we doing today?"

"Getting our ass kicked by autism," said County Attorney Darcy Fitzgerald.

"Been there myself."

"All rise!" said the bailiff. Family Court judge Gail Jackson entered the courtroom. "Good morning, people," the judge said. "What are we doing on the Fourniers' case? The family will be here in a few minutes."

"May we approach?" asked Fitzgerald. The judge motioned the group forward. "Judge, the county is willing to allow Evan Fournier to go home. To be blunt," she whispered, "the county can't deal with this child. None of our programs meet this child's needs."

Melendez opened her file. "This is only what I said last week. The county overreacted. These people have been through hell. I had no problem with investigating them. But pulling the kid?! You went completely over the top here." Melendez was pushing her point, and the judge nodded in agreement. "The mother has two children with severe autism. She was pushed to the limit and exhausted. The DA makes a statement and frenzy breaks out."

"All right," said the judge. "You've made your point. Let's reunite this family. We're doing an interim order—without admitting or denying?" Both attorneys nodded in agreement. "Good. Melendez, go talk to the family."

Melendez walked out of the courtroom and saw Veronica Fournier sitting on the oak bench, holding Tony's hand and crying.

The court officers got the Fourniers out of the building through a side entrance after the proceedings ended, avoiding the small pack of media people. Melendez emerged from the courtroom and saw Tony still sitting in the hallway. "Oh, you're still here?"

"You told me not to go. What happened?"

"Evan's going home. We got the family out of here. The County even agreed to give them some home-based services."

"Really? Someone finally came through for these people. They've been through enough."

"I agree. Hey, you want a cup of coffee?"

⚕ ⚕ ⚕

Tony and Melendez sat at a table in a small diner a block away from the courthouse. "So," Tony said, "do you just do family court stuff?"

"Actually, no. My husband and I have a fairly diverse practice. I do family. Carlos does criminal."

"Oh, so Melendez is . . . ."

"My married name. Do you know Carlos?"

"Chuck Melendez?" Laura nodded. "He was an ADA about ten years ago, right?"

"That's him. He's a knucklehead."

"I thought that he was a good guy. I wish he was still there."

"Yeah, but now we have the joy of running our own law office. We're starving. You a cop with family and kids, or are you a player?"

"Wife, kids, the whole nine yards. I even live in Winston. I'm boring."

"You started that program that helps find our wanderers, right?"

"That was me. I got a kid with autism, so I get what the families go through."

"I have one too. Little pain in the ass just turned six. I love him to death."

Tony laughed and the two talked about their kids. He had more in common with this lawyer than he had with most cops. His son's autism had changed him so much that he was even getting along with lawyers. Ten years ago, he wouldn't have been seen dead with an attorney who wasn't a prosecutor. When he started with the New York City Police Department twenty years earlier, having coffee with someone like Laura Melendez might get you fined by the brass.

"Did you start here in suburbia or are you another NYPD migrator?"

"That's me. Three years in the big city, then I came north for the big money, white fences, and low crime rates." Tony didn't want to talk about what happened while he was in the NYPD so he changed the subject. "Hey, what do you think about this vaccine thing?"

"We're doing those cases now."

"I mean the theory that vaccines . . ."

"Yeah, I know, cause autism. As I said, Carlos and I have started to take on those cases."

"Really? You guys have the kind of office to take on these companies?"

"You don't sue the companies. You sue the feds—Health and Human Services. It's called the National Vaccine Injury Compensation Program. It's supposed to be a no-fault program. It's like when you guys get in a car accident and spill your coffee and donuts and go out on worker's comp for ten years."

"Nice shot! If you do cop jokes, I get to do lawyer jokes."

"Okay, big guy. Give it your best shot."

"Okay. Here it comes. What do you call ten thousand lawyers at the bottom of the Challenger Deep?"

"What?"

"A good start." They both laughed. "So, do you think there's something to this vaccine thing? Why doesn't every vaccinated kid develop autism?"

"Because some kids are predisposed due to genetics or some other reasons. Think about it. Does every person who smokes die from cancer at thirty-five? No. Some never get cancer. Some develop some other health problem. Drugs affect different people differently. Too many reasonable people report that their kids regress after vaccines. The other side can talk about all of this being anecdotal reports from emotional parents who need someone to blame. But I talk to these people. Parents know their kids and know when something goes wrong."

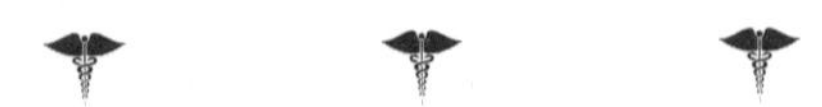

Although Veronica Fournier got her son back, her problems in criminal court lingered. Tony and his wife Anne helped get her through the months that followed. The only people who seemed to understand were parents who also had children with autism.

The DA finally agreed to dismiss the criminal charges but only after putting Veronica under supervision for a year. The services promised to the family were slow to materialize. Most of the people providing them did not understand what it was like to raise a child with autism.

Or to lose one.

CHAPTER 9

Diana Sampson sat in the back of a black limousine making sure that her baby boy, Jordan, was bundled up. She thanked the Secret Service Agent for opening the car door and whisked her son into the pediatrician's office building in Alexandria, Virginia. The receptionist directed Diana over to the well-baby side of the pediatrics waiting room. "Jordan has some sniffles," Diana said. "Should we hold off on today's shots?"

"Mention that to the nurse."

A few minutes later Diana placed Jordan on the examination table and began singing "The Itsy Bitsy Spider." Jordan giggled as the song was delivered with a tickle after every verse. The nurse entered and began shaking the vaccine bottles. "Congratulations to you and the senator."

Jordan smiled, pointed, and said, "Nurse."

"Mrs. Sampson, your son is gorgeous. He's going to be a lady-killer in twenty years. Keep him away from my daughter."

Jordan cried as the vaccines were administered just as Dr. Wohlman came in. "Mrs. Sampson, good to see you again. How's Jordan doing? He looks great."

"He's doing great. He has some words."

"Old Blue Eyes just pointed at me and called me nurse," the nurse smiled. "Yeah, he's got words, Doctor, and he uses them to charm women."

"Just like his dad," Diana said.

"That's wonderful," said Wohlman. "Any concerns?"

"He has a little cold. Oh, should we have given the vaccines?"

"Not to worry. You're doing everything that you should do." Wohlman began to examine the boy. "He has some language, good color. Sits up and looks like he eats well."

"Yes he does."

"Starting to walk?" Diana nodded her answer. "Good-looking kid. Mrs. Sampson, you have a happy, healthy baby boy."

That was the last time that Jordan Sampson would be described that way.

Later that evening, Diana Sampson heard a horrible scream coming from Jordan's room, unlike any sound she had ever heard before. She and her oldest daughter, Patricia, ran into Jordan's room. The boy was shaking and turning bright red.

"He's having a seizure! Get the phone!"

Russell Sampson was in a meeting with Utah Senator Ron McNair and some staffers when his chief of staff came in and whispered in his ear.

Sampson rose. "Senator, forgive me. I just got word that my son, Jordan, has had a seizure. I need to get the hospital."

McNair told his own chief of staff to order his car to the front of the Capitol. "And tell my driver to burn rubber!"

When Sampson arrived at the Alexandria Children's Hospital, he was immediately ushered into the emergency room. He was shocked by what he saw. His son was fully involved in a terrifying seizure. Diana and Patricia were hysterical.

"Daddy! Get them to stop! Jordan's dying!"

"He's not dying, Patricia. He's going to be fine."

One of the doctors turned to Sampson and whispered, "Please take your daughter outside."

Sampson held his daughter in the waiting room. He could hear Diana crying and the doctors working on Jordan. He felt completely helpless.

CHAPTER 10

Anne Colletti moved through the kitchen, preparing dinner with her usual intensity. "Sophie, let's get moving on homework. Anthony, get in here and start eating."

Sophie and Anthony were listening to the weatherman on SNN, who was predicting a nor'easter. Anthony couldn't say too much, but he knew that snow meant staying home from school and going sledding. He jumped up and down, flapping his hands and yelling, "Snow!"

"Sophie, we need to get your brother to speech. Turn the TV off and let's get moving."

"But Mommy, we need to get the forecast first so we can be prepared."

"This kid is telling me to get prepared," Anne muttered to herself. "I'll show her some preparation . . . " Anne was about to move away from the TV set when she noticed that SNN was covering a story about autism and vaccines. The report began, "We have news of a settlement in the Omnibus Autism Proceeding in the Federal Vaccine Court." That caught her attention.

"We are in front of the Centers for Disease Control in Atlanta, Georgia," the commentator continued. "The federal government—in what is called the 'Vaccine Court'—has conceded that vaccines did indeed cause autism-like symptoms. The case involves a ten-year-old boy named Carson Whittaker . . ." The camera panned to the family and their attorney at the microphone. All Anne had ever heard was that there was no link between vaccines and autism. Yet, right now on SNN, that was changing. The family spoke about their son's regression following the vaccines administered at a well-baby visit.

Anne dialed Tony at work.

"Tony, are you watching SNN?"

"Uh, no, Anne, I'm not. I'm having a crazy day here." Did she really think he sat around watching television? Tony asked himself. He and Forceski had just arrested a man on domestic violence charges. The perpetrator named Pollardi, who was well over six feet and built like a truck, might have killed his wife had the officers not gotten to the house in time. Pollardi sat handcuffed, screaming at Forceski. "Yeah! I was gonna kill her! Yeah! I said it! I was gonna kill that . . . "

"Sounds like it," Anne said. "Listen, SNN is saying that the government conceded that vaccines caused some kid's autism. When you get a chance, watch SNN."

"Okay, Anne, when I get a minute, I'll check."

A little while later, Tony knocked on the door to the chief's office. The chief was watching the TV weather report. "Looks like we're getting hammered again, Tony. They're talkin' about twelve to eighteen inches here."

"Here we go again. Hey, Chief, have you been watching SNN?"

"Why? What's going on?"

"Anne says the government conceded a case about a vaccine causing autism."

"Well, let's watch SNN. They usually run the same story over and over again."

After a few commercials, SNN had its resident medical expert, Dr. Nitton Geevarghese, talking about the federal vaccine court's finding. "Vaccine Court? What's that?—like a drug court or domestic violence court?" the chief asked.

"Actually, it's a federal compensation program for people who have suffered adverse reactions to vaccines. I talked to that lawyer on the Fournier case a little about it. She does these cases. You can't sue the drug companies, so you have to sue HHS—Health and Human Services."

The two men continued to watch the coverage. Dr. G, as he was known, was trying to explain the case to the anchor, a class action called the Omnibus Autism Proceedings. "It is hard to fathom. The government has maintained that there is no link between vaccines and autism."

The camera cut to a reporter named Sara Donovan in front of the CDC. "They are not quite saying that the child has autism. They are conceding that the nine vaccines he received at his eleven-month trip to his pediatrician . . ."

"Jesus," the chief said, "nine in one visit. Isn't that a lot?"

". . . somehow resulted in autism-like symptoms because Carson had a rare metabolic disorder . . ." The coverage then cut to Dr. Jennifer Kesslinger, the director of the CDC, who was walking into an office building. She did not look happy as she turned to comment to the reporters gathering around her. "I am aware of the case. While I haven't reviewed the file in depth, I'm advised that this child had a rare mitochondrial disorder that made him vulnerable. One should not look at this exceedingly rare case and draw the conclusion that vaccines are unsafe. This is a very rare case, very rare."

Donovan yelled, "Dr. Kesslinger, do vaccines cause autism?"

"No, they do not. Again, this child's case of autism-like symptoms has nothing to do with other cases. Vaccines do not cause autism. Vaccines are safe." With that, the coverage ended.

"Well, that's weird," said Tony. "It is and it isn't. They do and they don't."

"I know politicians, Tony. That lady looked nervous. Real nervous."

"And what is this autism-like crap?"

"I guess it's like a vaccine court version of a plea bargain."

"But they agreed to compensate the kid. Can you have symptoms of autism but not have autism?"

Later that night, Tony went on the computer in the living room and watched the coverage of the Whittaker case again. It left him feeling uneasy. It just didn't make sense. Anne strolled by in her bathrobe. "What are you looking up?"

"Coverage of the vaccine-autism case."

Anne looked over his shoulder. "The guy leading the press conference is Jack McLeod, an autism advocate from New York."

"This family is like so many other families that have reported the same story," McLeod told the camera. "Their child received some vaccines, became ill, lost skills, and was diagnosed with autism."

That's what Tony had heard. It's what he and Anne saw with Anthony. It was what Veronica Fournier reported, and what he had heard other parents say happened to their children. And yet, the CDC's Dr. Kesslinger came on to claim this was all rare and no one should draw any conclusions.

Anne shook her head. "Rare? She's full of it."

"What do you make of the autism-like comment?"

"Tony, if you have autism-like behaviors, you have autism. That's how you get the diagnosis."

"It's just behaviors?"

"Yes, you jerk. Don't you remember? It isn't like Anthony took a blood test and it came back positive for autism."

"Yeah, I remember. The psychologist told us to do a genetic test. Six hundred dollars later it comes back normal. Then he said it was genetic anyway and there's nothing he can do. I wanted to strangle him."

Anne went into the kitchen, and Tony kept searching the Internet. He found an autism blog that covered the Whittaker story. The Whittakers felt that the mercury in the vaccines had caused their child's autism. Tony never understood why you would put mercury in a vaccine. Mercury is toxic. Why inject it into kids?

A comment from another parent said her son had been compensated by the Vaccine Court too. Her son also had autism as a result of his vaccine injury.

The blog posted was the description of autism from the *Diagnostic and Statistical Manual*, the *DSM-IV*. Anne was right. If you have symptoms of autism, you have autism. Tony knew that there must be a hard medical description of autism somewhere. After searching, he found a paper that described autism as *an encephalopathy*—an impairment of the brain. The paper questioned whether the encephalopathy was static, meaning permanent, or one that was reversible. Could people with autism get better? Anthony had improved. Many of the people who commented on the blog said that their children also improved when they detoxified them and changed their diets.

The Internet was full of conflicting messages. Autism was genetic, but emerging evidence conflicted with that view and showed that environmental factors clearly played a role. Autism is treatable. Autism is a permanent, life-long developmental disability. Vaccines have been exonerated. Dr. Bryce Ramsey's MMR paper showed a link. Dr. Ramsey was a criminal who was responsible for dead children in England. The controversy was like a war. And today, the people who believed vaccines cause autism had won a huge victory.

Tony found something called the National Vaccine Injury Compensation Program Vaccine Injury Table. Encephalopathy was on the table of injuries, so the Program acknowledged that encephalopathy was a vaccine injury. As he read more, Tony saw that seizures were also on the injury table. His investigative instincts were cooking. Vaccine injury could result in encephalopathy that included autism. And many people with autism also have seizures. It seemed plausible that vaccine injuries could cause autism.

Tony learned that the NVICP was administered by the US Court of Federal Claims, and he found the Court's website. Many of the case decision opinions described dramatic regressions, seizures, and encephalopathy. One described a child who was "obsessively flipping the pages of a book . . . unable to speak or care for himself." The child "sometimes engaged in self-abusive behaviors." That sounded like autism.

The reason for the debate had begun to sink in. There were now hundreds of thousands of people—almost all of them young people—who had autism. Many researchers adamantly declared that there was no real increase in autism. There were always thousands of people with autism around. The increase in autism was because of better diagnostics. "Really?" Tony thought to himself. No one he grew up with had it. Where were all of the adults with autism now? He never knew what autism was until a few years ago.

Then Tony found an article detailing how the increase started when the vaccine schedule was ramped up in the late 1980s. The descriptions of the vaccine-injured people were clues. If vaccines were responsible, then the autism epidemic could have been prevented. But Tony still had trouble accepting this. "This can't be," he said to himself. "This is America. We would never let this happen." Was he becoming a conspiracy nut?

But the investigator inside of him knew it was plausible. The evidence was staring him in the face. As an investigator, he knew that you go where the evidence takes you. You keep asking questions until you get answers or until you run out of questions.

What would an industry do to keep a lid on this? But this was more than the pharmaceutical companies. This was the federal government, and all the states that mandated vaccines, and the pediatricians who administered the program. All of these powerful groups were lined up on this. No wonder the CDC director looked like a deer in headlights. So the real question became, what would these powerful groups do to deal with this problem? Or more to the point, what *wouldn't* they do?

The lawyers from McGaffey and Pierce arrived at SSN's legal department exactly at 9:00 a.m. They were there to shut down SNN's coverage of the Whittaker story. Leading the lawyers was the swaggering Charles Fontaine who wore a black cowboy hat.

The lawyers sat down in the conference room and piled their papers on the glass table. When SNN Journalistic News Division Chief Seth Millman came in, Fontaine greeted him warmly. "Well, hello, Seth, how are you doing?"

"I'm fine, Mr. Fontaine. What can I do for you?" Millman was a shrewd man with dark hair and thick glasses. He sensed that he was about to get squeezed. He knew Washington, he knew the news business, and he knew how to stay away from the nonsense that could derail good journalism.

"Seth, we would like you to let go of the vaccine-autism story."

Millman was right. The BS was going to flow. Someone wanted the news spun their way. He squirmed in his chair for a second, and then asked, "Who is the 'we,' Charles?"

"Every Child Safe for School."

"Who is that, and why should we not cover this controversy? You do realize that most news is controversy, Charles?" Millman was seething. This kind of thing was becoming a plague in the news business, and the old pros like him were growing increasingly resentful.

"Seth, most news is. But what happened here is the result of some good lawyering. Heck, I might hire these boys myself. They cornered DOJ on this one. Now we have piles of research here from peer-reviewed, high-quality journals. And all of it says that vaccines do not cause autism."

"But there was a press conference yesterday and the government conceded that, at least in one case, vaccines did cause autism."

"Actually, they conceded autism-like symptoms. Seth, my friend, this poor kid was dealt a bad genetic deck of cards and likely would have ended up this way anyway. That is the truth. And listen, this is your network, and we respect your rights to cover controversy. We're just asking that you move on to other controversies."

"Why?"

"Because vaccines save lives, and we need to have children safe and healthy to attend school when they turn five."

Millman returned to his office after the meeting and told his attorneys to review the studies even though he was sure that Fontaine was describing the research accurately. The legal division was going to shut the coverage down. Fontaine's subtle message—that SNN ran the risk of causing children to die from "vaccine preventable deaths"—scared everybody.

Millman researched Every Child Safe for School. It was a small Washington-based not-for-profit dedicated to ensuring that every child had his or her vaccines before starting school. Its 2008 budget was $350,000. And yet, this not-for-profit, which was really nothing more than an office in Chevy Chase, could pay a gunslinger like Charles Fontaine and his minions from McGaffey & Pierce to paper his office with research and legal briefs before the story even got going.

Millman wondered whether the other networks were being pressured too. Why hadn't ABC, CBS, and NBC covered the Whittaker story? He called his counterpart at ABC, Bill Ehrman, an old friend.

"The boys with the briefs were here too," Erhman said. It wasn't McGaffey & Pierce, though. It was another lobbying firm. "They scared the crap out of senior staff and they told us we weren't covering this thing. Seth, buddy, there is some real thick stuff here. Why does an industry that has its products mandated by every state in the union have all of these little piss-ant organizations to help them sell their products? Do the New York Yankees need twelve not-for-profits to tell the country how great baseball is?"

Robert Bangston spent the night alone, drinking Scotch in his Georgetown apartment. His wife and daughter left him years ago over this kind of behavior. He deeply regretted not knowing his daughter as well as he should, but they were both in California and had new lives. Soon his daughter would graduate medical school. He hardly knew her. Did she know him? Did she know how alone he was with the all-consuming Division of Vaccine Injury Compensation? No one understood the pressures of his "unique role," as he liked to call it. The director of Vaccine Injury Compensation was the keeper of a lot of secrets. And keeping secrets can change people.

The coverage of the Whittaker case was limited, only SNN and TNS, but it was still devastating. Kesslinger called him immediately after being cornered by the media and screamed about "being put in an untenable position." Bangston half expected to be fired when he got to his office. He looked and felt awful. His assistant brought black coffee with a short "Good morning, Dr. Bangston. Dr. Kesslinger is on line one." Bangston braced himself for another eruption. "Hey, Robert, sorry for going bat-shit on you. It isn't like I didn't know it was coming."

Well, that was different. "Phil wasn't able to squash all of it, Jennifer. These anti-vaccine kooks are fanatical."

"And now we have another problem. Hans Jurgenson wants more money."

"Crap, this is extortion."

"Robert, we should never have done business with this man. He's a terrorist."

Bangston felt as though he would puke his coffee and guts out. "I know, Jennifer. But he was the only person who could produce data. What are you going to do?"

"What I have to do . . . I think I sounded idiotic yesterday with that autism-like comment."

"So far no one in the press has really thought about it. I think it got us through. And by settling this nightmare, we can keep the problem from spreading into the rest of the test cases. We just have to hunker down for now."

"The White House switchboards lit up with calls from the autism community, so the president's people called me. They said that the president was confused."

They both burst out laughing.

Dr. Phillip Snyder had had enough. He was getting carpet-bombed by requests from journalists to comment on the Whittaker case. He had decided to settle on "no comment." But that was for now. He intended to come out swinging once things settled down. Snyder swore to Bangston that heads would roll. Snyder was now more of an administrator than an actual doctor at Silver Falls Hospital. He had become America's Vaccine Spokesman and could often be found promoting and defending vaccines. It was time to use his power and influence.

The anti-vaccine crowd had finally scored a legitimate victory. But most galling to Snyder was that the youngster's father was a doctor. That a member of the medical community had betrayed the rest of his community incensed him. Snyder made a note to ensure that "our own stay in line!" It didn't occur to Snyder that Dr. Whittaker was acting on behalf of his child or because a vaccine injury had actually occurred because Snyder genuinely didn't believe in vaccine injuries. Snyder believed that vaccines did not cause brain damage or seizures or any of the major side effects that were alleged. He believed that this was a bunch of nonsense created by attorneys to make money. He felt that the whole Vaccine Injury Compensation Program should be replaced by a tribunal of medical experts.

Snyder had heated arguments with Bangston over the years about adverse reactions. Bangston insisted that rare adverse reactions happened and had published a paper on adverse events from the MMR vaccines in the 1990s. But Snyder was a true believer and didn't buy that "rare event" nonsense. As far as Snyder was concerned, vaccines were delivered by God to man. They came down the mountain with Moses—they were sacred. They represented everything that is good about the medical establishment. What Dr. Whittaker had done was bad for the medical establishment.

Someone would pay.

Zvi arrived at work late the next morning. He had had trouble sleeping. He and Anya were up until midnight arguing about what he should do in light of the Whittaker case. He pounded his fist against the kitchen table. "I should come forward and tell the press! They had my research years ago but they did nothing about it."

"This isn't your problem. You told them. They made . . . decisions."

"That Kesslinger is no good. She's telling people that the autism reactions are rare. She has no intention of doing what should be done!"

Anya stroked his arm. "Zvi, we risked everything to become Americans. We have children. Think of what you risk. We left everything, everyone. You changed everything. You even changed your name."

"Maybe we are not really Americans."

Zvi sat down at his desk. He felt miserable. What should he do? Would they listen if he spoke out? How would these people feel if it came out that some long forgotten Soviet bureaucrat had figured this all out years ago? Would they call him a Communist? Would they treat him like that English doctor?

The Americans were just like the Soviets. And Zvi felt trapped in America.

CHAPTER 11

Lance Reed enjoyed a gin and tonic in his London flat and reflected on how amazing his career was. As long as he wrote negative stories about "the evil Dr. Bryce Ramsey," the money flowed. And it was good money for a journalist who wasn't really held in high regard by his peers. Reed could care less about his peers because he had no friends. There was an odd coldness about him.

Reed's writing always reflected the dark side of humanity. When other journalists saw the weak or vulnerable, Reed saw people trying to manipulate bad luck into financial gain. He got into the autism-vaccine issue years ago by doing stories about drug companies that produced bad drugs. People were hurt by the drugs, and then a few people were paid off. So what?

What really irked Reed was how people of a certain class in England always came out all right. Therefore, when the word came down that Bryce Ramsey should be dropped down a few pegs for damaging the reputation of the government's vaccine program, Reed was chomping at the bit. Who better than the man who covered some of pharma's past blunders? Reed took his new assignment with a twisted kind of joy. He decided that he was going to ruin that good-looking, upper-class bastard. And he loved watching Ramsey's little fan club of adoring American housewives wringing their hands in agony as he publicly gutted him. He knew that it was time to do it again.

And besides all that, the money was really very good.

"Sir, Lance Reed is on the line."

"Thank you, Donna," Calthorpe said as he lit a cigarette. "Lance, my old friend, how are you?"

"Cut the mushy tone, Lord Gordon. I was wondering when you'd call."

"I assumed you were waiting. It seems we have the flare-up, gratis the Americans."

"I get SNN too, sir. What the hell are the Americans thinking about?"

"Apparently, they had no choice. An expert witness was a problem. They had to cut a deal."

"If that deal was cut here we would at least have the common sense to seal the family away in the Falkland Islands."

"Yes, well, it is time for . . ."

"Mitigation. You need me to resume the slow broiling of Dr. Bryce Ramsey . . ."

"Fire up the grill, you mangy bastard."

Diana Sampson sat down next to Jordan on the living room couch and offered him his favorite cuddle toy, his older sister's Raggedy Ann Doll. Jordan loved the old doll and always dragged it around the house saying "aggedy Ann, aggedy Ann." She placed the doll in his lap but Jordan showed no interest. The doll fell to the floor. Jordan just sat there, looking out the glass door as though he was looking at something far, far away.

Diana hugged Jordan, but he seemed utterly disinterested. She called out his name, but Jordan didn't respond. He just stared.

This had been going on ever since she brought Jordan home from the hospital two weeks ago. Was it the seizure medication? Jordan looked and felt miserable. He had constant diarrhea and a terrible rash. He wasn't talking anymore. He wasn't interested in toys or television. It was as though her beautiful boy had disappeared, leaving a shell.

Diana found herself suddenly in tears. Scooping her son off the floor, Diana hugged and kissed him, rocking him slowly. "Jordan, Jordan, I love you, my darling boy. Come back to me."

But Jordan didn't respond. He just stared straight ahead as though he were a rag doll.

Diana had never felt such dread. Worrying about Jordan now consumed her. She had to call her husband. Diana knew that he was swamped, but she needed to talk to Russell. She left Jordan in the living room and went into the kitchen to make the call. While waiting to get Russell on the phone, Diana looked back at Jordan, who had picked up his toy fire engine. Thank God, he was interested in something again. But as she waited for Russell to come to the phone, she noticed that Jordan wasn't really playing with the fire truck. He was spinning the wheels of the truck over and over again.

CHAPTER 12

Tony turned on the computer at 11:00 p.m. Reviewing vaccine injury cases was tedious work but every now and then, he found something intriguing. In one case, a family alleged that their daughter had developed autistic behaviors after a vaccine injury. The final notation indicated a settlement after appeal, but the rest of the case disappeared from the website.

Tony had been making notations in a notebook about cases where autism was mentioned. He was up to six cases when he read one from 2003 that stunned him. The child was referred to as John Doe 15. The special master ruled that the MMR vaccine caused "brain injury that inexorably led to atypical autism." Tony looked up "atypical autism" and found it defined as "Pervasive Developmental Disorder-Not Otherwise Specified. PDD-NOS is an autism spectrum disorder." The special master stated: *"While this child does seem to have developed atypical autism from the brain damage that resulted from the vaccine injury, I do not see any relationship between this case and any other cases filed alleging similar circumstances."*

Tony thought that this was an odd ruling. Was the special master saying that this case was different than other cases alleging autism was a vaccine injury? And if so, then how so?

Laura Melendez got to her office in Pine Plains at 8:30 a.m. and began sifting through phone messages and emails. She smiled when she read an email from Tony dated this morning at 1:30 a.m. "This guy is nuts," she said aloud. Then she read the case decision and called him. "So I guess you're a vampire too. That's how you can dive into ice cold water and survive."

"Very funny, counselor."

"What the heck are you doing? Are you a legal research wannabe?"

"The Whittaker case got me thinking. And when you add that to the Hockleister case, the Lupannari case, and . . . "

"What cases are you talking about?"

"Cases where the Vaccine Court compensated kids for vaccine injuries that included autism."

"There's only Whittaker."

"Oh no, there isn't, counselor, there are more. Have you ever read these cases?"

"I'm a lawyer running a practice while trying to keep my husband from taking a dive off the Hudson River Bridge. You think I have time to read vaccine decisions? Where are you finding this stuff?"

"On the US Court of Claims website."

"Are you kidding me?"

"Now you sound like a cop."

"That would require donuts, fella. No donuts here. There's more cases?"

"Yeah, but I also hit a lot of dead ends. The website doesn't have everything. Some cases just disappear."

"Hey, listen, I want to talk about this with Herb Newman. He's been practicing in the program longer than I have. You mind?"

"Who's Herb Newman?"

"An attorney," she said with feigned drama, "who has been practicing longer in the program than I have. What do you think 'practicing' means?"

"Oh, I believe that you attorneys practice all the time. You just never get it right!"

⚕ ⚕ ⚕

Laura called Herb Newman at his New York City office later that morning. Newman had just finished humiliating a US attorney over an illegal search. It was what big, scary New York City criminal defense lawyers did. Newman wasn't just a defense attorney. He was a heavy hitter. His briefs in the Vaccine Court made jaws drop and special masters nervous.

"Hello, Laura. How's life in the suburbs?" Newman asked.

"Business is slow, but we're surviving. You?"

"I'm at war with some kid in the US attorney's Office. What else is new?"

"How're your vaccine cases going? What do you think about the Whittaker case?"

"DOJ got nailed for a change," Newman chuckled. "Don't think that this means they're surrendering. They cut this deal, bad as it was, so that they could go forward with the other cases. They're going to try to un-ring the bell. They have to."

"There won't be any precedential value from Whittaker?"

"These special masters pick and choose where they want precedent. There is no such thing as precedent in the compensation program unless HHS wants there to be precedent."

"Then what's the point of the Omnibus Autism Proceeding?"

"We shouldn't be having these proceedings. The statute says that we should only have to prove vaccine injury, and that's tough enough. But to show that a vaccine led to a behavioral disorder—and remember, that's how autism is defined—is a burden we shouldn't have to meet. I told the other lawyers that this was a trap. I'm not sure that they had a choice."

"Herb, I have something interesting that I want to send you. It's an email from an investigator I know who has been doing some research on previous vaccine case decisions."

"You guys hired an investigator to look up VICP cases? You have the money for that in the suburbs? I need to get an office up by you."

"The guy isn't an employee. He's a cop. Actually, I think he's a little nuts."

"A cop is doing this? What's wrong with the guy?"

"I think he leans a little to the compulsive," laughed Melendez, "but he's a good guy. He was the one who went into the frozen lake for that Winston kid."

"I remember hearing about that. Awful. Could have been any of our kids. You did good work for that family. Better you than me in family court, Laura. Forward the email."

Newman opened the email later that day and looked at the quote pulled from the John Doe 15 case decision:

> While this child does seem to have developed atypical autism from the brain damage that resulted from the vaccine injury, I do not see any relationship between this case and any other case filed alleging similar circumstances.

"Let me look this up," Newman said to himself. It was a fairly astonishing thing to put in a case decision. The logic was whacky. "Did this special master ever hear of the 'but for' construct," Newman wondered. "This kid has atypical autism, well, PDD-NOS, but it was the result of brain damage. The brain damage was caused by the vaccine, you idiot." Newman shook his head. The special master ordered compensation for this child for encephalopathy—brain damage. Clearly, autism was a result of the encephalopathy.

The expert witness who carried the day in John Doe 15, one of the world's premier pediatric neurologists, detailed how vaccine injury had led to brain damage and then to autism. Why on earth was an Omnibus Autism Proceeding even necessary? It had all been decided years ago.

But no one was saying that.

Tony was exhausted from staying up late reading vaccine cases. Just as he thought he could head home, news came that Randazzo had flipped his cruiser over on the ice on Hudson Street while chasing a speeding car. The chief, who was away at a conference, called Tony. "Go out and handle it because if Randazzo isn't dead from the accident, I might just kill him myself."

Tony and Forceski got to Hudson Street quickly. Randazzo was still in the cruiser—upside down. The cruiser had flipped over and slid on its roof until it wedged into heavy brush. Tony bent down to look into the wreck. "Hey, Dazz, how're you doing?"

"I am pretty pissed off, Detective. But I don't think I broke anything."

"What the heck happened?" yelled Forceski.

"Some punk in a Mustang was driving like a maniac. I started following back on Route 9. Chavez came back saying the guy had a warrant, I hit the lights, and the chase was on. I saw a patch of ice right as I broke to avoid a minivan. Next thing I knew, I flipped over and plowed in here. Can you get me out of here? My seat belt won't disengage. I'm stuck, and I have to pee."

"Good thing you wore your body armor and seat belt," said Forceski. "Otherwise, you might be all messed up."

"Captain, I really have to take a wicked piss."

Tony lay on his back looking at Randazzo. "Dazz, you are an absolute shit magnet." Forceski and Tony chuckled. "Now you got feeling in your legs and all that, right? I don't want to move you if you have spinal damage."

"Sir, I'm fine. I'm feeling everything, including the coffee I finished an hour ago."

Tony's cell phone rang while he was working on the seat belt lock. "Colletti here."

"Hi. I'm Herb Newman. Laura Melendez said I could call you about the vaccine program."

"How are you, Counselor?"

"Okay. Do you have a minute?"

"Detective, please, please get me out of here, or I'm gonna piss on you!"

Newman overheard and thought Randazzo was saying "piss on you" to him. "Hey, look, Colletti, I don't need that kind of crap! I've been dealing with cops for over twenty years and . . . "

"No, no, no, Counselor, look, I'll call you back later. I'm at an accident scene and someone's trapped in a car. I'll call you back."

"Oh, sorry. Talk later."

"Detective, please cut me out of this wreck, I'm begging you!"

Tony couldn't get the seat belt lock to disengage either. "Dazz, take it easy. I got my pocket knife." His cell phone rang again. It was the chief. "What's going on with Randazzo?"

"He's okay. It's amazing he wasn't seriously hurt. We're cutting him out of the cruiser."

"I need to pee!"

"And he needs to pee."

"Well, cut him out of the damned car! Make sure that he goes to the ER and gets checked out. Right now I need you to get on the county radio-band. County and Hanover PD have some hostage situation up there."

The belt finally released, and Randazzo crawled out and ran behind a tree.

"Don't they have hostage negotiators?" Tony asked. "What do they need me for?"

"Apparently," said the chief, "the hostage taker has a gun . . . and autism."

CHAPTER 13

Tony did not like what he heard over the police radio. A young man with autism named Stuart Abramson was shooting at the police and SWAT officers who hunkered down in the woods around his home. The Hanover Police Department called the county SWAT Unit, which responded in their usual understated way. They brought the "Tank"—an armored personnel carrier for SWAT—and parked it one hundred feet from the front door of the stately colonial house, blocking the driveway.

Nobody was getting out of 12 Iroquois Street.

Captain John Hunter peered at the Abramson home through night vision goggles. "Any visuals on Rachel Abramson?" he asked over the radio.

"Negative, sir," replied one of the SWAT officers.

Hunter was worried about the boy's mother, Rachel Abramson. It was believed that she was in the house, but she wasn't answering the phone and no one had seen her moving around inside. The father, Dr. Solomon Abramson, was on a flight back from Milwaukee where he had spent the week at the American Academy of Pediatrics.

How Stuart got access to a firearm wasn't clear. It appeared that Dr. Abramson was a hunter in his younger days and still kept a rifle or two along with a pistol, in his home. County records indicated that Dr. Abramson had gun permits. What was clear was that Stuart suddenly appeared outside on his porch with a rifle, screaming. The Hanover Police responded and tried to communicate with Stuart, but couldn't. Stuart walked back inside the house and the police moved up the driveway. Just as they reached the porch, shots rang out and the siege was on.

The hostage negotiators, who phoned Stuart twice, couldn't get him to talk. All Stuart would say was "Police go!" The hostage negotiators didn't know what to do. Hunter called Chief Lonnegan and asked for Colletti and Forceski. "Chief, I need your autism whisperer guys up here. We need to communicate with this kid."

Hunter had to do something. This siege couldn't go on forever. There was a residential facility called the French Heights School for Delinquent Boys just behind the Abramson home. Castleton County had a fair number of residential facilities going back to the days when New York City's young offenders were "sent up the river." The river was the Hudson, and the place of confinement was rural French Heights, the location of a small Revolutionary War battle.

"Tony, look at it this way," said Forceski while turning onto Iroquois Street. "One of our special kids has a whole facility of young criminals locked down."

"Irony, defined." Tony said. They parked their car and showed badges and identification to a blue-helmeted SWAT officer. "Hunter is waiting for you guys in the Tank."

"So I guess that the Abramson house would be the one with the Tank in the driveway," said Forceski.

John Hunter's voice boomed over a megaphone, "Winston PD! Get your Goddamned heads down!"

That tone did not indicate that things were going well. Nor did the smell. SWAT detonated a canister of oleoresin capsicum, and the area was blanketed in a shroud of caustic fumes. There was a lot of confusion when the event started. Some kids from The French Heights School came through the woods to see what was going on. When they refused to leave, SWAT let the OC canisters loose. The fumes were now rolling through the facility, sickening the residents and staff who were pinned down in classrooms.

The men entered the Tank through the rear hatch. "Hey, guys," Hunter said.

"Hey, Marine," said Forceski. "What the heck are we doing here?"

"We need you guys to get this kid talking or get him to come out. We don't know what the status of the mom is. We don't even know why he's shooting."

"We all don't know shit," said Hanover Chief Ambrose. "All we know is that we have a retard with a rifle and . . ."

"Hey, chief," said Forceski, "we both have autistic kids, and we don't call them retards!"

"Come on, Chief," Tony echoed. "We don't have to hear that crap."

"Let's chill out, gentlemen," Hunter said in military fashion. "We have a nightmare scenario here. None of us knows what the heck to do. I got hostage negotiators set up in the house across the street and they can't get anything going." Hunter was now shouting because of the noise from a helicopter that now hovered above the scene. Then one of the SWAT officers called over the radio. "Captain, I have a visual. The suspect is moving back and forth in front of the television, first floor family room. He's watching *Teletubbies*."

"What's he doing?" yelled Hunter.

"He's watching *Teletubbies*, sir."

"I can't hear this guy because of the damn helicopter . . . what?!

"*Teletubbies*, Captain! He's watching the *Teletubbies* on the TV!"

"John, can I get a look at the house? You got night goggles, right?" asked Tony.

"Yeah, take a look." Hunter pointed to the hatch above. "Just keep your head low. If you can see him, he can see you."

Tony poked his head up through the hatch. Searchlights kept sweeping over the house. There were half a dozen police cars with their overhead lights circling. The noise from the helicopter was incessant. The smell was acrid and awful, and the helicopter kept kicking it back into the air. "Look, we have to cut the chaos down," Tony reported. "There's no way that a kid with autism can handle this. He's gotta have sensory overload from all this."

"Okay," said Hunter, "we have to reduce the . . ."

Then a shot rang out. Everybody hit the floor. Then another shot. Hunter started screaming, "Down! Down! Everybody get your heads down!" Mayhem and obscenities ensued. "Where did the shot come from?"

"We think the kid!" barked one the SWAT team members over the radio.

Forceski and Tony's faces were inches from each other. Forceski said "He thinks it was the kid. What the . . ."

More screaming and yelling over the radios. Tony's cell phone rang. "Yeah," said Tony under the din.

"It's Newman. Hey, I ran a search through Westlaw. You're right."

"What?"

"Clear the freaking lines, people!" shouted Hunter. "I'm getting pissed off."

"I searched Westlaw," Newman continued, "and found eight more case decisions where the kid was described as having autism and was compensated by HHS."

"Uh, that's great, Counselor," Tony said. "But listen, can we talk later? We're being shot at right now."

Hunter was really angry now. "IDENTIFY THE SOURCE OF THAT LAST SERIES OF SHOTS, GENTLEMEN! WHO THE HELL IS SHOOTING?!"

Then over the radio, "Uh, Captain, sir, I saw movement on the south side of the property. I thought I saw a flash of something, but, well sir, it was a deer moving between trees with lights from a facility behind it and . . ."

"Copy that." Hunter was exasperated. "We bagged a deer."

Chief Ambrose was enraged. "You people come up here from Pine Plains and start shooting up my town! What kind of operation is this?!"

Hunter wanted to strangle Ambrose. "Don't you point your finger at me, you . . ."

"John," Tony said quietly. "Let's lose the helicopter."

"It isn't ours. It's News 13."

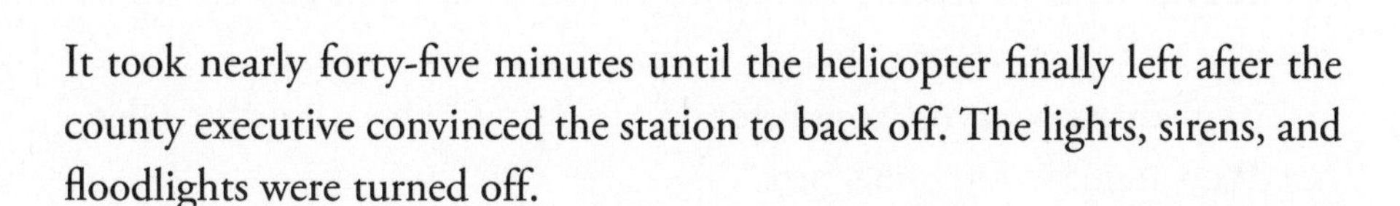

It took nearly forty-five minutes until the helicopter finally left after the county executive convinced the station to back off. The lights, sirens, and floodlights were turned off.

The Tank was now packed with cops. Hunter, Tony, and Forceski were looking over the house plans that Hanover Police had pulled from the town's building department. The hostage negotiators wanted to be closer to the house to plan the next move. "You think that he might just let us in?" said Demetrius Jones, a muscular African American officer and hostage negotiator.

"I think we have a shot," said Tony.

"Do we try to get the door open and bull the team through?" asked Hunter.

"If he lets you in, why not just take him in with as little drama as possible?" said Forceski.

"I'm not sure that I can communicate with him effectively," said Jones. My wife's nephew, Antoine, has autism, but I don't know him real well."

"Glen and I live with this," said Tony. "That's why we know you have to go low emotion here. No flash-bangs, battering rams, helicopters, or OC canisters."

"And that's why you guys go in," said Hunter. "We need to end this thing, and we still don't know the status of the mother. You two go in first."

There are times when it is completely reasonable to question one's career choices. That time had come for Tony and Forceski. Both men were moving quietly through the darkness down the driveway toward the front door with their guns drawn. In the house in front of them was an armed young man who couldn't communicate and who was under enormous stress. Behind them was a platoon of well-armed SWAT officers who had just spent hours freezing in the woods, stressed out, and sucking in the acrid OC fumes. Even with body armor, helmets, radios, and firearms, this was not exactly a good place to be.

"Guns in front of you, guns behind," said Tony. "This is horrible, Glen."

"You aren't kidding me, bro."

Once on the porch, the men took up positions on either side of the door. Tony listened for any activity. "TV's still on," Tony said into his radio.

"Tony, I think the door may be open," said Forceski. "Looks like it from my side."

"All right. If it opens, we move, quiet. You go left and I go right through the parlor. Once we clear that room, we go through the kitchen into the family room where we hope he is watching TV." Tony was talking to Forceski and to Hunter on the radio at the same time. Hunter moved his team toward their position.

"We will keep the door open. Everyone comes in quiet, with ears and eyes wide open. *Festina lente.*"

"Repeat last communication," chirped Hunter.

"Hurry slowly." Tony turned the door knob—it was open. Both men moved in quickly but quietly. Tony went right. Forceski cut left.

The parlor was clear.

Both men merged at the door into the kitchen. "Parlor is clear." They heard the SWAT team assembling on the porch. Tony nodded to Forceski. "So far, so good." They moved into the kitchen using the same approach. The lights were on and everything seemed normal. They could hear the television in the family room down the hall.

The two men huddled. "I think we ask SWAT to move into the kitchen and camp out here until we clear the family room. This way they have our backs. This is some house."

"Yeah, nice place. They got money, I guess," whispered Forceski.

Tony advised Hunter of the plan.

"Tony, I think he's watching *Bear in the Big Blue House.*

"That figures. It's my favorite kid show." They could hear the bear singing "I am just the shape of a bear . . ." "Let's do this."

The two men moved down the dark hallway and paused at the entrance to the family room.

Stuart Abramson, a tall, lanky teenager with a mop of frizzy hair, sat in front of the television, holding his mother's cramped, lifeless hand. Rachel Abramson lay on the floor, dead from a bullet wound to her head.

Stuart didn't notice the men yet. Forceski pointed to a rifle that was lying on the floor. He moved quickly and took it. Tony moved toward Stuart slowly, making sure that Stuart was unarmed. "Stuart."

The boy responded by screaming and punching himself in the head.

"Stuart. Easy. We're here to help. We are clear. Situation resolved!"

"Mom, Mom, quiet," Stuart said. Then he began to cry. "Mom. Mom."

The threat was over, but the scene was horrific. Stuart had blood all over his hands and clothes. There was blood splatter against the wall just past the entrance from a side hall. Mrs. Abramson must have been shot as she walked into the room. She may never have realized what was happening. The round took off most of the back of her head.

Tony felt his heart sink. It was one of the worst things he had ever seen in his life. He glanced at Forceski, who was also shaken.

"This is Colletti." Tony spoke into his radio. "It's over. Rifle secured. We have Stuart. It's over." Tony sat with Stuart on the couch and spoke quietly to him. "Stuart, what happened?" Stuart looked at him but couldn't really maintain eye contact. Finally, he said, "Call Daddy."

"Okay. We will."

Hunter and the other SWAT team members came into the family room. "Oh my God," Hunter said, "can he say what happened?" Stuart began hitting himself again, and Tony and Forceski had to restrain him. Hunter didn't know what to do. "Clear the rest of the house," said Hunter over the radio. "I guess we cuff him."

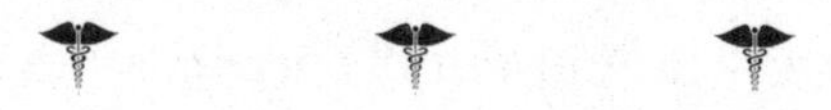

The rest of the evening was a nightmare. Tony sat with Stuart while other detectives tried to get him to describe what had happened. It was impossible to communicate with the boy, who was completely frustrated and continued his self-abusive behavior. The DA investigators had no better luck. It was futile. They couldn't use information from Stuart, anyway, as he clearly wasn't competent to waive his rights. Tony had Forceski call Laura, on the sly, and she sent her husband Carlos Melendez up to Hanover to represent Stuart.

It ended up being the strangest interrogation in the history of Castleton County. The perpetrator not only wouldn't talk, he couldn't talk. Finally Melendez told the detectives, "Guys, this is over. He isn't withholding. He really can't say what happened here." No one could really argue with him. It seemed that Stuart somehow got a rifle and shot and killed his mother. No one could determine intent. The incident was horrible and senseless.

Stuart would be held overnight in Hanover. He was photographed and booked. Booking is a tedious and tense process with regular offenders, and almost impossible to do to a person with autism.

Tony, Forceski, and Carlos Melendez never left his side. The men had become at least familiar to Stuart. At some point during the night, Dr. Abramson arrived. He looked ashen, as he entered the jail cell at 3:30 a.m. "I am Stuart's father," he said to Tony. "I am responsible here."

Tony stood up and acknowledged him, but didn't know what to say. Stuart suddenly became animated and started repeating, "Daddy, home. Home, Daddy."

"The officer outside said that you helped my son," said Abramson turning to Tony. "He told me you have a son with autism too."

"Yes," said Tony quietly, "I do."

"You may have saved my son's life."

"I am so . . . ."

"I am responsible, Officer. I am."

Tony didn't know what else to say. Leaving Dr. Abramson in the cell with Stuart, Tony and Forceski headed home. The two men said nothing to each other all the way to Winston PD headquarters where they reported what happened to Chief Lonnegan, who waited for them.

Tony got home after 5:00 a.m. at first light. Anne met him downstairs. "I heard about what happened. You look awful. Go get some rest."

Tony went upstairs and checked on Sophie and then little Anthony. They looked so sweet and innocent sleeping. He paused a minute over Anthony and brushed his hair and whispered ever so quietly to him, "Freedom. Freedom. I wish that you could have freedom." Then he kissed his son's forehead and went into his bedroom. Anne was back in bed and had already dozed back into sleep. He lay down next to her and closed his eyes. He couldn't get the image of Rachel Abramson out of his mind. Or the image of Stuart in the jail cell.

CHAPTER 14

As the Stuart Abramson case became headline news all over the country, Tony noticed more and more news stories about "dangerous autistics" committing violent acts and coming into contact with the criminal justice system. SNN replayed images of one young man with autism beating his head against the Plexiglas in the back of a police car in Michigan.

A young man with a hand gun was shot and killed by police in New Mexico after acting in a threatening manner in a mall parking lot. It turned out that the gun was a track pistol and that the man had autism. He may not have been able to understand the police's verbal commands to drop the weapon.

Reports of autistic children disrupting classrooms appeared in the *America Today* newspaper. "America's teachers were not handling the apparent increase in autism well." One teacher in Florida restrained a child with autism with duct tape, and other children began verbally abusing the child. Another child with autism wandered onto a road in Florida, and a teacher running after him was hit by a car.

The nightmare of autism was everywhere.

Radio shock-jock Brian Barbarino of the nationally syndicated "The Barbarian Hoard" ranted, "The autism epidemic was made up by incompetent parents so that their kids could get special attention. What do you mean your kid can't communicate when he screams like a maniac and can shoot a gun! And stop with all this autism epidemic bull (bleeped)! What we have is an epidemic of bad parents in a weak country where everyone needs a diagnosis to get special treatment."

The rant cost Brian the Barbarian several sponsors and several radio stations after Jack McLeod and his protestors from Fight Back for Autism picketed his New York City radio station. Tony liked McLeod. It was obvious that the guy had brass down there.

Tony and Forceski watched one television report where Phillip Snyder said, "There is no real increase. We are just better at diagnosing it now." Forceski shook his head. "Our school special ed budget is going through the roof. And they blame most of the cost on autism."

"How could all of these 'experts' have missed kids like Stuart Abramson twenty years ago?" Tony said. "It makes no sense. Were these clinical people really that stupid twenty years ago? It doesn't add up."

Once the coverage of the Whittaker Vaccine Court case stopped, a series of new studies were released "once again showing no link between vaccines and autism." Dr. Snyder again appeared in his white lab coat saying, "Mountains of evidence now refute a link." In one interview, Snyder admonished a reporter saying, "It is really irresponsible of you to ask about vaccines and autism. The controversy is over."

What was causing so much autism? No one knew. And no one asked.

But as winter began to loosen its cold grip on the Northeast, Dr. Abramson knew. And what he knew was destroying him. Abramson was wracked with grief and guilt. His oldest daughter tried everything she could to engage her father in help. But nothing worked. So one day in late March, he walked into his basement and took a hand gun out of his safe. He then went up to his study and wrote a letter. He then sealed the letter in an envelope and placed the envelope neatly on his desk.

And then he blew his brains out.

Chief Ambrose wasn't surprised when he got the call about Dr. Abramson. The suicide note left Ambrose confused, however. What was the NVICP? Why did Abramson feel responsible for his son's encephalopathy, whatever that was? Maybe Chief Lonnegan's guys could shed some light on it.

Laura Melendez pulled together a meeting with Tony and Herb Newman at her office to discuss Tony's investigation of Vaccine Court cases. "Tony, I got coffee but I forgot the donuts."

"Very funny, Counselor."

"Herb is on his way," said Laura smiling. "I think you'll like him."

Laura's husband, Carlos'/ea stopped by. "Hey, Tony, you did the right thing by calling me on the Abramson case."

The sadness of that night still hung in the air.

"Well, it was you or Bill Kunstler."

"Kunstler is dead," Laura said.

"But Herb Newman lives!" said Newman as he bounded into the conference room. Tony could see that he dominated any space he was in. "I assume you're the cop in charge of vaccine compensation program secrets."

"Yeah, I guess that's me."

Everybody sat down, except for Carlos who left to meet with a client.

"I made copies of the eight other cases beside John Doe 15," said Newman. "Here they are. This will be the beginning of our project files."

"Project?" asked Tony. "We're doing a project?"

"Well, yeah. That's what you in essence initiated here."

Tony thought about it for a moment. Why the heck was he doing all this? He was an investigator, but hardly a legal researcher. "Mr. Newman, where does all of this lead?"

"Call me Herb. Look, I think you're right. I think that are a lot of cases of autism that have been compensated by the program."

"It's an important finding, Tony." Laura said. "Some of these cases tell important stories. The descriptions of developmental regression following vaccine reactions are exactly what you hear at an autism treatment conference."

"How come none of the attorneys working in the program have reported this?"

"They're not allowed to talk about their cases," said Newman. "This is not a typical judicial setting. The rules are strictly enforced by the special masters."

"Well, how many cases with autism have you worked through in the past?"

"None," said Newman.

"Why not?" asked Tony. "I mean, if you think I'm right, then how come . . ."

"Because I started in the program after the Autism Omnibus Proceedings commenced. I wasn't involved prior to 2003."

"Almost all of the cases filed now are autism cases," added Laura.

Tony sat back and focused on Newman. "Counselor, what's your stake in this? Why do you care?"

"What's my dog in this fight?" said Newman directly. "Mr. Colletti, I am a liberal progressive and a criminal defense attorney. I am a cop's worst nightmare."

"And a great litigator too," added Laura.

"I have an uncle who was 'mentally retarded,' as people used to say. The government gave my uncle nothing. My family had to scratch and claw to provide him with a decent life and basic human respect. And I have a son who regressed after a vaccine—just like some of the families in the cases you found. Yes, my son has an autism diagnosis, but he has been injured by a vaccine and now has brain damage. Sometimes I think that autism is a diagnosis that was invented to label and discriminate against our kids. It's a slave word. And it's being used to deny children the help they need by people who are protecting their policy interests. Now you know what I think. I'm in the same boat as you Officer Colletti. I'm just fighting for my kid."

Tony regarded Newman in a different light. "Thank you. Now I know why you're in on the hunt."

"It's only right that you know. But you posed an important question: was autism a common feature of vaccine injury cases before the Omnibus

Proceedings, before people even realized that there was an autism epidemic?"

"What if Whittaker wasn't such a rare event?" Laura said.

"I got you," said Tony. "Would this project, as you call it, prove that vaccines cause autism?"

"No," said Newman, "this isn't science. This is social-legal research. But it would show plausibility. No one could ignore this study because, let's face it, the federal government compensated these cases for vaccine injury."

Tony nodded. This is why he was doing this. Newman and Laura were right. "In other words vaccine injury has nothing to do with autism, then how come . . . "

"All these vaccine-injured children also have autism?" Laura said.

"How many other cases have you found?" Newman asked.

Tony opened his notebook and leafed through his notes. "Well, there's Whittaker, John Doe 15, Hockleister."

"Hockleister?" asked Newman.

"Yeah," answered Tony, "the mom wrote an autism blog after Whittaker settled and said her kid with autism was compensated too. This case, Perlmutter, clearly states 'features of autism' but then ends without a decision indicating settlement. So I don't know. When I add my nine and your eight . . . "

"We have seventeen cases, and we've barely started!" Laura said. "Rare outcome, my ass."

Newman turned his laptop on and searched the Internet. "Make it eighteen. Perlmutter was remanded after appeal and the family was compensated."

"Where did you get that?" asked Tony.

"Westlaw, a legal database. We lawyers use it every day."

"To keep the police away," Laura joked.

"Hey," said Tony, "look up Hockleister."

Newman searched, but found nothing. "I bet it was settled without a decision. Is it on the Court of Claims website?"

"No," said Tony, "I checked. Hey, you know what? The Claims website only goes back to 1997. If the case was decided or settled before then,

then we can't find it." Suddenly he was worried. "How will we ever find all these cases? There could be . . . "

"Hundreds," said Newman. "There are cases going back to 1988, but how do we get to them?" He worked the computer as though it were plugged directly into his brain. "Department of Health and Human Resources Statistical reports . . . as of 2010, there were 1,300 cases compensated for seizures and/or encephalopathy since 1991."

"You mean that we're looking at 1,300 plus cases that could feature autism?" Tony said.

"This is huge," said Newman. "Huge."

"Oh my God," Laura gasped. "This could be a major scandal."

"It will be an important paper," said Newman. "And it will really piss off the feds!"

Tony felt uneasy as he drove home. "I'm a cop," he reminded himself. "I'm sworn to represent government authority, not tear it down." But what was going on didn't sit right with him. All of these children had their lives completely wrecked by autism. They were ending up in jail cells, abused, and even killed. Their parents were beleaguered. Their lives had become a series of catastrophes, viewed as a drain on society and even singled out as incompetent by radio talk show hosts.

And the consequences were happening close to home too. The chief had told him the other day that he didn't think his daughter's marriage would hold up under the strain caused by his granddaughter's autism.

Autism was like a freight train that's gone off the tracks and was wrecking life after life, family after family, and no one in authority was doing anything other than offering false assurances. It was the same messages over and over again: "There's no epidemic." "It's a genetic disorder. We're just better at diagnosing it." "There's no link to vaccines."

"Why should I care?" Tony wondered. "What am I doing hanging around with these lawyers? Maybe I should just take care of my kid and not deal with this."

Tony's cell phone rang. It was the chief. "Hey, Tony, I know you're off today, but I want to show you something. Can you stop by?"

Tony sat in the chief's office and read the Abramson suicide letter again. He was stunned.

"What do you think about that?"

"Abramson couldn't live with this, so he killed himself." Tony shook his head. "It's one thing to know that the vaccines you administer did this to your kid, but it is another thing to . . ."

"Cut a deal," said Lonnegan. "The guy cut a deal, took care of his kid, and then, well this is the really hard part, he represented himself as a pediatrician with a child with autism and told everyone that they should follow the vaccine schedule just like the AAP recommends. He even used his son . . ."

Tony finished the sentence. "As an example to support the system."

"Yeah. That's what this guy did," Lonnegan said while glaring at the American Academy of Pediatrics website on his computer. There was a photograph of Dr. Abramson smiling and a statement supporting the Academy and the vaccine schedule. Below his picture was a caption "Dr. Solomon Abramson, pediatrician, father of a child with autism."

"And all along," said Tony, "the guy knew. He had a case filed with the wonderful National Vaccine Injury Compensation Program. Stuart was compensated. And he has autism. I want to puke."

"So his kid gets access to his gun one day," said Lonnegan, "and accidentally shoots his wife dead. Unbelievable." The two men shook their heads. "Does this tie in with those cases you told me about?"

"It does. Had I known this, I might have shot Abramson myself."

Tony was seething when he left headquarters. He called Newman. "Hey, Herb, we now have twenty cases. And we are taking these drug dealers down."

CHAPTER 15

Robert Bangston sat in the back of a large hearing room nervously listening to Chief Special Master Carl Mantkewicz wrap up his testimony on the functioning of the NVICP before a portion of the US Senate's larger Health, Education, Labor, and Pensions (HELP) Committee. Mantkewicz, always polished, was completely at ease as he thanked the senators for their interest in the program. "I understand your concerns in light of the Whittaker concession, Senator."

"I have received dozens of phone calls from Iowans who have children with autism," said Senator Parker Smithson. "There are concerns about how you will deal with the thousands of cases alleging autism as a vaccine injury."

Smithson made Bangston nervous. The guy didn't trust the program. Bangston was glad that it was Mantkewicz up there because they couldn't challenge special masters too vigorously as they served a quasi-judicial purpose. They decided vaccine injury cases and their decisions were appealable to the judges on the US Court of Claims. However, much of the Vaccine Court's day-to-day business involved Bangston and his staff, executive branch employees. Bangston would be fair game if he ended up in front of Smithson.

"We share your workload concerns, Senator, but the statute is clear: the number of special masters is set at eight. We would need Congress to act to add more. So we have to handle what comes in. We have to do our best."

The hearing was winding down. The senators were shifting in their seats and chatting quietly with their aides. But Smithson wasn't done yet.

"Chief Special Master, thank you again for taking the time to talk to us today." Smithson lowered his glasses and peered intently at Mantkewicz. "I just have one more question. You have an extensive legal background. Do you feel that special masters should be fully integrated into the judicial branch, under Claims, beyond the influence of HHS?"

Mantkewicz anticipated such a question. "The independence of the special masters is crucial, and the Secretary affords us a great deal of independence. In fact, every secretary of HHS from every administration that I have been involved with over the past twenty years has always been respectful of our need to function independently."

"Yes, very good, Special Master," said Smithson, "but sometimes I do worry about the construction of this program. The same cabinet secretary who is responsible for promoting our vaccine program, and the CDC in fact, also administers the injury compensation program. So sometimes I just worry a bit. Old senators are known to do that."

The senator's comment triggered mild laughter in the room. Then Smithson looked up at the clock, and turned to his aide before speaking again into the microphone. "Thank you, Chief Special Master. You were most informative."

The committee adjourned.

Mantkewicz and Bangston left the Dirksen Building and crossed the Capitol grounds toward the Court of Claims. "Bob, what did you think about Smithson's last question?" Mantkewicz asked.

"The guy is suspicious. We should never have conceded Whittaker. And now we have another problem,"

"What?"

"Carl, Sol Abramson committed suicide."

"Oh no! That's horrible. What happened?"

Bangston pulled Mantkewicz toward a park bench across the street from the Court of Claims. "Apparently, he couldn't handle what happened to his wife. So he shot himself."

"Jeez. Who would have pegged him for a gun guy?"

"Listen," whispered Bangston, "just keep an eye out for anybody asking questions about his son's case."

"Not to worry. We don't let anyone see these files—ever. With all of the medical and personal information, we just don't allow it, you know that. Take it easy."

"I'm just saying, Carl . . ."

"Bob, we're fine, and everything is under control."

"I don't think that everything is fine. We've both been here since day one. I was standing next to you when Reagan signed the law. Carl, I don't know where the autism issue will end up."

"We've been doing this too long, Bob," Mantkewicz sighed. "We both know that some cases featured autism, but I can't accept that vaccines are responsible for all of the autism out there. The program saves lives, and we have to remember that. That's what counts."

"You're telling me what counts? Do you know what it's like to deal with Kesslinger? With Snyder?"

"That pain in the ass should shut up."

"Well he won't. He keeps bringing up the MMR encephalopathy paper I did in 1998. Half the time I think I might get the Ramsey treatment if anyone ever realized that my paper was still out there."

"Bob, what matters is the program. Vaccines are good."

Bangston grimaced. "Then why are we whispering?"

CHAPTER 16

It had been a long winter for Tony. Both his day job and what he now considered his night job were taking their toll, and his wife knew it. That's why Anne tossed Tony's judo uniform toward him as he walked through the front door. "Go do your training. You can have some soup when you get back. I got the kids. Get outa here."

Tony wondered why this gorgeous woman stayed with him and why she cared enough to always know what he needed. "Okay, you're right, I'm going. Need anything from the supermarket?"

"No. See you later."

As Tony drove, he thought about Abramson's suicide letter. He felt as though he were being dragged toward a conflict with an opponent that he couldn't define. He felt its presence in his dream after the Fournier drowning and he still felt it. "What am I thinking about?" he asked himself, then realized it was time to "empty his cup" at his old dojo with his sensei and friends.

He got to the dojo a few minutes early and smiled as he bowed to Sensei Saito. "Good that you are here tonight, Tony," said Saito. "We have evaluations scheduled for Victor, Susan, and Big D. I need you."

"I am here for whatever you need."

Saito whispered to Tony, "Give them nothing if they don't take it with sincerity."

Tony loved Sensei Saito. The man exuded serenity and compassion but could command a room full of vigorous young martial artists. It was said that Saito could walk through the toughest streets in Yonkers in complete safety; no one would dare attack a man who was referred to as the Wizard of Warburton Avenue. It was also said that Saito could stop a violent man with a glance and kill with a touch. The truth was Saito had never hurt anybody. He was a gentle man, completely committed to jujitsu, and to his neighborhood.

Tony was going to be taking a lot of throws, but that was what the class needed. He started with Victor, a tough, young Latino man who used to be a gang member until martial arts saved him from a life on the streets. Sensei watched Victor throw Tony more than twenty times making sure that Victor stayed focused.

Susan was a thin, quiet law student who had come a long way. She really worked the technique, and it was remarkable how someone so demure could suddenly unleash so much energy. Tony detected a small smile on Sensei's face as Susan perfectly deflected an attack.

Then Tony worked with "Big D"—all two hundred and sixty pounds of him. The problem with Derek Biggs was that he relied too much on strength and not enough on technique. Following Sensei's instructions, Tony did not give Big D the easy out. He would have to use technique. Big D attempted a hip throw, but didn't execute it properly. Frustrated, he rammed Tony against the wall with a loud crash. The entire room froze as Tony drove Big D back out into the middle of the floor and spun him to the mat with a loud snap.

Saito's voice pierced the room, "YAME!" Everyone stopped and stood at attention.

A short time later, Big D and Tony embraced quietly in the back of the dojo as the class wound down. "I apologize," said Big D. "I wasn't working it right, and I got frustrated. I'm sorry."

"You're going to get there," Tony said. "And when you do, it's going to be amazing." The two men embraced again.

Saito motioned to Tony to come over as he finished putting his coat on. "Officer Tony, let's go have coffee."

⚕ ⚕ ⚕

They sat in a diner overlooking the Hudson River Bridge. "Tony," said Saito, "what's going on with you?"

"I'm sorry about tonight, Sensei."

"No need to be sorry. You helped Big D hear what I'd been telling him for months. Never rely on strength! Less strength, more jujitsu. You taught him good." The two men laughed. "But something is troubling you. I know you for twenty years. Is it your son? Empty your cup."

Tony stirred his coffee. "It's my son. But it's more than just my son. I've come to the conclusion that my son wasn't supposed to have autism. He wasn't born this way. He became this way."

Saito nodded and then asked quietly, "Because of vaccines?"

"How did you know about this?"

"Susan came to the dojo one day with her brother, George, who has autism. We spoke about him at length. Susan says her parents, who are doctors, believe it was vaccination as well. She is very loyal to her brother. I have learned a lot about *Chugo* from Susan."

Chugo meant loyalty. It was one of the tenets of the Code of Bushido, the Samurai code of conduct.

"I see so many families who are like Susan's," Tony said. "These people inspire me."

"You are also one of these people."

"Sensei, there is more," Tony said quietly. "Our government has been lying. I think that they have built a wall of lies to keep people from figuring out this vaccination-autism connection."

"And yet, it seems that many people know. But they don't speak openly."

"Did you hear about that boy who won the case in the Vaccine Court?"

"I recall something. It was a few months ago?"

"Yes. The government claimed that it was just that one case. Well, I did some investigating, and found more. Then some lawyers I know searched some legal databases, and we found even more. Remember the Stuart Abramson situation?"

"Tragic. Such suffering."

"Read this." Tony took out his copy of Dr. Abramson's suicide letter and handed it to Saito.

Saito read the letter slowly. Then he folded it and handed it back, shaking his head. "I have seen this before, my friend," he said wearily. "Do you know where I am from? How I came to be in America?"

"I know that you came here as a child."

"Yes. But there were reasons." Saito's eyes softened with a faraway look as he recited,

"When I thought I was dying
And my hands were numb
And wouldn't work—
And my father was dying too—
When the villagers turned against us—
It was the sea
I would go to cry.

No one can understand
Why I love the sea so much
The sea has never abandoned me.
The sea is the blood of my veins."

Tony was dumbfounded.

"That poem was written by a fisherman from the town where I grew up, a place that I may never return to. Do you know about Minamata? It's a beautiful fishing village on the Shiranui Sea on the island of Kyushu. My family lived there for hundreds of years. The Chisso Company had a factory by the bay. Chisso means nitrogen in Japanese. The factory made fertilizer from the nitrogen and a waste product of the process was mercury."

"Mercury is in vaccines."

"The company dumped the mercury into Minamata Bay but told no one. The villagers—my family, my neighbors—ate the fish from the bay. At first, people noticed dead fish. But then sea birds fell out of the sky. Then cats began to get sick. They had all been eating the fish. They danced around as though they were possessed and then dropped dead.

"Then the villagers got sick. They couldn't talk, they couldn't walk, and they began to die of terrible convulsions. I saw my grandfather die from this sickness. My grandmother followed him." Saito had tears in his eyes. "Babies were born with terrible deformities. I had a younger sister . . . " Saito collected himself. "Tony, the people in Chisso knew what was going on. But none came forward. Chugo—loyalty—can have a dark side. Minamata needed Chisso. The company brought jobs and growth. Japan was still recovering from the war. Challenging the company was just not done. But a few people began to ask questions. The company printed studies showing that they were not to blame. When the studies were questioned, they blamed those who questioned them for hurting the company, for hurting Japan. Some villagers even began to shun the families of the sick. They blamed the families for bringing bad karma to the village. To be shunned in Japan is terrible. We take such pride in our communities, in being Japanese. Then, the truth came out."

"What happened?"

"A Chisso executive named Hasokawa learned that he was dying of cancer. He could no longer bear his dishonor. He confessed. The truth was revealed. So, you see, I have seen this before. You do not have to convince me."

"I'm sorry, Sensei."

"In the end, many died. And many people left Minamata forever. My father and mother decided to leave, and we came to America. Before my father died of cancer, he introduced me to Watanabe Sensei, and from him, I learned jujitsu in the traditional Japanese way. It was my father's way of giving me the best of Japan. This is why I teach jujitsu. It is my way of honoring my family and those who suffered."

Tony fumbled for words. "I am so sorry for the suffering you and your family have endured."

"The only way to understand suffering and not be defeated by it is through service to others. This is what true samurai have always understood. What do you intend to do about what you have learned?"

"I have to investigate this. The lawyers feel that we should publish a report. Sensei, you said that people turned against those who questioned."

"They did. Seeking truth often involves sacrifice. But it's the only way to achieve justice."

"I know. I want justice for my son and for all of those who have suffered."

"Then you know what you have to do. It's a matter of honor."

CHAPTER 17

Lance Reed waited in Calthorpe's dark office and brushed away the cigarette smoke. Calthopre entered and handed Reed two large packages. "Lance Reed, on time as usual."

"Afternoon, your Lordship. It's a perfect time for Ramsey to be kicked again as he is already on the ground."

"These bundles should help you keep your foot on his neck. Now get out of here you miserable little troll."

"You could've at least offered me some gin."

"There's enough in there to buy a lot of gin, my old friend. Now go and write some nasty articles."

Two days later, articles about Dr. Bryce Ramsey appeared in English tabloids alleging that Dr. Bryce Ramsey had altered medical records to make it appear that he had altered children's medical records in a study he authored. The allegation was that the children always had autism and that Ramsey made it appear that onset followed vaccination. The timing of the stories was a disaster for Dr. Ramsey who was already involved in a professional disciplinary hearing. Worse yet, it was alleged that Dr. Ramsey did this for financial gain.

None of it was true. But that didn't matter. The media in the United States picked up on the story, and the media immediately ran to Dr. Phillip Snyder.

"What I can tell you," offered Snyder, "is that this whole vaccine-autism thing is a dead issue, and it is time to round up those responsible for spreading fear."

"Isn't this confusing for parents who hear about the Ramsey scandal in the UK but see the government conceding vaccine-autism court cases here?"

"That child had a rare genetic condition and would have ended up with autism anyway. Look, lawyers can do great things for people," Snyder chuckled. "But the evidence is in. Autism is genetic. Vaccines don't cause it. Genes do. Vaccines are safe."

April was Autism Awareness Month and the media reported that another study had been published showing that scientists are closing in on the "Autistic Genes." The study reported "hot spots" on two genes and was repeated, with slight modifications, on every network. One version used some computer graphics showing the autism genes lighting up as if that was how the researchers actually found the "hot spots."

No one in the press picked up on the fact that, even if the findings held up to further review, that the "Autistic Genes" would account for less than 2% of autism cases. And when the study was evaluated further, it turned out that none of the hot spot genes had any statistically significant influence on autism. The genetic research was a dead end. But no one reported that.

Autism Awareness Month coverage then turned to a new study from the Norwegian Research Collective, a CDC-funded team under the direction of Dr. Hans Jurgenson. The CDC proudly announced that the study showed that autism rates in Norway had gone up after the removal of mercury in vaccines. Mercury in vaccines had nothing to do with autism.

Dr. Snyder addressed the media: "This is another marvelous piece of research showing that vaccination, or mercury in vaccines, has nothing to do with autism. This goes with the rest of the pile of research saying the same thing. This study won't make my new book, *The Autism Fraud*, but it validates the piles of science already on the books."

"Should Dr. Ramsey be criminally prosecuted in England for starting the autism-vaccine crisis?" asked one reporter.

"No legitimate member of the medical establishment should continue to engage in discussions that spread misinformation about the strong safety record of vaccines."

And the beat went on. Within a few months, the world had forgotten that the United States government had conceded that vaccine injury led to the Whittaker child's autism.

Back in England, Calthorpe surveyed the impact of the work from his dark office at Rollins and exhaled an avalanche of cigarette smoke. There was a never-ending string of pro-vaccine stories, and the words "Ramsey," "fraud," "vaccine," and "autism" were beginning to be used together regularly in the mainstream media. Now all that had to happen was to make sure that the Americans did the right thing in the Vaccine Court's Omnibus Autism Proceedings. "The Americans are such pompous nitwits," he said to himself.

But even there, he had Lance Reed greasing the skids. He had the folder of goodies for the lawyers defending the Secretary of Health and Human Services.

It was now April, and the mood around the Winston-on-Hudson PD had begun to improve. The snow was almost gone, Randazzo had not wrecked any more cars, and autism seemed almost under control.

Tony spent his nights looking up cases with Herb Newman and Laura Melendez. They found a few more that mentioned autism and some where the victim's behaviors were consistent with autism. Newman sent a Freedom of Information Act Letter to HHS seeking information about autism cases from the compensation program. "We are going to have to rip it out of them," he said. "You watch, they aren't going to give us anything."

"Herb, if that is the case," said Tony, "then some of these families will have to be located and interviewed. Getting these people on the phone is going to be a challenge."

"Getting them to talk won't be easy either," added Laura.

"Hey, guys," Tony said, "you do know that I know how to find people and get them to talk, right?" Everybody laughed. "So, let's keep digging."

"At some point," said Newman, "we'll need somebody to pull together a paper that we can publish, assuming the numbers keep building."

"Don't you write?" asked Tony. "I've read your work in *Autism Impact.*"

"No, we need a legal scholar for this," Newman said. "We need the Countess."

"Who's that?" asked Tony.

"Maria Contessa-Guevera at Columbia Law. She has written extensively on the program."

"You have to meet her," said Laura. "She is super busy and just had a second child. But I bet she'll like this project."

"Well, let's get the Countess on the phone," said Tony.

"We still need to get to the settlements," said Newman. "The website and Westlaw don't have all of the cases."

"Maybe we should put a notice about the project on an autism blog," Laura said. "We might catch a few families that way."

"I guess we should, but that might alert the other side that we're doing this," Herb said. "We know that they monitor the Internet activity of the autism community."

"Who would do that?" Tony asked.

Dr. Phillip Snyder smiled as he reviewed a contract with the pharmaceutical company he had partnered with for the past ten years. The distribution plan for his vaccine guaranteed healthy profit over the next two years.

Glancing over at his computer, he noticed an email from one of the Internet "monitors" that Calthorpe had watching the anti-vaccine crowd. It dealt with Newman's post about the "Vaccine Court Project" on an autism community blog. "Interesting," Snyder said to himself. "The whackos do have lawyers. There's some half-assed study of old Vaccine Court cases." He didn't give it much thought, but forwarded the email to Bangston for his reaction.

Bangston was actually happy for a change. His daughter had found Mr. Right and was getting married. His ex-wife was even nice to him. Then he saw the email. "Phil! What the hell is this?" was how he began his phone call to Snyder.

"I don't know. It came from one of the monitors. I thought you should know 'bout it."

"Phil, this could be a problem." Bangston put the call on speakerphone and paced around his office. "Do these people have access to the cases?"

"What cases?"

"Our closed cases. I don't want these people getting into my records!"

"Can they really do that? I don't see how they could, Bob." Snyder had a point. "These people can't just walk into US Claims Court and pull folders. You may be overreacting. We'll figure out which branches of the nut tree these whackos hang from and pull together some folders on them. We'll have a counterpunch for whatever nonsense they eventually put out. What are they going to find, anyway?"

"I don't know, Phil. This could be a problem."

"Bob, they're all nuts. Calm down." Snyder sensed Bangston's angst and felt for him. "Why don't you come out to the shore with me next weekend and play some golf? Get the heck out of DC."

"Okay, Phil. I'll calm down," Bangston lied, "Just throw me a fair handicap, will ya?"

"Call me later this week and we'll make plans."

Bangston hung up. It was useless to explain the situation to Snyder. The guy was the ultimate true believer and he didn't know the program's history.

But Bangston did.

Zvi Kokochashvili also noticed the description of the project on the *Era of Autism* blog and began making calls. Not everyone at the CDC and in HHS was convinced that vaccines didn't cause autism. There were whispers that a lot of cases that had been settled over the past twenty years featured autism. Word was that these children, now young adults, were so wracked by seizures from DPT vaccine injuries that autism wasn't really a priority for these families. Just keeping their children alive was an ongoing struggle.

Zvi went for a drive that night. From an old phone booth with an actual working phone he left a message on Herb Newman's answering service. "Mr. Newman, I am—never mind. I know of your project, and I believe that you must pursue case settlements. That is where you will find what you are seeking."

Then Zvi got in his car and drove away.

CHAPTER 18

Tony was scheduled to be off for a few days, planning to look after the household while Anne attended the Healing Autism Conference in New Jersey. He would also spend time on the project. He needed some time off and Anne had earned a break.

But the moment Tony got home from work, he saw something was wrong. Anthony was covered in gluten-free pasta and tomato sauce. Sophie, who was helping Anthony get through dinner alone, said "Mommy is sick. She's taking a nap upstairs."

Anne lay in bed looking miserable. "Tony, I've got fever, chills, the whole nine yards," she moaned.

"You don't have . . . "

"Yeah, the pukes."

"Oh, Babe, then how're you going to do the conference tomorrow?"

"Unless you believe in miracles, I'm not going," she moaned. "I called Mom. She'll come by to help. You go to the conference. I'm not wasting the money we put down for this."

"No, no, Babe," said Tony in a panic. "Cops don't do autism conferences."

"Well this cop will. Suck it up and bring back some information to help your son. I spent four hundred and fifty dollars on the conference science track, plus the hotel room. You think I want to learn about the methylation cycle?"

"Metha-flopping-what?" Tony sputtered

"Methylation. Learn it." Anne looked angry as well as sick. "You better come back knowing all about porphyrin testing and mitochondrial dysfunction."

"Mitocardria . . ."

"Mitochondria. This is about your son! We are trying to recover him. So pack your bags. The conference starts at noon tomorrow, so you have to leave early. Now get the kids to bed. I need sleep."

Tony arrived at the hotel at 11:30 the following morning. It was either register as Anne Colletti or pay extra, so now his nametag showed him to be a guy named Anne. Tony felt embarrassed and found himself thinking of Johnny Cash's "A Boy Named Sue."

Tony wandered through a crowd of people scurrying to different conference lectures. He couldn't find where the science track sessions were being held, and in his confusion he dropped his conference materials. Then he noticed Jack McLeod walking across the lobby. "Hey, Jack," Tony yelled. "You're Jack McLeod, right?"

"And you would be?"

"Tony Colletti. I recognized you from the Whittaker press conference on SNN. Thanks for smacking down Brian the Barbarian too."

"Oh, you're welcome," smiled McLeod. "It's what we do . . . Anne?"

"Oh, yeah, this," said Tony with some embarrassment. "My wife was supposed to be here but she got sick. Do you know where the Somerset Room is?"

"It's right behind you. Welcome to the annual gathering of the most dangerous people on earth! Come by the Fight Back for Autism booth later, and we'll kick it around."

Tony knew what McLeod meant. Although Dr. Snyder described The Healing Autism Conference as being "the annual gathering of anti-vaccine radicals and dangerous fringe pseudo-scientists," that already didn't square with what Tony observed. The conference attendees seemed to be regular middle-class parents, hardly dangerous. People who attended law enforcement conferences looked more radical than these people.

The first session was about testing for something called "porphyrins" in urine, the test to determine mercury levels. Tony had difficulty following the lecturer's thick French accent, but he picked up a test kit at the end of the session. As he left, he ran into Laura Melendez cruising through the crowd. "Hey, Laura," Tony yelled. "Are you in the science track?"

"What the heck are you doing here?" she asked.

"Anne got sick and . . ."

Laura laughed when she read his name tag. "Yes, I'm in the science track. You can follow along. Just don't act like you really know me," Laura teased.

The father-son research team who led the next session presented a study that showed that autism rates had dropped now that mercury has been removed from vaccines. The presentation featured a mix of science, politics, and even some discussion of Vaccine Court cases.

"How come this hasn't been covered during Autism Awareness Month?" Tony asked Laura.

"Didn't I tell you to stop acting like you know me?" Laura winked.

The next session, which was on the methylation cycle, was heavy science. The researchers showed that many children with autism have their "methylation pathway" screwed up. Methylation is an important biochemical process that is critical to gene expression. Children with autism were metabolic train wrecks. Metals, pesticides, and other toxins could cause real damage to a developing child and trigger autism. It was clear that injecting toxins into children predisposed to methylation issues was a recipe for disaster. The good news was that this metabolic pathway could be repaired to some degree through removal of heavy metals and other toxins.

Tony was impressed with the questions people asked. They were not radicals or fringe lunatics, just ordinary parents trying their best to understand what was going on with their kids and trying to heal them.

"Laura, why was this so threatening?"

"The 'Healing Autism Conference' by its very name implies that our kids have been injured. Mainstream medicine clings to the notion that autism is genetic so that they don't have to go down this road."

"None of the presenters have said that genetics isn't important. Didn't that French guy say some children may be genetically predisposed?"

"You caught that, did you?" Laura said. "You really getting all of this?"

"It's not that far over my head." Tony could tell Laura wasn't buying it. "All right, I thought my brain would melt when that guy brought up the Krebs cycle. I didn't know we had one. This stuff is so complicated, and everybody is really working hard to help their kids. I really respect our people. If this was a police conference, half the crowd would be liquored up by now."

"That doesn't mean we can't have a drink," said Laura. "I'm going to put my stuff in my room and drag Carlos out of the legal track. Meet you in the lobby bar."

Tony relaxed for a few minutes in his room and called Anne. She was still miserable, but sounded happy that he seemed to be learning things. On the way back to the lobby, Tony got in the elevator with a pretty blonde-haired woman in her early forties. A southern accent was evident as she talked on her cell phone.

Tony recalled the name on her nametag. As she ended her call as they left the elevator, Tony said, "Excuse me, but are you the Lana Hockleister who posted the comment on the *Era of Autism* blog about your child going through the Vaccine Court?"

"Are you a pervert?" she responded.

"No! I'm just a dad attending the conference."

"Where I'm from there are no men named Anne."

"My wife Anne couldn't come to the conference. She's not feeling well so I'm here instead. I'm Tony."

"You're a New Yorker, aren't you? You sound like a cop on *Law & Order.*"

"You're pretty perceptive. Hey, may I ask you a few questions about the compensation program?"

"It'll cost you a drink, but don't try hitting on me. My husband's a big old football coach, and he'll stomp you."

"I just want your thoughts about the Vaccine Court. I'm doing a project on it."

"It's a pretty dull thing to do a project on. The whole process was long, frustrating, and boring."

Tony didn't notice Laura frowning as she watched Tony buy Lana a drink at the bar. "What was your special master like?" Tony asked Lana as they found seats.

"He was all right, I guess. We only met him once to sign the settlement papers."

"You never had a hearing?"

"They were coming down to Mobile to hold the hearing when the Justice Department settled."

"They were going to have the hearing in Alabama?"

"Our attorney said they try to have hearings near where you live so that you aren't made to travel with a disabled kid. They do that for everybody, he said."

"So you never met any other parents going through this?"

"Nope, you do it alone."

Tony wondered whether this procedure was also a way to keep families isolated. "How's your son now?"

"He's sixteen now but still needs us with him all the time. He's started to talk some."

"How's he doing physically?"

"He still has seizures and autism. He still obsesses over *Sesame Street* videos and has meltdowns if you try to take him someplace new."

"My son does that too," Tony said. "I have a big Italian family. They're good, accepting people, but I can see that they just don't get Anthony."

"I know whatcha mean," Lana said. "You feel everyone's eyes on you. It gets tougher as they get older because it's one thing for five-year-olds to go off, but people get spooked when a sixteen-year-old acts that way. They get bigger and they just ain't cute anymore."

"It doesn't get any easier, does it?"

"No. And I worry all the time because I won't live forever, and I fear dyin' without having someone to take care of him."

"That's my fear too."

"But you've gotta have hope. That's why I'm here. Maybe something will help my son."

"Did the special master and all the lawyers know that he had autism?"

"Yeah, they all knew." Lana took another sip of bourbon. "They said that the autism was a sequela. You know that word?"

Tony nodded. "A condition resulting from a disease, condition, or traumatic injury. I've heard an attorney use the term. Did the autism sequela seem like a big deal to them?"

"No, they didn't care too much. They seemed like they had done this lots of times."

Tony swirled his Scotch. "Why do you think that you won?"

"Our lawyer said we had an open-and-shut case because my son met the criteria for encephalopathy, which is basically, brain damage. They have this thing called a 'Table of Injuries.' If your case meets the criteria, then you eventually get compensated. So it only took us five years."

"Five years was quick for an open-and-shut case?"

"Well, sure, we ended up in an emergency room. My son had seizures and almost died within an hour of the vaccine. Everything was documented up the wall. And our lawyer said we were lucky. Some cases take eight or nine years." Tears filled her eyes. "Yeah, my son was lucky. He'll never have a job, never play football or baseball or write something about himself. He'll never have a girlfriend or be a father."

They looked at each other for a moment, saying nothing. What had been taken from her family could never really be "compensated." And the Vaccine Court secretive functioning only made the experience more unnatural.

"Lana, has anyone from the program ever called you to follow up on how things are going?"

"Never. Once it was over, it was over."

Tony wondered if the program sought to silence or intimidate families. "Did they ever tell you not to talk about your case, about your son's autism?"

"We were told to keep our case quiet. But they weren't going to threaten me and Billy Joe. My husband had just retired from the Oilers, and he's a pretty big dude."

Tony vaguely recalled a player named Hockleister and put it all together. "He was a linebacker, right?"

"Yep, that's him. Big and dumb as a man can come, but I love that horse's ass. And he's a great dad." Lana laughed and finished her drink. She stood and offered her hand. "I hope I helped you learn something."

Tony spotted Laura and Carlos with Herb at a table near the bar. Laura scowled at his approach. "Wow!" he said. "I just had a great conversation with Lana Hockleister."

"I bet you did. Did you get her number?"

"Do you think I should have? I learned a lot from her."

"That is a nice way of putting it. You have a wife sick at home taking care of your kids. You're not supposed to go to these conferences to pick up blondes at the bar. You are really a . . ."

"Laura," Tony said quietly, "she has a kid with autism, and she went through the compensation program. Her son's case is one of the cases in our count. She is *that* Lana Hockleister."

"Oh." said Laura sheepishly. Carlos and Herb burst out laughing.

"You are one piece of work, Counselor," Tony laughed too. "You really are. So, do you think I could've scored with Lana?"

Laura punched Tony in the arm.

The conversation with Lana was fascinating and sad. There was a lot Tony needed to understand better. It was clear that families never interacted with other families going through the program. Tony wondered whether taking the hearing to the subject's home town was actually a crafty way of concealing the program's functioning. While the program wasn't exactly the secret court as some critics described it, it certainly wasn't an open forum.

"Herb," Tony asked, "why haven't more families spoken out about their cases?"

"Why would you?" Newman answered while working on his laptop. A half-finished beer was at his elbow. "Think about it. These people have been through hell. The cases take years, and believe me, Lana *was* actually lucky. I've heard about cases where parents are accused of child abuse, where medical experts have their credibility viciously attacked. Forget all that nonsense in the act about cases being handled with compassion. I had a case where the kid died from a vaccine. DOJ used everything from sudden infant death syndrome to shaken baby syndrome against the family. Even the special master said enough was enough. What do they get? Two hundred-fifty thousand dollars. That's all that the act—the *compassionate* act—allows for the life of a human being."

"That's it?!" Tony said.

"This isn't justice," Newman said. "You watch what happens with the Omnibus. They have to win now. They have no choice."

"You really think the whole thing is a sham, don't you?" Laura said.

"They have to protect the program. They have to protect their policies . . . the war is just beginning." Newman continued his search on the Internet. "Why can't I find any records about the settlements?"

That weekend, as the conference attendees sought answers about autism, two representatives of the United States Department of Justice met with Lance Reed in a London hotel room. "Here are the bundles, my friends,"

Reed said with a knowing smile. "Selected records from the English litigation on vaccines and autism."

"They're enormous," said the female attorney, "how'll I read this in time to prepare? The hearings start Tuesday."

"Lady," Reed answered, "that's your problem. But you'd better read them."

"Well, aren't you a peach," said the male attorney

Reed looked at them as though they were insects. "I think that you're utterly unprepared. You were completely unprepared when Whittaker's lawyers pulled your pants down around your ankles too."

"What do you know about that, Mr. Reed?" the male attorney said angrily. "We can't bury expert reports. We can't manipulate every aspect of the system just to produce the outcome we want. We do have rules that we have to follow."

"Really?" Reed smirked. "Then why are you here?"

CHAPTER 19

Tony began the next day of the conference, sitting next to Laura, in a presentation about autism and gut issues. The slides used by the gastroenterologist in the presentation made Tony happy that he had not eaten a big breakfast. It wasn't the photographs of feces and diarrhea. It was the photographs of suffering children with autism who were clearly undernourished and emaciated. Their eyes were haunting. The doctor then showed some of the same children after treatment and after their diets were changed, usually to a wheat-and dairy-free diet, and the positive changes were obvious. "Thank God that Anne put Anthony on a gluten-free/casein-free diet."

"My guy also improved after changing his diet," Laura said.

Tony noticed that Laura had tears in her eyes. "What's wrong?"

"I had to represent an autistic child who looked like those children in a family court proceeding a few weeks ago. He was removed from his home for good reason. But the doctors involved don't believe changing his diet will help him."

As the session ended, the room filled up with even more people. The hotel staff removed the dividers so the hall could hold more people. Dr. Bryce Ramsey was about to address the audience about his recent research and disciplinary proceedings in England. Tony noticed that a television crew had assembled in the back of the conference room.

The room had a definite buzz about it. Tony and Laura were joined by Jack McLeod.

"What do you think about Ramsey?" Tony asked McLeod.

"I think he told the truth and got skewered for it. Doctors are being given a message: criticize vaccines and what happened to Ramsey will happen to you."

The tall, good-looking Bryce Ramsey was introduced to a standing ovation. "My friends," Ramsey said, "it seems that I have committed the ultimate sin. I listened to my patients' parents. Even worse, I treated their children. And, as many of you can attest, the children who have been treated have improved." The audience again stood and applauded. "Many of the parents I know report that their children regressed after a vaccine. This has been observed over and over again. One report is an anecdote. Hundreds of reports are a pattern." The applause resumed. "It may well be that the government knew about autistic regressions after vaccination and we have asked for the data on this for years. And for years we have been refused. I call on the CDC to finally release the Vaccine Safety Data Repository to independent researchers!" This brought tremendous applause from the crowd and chants of "CDC Transparency! CDC Transparency!"

"What is the VSDR?" Tony asked McLeod.

"Data that belonged to US taxpayers that was handed over to a pharma trade group. The data is believed to show a connection between vaccinations and autism. Pharma said they won't give the data—something about business interests or some silly crap like that. Now they say they lost the data."

Then Ramsey asked the audience to raise their hands if they believed that vaccines played a role in their children's regression into autism. Everyone in the room raised their hands. It was a stunning sight. Tony was close enough to the television crew to hear the television cameraman say, "Wow!"

While exiting the session, Tony described the project to Jack McLeod. "You found twenty-two cases already?" McLeod asked incredulously. He pulled Tony off to a quiet corner of the lobby. "Tony, this is explosive stuff. You need to keep what you are doing quiet. Loose lips sink ships. Trust me on this, not everyone here is really with us. If the other side catches wind of this, they will try to stop you."

"What are you saying? We have, like, spies here?"

"Not like," said McLeod.

Later that afternoon, television journalist Sara Donovan was showing Seth Millman the footage of her interview with Bryce Ramsey and his speech at the conference. The footage of an entire room of parents, just regular Americans, raising their hands in response to Ramsey's question was powerful.

Sara Donovan was a serious investigative journalist. Now in her early forties, the attractive Donovan was regarded as a top journalist talent. She lived for the hard investigation side of the news. "Seth, these people believe this. They know what happened to their kids."

"Everyone in mainstream medicine says they're nuts," Millman said. "Is it possible that there's a sort of group influence thing going on?"

"I don't think so. They don't say that their kids got a vaccine and became instantly autistic. They talk about serious illnesses, seizures, and emergency room drama following vaccine administration. Many can document this phenomenon in medical records. The kids regress, lose skills and language, and eventually get an autism diagnosis like in the Whittaker case."

"All these families report that?"

"Not all, to be accurate." Donovan said. "Some report a more gradual descent—or regression—into autism."

Millman rubbed his eyes and leaned back in his chair. "This is a complicated story, Sara. It won't be easy to convey this complexity in a three-minute segment."

"It's an important story, Seth."

"If anyone could do it, you could. Is anyone at Johns Hopkins willing to talk about these regressions on the record?"

"They say that these regressions don't happen."

"Really?"

"The neurology director says that the children are born autistic but that parents don't realize it for a while. Actually, he claims that the parents didn't pick up the signs."

"Oh, come on, Sara," Millman said shaking his head, "that makes no sense to me. I have three daughters. I may have been riding midnights around here or kicking around the Middle East ducking scud missiles, but my wife would never, never have missed something like autism. She could tell when my daughter had an ear infection before the doctor looked in her ears. That neurologist is disrespectful."

"I agree. Seth, these people are credible."

"That doesn't mean that they're right. But it does mean that they should be heard."

Thirty minutes later, Charles Fontaine and two assistants appeared in the lobby with folders full of briefs. Once again, Fontiane's clients wanted coverage of the vaccine-autism controversy suppressed. Fontaine didn't want Ramsey's speech and the footage of all of those parents raising their hands on the nightly news. Millman refused to meet with him and continued working on the Ramsey piece for the evening news. The piece was about to be finalized when the head of the legal division burst into the production room and told them to pull the story.

"Ralph, this is crap!" Millman shouted. "We aren't saying these people are right, but it is news!"

"This is disgusting!" said Donovan. "We're supposed to let our audience make these decisions!"

"Look, people, SNN is not taking the rap for a disease outbreak!"

"Oh, come on!" Millman shouted as he flung his coffee into a garbage pail.

The story never ran.

Tony met McLeod, Newman, and Laura at the bar to continue their conversations after the presentations ended. The conference was still buzzing from Dr. Ramsey's speech.

"I see that you have a new laptop or iPad or whatever," Laura said to Newman.

"Yes," Newman said proudly, "this just came out. It has everything."

"Of course it does," Laura teased.

"Hey, man," McLeod said. "I bet that the entire Internet, national defense, and NSA satellites are now directly under Herb's control."

"It has enough processing power to do that, actually," Newman said while sipping wine.

"Of course, it does," Laura said.

"Hey, Herb," McLeod said, "can you get me off the terrorist watch list with that thing?"

Everyone laughed but Tony didn't see the humor. "Jack, are you serious about that?"

"Yeah," McLeod said. "I had to take a business flight to Montreal last month and got the TSA buddy treatment."

"You kiddin' me?" Tony asked.

"It was the Whittaker press conference," Newman said looking at his laptop. "I'm not surprised. We're a threat to the vaccine program so I'm sure that some federal bureaucrat came to the conclusion that Jack is a potential threat to national security."

"This is nuts, people," Tony said. "You're telling me that the people here eating gluten-casein-free diets are a threat to national security?"

"That's what I meant when I told you we were the most dangerous people on earth," McLeod said.

"I've heard some in our community argue that what's going on is like the Holocaust. I bristle at that," Newman said, "and I think that those kinds of comments make us look like fringe kooks, which feeds into how we are painted by the other side."

"I agree, Herb," Laura said, "but there are elements in common."

"Yes, there are," Newman said. "When you look at what is going on, it's clear that the other side uses distance and concealment to keep the reality of vaccine injury away from the public. The German people knew about the persecution of the Jews, but it was still logical to build the concentration camps away from the centers of towns and cities. It helped keep the ugly reality away. America's not so different. You don't see maximum security prisons in Scarsdale, do you?"

"No, we don't," Tony said. "The whole program accomplishes this. The families go through it alone. It's not an open court in a public building."

"That's right," Newman said. "The use of propaganda to further policy goals is another common element. The press is continually told that we're crazy. Again, the strategy is to use that sort of picture of us to keep us at arm's length in the public consciousness."

"Can you imagine the publicity of an open civil trial with the press reporting on events like we saw with the tobacco industry?" Laura added. "That would do real damage."

"That's what they desperately seek to prevent," Newman said. "Keep in mind that Big Tobacco won most of the civil suits, but the net effect was a decrease in cigarette smoking and a decrease in profits. That's why I believe that the only reason that there's an Omnibus Autism Proceeding is because they intend to publicly dismiss the autism issue. The Whittaker case—and Jack here did an amazing job in bringing that to light—was a complete mistake. They got caught with their pants down. I can't talk about why; we're under a directive to be silent about it."

"You are?" asked Tony in amazement.

"Yep," Herb replied.

"This is unbelievable," Tony said, shaking his head.

"Tony, I want to introduce you to Maria Contessa-Guevera—the research scholar who'll write the paper for us." Laura said.

Laura walked Tony toward a woman seated by a waterfall in a portion of the hotel lobby that featured lush plants. "Maria, this is Tony Colletti, the man I told you about who started . . . "

"Oh!" said Tony, red-faced and embarrassed.

"I see you're not used to women openly breastfeeding their infants," said Maria Contessa-Guevera with a slight Latino accent.

"You could say that, I guess," he mumbled.

Laura laughed at Tony's discomfort. "I'm going to get Carlos and join you in a few minutes."

Maria looked at Tony and smiled. "This is my son, Antonio. What do you think?"

Tony began to relax a little. "I think that he's beautiful. My son is named Anthony too."

"I may selectively vaccinate him after age four," Maria said. "I will do vaccines my way this time because my older son regressed after his vaccines at eleven months old. My husband and I have had to go to great lengths to recover him. I don't want to make the same errors again. Please sit down." Maria was a beautiful, dark-haired woman with beautiful brown eyes. She exuded serene wisdom. "I understand that you've been doing some research on the program and finding a hidden history."

"Yes, I have," Tony replied. "Herb and Laura are helping a lot."

"They are excellent lawyers. I've been studying this program, as well, from a scholarship perspective and also because of my personal interests. I think that you have found something worthy of publication."

"What does that involve exactly?" Tony asked.

"A great deal of work: building a case, fact-checking, assessing information, and reaching conclusions that you can sustain. The paper would have to go through peer review." Maria cuddled her son, who had now fallen asleep.

"I work in law enforcement, so I understand what it means to build a case."

"Yes, I heard that you're a policeman. But there is a significant difference between proving an individual's guilt and proving the guilt of a government program." Maria buttoned her shirt and sat back holding her sleeping son. "I've seen what happens to people who challenge their government. It's not done without cost. And for people—perhaps people such as you—who are representatives of the hegemony . . . "

"You mean the government?"

"Well, an indirect representative of the authority of government. The experience of suddenly being opposed to that authority can be especially difficult." Maria drank some water and looked Tony directly in the eyes. "In Argentina I saw many protestors jailed for speaking out against the government. However, the government officials who joined them were not just jailed. They were executed or made to disappear. My father was such a man."

"Your father was a cop?" Tony asked.

"No," Maria shook her head sadly, "he was a judge. One day he never came home. We searched frantically for him but no one would help us find my father. Everyone turned their backs on us. Eventually, we realized that the government made him disappear."

"Your father was a judge, and no one helped you?"

"Argentina was under the rule of corrupt people. If you challenged the government, you became one of the desperadoes, the Ones who Disappeared." Maria gently rocked her son.

"America doesn't do those sorts of things," Tony said.

"America does things differently. These are powerful people who will be threatened. If we find more cases, they'll use the devices available to them to push back and discredit those who oppose them."

"Like what they did to Dr. Ramsey."

"Exactly. What's been done to Dr. Ramsey is not just about Dr. Ramsey. It's a message to others not to question the established order. Now it's true that he has not been killed or jailed. However, he's been attacked and ostracized to such an extent that he can't return to his own country and live and work in peace."

Tony looked out the windows of the hotel lobby and found himself thinking about how similar this experience was to what Sensei described as having happened in Japan. He turned back to Maria and looked at her holding her son while he slept.

"Are you willing to write and publish what we find?"

"Of course. However, I will not publish something that is not fully supported by facts. We must have facts, not suspicions."

"I agree." Tony sat quietly and reflected on how beautiful it was to watch Maria gently rock her son.

⚕ ⚕ ⚕

Tony had trouble sleeping that night. He had vivid, disturbing dreams that he was back with the NYPD, in the old Bronx 42nd Precinct, chasing a man who had shoved an old lady to the floor, beaten her, and taken her pocketbook. Suddenly the man turned and shot at Tony. Tony returned fire, and the man fell to the floor. He found himself surrounded by angry people. The young man's mother was lying in the street, holding the dead man in her arms. "You killed my baby! You killed my baby!"

"But he tried to kill me."

"You killed my baby! My baby is gone!"

"My life was in danger. I did what I had to do."

"You took my son!"

Tony kept seeing Maria's intense dark eyes.

"They made people disappear."

Tony woke up at 4:45 a.m. and looked out into the predawn darkness. It had been years since he had these dreams. He showered and went for coffee at the lobby restaurant, which was just opening. Laura was sitting at a table drinking some coffee and working on her laptop.

"What're you doing here?" she asked.

"I couldn't sleep," Tony said. "What're you doing down here?"

"I run a business. I've got briefs and research to do," Laura said. "I didn't want to wake Carlos. One of us has to sleep. You look like crap."

"Laura, I killed someone once."

Laura looked up from her laptop. "What are you saying to me?"

"When I started with the NYPD, I got in a shootout." Laura gasped. "It was a 'good shoot' as they say in my line of work, and I was cleared. But I killed a man who tried to kill me."

"I didn't know. Have some coffee."

"When something like this happens in law enforcement, a procedure takes place. The officer involved gets immediately removed from the scene in an ambulance for medical reasons."

"And to give you time to get your story straight."

"Well, yeah. I was in shock. I couldn't process what had happened. I might've said anything."

"They're smart, Tony, because it might be the job of someone like me to use whatever comments you made against you."

Tony nodded to Laura. "I know. No one has their post-shooting protocols together like the NYPD."

"You're giving me those sad freaking eyes of yours. What are you feeling?"

"I never got a chance to really process what had happened. There was this horrible thing, and I was whisked away. I was never allowed to really see the effects of what I had done, to know what the guy's family went through. That criminal was someone's kid. A mother lost her son at my hands. Yes, it was legal. And my only choice would've been to accept that my mother would lose her son."

"You made the right choice, Tony. Your mother raised a good kid. Look at all the good you have done for people."

"Maybe that's what Dr. Abramson thought." Tony looked down. "I was so angry at that man. Now I understand that he was doing what everyone does—keeping the painful reality at arm's length."

"You're a good guy doing your best, Tony. You're a good man."

"Thanks." He smiled at her and felt a little better talking about it. "You know, this is the weirdest situation in my life, sitting here at this conference with all of you: lawyers, people on terrorist watch lists, blacklisted renegade doctors, people who are ordered to silence themselves, refugees, breast feeders."

"That was hysterical! Yeah, I guess that we are stretching you out a bit."

"But you know what?" Tony said. "Everything that I'm hearing here ties into what is really going on with this autism war."

"How so?"

"Pulling me away from the shooting allowed me distance from what I had done. That's what this compensation program is about. The Germans knew what was going on with the camps, but the camps were out in the woods so the regular people didn't see their connection to it. The Japanese who dumped mercury into Minamata Bay and poisoned people knew too. But everyone was told to support the company because the company was good for the community. The Argentineans made people disappear. They just took the problem people away and 'disappeared' them. And people did nothing because they were afraid. Now our government is making vaccine-injured children invisible."

"That is why they deny the epidemic," Laura said. "America is making us the mothers of the invisible."

CHAPTER 20

Laura Melendez sat next to Maria Contessa-Guevera in the back of the Court of Claims hearing room on the first day of the Omnibus Autism Proceedings. Laura rolled her eyes as she watched the three special masters, led by Carl Mantkewicz try to explain why they were allowing the surprise evidence from England but not allowing the petitioners time to assess them.

Wilson Garrison, a gray-haired African American with a chiseled jaw, and Herb Newman were visibly upset over being bushwhacked.

"It is time to commence these proceedings, Mr. Newman," Mantkewicz said. "There's been years of preparation."

"Well then, Honorable Special Master, what harm would a few more weeks really do? We need to assess these documents. The act states that these vaccine proceedings are supposed to be compassionate and informal."

"And they are informal, Mr. Newman. You need only prove your case by a preponderance of the evidence."

"That is simply fifty percent plus the weight of a feather," chimed in Special Master William Riley.

"With respect," countered Garrison, "fifty percent plus the weight of a feather isn't real if you've hidden the feathers."

Mantkewicz glared at Garrison. "Counselor, please move on. We have made our decision and will admit the papers from England."

"Honorable Special Master," Garrison pressed, "we feel that it is essential then that all the parties have access to the critical material of the Whittaker case so the material can inform the rest of these proceedings."

"Mr. Garrison," said Mantkewicz with growing impatience, "the Whittaker case is no longer a part of these proceedings. Terms of the settlement were the withdrawal from these proceedings."

Sitting nervously a few rows behind the Department of Justice (DOJ) attorneys was Robert Bangston, who didn't see why DOJ wanted him there. Elyse McCormick, the petitioner child with autism, sat in a wheelchair looking directly at Bangston. The young girl kept staring at him while obsessing over her fingers. Bangston felt paranoid. "Stop looking at the kid, Robert," he told himself.

"Chief Special Master," Garrison said, "I ask that you rule on the motion for transparency that I filed after the Whittaker settlement. I understand that there may be many conditions to *Whittaker*, but the facts of the case are important—I think vital—to the rest of these cases and any future ones that come before the program. They should be aired. My esteemed colleagues from the Department of Justice have indeed decided to compensate a case where the vaccine injury is autism. They have conceded such."

Senior Assistant Justice Department Attorney Rick Lavin immediately rose in opposition, "We proffered a settlement, Honorable Special Master, for autism-like symptoms that accompany encephalopathy. However, the case centers on encephalopathy. We are here to determine whether autism, not encephalopathy, was a result of vaccine injury."

Laura leaned over to Maria and whispered, "This is convoluted."

"Petitioners should only have to prove that an injury occurred," Maria whispered. "This is a trap. Garrison knows that, and that's why he filed his motion."

That night Sara Donovan's segment on SNN about the start of the proceedings reported that the special masters had tabled a decision on

Garrison's motion for transparency. "The proceedings seem odd in light of the recent concession of HHS on the Whittaker case," she commented, "where the government conceded that vaccines induced her autism-like symptoms." Donovan interviewed a retired HHS official who admitted that "vaccine-adverse reactions are not actively monitored. I find some of the vaccine safety assurances made by members of the medical community to be over the top." Donovan then interviewed Clyde King, the author of *Mercury Rising*, a book that focused on mercury in vaccines and the autism epidemic. King told viewers that the Vaccine Adverse Event Reporting System captured very few of the adverse reactions to vaccines "because the majority of families don't know that there is a reporting system and don't even know that there is a National Vaccine Injury Compensation Program."

Donovan and Millman got the story aired before Fontaine and his minions could suppress it.

Philip Snyder, who watched the SNN coverage, went berserk. He called Calthorpe's office only to hear that he was at a polo match. Snyder immediately called Jennifer Kesslinger and screamed, "We can't have these people looking legitimate, Jennifer! For God's sake, your guy made the other side seem reasonable. And I want Clyde King stuffed in a suitcase and dumped in the Potomac!"

"Phillip," Kesslinger replied reasonably, "I can't fire the man. He's retired. You can't fire a retired employee."

"We can't have these people looking legitimate, Jennifer!" Snyder bellowed again.

"What do ya want me do, Phil?" Kesslinger screamed back. "You think I can just order the proceedings shut down? This is the system we have. Congress wanted this program because industry kept whining about lawsuits. Keep in mind that because of this program, you and your pals have no exposure to tort liability. Zero. Zip. Nothing. Nada."

"This is bullshit, Jennifer," Snyder screamed louder. "What about the *Cornachio* case being reviewed by the Supreme Court? We don't have full immunity from liability. Texas says that the Cornachios can sue Binghampton Pharmaceuticals because they rejected the Mantkewicz dismissal. How can that be allowed?"

"Phil," Kesslinger said with exasperation, "the Cornachios can do that because the law says that they can. Have you read the act?"

"Don't give me legalese and that all-knowing, inside-DC crap," Snyder snapped back. "We need a panel of medical people to decide these things. This whole thing is a sick joke. These kids are genetic mutants and . . . "

Kesslinger reached her boiling point. "Phil, you *cannot* run around saying stuff like that!"

"They have bad genes, Jennifer! Every population has them. But in America, the lawyers show up and blame vaccines!"

Kesslinger looked at the pile of unfinished work in her in-box. "Phil, I've had enough. Calm down."

"Look, these anti-vaccine people rip into me every day. They call me greedy. They say I don't care about kids. They call me a toad. My wife sees this stuff. I mean, come on. Jennifer, did you see the recent poll numbers?" An internal CDC study of vaccination uptake had revealed that twenty-three percent of those asked believed that vaccines were unsafe. More ominous was that vaccination rates were declining, particularly among well-educated parents.

"We're not happy about them either."

"It's these anti-vaccine kooks," Snyder said. "They need to be destroyed."

Even before he returned to his office Calthorpe was well aware of Snyder's messages and the urgent phone calls from pharmaceutical executives. He had Donna call them back and advise them all that Rollins had matters well in hand. The woman at SNN had to be bottled up better. There was a plan in motion for that already.

The larger issue of public faith in the vaccine program—the internal study from America's CDC—was a bit more of a concern. Calthorpe saw the other side had begun to impact public perceptions of the issue. He decided to arrange for more articles in the print media that again questioned whether there was a real increase in autism. Most publications craved cheap content, and Calthorpe's people would do the writing for them. Creating doubts about the validity of the autism epidemic was a vital concept because it reassured the public that nothing frightening was going on. It was a valuable technique to keep the concept of an "Autism Epidemic" out of the public consciousness.

Calthorpe finally called Snyder. "Phillip, how are you?"

"Angry."

"Be assured, my friend, we *are* adding a new ingredient to the mix. There will soon be articles appearing all over America that will describe these parents as selfish and reckless. This will get the ball down the field to the "danger" concept we have spoken about."

"Good idea. These people *are* dangerous."

Calthorpe allowed himself a smile. "Phillip, you do realize that anything is possible when a government believes someone is dangerous."

CHAPTER 21

Senator Russell Sampson and his wife Diana had been looking forward to the black-tie gala at the Washington Hilton honoring John DeRario, the retiring US ambassador to Italy. DeRario was a long-time New York Republican Party leader, and Sampson's old friend, Governor Lou Miller, would be the master of ceremonies.

Now that they were there, the senator mingled easily with Washington's elite, but Diana was a nervous wreck. She hadn't left their son Jordan alone for nearly two months. Jordan had become impossible to deal with. He had a favorite electronic toy and kept pushing the same button over and over again. Diana found the repetition maddening.

Diana had taken her eyes off Jordan for a few minutes earlier that afternoon so she could do homework with her daughter when she heard a thump on the front porch roof. Jordan had taken off all his clothes and had climbed out of his bedroom window. Diana had to go onto the roof and pull Jordan back in.

The couple had moved to Washington temporarily, renting a colonial on the outskirts of Georgetown so that Russell could be on hand to help with Jordan's crisis. He had been working nonstop in the Senate, but knew that he needed to spend some time with Diana. She needed a break. Even though Diana was shy, Russell hoped she would enjoy a glamorous night out. And, as New York's irascible governor took to the podium, Diana began to enjoy herself. Lou Miller was in rare form.

"Tonight, my friends, we celebrate the service of a great man, John DeRario, the best ambassador to Italy New York has ever produced. John left Wall Street for Italy for one reason: the food." Laughter erupted. "And he's going back to Wall Street for one reason: the money." The crowd applauded. "You think I'm joking about the food thing? Every time I called John's cell phone the guy was eating. 'Lou, can't talk right now, I'm in Vincenzo's. You have to try this *Mozzarella en Carozza.*' John ate at every restaurant in Rome in the service of US foreign policy while yours truly ate a bagel made by a Mexican in Albany." The room burst into applause and laughter.

Russell smiled lovingly at Diana. "You look lovely tonight."

Diana caressed Russell's knee. "You look pretty good yourself, Senator."

Miller was just warming up. "Now, John became Italy's ambassador because our previous senators pushed the president hard for John to get this job. I remember Senator Lombardo whining, 'We need a real Italian New Yorker to be our Italian ambassador.' I wonder if our new senator would consider whining a little for a good Jewish New Yorker to become the next Israeli ambassador."

As the evening ended, Diana received a text message from Jordan's nanny about a problem she couldn't handle. The couple rushed home to find their son asleep in his bed. Diana took one look around, ran to the bathroom, and vomited. Jordan had smeared feces all over himself, his bed, and the walls of his room.

Russell took off his jacket. "I'll clean it up."

"Something is really wrong!" Diana cried. "I don't know what to do. What is wrong with him?"

"I'll make some calls. We'll get the best people, the best doctors."

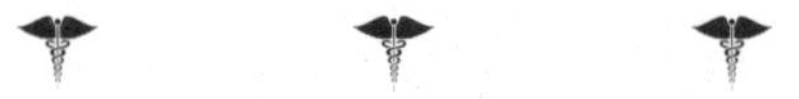

The Sampsons sat in the otherwise-empty waiting room of Dr. Rudolfo Saracino, a renowned child psychiatrist at Johns Hopkins. They could hear Jordan screaming in an adjoining examination room where he was being assessed by the doctor and his staff.

Finally, Saracino called the couple into his office. "Please have a seat. Coffee?"

Diana shook her head no. "Black, please," Russell said.

Saracino poured Russell a cup. "How're you two doing?"

Diana began to cry. Russell put his arms around her, on the verge of tears himself. "We're worried sick about him."

"Just a few months ago, he was a dream child," Diana said. "He was perfect."

"What do you think?" Russell asked with pleading eyes.

"I'm concerned," the doctor replied. "While it's too early to assign an autism diagnosis, that's where we're heading."

Diana sobbed louder. Russell shook his head in disbelief, "What does that mean really?" Russell asked.

Saracino handed Diana a box of tissues. "It means that Jordan's not going to have the kind of life that you wanted for him," Saracino said honestly. "I won't lie to you. This is going to be a significant challenge in your lives and certainly for Jordan as well."

"What happened? He was doing so well, just like our girls," Russell said.

"It was those vaccines he got when he was sick," Diana said.

Saracino's response was something that Diana and Russell would never forget. "I believe you. I've heard this before."

"You do?" Diana said.

"However, please understand that most doctors won't believe you. They wouldn't even consider what you're saying, and they would be angry with me for believing you."

"What the hell are you talking about?" Russell wanted to know.

Diana knew exactly what Saracino was talking about. Her worst fears had been confirmed. "Russell, I've spoken to other mothers. People know this happens."

"What does that mean? People know this happens?"

"They do. And it happened to our son. I shouldn't have let him have the shots when he was sick. It's all my fault!"

"No, it's not," Saracino said.

"I'm supposed to protect my children. It *is* my fault!"

"Mrs. Sampson, it's not your fault." The doctor's words didn't matter, for Diana was inconsolable.

Russell was still in shock. "What do we do?"

"I'm going to make some referrals to people who will provide you the very best therapies available. Therapies that no one would question, applied behavior analysis—ABA—speech therapy, and physical therapy. I'm also going to connect you to some professionals that my colleagues would object to. I know of cases where they've come up with treatments that work."

"Thank you," Diana said between tears.

"Let me ask you, did you observe anything unusual about your son prior to the regression?" Saracino asked.

"He was normal, adorable," Diana said.

"He was the most social little bug you ever saw. He loved to sing," Russell added.

"He smiled," Diana said. "He reached up for me when I walked in a room. He loved me."

"He was a normal child," Russell said choking back tears. "We've raised three other children. We know what kids are like."

"I believe you both," Saracino said. "It's important to tell the doctor I refer you to about the vaccine reaction. It will give him insight into what to do." Saracino wrote down names and phone numbers on a pad next to his telephone. "Call the man at the top of the list. I've sent families in your situation to him before, and he's done some good work. I'm not doing this because you're a senator—I'm doing it because I think this is the right thing to do."

"I am confused. What do you mean?" Russell asked as Diana took the papers from Saracino.

"I could draw a lot of criticism for sending you to these people. In medicine, like politics, reputations are everything. You'll see what I'm talking about when you start doing some of your own research."

"What do you mean?" Russell asked.

"Senator," Saracino said, taking his glasses off and rubbing his eyes, "right now you both must do a lot of work. You'll have to do this while grieving what has happened to your son. That won't be easy, and you both already lead intense, complicated lives. What you are about to deal with is unlike anything you've ever experienced. I would like to keep talking with both of you as you work through this. I'm not putting you on the couch or anything. But let's stay in touch. I spoke to a mother of an autistic child last week who said she felt as though she'd fallen into an alternate universe. You know, like when Alice fell down the rabbit hole into Wonderland. You'll see why."

"Why?" Russell wanted to know.

Saracino shook his head. The two men looked at each other in awkward silence.

Diana and Russell soon found out what Saracino meant. Within a week they met with a doctor who immediately implemented a wheat-and dairy-free diet. Once the diet was in place, Jordan would start hyperbaric oxygen therapy. Russell thought the whole thing was crazy but went along with it because Diana laid it on the line. "Russell, I love you, but I will kill you in your sleep if you don't back me up on this. We're saving our son," she told him one night as the couple went to bed.

Their tacit arrangement was that Diana took the lead with the children and kept her husband informed. His career was simply too intense and frenetic for it to really be any other way. However, the controversial interventions that they had started were not popular with mainstream medicine. And Russell Sampson was a mainstream kind of guy. He didn't want word about his son being on a gluten-free/casein-free diet getting out. He might be a New York Republican, but he was still a *Republican.*

Then there was the vaccine-autism issue. Russell did some research on the political aspects of the controversy. He was alarmed by what he found. Within two hours he realized that the nation's vaccine program was dominated by the pharmaceutical industry and rife with conflicted interests. And most of the people in his own party were unwilling to talk about it. So he did something that was almost unthinkable in the current political climate.

He called a Democrat.

Walking past the bar at Martin's Tavern in Georgetown, Russell knocked four times on the door that said "Staff Only." A waiter opened the door and escorted him to a dimly lit room. Sitting at a small table was Senator Parker Smithson.

"What are you drinking, Russell?"

"Scotch."

"Make it an Aberlour for my friend," he told the waiter "How're you doing?"

"I've been better, Senator."

"Call me Parker. McNair speaks highly of you, and I trust that old coot. We're about as different as night and day politically, but I admire the guy. He has the balls of a lion. Let's talk about why we're here."

"You recently held a brief hearing on the vaccine program. I think we need to look at it harder."

"I agree, but the vaccine program is the one big government program that we all can still shake hands on. We mandate these drugs, pharma supplies 'em, and everybody makes money. It's a win-win. Unless you're injured."

The drinks arrived, and Russell held up his glass in a silent toast. "Two months ago my son had some shots at the pediatrician's office. That night he had a seizure and almost died. Jordan never recovered. He can't talk anymore. He obsesses over objects and flicks the lights on and off over and over again. I have a full-time nanny helping my wife, but we still can't keep him safe."

"Jesus. I'm sorry, Russ." Smithson looked hard into his drink. "I hear similar stories from my constituents. My district staff says we don't have a week go by without a family calling for help. And local government isn't getting it done."

"What are we going to do?"

Smithson sighed. "You know that I'm called a whacko for supporting alternative medicine and all that."

"I sure do. We Republicans are the ones calling you that."

Smithson chuckled. "Washington's all about irony, Russ. We're supposed to be about making sure people are protected. Making sure they're safe. If vaccines were so damn safe, why do we have a National Vaccine Injury Compensation Program anyway? I'll tell you why. Because we're full of shit."

"Pharma has enormous lobbying influence."

"Those bastards act like they own the Hill. Thanks to them, if we even talk about vaccines and autism, we scare people and get labeled nuts. As a member of the Senate, a label like that could end with you being *un*elected. You remember Congressman Tully from Indiana? He held hearings on mercury in vaccines nine years ago. The hearings led to the conclusion that mercury in vaccines could well be responsible for the increase in autism. Neither party did a damn thing about it. Tully got primaried in a district he owned for years. Yeah, he won, but he couldn't make headway on the issue. There's still pharma money for any candidate who'll run against him. You know the world of crap I got for that one hearing I held? They don't want anybody digging around the VICP. There's something wrong over there. I can feel it."

"And you can't sue a manufacturer," Russell shrugged. "Case law describes vaccines as 'unavoidably unsafe'?"

"Yeah, I was here when we passed the law. The manufacturers whined about lawsuits so much that we changed the playing field," Smithson drained his glass. "We protected them. Now you have to sue the Secretary of Health and Human Services instead. Got a vaccine injury? Go sue the lady having lunch with the president of the United States. We screwed the planet on that one."

"There's a vaccine injury case—Cornachio—headed to the Supreme Court."

"And those DOJ bastards are going to argue that Congress completely preempted the right of citizens to sue a manufacturer."

"That's not what the act says."

"Russ, I've been around here too long. I've learned a thing or two. These people have too much power."

"This isn't a free market system, Parker. And I still don't understand how they feel they can mandate people to take these products. I don't understand how my party feels comfortable with this."

"Pharma writes checks, Russ. You know that as well as I. Write a big 'nough check and Libertarians become Socialists. It's always the money."

"We're the problem. To fix this, we have to fix us."

"Good luck! It's gotten so bad that your son got injured and we're meeting in the back of a bar so we don't piss off our caucuses."

"There has to be a chink in their armor."

"Imagine having a product line where you control the approval process, set the price, and get the government to mandate it. *And* you have no liability. What would you do to protect that kind of business? What would corporations with unlimited resources, power, and influence do to protect it?"

"What wouldn't they do? Mr. Chairman, we have a problem. What're we going to do about it?"

"This is Washington, my friend. For now we'll drink another round. And lie in wait."

CHAPTER 22

Tony, Laura, Herb Newman, and Maria Contessa-Guevera began an evening conference call to focus on the problem of missing cases. "We've searched the federal court case management system and the Court of Claims website," Tony said. "No luck."

"I've got an intern running searches through Westlaw," Laura added. "We're still not finding the missing cases."

"I've looked at the program statistics," Tony said. "There has to be thousands of cases. But we're not finding them."

Herb Newman broke in. "I did get a fascinating phone message last week. Seems we have a whistle-blower of sorts. Listen." He played the tape over the phone:

> *Mr. Newman, I am—never mind. I know of your project, and I believe that you must pursue case settlements. That is where you will find what you are seeking.*

"The voice sounds Eastern European," Laura said. "Sort of mysterious."

"He must of have seen the notice we posted on the autism community blogs," Newman said.

"That confirms it. The missing cases are settlements," Tony said. "The question is how do we get to them?"

"Did he leave any way for us to contact him?" Laura asked.

"No," Newman said, "but isn't that call interesting?"

"It is," Maria said, "We need to get these settlements. What happened with the Freedom of Information application?"

"Some bureaucrat in Health and Human Resources responded that we could get the redacted information in about five years," Laura answered.

"That's outrageous!" Newman shouted.

"It gets worse," Laura went on. "The information will cost us five hundred thousand dollars."

"Aw, come on," Newman moaned. "And what were they going to redact?"

"Personal information, medical and psychiatric information—all the information that would be useful to us," Laura said.

"Are there more published case decisions that mention symptoms of autism?" Maria asked.

Tony answered. "The Wizwer case details repetitive behaviors, self-abusive behavior, and even digestive problems."

"*Max Wizwer v. the Secretary of HHS*," Newman said. "1989."

"He's got the laptop on again," Laura explained.

"It always is. This case is interesting—one of the first to go through the program. Laura, guess which DOJ attorneys worked on *Wizwer*?"

"I was in law school then. Which ones?"

"Dumbrowski, Stone, and Reynolds," Newman answered. "All three of them are still working in the program. Doesn't anyone ever move on to another bureau at DOJ?"

"Or get a job outside of government where they have to actually work for a living?" Laura's voice dripped with sarcasm. "No offense to you, Tony."

"None taken. Hey, what were the first names of the parents in the Wizwer case again?"

"Leopold and Janet," Newman said.

"How many people named Leopold Wizwer could there be?" Tony asked.

"What's your point?" Newman said.

"Didn't I mention to you guys that I find people for a living. Finding someone named Leopold Wizwer in a country of three hundred million people is possible. Finding a guy named John Smith isn't." Tony leaned over to his desktop computer. Anthony sat next to him on the couch listening to his music, looking cute with the big earphones on. Tony looked up Leopold Wizwer on Yahoo! People Search. "Hey guys, guess what? Leopold lives in Corpus Christi, Texas. Yep, so does Janet Wizwer. So who wants to call them?"

"We can't," Laura said. "We're practicing lawyers in the program. We might be calling other people's clients. You have to call."

"Me? What do I say to them? What do I ask?"

"First you tell them who you are and why you're calling," Maria said. "We're not like our opponents. We must be transparent and ethical. I will not be a part of any deceptions."

"Make sure that they fully consent," Newman added. "Their participation in the interview must be completely voluntary."

"Don't sound like a scary, freaking cop," Laura added. "Lose the New York tough guy voice."

"New York tough guy voice? Who? Me?"

"I know what you're capable of. You know martial arts stuff. Don't be intimidating."

"Yes, I agree with Laura," said Maria. "Don't sound like a scary policeman."

"And don't call while you're being shot at," Newman said.

Everyone laughed.

The following evening Anne was out at a yoga class with Veronica Fournier, so Tony was alone with the kids. He worked on homework with Sophie at the kitchen table while having a devil of a time keeping Anthony out of the cupboard. The child wanted chocolate chip cookies that weren't gluten-free. Tony hid them in the bathroom, but that didn't keep Anthony from looking.

Sophie went upstairs to start her bath, and Tony had Anthony listening to music. The household seemed to be calm enough for Tony to make that phone call. "Well, here goes nothing," he mused as he dialed the number.

A raspy female voice answered. "Hello?"

"Good evening. My name is Anthony Colletti and I am calling from, uh, from New York. Do you fully consent to this interview?"

"Who is this?"

"I'm Tony Colletti. I'm looking for Janet or Leopold Wizwer."

"Yeah, you got Janet. What do ya want?"

"I'm looking for information. You have a minute?"

"I'm talking now. Who are you?"

"My name is Tony Colletti, and I'm doing some research on the Vaccine Injury Compensation Program and—oh crap!" Anthony, who had followed his sister upstairs, had found the chocolate chip cookies and was devouring them in front of his father. "You sneaky little pain in the ass!"

"'Pain in the ass?' You call me from New York to curse at me?"

"Mrs. Wizwer, I'm so sorry."

Leopold Wizwer broke in on an extension from somewhere in the house. "What's this about? Who the hell's cursing at my wife?"

"I apologize. Look, I'm a dad, and I'm trying to keep my son who has autism from eating something he shouldn't eat. I guess I'm not a very professional caller."

"Well, heck, my Max has autism," Janet said. "We couldn't keep him out of anything when he was younger. You got your hands full there. What is it you want to know?"

"Did you say that Max has autism?"

"You got a hearing problem, mister?" Leopold said, "That's what my wife said. You got a kid with autism too?" The conversation then took off. Once Janet and Leopold understood who Tony was and why he was calling, nothing else really mattered. "How did you find out about our case? Our lawyer said Vaccine Court stuff wasn't public."

"It's posted in a legal database," Tony said.

"You're the first person who ever called to talk to us about the case. Max still has seizures. It's a struggle for us just to keep him alive. We're getting older now, and we worry every day about what will happen to him when we've gone to God."

"The money from the settlement dried up years ago," Leopold added. "It was never really enough to provide what Max needed. We're all he's got."

Tony looked over at smiling Anthony who was on the couch bopping to music. "I have the same worry."

"Does your son talk?" Janet asked.

"A little. His language has improved lately."

"May I speak to him?"

Tony handed over the receiver. "Anthony, say hello to the Wizwers."

"Hewwo, Wizmers," Anthony cooed.

"Hey, darling. You can call me Auntie Janet. It feels so good to hear you talk. You listen to your daddy now." Tony got back on the phone. "Thank you," Janet said. "Kids make me feel young again."

"Lookin' at Sophia Loren makes me feel young again," Leopold said. "How'd you come up with the idea to call us?"

"A few months ago I started doing research on the Vaccine Court after it came out the government admitted that vaccine injuries resulted in one kid's autism. My associates and I found a bunch more so far."

"What a surprise," Leopold drawled. "The government is lying to people."

"Well, the attorneys I'm working with suggested I call you. I looked you up online."

"You're a cop working with lawyers?" Leopold asked.

"This is what my life has come to."

"Just like an attorney—sending the workin' jerk out to do the heavy lifting. Hey, I got a joke for you, what do you call ten thousand attorneys dropped into the Challenger Deep?"

"A good start."

"Ha! You know that one too!" Leopold said. "Hey, you know what? No one from the federal government ever called us to see how things were going. You're the first guy I've talked to about this in years. You can't count on the government, they could care less, but you can count on your family. I can see that you get that, even though you're a cop. Now lemme give you some good advice. Stand by your son. Keep your family together. It isn't easy, but it's the right thing to do. A man takes care of his family. I love my son and I'm blessed to have him. I'm blessed to have my other kids too, even though they make me nuts. Know what I'm talking about?"

"I do, sir. Exactly."

"You call me Leo. Call us whenever you want. We're happy to help you."

"Give your son a hug for me," Joyce added.

As soon as he hung up, Tony phoned Laura. "I just spoke to the Wizwers. Their son has autism!"

"Hold it! You got them on the phone? They confirmed it?"

"Yes!" Tony said. "They're great people. It went really well!"

"This is the first call, and the kid has autism! There could be hundreds."

CHAPTER 23

Investigative journalist Clyde King stood impatiently at the DC Marriott registration desk. He was there for the Immunization Day Conference. The author of *Mercury Rising: Vaccines and Thimerosal*, King was often accused of being "anti-vaccine." In truth, King supported vaccination, but had come to the opinion that the vaccine program was becoming its own worst enemy because of industry spokesmen like Dr. Phillip Snyder.

A good-looking, athletic man in his mid-forties, King had a press pass from the *Pulsipher Post* to follow up on his coverage of the Whittaker case. However, the conference sponsors objected to his presence. "You're not excluding journalists who might ask tough questions are you?" King said.

The woman behind the desk had King's name on the "Not to admit list." She didn't want a scene. "No antics, Mr. King."

"I'm an investigative journalist, lady. I don't do antics. I ask questions and write."

King was finally issued a ticket in time for Dr. Snyder's keynote address. Snyder was introduced to friendly applause by a female CDC official. The conference room was half-filled with an audience composed primarily of public health officials, a few parents, and reporters from the *New York Times*, the *Wall Street Journal*, and *America Today*. "Good morning, my friends," Snyder began. "I want to thank Every Child Safe for School for sponsoring this conference." He began by showing slides of children who were horribly disfigured and sickened by vaccine-preventable diseases. "This is what we are up against in our war against disease. We are also up against this." A slide of Dr. Bryce Ramsey appeared. "This man, Bryce Ramsey, has published a paper that purports to show a link between vaccines and autism, and he has done a lot of damage. Bryce Ramsey has been refuted again and again. My colleagues in pediatric practices tell me that a day doesn't go by where a parent refuses a much-needed vaccine because of the lies spread by this man. Many parents are now off the recommended vaccine schedule. As someone who has developed vaccines, I can assure you that vaccines have an incredible safety record. We have parents who worry about receiving more than one vaccine at a time. I know for a fact that you could give several hundred vaccines at once and not see any negative reactions beyond a low-grade fever."

"That's an incredible statement," King thought to himself.

"These people falsely linking vaccines and autism are becoming a threat to us all," Snyder continued. "In fact, they're dangerous!" There was a smattering of applause. "It's time we begin to fight back and state loud and clear that these people are a threat to our nation!"

Snyder took a series of questions as he moved toward the end of his keynote. Most focused on how public health officials could better communicate the value of vaccines and the majority began with, "Thank you Dr. Snyder for all you do." King suspected that the whole event was "packaged" by a public relations firm.

King raised his hand. Snyder took the question before he realized who was asking it. "Dr. Snyder, thank you for all you do," King began, as Snyder glared. "I'm curious about your statement that you know for a fact that you could give several hundred vaccines at once and not see any negative reactions beyond a low-grade fever. What science do you base that statement on?"

Snyder leaned over to the CDC representative who had introduced him. "Clare, I thought that we were keeping these people out of here." The woman spoke into a small microphone on her sleeve.

"Dr. Snyder, I support vaccines, but I must ask you what you base that assertion on." Two security guards moved toward King from the rear of the hall. "Dr. Snyder, thank you for all you do. Please respond to my question."

"Okay, buddy, you gotta go," said a beefy security officer.

"I have a ticket and press pass, pal." King looked up at the speaker. "Dr. Snyder, I would like you to answer my question before I'm removed."

"No way, buddy. Let's go." The other officer grabbed King's shoulder.

"Get your hands off me! I'm a journalist. I was issued a pass, and I'm asking a legitimate question." The guards pulled King out of his seat. "Get your dirty hands off me. Thank you for all you do, Dr. Snyder!" When King resisted, they dragged him out of his seat and out of the hall. Once they got him out of the audience's view, they roughed him up even more.

Many in the audience applauded King's removal. Many did not, but no one dared speak against what had happened. The journalists from the *New York Times* and the *Wall Street Journal* didn't mention the forced removal of a fellow journalist from the proceedings in their lackluster coverage, although *America Today* mentioned a disturbance caused by an anti-vaccine activist.

The autism community went ballistic on the Internet over the King incident and Snyder's ridiculous statement about giving hundreds of vaccines at once. The *Era of Autism* blog ran story after story about the conference, Dr. Snyder, and what a hoot Immunization Day had been for Clyde King. While the vast majority of the mainstream media said nothing, Sara Donovan ran a short piece on SNN featuring an interview with King, who proudly sported a bruised, puffy cheek and a cracked lip.

Donovan: "So what you are saying is that you asked a question about Dr. Snyder's claim that a child can take hundreds of vaccines at the same time—and not suffer any consequences—and got forcibly removed from the conference room?"

King: "Yes. I just felt that he had a responsibility to answer that question. I ended up—as you can see—being assaulted. I'm finding that the supporters of the vaccine program are becoming increasingly resistant to any questions about vaccine safety. That is a problem because these are the only drugs our government mandates children to take."

Donovan: "None of the other journalists have covered what happened to you?"

King: "None. And, more important than covering what happened to me, few journalists are willing to ask meaningful questions about vaccine safety."

Robert Bangston saw the SNN coverage that night in his apartment. Snyder and the people running the conference had gone too far—Bangston knew that Snyder's "hundreds of vaccines" comment was reckless. Snyder and other public health leaders had lost any hint of objectivity and now sounded as though they were fighting for a religion. The "autism war," as Bangston had taken to calling it, was becoming a jihad. What happened at Immunization Day was completely wrong. Bangston felt trapped in a situation that was spinning out of control.

Tony decided to take a break from going through case decisions. Reading what happened to the children was taking a toll. Many cases ended with young victims permanently disabled or dying. Tony saw the same pattern in case after case of vaccine injury; the child let out a horrible, piercing scream followed by seizures. And the lives of the children and their families were forever changed.

Instead Tony began reading through research that people in the program had published based on Vaccine Court cases. Newman had dug up a bunch of papers all published by one doctor—Robert Bangston. His 1998 *Pediatrics* paper concluded that the MMR was causing encephalopathy and death. Tony found himself wondering what would have happened to

Bangston if he came out with a paper about MMR causing encephalopy today.

Bangston had been criticized by some doctors. One letter to *Pediatrics* questioned the wisdom of studying vaccine safety outcomes because "we shouldn't give the impression that this could really be happening." Although it was after 11:00 p.m., Tony called Herb Newman. "Herb, I didn't wake you, did I?"

"No. I'm up. Working on a brief."

"Who's this Robert Bangston guy?"

"He's the dark lord of Vaccine Court secrets."

"Seriously, who is he?"

Newman yawned. "He's the director of the Division of Vaccine Injury Compensation. All the cases that enter the program go through him. Ultimately, he has a lot of influence over what gets settled and what goes to hearing."

"Okay, when you file a case, what's in the file?"

"Medical records, the petition, supporting documents. That sort of stuff."

"So, if anyone knows what's been going on, it's Bangston—right?"

"Yeah. He and Chief Special Master Mantkewicz. They've both been there since day one."

"Is there any way that those two could've missed the word 'autism' in folder after folder for all these years?"

Newman yawned again. "I think you know the answer to that question."

CHAPTER 24

Robert Bangston nervously watched Maria Contessa-Guevera taking notes on the start of the third week of the Omnibus Autism Proceedings. Bangston feared that Maria was documenting the issues with the government's expert witnesses and their over-reliance on the research of Hans Jurgenson, which he knew to be garbage. He cringed every time a government witness cited it.

Sitting next to Maria was Professor Herman Tyler, a scholarly African American with a small goatee, from the Georgia Southern Civil Rights Clinic. He was observing at her invitation and out of respect for one of his heroes, attorney Wilson Garrison. Tyler's nephew had autism and his sister blamed vaccines.

"I see your point, Maria," Tyler whispered. "This does have the feel of a Stalin era show trial."

"The exception being that the petitioner's attorneys are not going down quietly."

"Yet another government witness who refused to examine Elyse McCormick!" said Herb Newman pounding his fist on the table.

"I object again," said Department of Justice attorney John Dumbrowski.

"Mr. Newman," said Chief Special Master Mantkewicz sternly. "You knew that. We *all* knew that prior to Dr. Francois being sworn in. Move on."

Dr. Jacques Francois, an epidemiologist with a pronounced Quebecois accent, was the twelfth government witness to testify that a vaccine could not have caused Elyse McCormick's autism. "I didn't have to examine the subject. The epidemiology is clear."

"Epidemiology—the study of disease in a population—can't decide what has happened to *this* child," Garrison said. "Once again, Honorable Special Master, I move that this witness be disqualified because he hasn't examined this child."

"You are pushing it, Mr. Garrison!" Mantkewicz lifted the gavel. "Substantive questions, please."

Newman rose. "Then let's get into the substance of the Norwegian study you're relying on. Jurgenson compares two different populations, doesn't he?" Francois said nothing. "I asked you a question." Francois continued to remain silent. "Honorable Special Master, I asked this epidemiologist a question."

When there was no reply from the bench, Newman glared at Mantkewicz. "Fine. First, Jurgenson counts hospital emergency room admissions for autism. That is a low number because I imagine that it's rare for people to show up at a hospital emergency room saying "My child has autism." That's not what people tend to do. Not even Norwegians. And then the study counts a separate population registering upon the opening of the Oslo Autism Clinic. More people show up at an autism clinic to register their loved ones because they're likely to receive the clinic's services. Obviously, these are two separate populations driven by different circumstances. Then Jurgenson counts the clinic registrants. To no one's surprise, he finds more than one would from ERs and then declares that the Norwegian autism population increased after mercury was taken out of the vaccines. Hence, vaccine mercury isn't the culprit. How did this study get published?"

"Mr. Newman," Mantkewicz said, "this is a peer-reviewed, published paper that was accepted by . . ."

"Honorable Special Master, it was accepted for publication only after the CDC pressured the journal to publish it. We have the correspondence from the CDC to support my statement. You can drive a truck through the holes in this study!"

"Mr. Newman, it's peer-reviewed!"

"So was Dr. Ramsey's paper," Garrison interjected.

"Don't compare this paper to the work of that vile Englishman!" Francois said loudly.

Mantkewicz pounded the gavel. "That's it! All of you, outa here! We're done for the day!"

Bangston called CDC Director Jennifer Kesslinger that afternoon after the drama in the autism hearing. "Jennifer, these attorneys are taking an axe to Jurgenson's research. How the hell did they find out that we pushed for publication?"

"An anti-vaccine activist sent a Freedom of Information letter, and one of my bureaucrats followed the stinking rules. I can't monitor every letter that the CDC gets."

"They are killing that paper and Mantkewicz can't seem to shut them down."

"It gets worse," Kesslinger added. "Jurgenson wants even more money."

"It figures he'd extort more money while the autism cases are being decided."

"The guy's a criminal. He's driving around Emory on a Harley with his hot-blonde 'research assistant.'" Emory was widely known as "CDC University" because of the university's close association with the federal agency. "Last week he came into the Research Dean's office, drunk off his ass, and pissed in his garbage pail."

"We can't have this. Put him on a plane back to Scandinavia."

"Phil Snyder keeps saying that the guy's published great stuff, but Snyder doesn't have to live with his antics and he doesn't have to pay him. And someone will eventually figure out what he is doing with the rest of the grant money."

"What *is* he doing with the rest of the grant money?"

"I'm not answering that."

Newman and Garrison met Maria and Herman Tyler under the statue of General Lafayette for a picnic lunch in President's Park across from the courthouse and the White House North Lawn. It was a fine May day with a handful of tourists snapping pictures.

"Well, that went well," Newman said as he turned on his laptop.

"We're likely to become the first attorneys in the history of vaccine law to be held in contempt." Garrison said.

"What questions *will* they let you ask?" Maria said as she handed around sandwiches and bottled water or iced tea.

"These are unlike any proceedings I've observed," Tyler said. "These special masters seem hardwired not to listen."

"At this point we're just creating a record for appeal," Garrison explained.

"They're serving public health policy—Elyse McCormick be damned," Newman said. "A child with autism is opposed by an industry that has managed to get the federal government to defend its interests. One child stands against all that power. It's disgusting."

"I agree." Tyler nodded. "What's happening here is a threat to justice everywhere."

Newman scanned the federal court system case-search screen on his laptop later that afternoon to find a way to the Vaccine Court settlements. To do so he needed the names of the litigants or the attorneys who worked on their cases. Locating either of those two variables would lead to the case history reports, or CHRs, that contained all official case activity. The CHRs would show whether a case was compensated because of an entry indicating that the case was settled and for how much. Colletti's conversation with the Wizwer family nailed it for him. Newman firmly believed there were hundreds of cases featuring autism compensated in Vaccine Court.

Newman ran a report of cases by his name to determine if the system would provide a report that accurately captured all the cases that he represented in the Vaccine Court. Sure enough, the system created a report that had all of his cases. He could click on the case name and then view the CHR. Then he ran Wilson Garrison and the system created a report of his entire caseload.

And then he remembered the conversation with Tony, Maria, and Laura from a few nights ago about the Department of Justice attorneys. Many of them were in the program since day one. "What if I run the caseloads of the DOJ attorneys?" he thought to himself. Newman entered John Dumbrowski's name and found a list of over four hundred cases. Running the names of other DOJ attorneys provided access to hundreds more.

Newman called Tony. "We hit the mother lode, baby! I figured out how to get the CHRs on hundreds and hundreds of cases!"

"Yes! That's great, but how am I gonna call all these people?"

"Shoot. I haven't considered that."

"Hey can I call you back? I have to arrest a sex offender on a probation violation warrant."

"Give him my card. Talk later."

Tony and Forceski were backing up the probation officers to arrest Tommy Pittaluga, one of Winston's few registered sex offenders. Pittaluga, who lived with his wife in a run-down turn-of-the-century house, was notorious for having sexually abused a thirteen-year-old boy. Forceski and a probation officer knocked on the front door while Tony and the probation supervisor moved to the rear of the home. The beefy Pittaluga burst out the back door and ran right at them. Tony intercepted him with a palm-heel strike, and Pittaluga landed on his back. "You're under arrest, Tommy," Tony said. "Roll over so we can cuff you."

Pittaluga complied. "This isn't fair! I want a lawyer!"

"Funny, we were just talking to one who's interested in your case," Tony replied.

Pittaluga's wife began tossing computer parts out of the first floor window onto the lawn. "Take your Internet kiddy porn and your filthy computer with you, you pervert!" she yelled. "I hope they lock you up for a hundred years."

"You rotten hag!" Pittaluga screamed back.

Forceski and the other probation officer ran over. "What's going on?" he said.

"Pick up those computer parts," Tony said. "We'll get a judge's order so we can search them."

"She's drunk! She doesn't know what she's saying." Pittaluga screamed. "You screwed me, you whore! When I get out, I'm gonna . . ."

His wife leaned out of the window. "I'm serving you with divorce papers, you creep! And when they see what's on that hard drive, you're done. You and your sick pervert friends better stay away from me!"

"What a lovely couple," Forceski scooped up the computer hardware. The officers put Pittaluga in the police car and drove him to court.

No one realized how significant the arrest would be.

CHAPTER 25

FDA employee Victor Petrov, once known as Zvi Kokochashvili, reviewed the initial safety data of a new vaccine called "Vax—Powder," innovative because it didn't rely on a liquid-injection delivery system via hypodermic needles. Instead, the vaccine was delivered in a powder that was scraped into the skin with a device that looked like a thimble with a bristle cupped under it. The bristle pushed the vaccine's antigen into the body, mimicking the way humans naturally develop immunity when bacteria and viruses come into contact with skin, mucous membranes, and the digestive tract.

Vax—Powder impressed Zvi, who knew that the product would be safer than standard vaccines that used liquids containing mercury, aluminum, or live viruses. Although vaccines were an accepted medical practice, few people contemplated that natural human immunity did not evolve to engage substances directly injected into the body. Vaccines bypassed natural mechanisms that developed to build immunity.

Zvi's opinion was that vaccine technology was antiquated and that safety improvements could be realized, but only if the industry wanted them. Although it was unclear that Vax—Powder achieved the desired levels of immunity, the product gave Zvi hope that the vaccine industry was considering developing safer immunizations.

The word around the agency was that the petitioners would lose in the Omnibus Autism Proceedings. Maybe it didn't matter, Zvi hoped. The Supreme Court had just announced that it would hear the *Cornachio* case to decide the government's dubious claim that civil court action was "pre-empted by Congress" from leaving the federal compensation program. Zvi wasn't a lawyer, but he read the statute and knew what it said. It would take a miracle for the government's lawyers to convince the Court that a family couldn't sue a company for a vaccine injury if they felt that they had been denied justice in the VICP.

"The law says so," Zvi thought to himself. "And America is a nation of laws."

Anne Colletti and Veronica Fournier chatted about kids, husbands, and autism therapies over lunch in the Route 9 Diner. "Has the gluten-free diet really helped Anthony?" Veronica asked.

"We also cut out dairy, but yes, it helps." Anne said. "Tony came back from the conference with something called GABA. Little Anthony climbed the walls within ten minutes of taking it, so I flushed it down the toilet. That's what you get when husbands go to autism conferences."

Veronica laughed. "Robert would never go to an autism conference. That's just not what accountants do. I wish I got more help from him. He's so shut down emotionally. I feel alone with everything. Sometimes I feel trapped with Ian."

"Your guy has to step up," Anne agreed. "No one should fight the autism war alone."

"He's never handled it well. I don't know that I have either." Tears welled in Veronica's eyes.

"And you're still grieving," Anne said. "I'm with you, Ronnie. I got your back."

Veronica composed herself. "Ian's new shrink doesn't believe in changing diet. He's a proponent of light therapy."

"I never heard of that."

"Ian is lightly sedated and watches some changing light patterns on a table in a dark room. It's a new protocol that Dr. Portnoy is developing with the American Psychiatric Association. Cutting-edge stuff."

"Can I come with you to see this?" Anne asked. "I'm willing to consider alternative treatments, but I research everything first."

Veronica smiled. "I'd love it."

When the hearing resumed, Robert Bangston worked at avoiding eye contact with Elyse McCormick. He looked at Maria Contessa-Guevera, but quickly glanced away when she turned toward him. "That damn woman is still taking notes," Bangston muttered to himself.

Maria shook her head at the drama playing out in front of her. Special Master Mantkewicz's face was beet red as Newman and Garrison pushed the legal envelope. The two lawyers were going down swinging, providing pages of issues that could raise eyebrows at the US Court of Appeals.

Dr. Catherine George, a government expert witness, was exasperated by Garrison's ferocious questioning. The middle-aged psychologist who specialized in autism was on the verge of tears.

"Mr. Garrison, I won't allow expert witnesses to be abused," Mantkewicz said.

"I concede that the witness has remarkable credentials, Honorable Special Master. However, I want to know why a woman who has evaluated thousands of children with autism refused to examine Elyse McCormick but yet appears here as a witness for the government?"

"I stand by my work!" the witness said loudly.

"Please remain quiet unless you are asked a question, Dr. George," Mantkewicz advised.

"I see that she now has two lawyers," Newman said sarcastically.

"Watch it, Mr. Newman," Mantkewicz warned.

"Dr. George," Garrison asked slowly, "How do you know that a vaccine injury didn't lead to *this* child's autism?"

"I know because autistic regression is a myth. Parents simply miss the earliest signs of autism. The disorder appears at a time children are being vaccinated a lot, and a false connection is made."

Newman rose. "I have had the opportunity to review past cases from this program, Dr. George. Many of the cases compensated for encephalopathy detail developmental regressions. Are you saying that we've learned nothing about vaccine injury since 1988?"

Mantkewicz pounded his gavel. "There is no precedent from previous cases that applies here . . ."

A shout from Elyse McCormick's mother suddenly interrupted the proceedings. The child writhed in convulsions. She was having a seizure. As her father moved Elyse out of her wheelchair and onto the floor, Garrison and Newman strode over to offer assistance. "I'll call for help," Newman said.

Special Master Amy Tychyn whispered over to Mantkewicz, who rapped his gavel. "We're adjourned until tomorrow," he ordered, after which he and the other special masters quickly left the room.

Maria noticed Bangston standing in the back of the room, then approached him. "Dr. Bangston, there's a child here who needs your attention. Please help."

Bangston looked at Maria in shock. "You want me to render assistance?"

"I want you to help this child." Elyse McCormick was now fully involved in the seizure, and her lips were turning blue.

"I . . . I really don't practice anymore and . . ."

"You will help these people now! You're a doctor!" Maria said between clenched teeth.

Bangston placed pillows from the back of the wheelchair under Elyse's head. He made sure the child could breathe. Then he saw to it that no objects around her would restrain movement or cause injury. "She's coming out of it," he reassured the parents.

Bangston knelt down and looked into the eyes of the child who had so unnerved him during the proceedings. "Elyse, please lie still. We're taking care of you. You're going to be okay." He looked up at the parents. "I'm sorry you have to go through this."

By that time EMTs arrived and took over. Bangston turned to walk away.

"Dr. Bangston," Maria said. "Thank you."

Bangston nodded, then turned and walked out of the room.

CHAPTER 26

Tony entered the Route 9 Diner on a warm, humid June evening. Forceski motioned him to the rear of the restaurant. "The manager gave us the back room."

"Good. Anyone here yet?"

"Johnny Mo's here, asking for coffee already. Raffy's pullin' in now."

"How you think this'll go?"

"Our crew is gonna be pissed when you tell them what this is about. It'll be interesting to see how they handle your 'ask.'" Forceski smiled as County PD Detective Raphael Molea came through the door. "Hey, Raffy, we're back there."

Raphael Molea, a brooding, six-foot-four man with dark hair, was known for his toughness. "Hey. I'm here for the autism dad support group."

John Morris, a slim, anxious man with graying hair, came out of the restroom and greeted the other men. Morris had just retired from the Pine Plains PD and was still a caffeine junkie. "You havin' coffee, Raffy?"

Marge Riley, a detective from the Port Chester PD entered next. Riley was tough, blonde, and Irish. "Boy, this is some crew here," she said with her signature smile. "Hi, Glen. Hey, Tony. You guys still ice fishing?"

Tony laughed, "I see you've been taking sensitivity classes. How're you doing?"

"You know, taking in the sights of Port Chester and taking care of my son. What's this about?"

"You'll find out as soon as the rest of the dream team gets here."

The group fell silent when Chief Lonnegan walked in. A chief is brass, and the group wasn't prepared for his presence. Tony looked at Forceski in surprise. "The chief asked me if he could come," Forceski whispered.

"Hey," Lonnegan said as he sat down. "I'll have a cup too. So all of you know, my granddaughter has autism. I thought I could help with what Tony's gonna to talk to you about."

"Hey, Raffy," Morris said with a sly smile, "I thought you county PD guys didn't go anywhere without your Tank."

"Don't bring up the Tank," Tony joked. "Glen and I never want to see that thing again." The group chuckled and broke into small talk until Laura Melendez and Susan Miller, the young law student from Tony's dojo, entered.

"Everybody," Tony said, "this is Laura Melendez, an attorney who's working with us."

"I know you," Morris said. "You broke my braccioles on that child abuse case from the Fromer Avenue Projects years ago."

"That was me," Laura said not the least bit intimidated. "Pour me some coffee, Morris."

"Call me Johnny Mo, Counselor. I guess we can have coffee together. I'm retired now."

"This is Susan Miller, a young lawyer who's also helping us," Tony said.

"Well, I didn't graduate yet," Miller blushed.

"You will," Tony said. "So that everyone knows, Susan has a brother with autism. Laura also has an affected son."

"What're we agreeing to here?" Raffy asked.

"You didn't agree yet," Tony answered. "Let me tell you what's been going on." He reported on what he and the lawyers had discovered about the Vaccine Court. The group was silent for most of his speech but Tony could tell that they were intrigued.

"I have a question," Riley raised her hand. "You mean to tell me that these people make announcements about how vaccines don't cause autism, but all along cases are compensated in this—what is this thing again?"

"The National Vaccine Injury Compensation Program," Laura said.

"Okay, the program. And all along they're compensating these kids for autism?"

"Not exactly," Laura said. "The compensation is for brain damage and seizures."

"But many children also have autism," Tony said. "Autism is a behavioral disorder that follows brain damage."

"Sure is behavioral," said Morris. "My kid still can't leave the house. He's a social disaster."

"So are you, but your guy has some pretty good language, as I recall," said Raffy. "You and your wife did an amazing job with him."

"Thanks. But he's still profoundly disabled. He can't work or live independently. I'm spending my early retirement waiting for a day placement for him. It's a struggle to find a meaningful program for your kids when they age out of school."

"I hear you, Bro," Forceski nodded. "I really worry about the day when the school bus no longer comes. I don't know what we're gonna do for my guy."

"The issue in the Vaccine Court," Laura said, "is that these kids were injured by vaccines. The feds conceded these cases, so there's no disagreement. And these same kids have autism."

"That's not supposed to be," Riley said, clearly angry. "These people are deceiving the public. This should've been disclosed. This is bullshit."

"Complete bullshit," Lonnegan echoed.

"If you follow the media coverage, they make it seem like this is all nonsense—that people are crazy for even talking about it," Morris added.

"And all the while, behind closed doors, they cut deals," Raffy shook his head. "This is unbelievable. My wife swears that it was vaccines. I never wanted to believe her. Now it looks like she was one hundred percent right. Even I wouldn't listen to her."

"We're trained to trust authority," Tony said. "Cops are wired to."

"We even joke about it. 'I'm from the government and I'm here to help you.' How many times have we used that line?" Riley said.

"How's this program run?" Morris asked. "Are the cases reviewed by professionals? Do they go through a central point?"

"They're all reviewed by the Division of Vaccine Injury Compensation," Tony said. "Some doctor named Robert Bangston. He's been there since 1988."

"I assume," Riley said, "that the files come in with a lot of medical reports, clinical evaluations, and tons of paper."

"I get what you're saying, Margie," Tony said. "My opinion's that Bangston has seen the word 'autism' in case after case."

"And he's never disclosed this?" Raffy asked.

"No," Laura said.

"The guy's goin' to hell," Raffy said.

"Isn't there some requirement to report trends from the data? The feds always have those sorts of rules." Lonnegan asked.

"The statute indicates that the program should do stuff like that," Laura sighed, "but it doesn't absolutely require it."

Tony then explained why he had gathered the group. They were being asked to contact the hundreds of affected families. "They have to consent to the interviews and be fully advised about what we're doing. Cases will be assigned numbers and identities protected. The family's wishes are paramount. I called on all of you because you're superior interviewers and investigators. All of you know what it is to hunt for the truth, and all of you know what autism is about. This is for our kids."

"I'm in," Raffy said.

Morris put his coffee down. "Why not."

"Let's drag the truth into daylight," Riley cheered. "And then let's drag these bastards out of their nice offices in handcuffs."

Within a few days, the calls began.

CHAPTER 27

Maria continued taking notes as the Omnibus Autism Proceedings wound down. She glanced up to see that Bangston was gone and that new people sat behind the DOJ attorneys. Officially they were spectators, but rumor around the Court of Claims was that they were lawyers from pharmaceutical companies.

The mystery attendees were joined by another noteworthy figure, the journalist Lance Reed, who had been there for the last two weeks. Maria observed that the government attorneys targeted Bryce Ramsey whenever Reed was in the room. Reed gave Maria chills. He always looked detached yet malevolent. He often glared at Donna and Elyse McCormick. Donna McCormick noticed it too. "There is something wrong with that man," McCormick whispered to Maria. "He gives me the creeps." A few minutes later, Reed walked up the center aisle and glared at Donna McCormick again. "Is there something you want to say to me, Mr. Reed?" she asked. Reed stopped and looked at her but said nothing. "Good. Then keep walking, you eel."

When Garrison and Newman finished their final arguments, the special masters thanked the McCormick family and reminded the attorneys about the deadline for their final briefs. The DOJ lawyers, their assistants, and their mystery guests picked up their files and quickly left the hearing room. Wilson Garrison closed his briefcase and Newman unplugged his laptop. Both men embraced Donna, Robert, and Elyse McCormick. "Thank you," Donna said. "No one could've fought better."

Newman had tears in his eyes. Garrison bowed. "We were honored to represent you."

In the weeks that followed the end of the proceedings, Tony and the project team telephoned families who had children who had been compensated by the Vaccine Court for brain damage. Many of the children had autism.

The numbers were building.

One morning Tony and Forceski drove around Winston collecting statements about a recent rash of burglaries. "From what you're saying," Forceski said, "it looks like at least forty percent of the cases have autism."

"Yeah," Tony said. "Incidentally, last night's call was awful."

"What happened?"

"I got the kid's father on the phone. The vaccine-injured child was severely autistic. Suffered horrible seizures, in constant pain. The kid punched and bit his mother every day of his life. Their lives were hell."

"That kind of story's not in the happy headlines during Autism Awareness month."

"His wife gave their son an overdose of sleeping pills and then took the rest herself. The lady couldn't stand to see her son suffer anymore and knew she couldn't live with the guilt. Vaccine injury destroyed this family. I verified the story in the San Jose newspaper online. May, 2008—'Mother kills autistic son, then self.'"

"I bet the reporter didn't say how these people ended up in this situation," Forceski said. "I've read dozens of autism tragedy articles. Our families suffer in silence, and no one in the media asks why."

Tony snorted. "Remember Mike Wallace, the *60 Minutes* guy? When I started in the NYPD we used to joke that he was gonna come into Police Plaza, interview the commissioner, and blow the lid off the corruption. No one does that kind of reporting anymore."

"Wallace did a *60 Minutes* report in the 1970s on the swine flu shot. He exposed everything. People got injured from the vaccine, and the outbreak of swine flu could never be verified." Forceski was Tony's semiofficial "project media watchdog." "Newspapers are running a new batch of pro-vaccination stories, and every story has the same message: you're irresponsible if you don't follow the vaccine schedule to the letter. It's like they're written by the same people. Here's Snyder saying you're dangerous if you don't give your kid a shot. Freakin' guy's everywhere."

"Wasn't that guy all over the measles outbreak in Illinois?"

"Tony, it was six cases of measles, and they're acting like bodies litter the streets of Chicago. I caught measles when I was kid and got over it in a week. Snyder blames the "irresponsible unvaccinated."

"He means us. Except that our kids were fully vaccinated. And look what happened."

"This week it's New Jersey's whooping cough outbreak. Snyder blames us again. So their legislature is planning to ban vaccine exemptions." Forceski shook his head. "And they just made the flu shot mandatory in response to the whooping cough outbreak. There's government logic for you."

The pro-vaccine coverage was endless, but every now and then a journalist did a thorough job. One from the *Newark Journal* obtained health department records that showed the whooping cough outbreak in fact occurred in young people who were vaccinated for the disease. Although the story was confined to just the *Journal,* Jennifer Kesslinger's CDC went into overdrive analyzing the outbreak. The Center issued a report that the bacteria "shifted" and was increasingly resistant to the vaccine. Although the stories received marginal coverage, Phillip Snyder went on the attack. "The disease outbreaks are the fault of Dr. Bryce Ramsey and those dangerous anti-vaccine conspiracy people."

Lance Reed authored a series of new articles claiming Bryce Ramsey had committed "outright fraud to pad his pockets." Reed connected Ramsey to the Illinois measles outbreak and reported on an interview with a man who had not vaccinated his son "because I believed in the work of Dr. Ramsey." Ramsey responded in an interview on NBC that went badly, the interviewer calling Ramsey "a baby killer."

Rollins Public Relations was pouring it on now and working its magic to reconstruct public trust in the vaccine industry. E. Gordon Calthorpe, who reviewed the progress of vaccine industry issues on a daily basis, had revolutionized the concept of product trust, and the vaccine industry was the ultimate test of his public relations model.

The mantra "autism-vaccines-Ramsey-fraud" was working. To Calthorpe's surprise, however, trust in the vaccine program was not improving. None of the "measures of trust" that Calthorpe's research team assessed showed improvement, and the "non-anti-vaccine public" was increasingly suspicious of vaccines. Calthorpe was perplexed. It seemed that the more pro-vaccine messages went out, the lower public trust fell. Industry leaders complained to him that profits were not meeting expectations. Calthorpe countered that he had been brought in to manage the anti-vaccine impact, not profitability issues. But he was concerned about an elusive variable in the "trust equation."

A few weeks later, the Vaccine Court's special masters issued a scathing ruling denying Elyse McCormick compensation. Special Master Tychyn's opinion described the McCormicks, their doctors, and their expert witnesses as having engaged in "magical thinking" and insinuated that the doctors committed malpractice.

It was as though the government had never conceded that the Whittaker child's autism was the result of vaccine injury. They had un-rung the bell.

The decision, which received national media coverage, dealt a devastating blow to the McCormicks and the rest of the autism community. Tony, Newman, Laura, and Maria wasted no time pulling together a conference call to discuss the implications the ruling would have on their project. "This work is now more important than ever," Newman said.

"Is there any way to get published before the Supreme Court hears *Cornachio* in October?" Laura asked.

"I don't know," Tony said, "the numbers are building, but this work takes time. However long it takes, we're hunting down Robert Bangston."

Senator Russell Sampson watched the television coverage in his office and shook his head. The images of Elyse McCormick left him on the verge of tears. He shut his office door to collect himself, and then Diana called. "I saw it, Diana. I haven't read the decision yet, but one reporter said they mocked the family. I was hoping they'd win. We could've stood with them."

"We still could, Russell," Diana said plainly.

That hurt. "The other side looks for anything to attack us, Diana. You know that." Russell said through clenched teeth. "They'll call us crazy!"

"I know, Russell, but this is our son. What happened to that child, happened to our child."

"I'm working with Smithson on this but we have to be careful."

"I told my dad today that Jordan has autism, Russell. He was so confused. He kept saying that there was a mistake. He insisted that Jordan was fine, that nothing was wrong. Jordan just sat there humming and spinning the wheels on his toy cars."

"Diana, this is not the right time to attack the issue."

His wife was silent for long seconds. "When will it be? Is this the country you risked your life for? A country where children's brains and futures are snatched away? Where grandparents' dreams are crushed? A country where half-assed judges mock families who fight back, all the while protecting multinational corporations? Why did we come to Washington? Huh? Tell me that?"

Kesslinger called Bangston on his cell phone as soon as she heard the decision. "Robert, they ruled in our favor. Hallelujah! What do you think, fella?"

"I guess it's good, but we have more hurdles, Jennifer."

"True, true," she admitted, "but the tide is turning and you were a huge reason for it."

"I suppose."

"I'm gonna remember you when I'm out of government. You came through for us."

Bangston sensed that Kesslinger had had a few drinks. "Well, thanks."

When Kesslinger hung up, Bangston went through yet another file describing a child regressing into autism by age three. This case was submitted by a family without an attorney. This family had no chance of compensation. He stamped it "Rejected" and tossed it onto the growing pile.

Zvi read the decisions on his home computer and shook his head with disbelief. How could the special masters mock the McCormick family for listening to doctors who believed that vaccines triggered Elyse McCormick's autism? Media coverage described the story as a huge victory for the vaccine program, which was described in glowing terms. A triumphant Dr. Phillip Snyder appeared on several networks. "These rulings are the final nail in the coffin of the vaccine-autism myth."

Zvi was captivated by the images of the McCormick child. She was so similar to the children he saw in the Soviet Union. She was also similar to the two children with autism on his street.

The next day Zvi's supervisor informed him that Binghampton Pharmaceuticals bought Vax—Powder and shut down the research. There would be no next generation of safer vaccines and nothing that the old vaccines could be compared to. Zvi wondered if Binghampton shut it down because they knew the ruling was coming.

That evening Zvi stood at the entrance to his living room, a glass of vodka in his hand. He liked what he saw. His family was safe and happy. Anya worked part-time to help manage Georgi's medical school costs. America had been good to Zvi but he had to do something.

But what would happen to him if he came forward with what he knew? Zvi noticed the uptick in media attacks on Dr. Ramsey. The attacks seemed planned. It reminded him of the old Soviet propaganda machine and how it was used to justify government actions. He looked at himself in a hall mirror. Zvi looked like a foreigner. Was he the kind of messenger from whom Americans would accept this information? Would they call him dangerous? A Communist?

An enemy of the people?

Zvi thought of children living safe lives full of promise, so very different from what had been taken from the McCormick child and the children with autism on his street. He felt guilt all the way through his guts.

He waited for Anya to fall asleep, and then went out to the garage to look in his old file cabinet for the DPT paper in his records. At least he could re-read his study before deciding whether to take the risk of showing it to the media.

He slid open the file drawer, then leafed through the folder where he kept the paper.

The paper was gone.

CHAPTER 28

Tony, Forceski, and Probation Supervisor Eddie Mendoza entered Joe Pittaluga's dark cell in the Special Housing Unit at the Castleton County Jail. Pittaluga had been in Special Housing for months because a pedophile might not be safe in the regular jail population. Looking at eight years in state prison because of the horrendous child pornography on his computer, he would spend the rest of his life marked as a notorious Level III offender on the state's Sex Offender Registry.

"What do you wanna talk about, Joe?" Tony asked.

"I can't do the eight years."

"What do you want us to do about that?" Forceski asked.

"We asked you to work with us weeks ago," Tony said. "You blew smoke and now you're lookin' at eight hard."

"Maybe something could come off the time if I tell you some stuff."

"It's gotta be good stuff," Mendoza said. "I'm not going to do anything for you with the DA if it isn't."

"One of the guys running this thing is a bad dude. He finds out that I'm working with you, I'm dead."

"New York's a big-ass state, Joey," Mendoza said. "There are ways to keep people in different prisons."

"Eight years is a long time for a sex offender," Tony said coldly. "What do you have?"

⚕ ⚕ ⚕

The man named by Joe Pittaluga was John "Slag" Fusco, and he was indeed a bad dude. Fusco was suspected in two homicides and was on probation for sexually abusing his ex-girlfriend's daughter. One of the homicide suspicions was that of his ex-girlfriend. The other was a dead biker in upstate New York.

"Fusco's one of ours too," Mendoza said. "He reports and does what he's told, but everyone knows the guy's a psychopath. We think he's been in a biker's gang and has white supremacist tattoos."

"Freakin' guy abuses his girlfriend's daughter and then decides to kill her," Forceski said. "Nice human being."

"Dutchess County couldn't make the case," Mendoza said. "It's been two years since they found her body."

"So now Fusco is peddling child pornography disks," Tony said.

"What was on the one we saw was more than child porno," Forceski said. "That was grotesque."

"What'd you make of Pittaluga's statement about the victims?" Mendoza asked.

"He said that they were all retards," Forceski said. "Don't know how I didn't put one right between his eyes after that."

"Eddie, Glen, and I have disabled kids. This is our worst nightmare."

"I'm sorry," Mendoza said. "This must be horrible for you guys."

"But Fusco's not the guy on the disk," Tony said with disgust. "That's some other ghoul."

"These guys have figured out that the Feds monitor the Internet and they can get caught emailing videos and photographs," Mendoza said. "So they adapt their business model. I guess there's big money in private collectables."

"A 'private disk' like that goes for thousands." Mendoza said. "I bet Fusco is funneling these disks to a whole network of sex offenders."

"Eddie, how do you handle working with these creeps?" Forceski asked. "I couldn't do it, bro."

"Someone has to," Mendoza said.

"That disk is a horror show," Tony said. "We have to find the guy with the Wolverine mask before he puts another kid on that table."

Dinner at the Colletti house was just over when Marge Riley telephoned Tony. "We got another autism case!" she announced happily.

"Great goin', kid," Tony said. Anne rolled her eyes. Tony was now working into the wee hours of the morning on the project, and she was worried that he was getting exhausted. "Which family?"

"Carla Liscombe out in Utah. Terrence Liscombe, the kid who got compensated by the Vaccine Court, answered the phone. Sounds like my Billy. The mom consented, and we talked for about an hour and a half. Nice lady. I'm enjoying doing this work."

"I know. I had a call go past midnight last week."

"Her son had a seizure within ten minutes of the vaccine and almost died. It's the usual pattern: horrible seizures, serious illness, developmental regression, and then permanent disability. The mom's gonna scan some records and email them to me."

"Getting documentation is critical."

"She mentioned something that she said made her son's case go pretty quickly, if you call four years of legal bullshit quick. He had a nasty reaction to his first DPT that was also documented. Then the second shot really pushed him over the edge."

"Herb mentioned cases like this—they document a challenge and re-challenge effect."

"Meaning?"

"It shows that the vaccine really did it. Science and law both recognize challenge—re-challenge as proof of a drug's effect, good or bad."

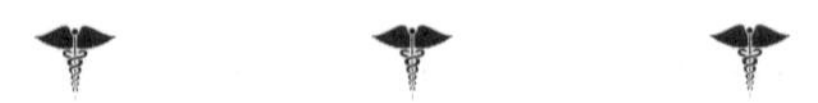

Raphael Molea ended his two-hour phone conversation with George Babakian of Roanoke, Virginia, at 10:45 p.m. The interview was gut-wrenching, and Raffy was exhausted. He wept as he filled out the last few lines of the interview form.

The child compensated by the Vaccine Court, Alison Babakian, age fourteen, died just three weeks ago. She suffered her entire short life from seizures and autism triggered by a vaccine administered when she was an infant. Raffy was a devout Catholic, but he was deeply troubled by what he heard.

Even though it was after 11:00 p.m., he called Tony. "Tony, the Babakian kid had autism too."

"What do you mean by 'had'?"

"She died three weeks ago from a seizure. I spoke to the dad for two hours. I cried my eyes out when I got off the phone. What has happened to these families is challenging my faith."

"I feel it too, Raffy. I wish that I could un-know what I know. There's such darkness to all of this."

"Do you go to church?"

"Not as often as I should."

"Would you pray the Rosary with me for this kid and her family?"

"Of course."

The two men prayed together. "Our Father, who art in heaven . . ."

John Morris finished his coffee and felt deflated. He had just called five families, and no one had answered the phone. It made him wonder whether Tony was sending him all the clunkers. Then the phone rang and displayed the name of one of the people he left a message with. "Johnny Mo," he answered.

"Sandra Chartier here. A John Morris called me about a research project?"

"Yeah, that's me. I'm Johnny Mo."

"How can I help you?"

"Well, like I said, we're doing a research project, and we're trying to contact families who went through the National Vaccine Injury Compensation Program. Are you the mother of Paul Chartier?"

"Wait a minute, Mr. Mo. Would you mind telling me how did you get information on my son's case, and how did you got my number?"

Thump, thump. John's son entered the kitchen, humming loudly as he whacked an empty water bottle with a wooden spoon.

"We googled you after we looked at public records from the program. Sorry about the noise."

"What is this?"

"This is a professional research study, lady. It's completely voluntary but we're wondering if . . ."

"Excuse me, Mr. Mo," Chartier interrupted, "but do you have a child with autism with you?"

"As a matter of fact I do. That's my little John. He's six feet tall actually." Morris put his hand over the receiver. "John, can you make that noise in the living room? Sorry about that."

"Isn't that something?" Chartier said. "My son makes a similar noise when he flips through the pages of books and magazines. We call it 'stimming.'"

"Your kid stims too?"

"It is what people with autism sometimes do, Mr. Mo. I think you know that."

"Your kid has autism?"

"I just said that."

"Nailed one!" Morris said with glee.

"Mr. Mo, you're from New York, aren't you?"

"How'd you guess?"

"I'm a psychologist. I'm supposed to be perceptive. I guess I'll answer your questions."

"Thank you so much, Ms. Chartier."

"Please call me Sandra. How's your son doing?"

"He's happy. Loves to read. Can tell you the entire history of the Civil War—whether you want to know it or not."

Chartier laughed. "My son can be that way too. He can tell you what day of the week June 12, 1735, was."

"You know, even with all the quirks, I'm proud of my kid."

Most of the students had left when Sensei Akinori Saito walked through the men's changing area in the back of the dojo. Wearing his ghi, Tony sat on the bench lost in thought.

"Spending the evening or just hoping that I would make some tea for you?"

"That would be great, thank you."

Saito shut the door. "Your mind goes to another place the minute you step off the mats, my friend. You are troubled. Empty your cup."

"The families we are finding have been through so much pain. Some of the children died after years of suffering. All this from drugs that our government says children must take. And now my partner and I found out that criminals are making money by sexually abusing disabled children."

"The weak are often victimized by those willing to abuse power. That's why good men like you are so important."

"I just hope that I can make a difference. That some good comes from all of this."

"There are good people all around you. Always keep that in mind. But it will be good for you to step away for a few days and take some time to enjoy your family. And some tea."

It was the Fourth of July, and Tony and Anne brought Anthony, Jr., and Sophie to Winston's Independence Day Parade. Tony spied Chief Lonnegan in his dress uniform watching the fire department line up its personnel and equipment in the elementary school parking lot. "Hey, Tony—brought the whole clan, I see."

"All the Collettis are present and accounted for, sir," Tony said. "This old river town looks beautiful today, doesn't it?" Lonnegan nodded in agreement. The red fire trucks sparkled, and many of the townsfolk were waving small American flags. The blue of the Hudson River framed the old colonial homes.

"Fire trucks!" little Anthony said while jumping up and down.

Lonnegan's Irish eyes twinkled. "Hey, Anthony, would you like to ride in one?"

A few minutes later, Tony found himself sitting with Anthony, proudly riding down Old Bedford Road in an antique fire truck cabin. "He's enjoying this like any other kid would," Tony said to himself, and he kissed his son on the cheek.

"Mommy, look at Daddy and Anthony riding in the fire truck!" Sophie exclaimed.

Anne switched her iPhone to camera mode. "Wave your flag, Anthony!" she shouted.

"What do you think about the Fourth of July, Buddy?" Tony said to his son.

"Fire trucks!"

"Yeah, but what did they tell you in school about what the Fourth of July meant?"

Little Anthony smiled. "Freedom! Freedom!"

CHAPTER 29

On a sultry August Monday in Memphis, Tennessee, the South Side Community Health Clinic waiting room was full of families getting their children back-to-school shots. The clinic was a bit run-down, but warmly regarded for providing solid health care for the city's poor and working-class people.

Dr. Ronald Washington, a young African American pediatrician cruised through the examination rooms giving kids high-fives for bravely taking their shots. The Johns Hopkins graduate could have written his own ticket to any number of top-shelf jobs but chose to serve the community where he grew up.

Washington put down a cup of coffee when he heard a scream from down the hall. A child had passed out in examination room #6. Then another child fell unconscious in #3. As both children were tended to by nurses, a third fell to the hallway floor in a seizure.

Nurses and aides ran to and fro dealing with children having seizures or blacking out. "Stop all procedures—stat!" Washington shouted. "Someone call 911 now. We need back up from Holy Family now." Washington ran between rooms, calling out instructions, focusing staff. "Maureen, it may be the vaccines. Pull them now."

"Which ones? We're giving some kids five plus to catch them up."

"All of 'em! Stat!"

"Oh, no!" a nurse gasped, as another child convulsed in the waiting room. Panicked parents scooped up their children and fled the clinic.

Washington went to the child lying face-down between toppled chairs. Her windpipe was obstructed, and he struggled to clear it. "Come on, child. Breathe!"

"My baby!" her mother cried.

Two police officers carrying a crash bag burst into the waiting room. "We got people running down the street saying children are dyin' here. What's happenin'?"

"Not sure," Washington said as he worked on the child. "We were giving routine immunizations when kids started having seizures." An officer handed him a bag valve mask that he affixed to the child's face. "We can't wait for an ambulance."

"Let's get her to our car."

Washington carried the girl through the clinic doors and into the backseat. One of the cops got in with her as the other officer gunned the engine.

Washington ran back into the clinic as ambulances flew down Beale Street, sirens wailing.

Although Dr. Washington and his staff saved the lives of seven children that day, the one heading to Holy Family Hospital died in the police car en route. Local media descended on the clinic after the city released her name along with a statement that the matter was under investigation. The health commissioner told the press, "We should not assume that the vaccinations being administered caused the outbreak of seizures. We are working with the Centers for Disease Control to further assess the event."

The story rolled up the media food chain until it landed on Sara Donovan's computer screen at SNN. Donovan printed it out and ran into Seth Millman's office. "Seth, look at this."

Millman lowered his glasses and read. "Oh man, Sara, you know they're going to try to block this one."

"I want to go."

"You think I can just dial up a three-person crew and fly you to Tennessee? With all the budget nonsense I'm having trouble getting crews to go to New York and LA."

"Give me one cameraman. Come on, Seth! Just one!"

"And just how am I going to get this by the new 'medical issues team' here?"

"Seth, this is what we do. It's a huge story. A kid is dead and . . ."

"Dr. Randall Cooke and the medical issues team are here to contain us, Sara." Millman was fuming. "Come back with this, and they'll descend on us like the wrath of Khan!"

"Oh, I get it," Donavan dripped sarcasm. "SNN runs stories about nutrition and breastfeeding while the hard stuff gets squashed. This is crap and you know it. A child is dead and half-a-dozen more are injured—possibly for life!"

"You know the new rules, Sara. You can cover government fraud, corrupt politicians, and military screwups, but vaccines are *verboten*." Millman got up and looked out his office window at the Connecticut Avenue traffic. "I don't want to spend another week looking at Charles Fontaine in meetings with our legal staff. And I'm sick of Phil Snyder's nasty-grams."

Come on, Seth. Just one cameraman." Donovan pleaded.

Millman thought long and hard, and then shrugged. He knew when he was beaten. "All right. Tell production you're taking Tommy and go to Memphis."

CHAPTER 30

Tony and Forceski sat in an unmarked car in a parking garage across the street from John Fusco's apartment in Croton Manor, the town neighboring Winston. It was a hot August day, and the men appreciated the shade and cover that the parking lot afforded them. Eddie Mendoza's probation officers searched Fusco's apartment the week before, and found a small quantity of marijuana but nothing related to child pornography. How Fusco was producing and distributing the pornographic child abuse disks was still a mystery. And now Fusco knew that law enforcement was watching him again.

"This guy's gone underground," Forceski said.

"He's gonna start doing his thing at some point, Glen. Guys like this don't change."

Chavez chirped on the radio. "Detectives, we got a disturbance at the Fournier house.

Veronica Fournier says that her autistic son, Evan, assaulted her."

"Uh-oh," Tony said. "We're going. Chavez, who's responding?"

"Randazzo and Wanda."

"Let 'em know we're on the way."

The men arrived in front of the Fournier house a few minutes later. Randazzo and Veronica Fournier were at the police cruiser where he was placing a bandage on her forehead.

"Hey, Veronica," Tony said. "What's going on?"

"Evan's just been so agitated. I don't know what triggered him. He started punching himself in the head after watching television. I guess that the new shrink in town is no better than the old one—the medication is making him worse."

"You all right?"

"Officer Randazzo is very helpful," she said smiling.

"Let me get you a cold pack," Forceski rummaged through the first aid kit in the back of Randazzo's cruiser.

"Where's Evan?" Tony asked.

"He's still in the house, Detective," Randazzo said, "Wanda's in the backyard to make sure he doesn't run out the back. We didn't want another trip to the reservoir."

Officer Wanda Burke's voice came over the radio. "Suspect exited the rear of the house brandishing a knife."

"Oh crap," Randazzo said. Tony motioned for him to go around the right side of the house. Tony took to the left side. The two men arrived in the backyard at the same time.

Wanda Burke, a young African American officer, had her gun out. "Police! Drop the knife!" Evan Fournier waved a long carving knife and moved toward the retreating Burke.

Randazzo drew his gun. "Stop! Police! Drop the knife."

Tony moved closer to the teenager with his hands open. He did not draw his fiream. "Evan! Put the knife down!" Tony said firmly. The boy turned and ran at him, screaming and swinging the knife in the air.

"STOP—POLICE! STOP—POLICE!" Randazzo shouted.

Randazzo fired once at Evan's torso but pulled the second shot to the left when he realized that Tony was now in the line of fire. Evan kept charging Tony who felt a burning sensation on his right leg. He grabbed Evan's knife hand and spun the boy to the ground with a thud. Kicking the knife aside, he immobilized Evan in a restraint hold. "Okay, son. I got you. We're going to calm down together, buddy." Evan cried and moaned as Tony held him. Tony looked Evan over as the other officers closed in. "I don't see any wounds. Is he hit?"

"I don't see any blood," Randazzo yelled.

"You're okay, Evan." Tony experienced so many emotions at once that he didn't know what to feel. Evan seemed to be uninjured. He winced at a stinging pain in his right thigh, but his leg seemed functional. Glancing down, he saw that his pants were shredded. But relief swept over him as he realized that Evan had not taken a bullet.

"Detective, are you all right?" Randazzo shook from stress.

Forceski arrived on the scene. "What the hell happened!? I heard shots."

"Randazzo had to shoot when he charged Detective Colletti with that knife," Burke said.

Forceski examined Tony then Evan "I think I'm okay," Tony said. "But I must have taken one in the leg. Dazz, holster your weapon."

Burke was on the radio. "Officer down! Ten-thirteen! Officer down!"

"Oh crap! You've been hit." Randazzo yelled. He looked more closely at Tony's right leg. "Detective, hold it, there's hardly any blood."

"Let's get Evan cuffed," Forceski said. "We're gonna need three ambulances, Wanda."

Tony and Forceski sat Evan up and cuffed him. He was rocking back and forth while Tony kept him under control.

Veronica Fournier ran up waving her hands and screaming. "Oh my God! My son!"

"Veronica," Tony said, "We're all right. Evan's safe."

"Detective, it's like the bullet grazed you. It looks more like a burn than a bullet wound." Randazzo half-smiled. "Remarkable, really."

"Remarkable, my ass! You just shot me in the leg. It'll be remarkable if I don't strangle you."

"You shot at my son!?" Veronica screamed. "Oh my God! Is Evan hit?"

"No, he's not," Forceski said. "He's okay. But he's going to the hospital so they can check him out."

"You shot at my son!" Fournier screamed at Randazzo. Forceski restrained her from lunging at Randazzo.

"He was running at the detective with a knife. I feared for his life," Randazzo said.

Tony nodded in agreement. "Veronica, it got intense for a minute. Randazzo responded like he's trained to. But it's okay. One round hit my leg and the other went somewhere else."

"You're shot! My God!"

"It's a flesh wound," Randazzo said, still shaking.

Tony glared at him.

"Mrs. Fournier," Burke interrupted, "let's give everyone some room."

As sirens wailed in the distance, Tony got up and grabbed Randazzo around the shoulders as though he were grabbing him by the throat. "Listen to me, when the ambulance gets here, you get in and you shut up. You go to the hospital and get checked out. Glen will call Pooch and the union lawyer, and you say exactly what you just said, you feared for my life. You used verbal commands first. Stay away from the chief for a few hours because he may shoot you and he won't have a legal defense. I loved these pants. Now you shot a hole in 'em. You're gonna buy me some new pants, Randazzo."

Chief Lonnegan was seething. Media was pouring onto Reservoir Road—again. He had two officers on the way to the hospital again, and the town supervisor was apoplectic. "Wanda," he barked, "tell me what the hell happened here!"

"Chief, Colletti got wounded but still safely unarmed this poor freaked-out kid. He somehow managed to keep himself and everyone else together. It was the bravest thing I've ever seen. I don't know that I know how to write that in a report." Burke's voice trembled with emotion.

Lonnegan put his hand on her shoulder. "You write it just like you told me, Wanda. Just like that. We're all okay. You did good work, and everyone's going home tonight."

The chief called headquarters. "Chavez, put out a request to have other departments send us officers who've been through deadly physical force situations. I want them talking to our officers. Call in all the brass, too. I want everyone backing each other up."

"Yes sir."

In law enforcement, silence could become a silent killer. Winston-on-Hudson had just had its first police shooting in over forty years. Lonnegan knew how important it was for everyone to talk about the incident and understand what could be learned from it.

Tony spoke to Anne on his cell phone as the doctor and nurse cleaned out his wound. "Babe, I'm fine, really. It won't even leave a scar." The nurse indicated a small scar. "Well, maybe a small scar . . . Yes, it was Randazzo, again . . . No, I can't shoot him back. He actually responded reasonably. The kid was running at me with a knife. What's the guy supposed to do? I know you don't want to hear that. Listen, I'm okay. Just tell Sophie that Daddy had a little accident. I promise you I'm okay. Evan Fournier is okay. Veronica mentioned that Evan is seeing a new shrink. Whatever he's giving Evan, it isn't working." The chief and Forceski entered the room. "Gotta go. See you in a little while."

"You told Anne?" Forceski asked.

"Yeah. She wants me to shoot Randazzo."

"No, I get to do that," the chief drawled, "right after he's done giving his statement. You all right?"

"I'm okay. It got real interesting there for a few seconds. Evan never gave Dazz a chance to do anything other than shoot. We got to the backyard at about the same time, and then the kid charged at me with the knife."

"This is classic. Shootings happen when there really are no other choices or time to make them," said Forceski. "This is why we need Tasers. It's time for the town to find the money in the budget."

"Poor kid was so freaked out," Tony said shaking his head.

"He's settling down over at the medical center psych wing. How bad was he?" Lonnegan asked.

"He was really amped," Tony said. "He was pounding his head with his fist. Then he started swinging the carving knife around and everything escalated from there. Veronica has been taking Evan to a new psychiatrist in town. I wonder what he's giving the kid."

As Tony prepared to leave his hospital room, a pale and nervous Randazzo appeared in the doorway. "Hey, Detective," Randazzo asked, "how're you doing?"

"I was shot in the leg. How do you think I'm doing?"

"I'm so sorry, man."

Tony realized he was being unfair. "Hey, it's okay. We'd all feel really terrible if the kid had been hit or—worse—killed. But none of that changes the fact that you responded the way you were trained. Many cops go through their whole careers and never know if they could really do what they have to do in a moment like that."

"But you never drew your gun," Randazzo said. "You committed to hand-to-hand action right from jump."

"I might have shot him, Bobby," Tony said looking down. "I've been there. But that's for another time. I focused on dealing with the situation with hand techniques."

Randazzo sat down in a chair near the door. "That was what I wanted to talk to you about. How did you do that? With everything that was happening, you just focused."

"It takes training, Dazz, hours and hours of training. We all need to be better at hand-to-hand self-defense if we're going to be dealing with more kids like Evan. This is going to be a big issue in our line of work."

"I've never been good at focusing."

"Look, it's not like you don't have the guts for this work. It isn't every man who commits to action like you do. Everybody knows that."

"I can't even begin to describe how horrible I felt after I shot. I never want to feel that way again."

"I've been there. Why don't you come with me to the dojo?"

"The what?"

"'Dojo' is Japanese for 'the place of the way.' You'll see."

CHAPTER 31

Sara Donovan walked out of a late summer downpour and into the lobby bar of the Memphis Hyatt. Spotting Dr. Ronald Washington, she sat down at the table he occupied. "Thanks for agreeing to talk," she said.

"I'm not the kind of guy who would normally do this," Washington began.

"What do you mean?"

"Be a whistle-blower. I had no intention of talking to the press, but I felt I should talk to you after the attitude that the CDC investigation team took."

"What sort of attitude?"

"They confiscated all the vaccines. I expected that," Washington said, "but when they began interrogating me and my staff as though we're criminals, I got suspicious."

"Oh?"

"We were all interviewed separately and they fired questions at us. I felt intimidated and so did the staff. I told one CDC guy to watch his tone or I'd throw all their asses out of my clinic. We didn't deserve that kind of treatment after what we'd all been through."

"I'm sorry. I can't imagine what that day must have been like."

"We love our community. What happened to these children was . . ." Washington paused a long minute before drinking from his soda glass. "Sorry."

Donovan smiled. “It’s okay.”

“Every other question came with a comment attached like ‘you know that vaccines don’t cause that’ or ‘why weren’t you aware that the children had histories of seizure disorders?’ None of the kids had seizure histories.”

“So, the questions weren’t open-ended? Like the ones I’m asking you?”

“They were questions, but with messages embedded. They seemed to be working off a script. It’s like they needed someone to blame.”

“Any idea who?”

“Anybody and anything other than the vaccines.”

“Why do you think they took that tone?”

“The children, the clinic, and my community got screwed. We got a bad batch of vaccines. It’s important to resolve what happened here. The medical community and the public need to know because vaccines are important. If there’s a problem, it should be disclosed.” Washington leaned in and whispered. “I made some calls, and was told that they call a batch of bad vaccines a ‘hot lot.’ I asked the CDC people about that term. They denied that term existed and were unwilling to admit that a ‘hot lot’ could even happen. But there have been other events like this.”

“I’ve checked and heard the same thing,” Donovan said. “One would think that there would be a report issued, like what the Federal Aviation Authority does after a plane crash. But, the CDC doesn’t do that.”

“The people who came to my clinic are not going to issue a report on their findings, I can tell you that,” Washington shook his head. “I think that they intend to sweep this under the rug. But what really angered me was when they started talking about the episode being a ‘psychological event.’ Like a form of mass hysteria.” Washington shook his head. “How do kids transfer seizures to each other psychologically? That’s nonsense because the first two kids had seizures in different offices on different sides of the clinic.”

“I agree. That makes no sense.”

“No sense at all,” Washington echoed. “And this morning a psychiatrist interviewed on local TV said that the event may have been ‘psychological.’ This doctor is a friend of the health commissioner. Psychiatrists don’t know about vaccine reactions in children. *He* was allowed to discuss the event, but I've been restricted from making public comment. I could get fired for even having this conversation with you."

"Has the CDC communicated that or did it come from your direct supervisor?"

"From the health commissioner himself. But I'm sure he was feeling pressure from the CDC people. They wanted us to know that we were accountable. Instead of open-minded investigators, we got agents delivering a message."

"And the message was?"

"'Shut up about this.'"

The next day Donovan went to the home of Ray and Leanna Yearwood in downtown Memphis. It was clear that two-year-old Daniella, one of the children who had suffered seizures at the clinic, was not well. Even though she had been discharged from the hospital, the seizures had not yet stopped.

"A few days ago, my daughter could talk and walk and was pretty much potty trained. Now . . ." Mrs. Yearwood began to cry. "It's like she's a Raggedy Ann doll. She's so sensitive to light. When we switch on even a lamp, she begins to scream. It's just terrible. My husband is so angry. He hasn't slept in days."

"I'm so sorry," Donovan said. "Have the doctors given you any idea as to when she'll get better?"

"No, they keep talking about controlling her seizures. They say that she has an encephelopa . . . an encephelopa—something."

"An encephalopathy?"

"That's it. Do you know what that is?"

"I have an idea, but I'm not a doctor."

"They don't really give much information," Yearwood cried. "We don't know what to do. We're so worried."

"Has anyone reported the adverse event to VAERS for you?" Donovan asked.

"What's that?"

"It's the Vaccine Adverse Event Reporting System, the government's reporting system for vaccine injuries." Yearwood shook her head. "Did they tell you about the Vaccine Injury Compensation Program?"

Yearwood looked blank. "No. They didn't."

Donovan shook her head in disgust. The family had not been told about their legal options despite clear indications that their daughter's injuries were vaccine-related. And the doctors didn't even tell the Yearwoods that they could report the vaccine reaction.

As soon as Donovan's flight touched down at Reagan Airport, she immediately headed to the SNN production office. The interviews had already been sent to Seth Millman and the production staff, who were hard at work pulling together the piece for the nightly news.

But there was a problem. The medical issues team found out and was raising a stink. "They know," Millman said as he ushered Donovan into his office. "We're in for a fight."

"Then I say we fight, Seth. What happened in Memphis is a huge story."

Dr. Randall Cook waited with his team members in the conference room with the SNN legal staff. A thin, good-looking man in his late fifties, Cook wore his obligatory white doctor's coat and looked like everybody's attending cardiologist. The three lawyers—two men and one woman—looked grim in their business suits.

"Hi, Randall," Donovan said as she entered the room.

"Hey, how are you?" Cook asked.

"Oh great. We're about to have some real bullshit here, aren't we? I see that you're wearing your doctor's uniform again. Seeing any patients here at SNN?"

Cook played it cool. "Would you like some coffee? It's a fresh pot."

"Don't try to placate me. Seth and I know what this is about. This is censorship, and you're just an industry agent in a lab coat!"

"Look, Sara, the word from Memphis professional circles is that the whole thing was a psychiatric event. There's no story here."

"You have to be kidding me. The people I spoke to in Memphis are credible. They know what they experienced. The clinic people went through hell."

"This is completely reckless!" Cook lost his cool. "We're going to scare the public for no good reason. There's no way to say that vaccines caused this event, Sara. It's reckless."

"A child died, Randall! Are you saying that the child died from a psychiatric event?"

"No! I'm not. The kid had a seizure. That one seizure was real. Then it set off the other kids."

"Kids who didn't know what was going on in other rooms around the clinic? That's preposterous!"

"Don't you raise your voice to me," Cook shouted back. "I went to Johns Hopkins, you snide little . . ."

"So did Dr. Washington! He was there for the whole thing, and he knows what he saw!"

"Your loyalty to your profession is interfering with your thinking about this story!" Millman said pointedly. "We are not here to defend the AMA! Come on! We're supposed to be journalists here. So are you!"

"This is irresponsible!" Cook said, lowering his voice. "Think about how important vaccines are and how much this network risks by running this story. Vaccine injury is just conjecture."

"By your standards, Randall, there is no way to ever prove that a vaccine could cause an injury," Donovan said.

"Officially, they don't," Cook said.

"And I take it that you are the official word, aren't you, Randall?" Millman said.

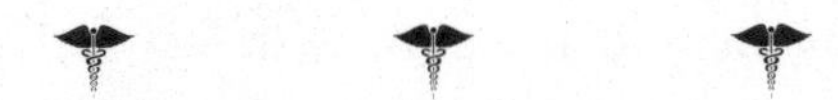

The story that Dr. Cook ran on SNN that night focused on the growing consensus that the whole sad Memphis affair was a "psychiatric event triggered by one child who, tragically, suffered a fatal seizure," a gray-bearded psychiatrist named Max Zissner said reassuringly into the camera. A CDC official commented, "The vaccine issue will be fully evaluated, but the vaccine-seizure connection looks increasingly remote."

On another network, Dr. Phillip Snyder appeared in another piece about the Memphis incident. "I once saw an infant boy have a seizure on the examination table before I started immunizations. It was later revealed that the child had a genetic disorder. You can understand why parents get confused. This is why we advise families to listen to the experts."

Donovan and Millman left the office right after the nightly news ended and got drunk at a local bar. Both decided that they still had important journalism to do, but they were done covering vaccines. They took cabs home and got to the office late the next day.

Sitting at her desk that afternoon, Donovan worked on some of her other stories. At 3:15 her cell phone rang. It was Dr. Washington.

"Sara," Washington said, "what happened to the story?"

"I don't want to talk about it, Doctor. I am sorry about this. I really am." Still hungover, Donovan got up unsteadily and shut her office door. "They wouldn't let me run it. I tried. I really did. It's no reflection on you."

"I'm afraid it is a reflection on me," Washington interrupted. "I just got fired."

Donovan's headache disappeared. "What?"

"They fired me. The health commissioner just hung up the phone."

"Oh no! Excuse me. I'll, I'll call you back." Donovan fought against tears but quickly composed herself. She walked into the office kitchen where a nice fresh pot of coffeemaker in the coffeemaker. She removed the pot and went across to Randall Cook's office.

Cook was sitting behind his desk with his feet up, talking on the phone. "Phil, that's such good news. I'm so happy for you. When will you be inducted?"

"Don't worry. It's a fresh pot," Donovan said as she poured the coffee onto Dr. Cook's lap.

"Ahhh! Ahhh! You burned me!"

"No, I didn't." Donovan felt better than she had in days. "Your symptoms are just psychological, Dr. High-and-Mighty, Johns Hopkins Graduate. Any association with the coffee is purely coincidental."

CHAPTER 32

Dr. Robert Bangston sat in a conference room in the Health and Human Services Building in Washington. He tapped his fingers as he watched Department of Justice attorney Terrence Stone present the latest statistics to the members of the Advisory Commission to the National Vaccine Injury Compensation Program. Since the rulings against the petitioners in the Omnibus Autism Proceedings had been announced, the tension around the program had ebbed. "In summary, special masters are now dismissing autism claims on a regular basis, that's why you are seeing such a significant decline in cases," Stone told the group.

The recording secretary said, "As per the agenda, it's now time to offer the public listening on the conference line opportunity for comment. First caller, please identify yourself."

"This is Wayne Brodie from Saint Paul, Minnesota. Is it wise to dismiss the autism cases when all the science isn't in?"

Bangston wasn't surprised by the question. "The special masters ruled that vaccines don't cause autism. The rulings are clear, precise, and strong. They relied on peer-reviewed science to evaluate the issue."

"What about the Whittaker case? In that case vaccines were determined to have caused autism."

"Not correct. There were just symptoms of autism," Stone responded.

"That makes no sense," the caller said. "There's a lack of independent science on vaccine injury. We need independent, non-pharma sponsored . . . "

"Thank you for your comments. You have used your time allotment," the recording secretary interrupted. "Second caller, please state your name and address for the record."

"Anthony Colletti, Winston-on-Hudson, New York."

"Please begin your comments, Mr. Colletti."

"I have a question for Dr. Bangston."

"Yes, Mr. Colletti."

"In the 1998 paper in which you and other researchers at the Division of Vaccine Injury Compensation reported that the MMR vaccine was associated with encephalopathy, did you determine whether any of those cases also featured autism?"

"I'm sorry. Could you repeat the question, Mr . . . ?"

"Colletti."

"I see, Mr. Colletti." Bangston shifted nervously in his chair. "The question again?"

"Yes, your 1998 paper in which you found that the MMR was associated with encephalopathy, did you determine whether any of those cases also featured autism?"

"Well, we, uh, weren't looking for autism."

"Dr. Bangston, that wasn't the question. Did you find that any of the cases featured autism?"

"I will have to dig up my old research notes on that and, um, get, get back to you on that issue."

"Certainly you and the other researchers had extensive medical records," Tony said. "On those cases where you determined that encephalopathy had been vaccine induced, did you find . . . "

"Your time is up, sir. Thank you for your call."

After the meeting, Bangston cornered Stone in the hallway. "Terry, can we please institute a screening system for these callers? How many times have I asked for that?"

"Bob, what's the problem? We all know that the whackos come out for these calls. Who else is going to call some insignificant committee attached to this ridiculous program?" Stone loosened his tie. "Relax, Bob."

Bangston, still upset, telephoned Phil Snyder.

"Robert, how're you doin'?"

"I'm steamed. I'm sure that one of the callers was one of those people who were doing that project on the cases settled prior to the Omnibus. The guy's name sounded familiar. He asked about my old MMR paper."

"I never liked that paper."

"Phil, that's not the point. We don't need these questions."

"What's the big deal?"

"Look, is there any way to stop them from digging around too much? I really want to move past the autism thing."

"They're on their last legs, Robert. They're done. I really wouldn't worry about them bugging you. Heck, they have me to kick around. Did you hear about that little punk with Asperger's who writes all those articles about me? Called me the "Dark Lord" on the *Era of Autism* blog. I've prevented thousands of children from getting vaccine-preventable diseases, and I'm called the "Dark Lord." These people are lunatics."

"I don't need them pestering me either, Phil. I don't have product royalties coming in. I'm slaving away here in government. Could some of your connections to do something about this guy? He sounded like he was going to interrogate me."

"All right, let me make some calls. Maybe there's something we can do."

⚕ ⚕ ⚕

A few weeks later, Maria Contessa-Guevara detected a clicking sound on her home phone. Tony noticed that his phone was behaving oddly as well. Then a few nights later as he was on a conference call with Johnny Mo, Marge Riley, and Raffy, he happened to look out his bedroom window. A black van was parked at the end of the street. Tony knew all his neighbor's cars, and it wasn't one of them. Through binoculars he noted that the car had tinted windows and New Jersey plates. He quickly ended the call. The van left a minute after the call ended.

The next night, the van was back.

A meeting was held the next day at Laura's office to address the group's concerns. "I'm completely freaked out," Laura said. "But so far, my phone seems normal."

"I'm really getting paranoid now," Herb responded.

"You've always been paranoid," Laura joked, and everybody laughed—except for Maria. Later that night she called Tony from her new cell phone.

"I'm worried, Tony," she said. "I've seen people disappear. The others have not. But I have seen terrible things."

"I understand, Maria. I'm a detective. I've been a part of this kind of work. I'm not enjoying being on the other side of a surveillance."

"There is no rationale for a government to spy on its citizens this way, Tony. I can't envision a judge who would permit spying on citizen's doing research."

"I'm not sure that this is the government. You mentioned that there were pharmaceutical industry attorneys at the McCormick hearing."

"That's what was rumored. They certainly looked like attorneys."

"I bet these people in the van and tapping the phones are with the industry."

"That makes sense. The government has become a vassal of the drug companies. But it still scares me. It brings back the memories and the horror."

"Do you want to back off the project for a while?"

"You know I can't do that. But I think we need to take precautions."

"What do you mean?" Tony wanted to know.

"We must insure that our work gets into the hands of people who will see it isn't buried."

"How?"

"It's time we connected to certain journalists. I will make some calls tomorrow—from my new number."

Tony hung up. The house was quiet. Anne and the children were sleeping peacefully. He looked out his bedroom window into the darkness. No van tonight.

But he knew that they would be back.

CHAPTER 33

Herb Newman's office was a maze of bins stuffed with paper and stacks of files obscuring a bronze desk plate that read *A messy desk is a sign of genius*. When the phone rang, Newman recognized the Atlanta area code where he once worked for the US Attorneys Office. "Herb Newman, attorney-at-law. How can I help you?"

"You're the attorney working on the autism project?" said a man in an Eastern European accent.

Herb stopped typing. "You've called before, haven't you?"

"Indeed. I need to talk to you."

"Very well. What's on your mind?"

"Have you located the settlements?"

"Sir, I don't want to seem paranoid, but you must understand that I have reservations about talking about this matter over the phone."

"My name is Victor Petrov. You are at a computer? Look me up. 'Google me,' as they say."

Herb made a few keystrokes. "Okay . . . I see you've published some papers. First glance, you've been involved in the FDA approval process of several drugs."

"Indeed. Now you know who I am. You have my name and you know where I work."

"Yes, but I have an agreement with everyone else that I'm working with not to disclose certain . . ."

"That is fine. I assume that by now you have discovered that the United States government has been compensating many children with vaccine-induced encephalopathy for many years."

"Mr. Petrov, we're at a critical juncture in our work and we must protect . . ."

"And these encephalopathy cases frequently feature autism diagnosis as well."

Newman paused to wonder how to respond, then went ahead. "You're correct, Mr. Petrov."

"I know what it is to present things under false pretenses, attorney Newman. What it is to hide truth with phraseology in such a way as to disguise reality."

"I can see that. But you've called for a reason. What can I do for you?"

"You could promise me that you will keep your knowledge of me a secret."

"Agreed. I will do so."

"There is more. Just as a vaccine injury that results in autism-like symptoms is called something else, so is 'Victor Petrov.'"

"I don't understand."

"My real name is not Victor Petrov, it is Zviad Kokochashvili. You are the first person that I have told my real name to in many, many years."

Newman was puzzled—and nervous. Why was this man disclosing this information to him? He typed "Zviad Kokacashvili" on Google, assuming that it was spelled with a "K" but . . .

"I hear your typing. You will not find my name on the Internet. I have been erased. Zviad does not exist. It's because of the kind of research that I used to do for the Soviet Union."

"You worked for the Soviet Union? Now you work for the FDA?"

"I have had many assignments since defecting. But now that I see what is really happening, I understand that I am actually just a comfortable hostage."

"A hostage?"

"In a manner of speaking, my friend. I wrote a paper many years ago about how Soviet victims of your old DPT vaccine became what we called 'ghosts.'"

"Ghosts? What do you mean?"

"That was what we called them then. Today you would say that they had autism."

"People with autism, ghosts?"

"Indeed. Then Zviad became a ghost of another sort and eventually the entire Soviet Union became a ghost. I would like America not to end up as a ghost. But to do that, we need to meet. I need your help."

Tony and Newman crossed into Maryland on I-95 en route to their meeting with Dr. Zviad Kokochashvili ahead of schedule. Tony's time in the car with a criminal defense lawyer once again brought him in touch with how strange his life had become. The two men had become the ultimate odd couple. For one thing, Newman liked to drive fast—real fast.

"Herb, slow down." Tony cautioned several times.

"You afraid we're gonna get a speeding ticket? Just show your badge."

"Never gonna happen 'cause the Jersey Troopers can't catch you. Their vehicles don't have warp drives. Now slow the hell down!"

"Why, do you think the people tapping our phones are chasing us?"

Tony didn't reply. That wasn't funny at all. They pulled into the Maryland House rest stop near Havre de Grace and found a booth in the Pizza Time section and waited. "So where's Vlad the Impailer?" Tony asked as he folded a slice of pizza.

"He'll be wearing a trench coat and red tie," Herb said looking around. "I don't think he'll chicken out." Almost on cue, a man walked over to them. "Mr. P?" Herb asked.

"How are you, my friend?" Zvi responded, his hazel eyes darting around the room. "I am most pleased to meet you." The two shook hands and Newman introduced him to Tony. "Happy to meet you as well, Officer Tony."

"Same here," Tony said. "We gotcha a soda."

Zvi sat down. "So, you are the policeman who figured this out."

"I couldn't have figured out anything without understanding how the Vaccine Court works. And my friend Mr. Newman here helped provide that understanding."

"You saw past what is presented overtly and into the underlying reality," Zvi said. "People in the Vaccine Court do not want to admit what you know."

"They are dogged," Newman said. "No question about that."

"Those who oppose you will go to any lengths to ensure that their policy interests are protected." Zvi furrowed his brows ominously. "At some point over the past few years, they entered my home and removed my paper on the DPT injuries in the Soviet Union."

"Are you sure—really sure—that you didn't misplace this document at some point?" Tony asked.

"I do not misplace documents, officer Tony. I understood that my research was why the Americans went through the trouble of helping me defect. I brought everything I wrote with me. I left my country in fear for my life. I took a huge risk. I could easily have been caught with my family. We all would have been made to disappear. When you are in my situation you do not . . ."

"I got you," Tony interrupted. "I never leave a question unasked."

"How can we help you?" Newman asked. "No ghost stuff, we're all nervous enough."

"I need you to get my paper back."

"But how?" Newman asked. "This isn't the kind of thing you send a Freedom of Information request for. We just can't walk into the CDC headquarters in Atlanta and ask for it."

"I understand that," Zvi sighed. "And I doubt that the CDC actually has it in their official files, my friend."

"Describe your paper again." Newman said.

"Essentially, we looked at Russian families who had their children vaccinated with the DPT and compared them to Russian families who did not."

"Oh, hold it," Tony said, realizing the importance. "You basically have a . . ."

"Vax/unvax study," Herb said nodding. "A comparative analysis of health outcomes between those who receive vaccines and those who don't. We've been advocating for this type of study for years."

"Did you look at other vaccines?" Tony asked.

"No, just the DPT," Zvi said. "There were only a few vaccines in Russia at that time. It was not like America is today. Here you have a vaccine for everything. We only looked at the DPT and saw problems in the vaccinated population that didn't occur in the non-vaccinated population."

"Go on," Newman said.

"Children died." Zvi shook his head sadly. "More than you would think. We also had many children who were just completely devastated and spent their lives bedridden. Many were institutionalized. It was terrible. We also saw that many of these children had what we call autism here."

"Did you call it autism?" Newman wanted to know.

"No, we didn't know what autism was. No one in our research collective had ever seen the disorder before, so we didn't call it that. We described the behavior in detail, and we called the children ghosts."

"What were the symptoms?" Tony asked.

"These children lost all language skills, and some never spoke again. They regressed after the DPT was given. Families reported a scream, a horrible scream, then seizures and prolonged illness. Eventually, they engaged in obsessive and repetitive behaviors and made strange noises. Many walked on their toes—a very odd thing, and they would flap their hands when they were stimulated by something."

"That's autism," Tony sighed.

"And you recorded these symptoms?" Newman asked.

"In great detail, my friend," Zvi said with obvious pride. "We felt that we were describing something new, and we took great pains to record what we observed. I described their autism quite clearly. We took great pride in our work. Unlike your scientists here, we didn't work for the company that offered the most research money. We worked for the people, for their health."

"No pressure for your work to focus on the idea of herd immunity for the greater good?" Newman asked.

"We always focused on the greater good. The greater good is healthy children and healthy adults!" Zvi pointed his finger in the air. "What you now have in America is a system out of balance, out of control. I don't devalue what's been built here, my friends. I risked my life, my wife's life, and my son's life to come here for freedom. Do you not know that this food court would be the finest restaurant in my entire village? Americans do not understand such things. They think everything is easy. Everything quick. Want supper? Go to Pizza Time. Want health? Get a vaccine!"

"I hear you, Dr. Z," Tony said.

"My children have lives I could never have dreamed of as a young man in Georgia. I don't want to lose it for them, but I cannot accept what is going on and do nothing. Not anymore. I now feel that I bought our freedom and my children's futures with the lives of other children. I did not agree to that. I would never have agreed to that." Zvi sat back in his chair and shook his head while looking down. "I fear that I have not been the best American I should be."

"You are today, Dr. Z," Tony said.

Zvi looked across the table at Tony and came to a decision. "I need my paper, but I can't go back to Russia to get it."

"Who can go?" Tony asked.

"You can."

Tony arrived home after 10:00 p.m. to find a very unhappy wife. "The boys in the black van were on the corner tonight."

"Jesus," Tony said quietly. He was physically and emotionally drained, as much from arguing with Hot-Rod Newman about who should drive home as from the meeting and its implications.

"How did it go with that guy?"

"It was interesting. And then some." Tony looked out the window. No van—for now. He sat on the bed. "Anne, I need to go to Russia."

"What the heck are you talking about?" Anne said, looking at him as though he were insane.

"I need to go to Moscow with Herb to dig this man's paper out from some research institute."

"What is going on here?" Anne said between clenched teeth. "We're being stalked by mystery vans, you're digging up all this stuff about the government—and since you've obviously forgotten, you *work* for the government! You're a cop. You have other cops calling all these people. Now you're going to Russia? Russia! What the hell are you doing?"

"Anne, not now. I'm wiped."

"No! Now! Right now! Why're you doing all this?"

"I have to. For Anthony. For Sophie too. Tony's volume level rose. "I have to do this, Anne. People have to know!"

"Anthony Colletti, lower your voice. I'm the mother of your children."

Tony sat down on the bed. "All right. I'm sorry. I never thought for a minute this would get so crazy."

"Well, it apparently has, hasn't it?"

"You remember when we first got Anthony's diagnosis? I felt so depressed. I felt trapped, and I couldn't stop worrying about Anthony, about his future. I was afraid for Anthony, and I was afraid of autism. For the first time in my life, I was frozen by fear. Then I saw you fight back. You got me moving. You got us all moving. Look at him now. He's talking more every day, and he's happy. He's such a happy kid. He was a ghost and you brought him back to life. Maybe not the life we wanted, but he's so much better than he was."

"And this has what to do with going to Russia?" Anne said quietly.

"This guy's paper is in the archives of some research institute in Moscow, we hope." Tony began to whisper. "He can't go to Russia because he fled from there years ago. He was a researcher, and the Russians realized that they were having problems with the old DPT. So they did a study. Only the vaccinated children had autism."

"That's the kind of study our country won't do."

"Yeah, well, the Russians did it, and then we Americans hid it. He has a contact there, some old Russian doctor, who's agreed to help."

Anne sat next to Tony on the bed. She put her hand on his knee. "What if you do all this and nothing changes?"

"That could happen—I know that. And if we do get the press to look at this, we're going to be attacked. It's a war, after all."

"Yeah, the autism war. They're going to attack all of you. Look at what they're doing to Dr. Ramsey." Anne said. "If they could, they would hang him."

"I know, but this has to be done. Anne, I want Anthony respected. There's a respect that people will give him that they will give all these kids and families, but only when they understand the truth about what really happened to them. When people know the truth, there can be justice. I want that for Anthony. It may be the only meaningful thing that I can ever give him."

CHAPTER 34

Nervously watching technicians setting up video cameras, Dr. Robert Bangston sat in the back of the special masters hearing room where the Omnibus Autism Proceedings had ended a few months before. The Secretary of Health and Human Services was holding a press conference to commemorate the twenty-fifth anniversary of the passage of the 1986 National Vaccine Act, which established the National Vaccine Injury Compensation Program. The event was to be led by Chief Special Master Carl Mantkewicz and CDC Director Jennifer Kesslinger who insisted that Bangston attend.

The press release described all the good that the 1986 act had done: the country now had an ample supply of vaccines, and the threat of pharmaceutical companies walking away from vaccines over litigation threats had evaporated. The few children who had been injured by vaccines were "compensated swiftly, fairly, and with compassion," just as Congress had promised in 1986. At least that was how the Secretary of Health and Human Services saw it.

Bangston thought that the press conference was a terrible idea and said so in a conversation with Kesslinger the day before. "There's still too much bitterness over the autism hearings, Jennifer. Issue a press release and call it a day."

"We won those hearings, Robert, and we should thump our chests a little."

"Children weren't compensated, but that hardly means that anybody 'won' anything."

"What're you saying? We should apologize? Why do you feel we have to stay in the shadows?"

"The program works best away from the spotlight, Jennifer."

"The Secretary wants this. We're doing the press conference."

The press conference began with Kesslinger's telling the media, "We are at war with disease. And this war is unending. Vaccines are the cornerstone of American public health policy and today we commemorate the visionary law that has resulted in the end of virtually all vaccine-preventable diseases in the United States. This law—this program—has been so successful that most of the country has forgotten what diseases like polio look like. This program shows that science and modern medicine, when supported by good public health policy, can triumph over disease."

Mantkewicz then spoke about the role of the special masters within the compensation program. "Vaccine injuries are rare and complicated. Special masters have unique expertise and knowledge that we bring to these cases. Independence, compassion, and fairness are the cornerstones of our program and guide our decision making on these difficult, tragic cases."

Most of the assembled reporters, who had no idea what the National Vaccine Injury Compensation Program really did, asked a few questions about the number of cases and how much money was paid out in injury claims.

Then investigative journalist Clyde King emerged from the back of the room and directed a question to Chief Special Master Mantkewicz. "Do you plan to issue a ruling responding to the motion for transparency filed by attorney Wilson Garrison so that we can understand what occurred in the Whittaker case where the government conceded that vaccines caused the child's autism-like symptoms?"

Bangston buried his face in his hands. "Here we go," he thought to himself.

"Perhaps you're not aware," Mantkewicz said calmly, "that the Omnibus Autism Proceedings ended with rulings stating that vaccines do not cause autism."

"I am aware of that," King replied. "And it is difficult for me as a journalist to reconcile how the program compensated one child with autism yet issued such stinging decisions on the other cases."

"Vaccines do not cause autism," Kesslinger said sharply.

"Except when they do," King responded.

A woman stood up in the front row and cleared her throat. "Honorable Special Master, my name is Donna McCormick. I filed a petition eight years ago seeking compensation for my daughter's injuries. Elyse developed autism after a series of vaccines were administered just before age one. I am a college graduate, and my husband is a Marine. When my husband isn't deployed, he works keeping our nation's borders secure with the Immigration and Naturalization Service. We sacrifice every day for our country."

Kesslinger interrupted, "This is a press conference about the 1986 law and . . ."

"Please allow me to continue." McCormick went on. "My family, like thousands of others, filed our petitions here in good faith. The rulings that were issued by the special masters mocked us and painted us as irrational. We are not. We are just regular Americans who saw something happen to our children after immunizations, and sought justice from this program. We should not have been ridiculed and insulted. We should have been treated the way Congress intended, with fairness and compassion."

"I knew we shouldn't have done this," Bangston whispered to himself.

Kesslinger glared at Donna McCormick and turned to Mantkewicz who simply said, "Thank you."

The press conference ended.

Donna McCormick's courageous speech was not covered by the majority of the media that attended. However, one local Washington station did run her comments and Clyde King wrote an article about it on the *Era of Autism* blog.

Wilson Garrison watched the clip of his client's mother in his office. "Your child deserved better, Donna," he thought. Garrison emailed the link to the piece along with Clyde King's article to his friend Herman Tyler at the Georgia Southern Human Rights Clinic with a note:

> *Herm, please take note of this act of courage. I hope that it lifts your heart, my friend. Lord knows you deserve a boost to your spirits. I pray for you every day and I am with you in your loss.*

Professor Tyler showed the video to students who were inmates of the Georgia Department of Corrections. The class was in a program called Changing Lives Through Literature. Tyler enjoyed watching and listening to the men thinking about the books they were reading. The class was now on *Parting the Waters: Martin Luther King and the Civil Rights Movement 1954–63* by Taylor Branch.

"Gentlemen, I ask you to consider," Tyler said, "whether this woman is part of a legitimate movement seeking justice and challenging the government in a manner similar to Reverend King."

"I need to know more," said a student named Daniel. "I can't evaluate her statement based on this one story. I would need to learn more about her claims. More about the vaccines and how the government is doing all this."

"My mother says that my little brother got that autism after vaccines," a student named Kienan said. "Somethin's going on with this, and society and the government are afraid to talk about it. Woman's speaking truth to authority. I respect her."

"My sister also has a child with autism," Tyler said. "She also feels that vaccines were involved."

"But aren't vaccines good?" said Daniel. "Isn't that why they're mandated?"

"What if they're good for some but damage a minority?" Kienan said. "I thought that we learned from our history that a minority should not bear the burdens of those in power."

"Well stated," Tyler nodded. "Taking the *Parting the Waters* to heart, I see."

"People need to talk about this openly," Kienan said. "Like this woman did, but people are afraid."

"Why is that?" Tyler asked. "Why are people afraid to talk about this?"

"It challenges what people are told to believe," Kienan replied. "I know that people view us as thugs 'n' crimnals. It's what they're told to believe in the messages they get. They don't think to look past what they're told and really listen."

"What does it take for people to listen?" Tyler asked.

Tyler went home that night to a quiet dinner with his mother. His mother had moved in to help after Tyler's wife died suddenly six weeks earlier. The coroner's report indicated an adverse reaction to an asthma medication. Tyler's mother was now the rock of his existence. "Mom, I couldn't have made it through . . ." he began over dessert.

"Herman," his mother interrupted, "this is what family's about. We stand together. I love you, son."

Later that night Tyler watched his son sleep from the doorway of his room. He considered the controversy around vaccines and autism, his nephew who had the condition, and what his sister had told him about autism and vaccines. Then he thought about what Donna McCormick had said to the special masters and about what had happened in the Omnibus Autism Proceedings. Martin Luther King's words pulsed through his heart. *"Injustice anywhere is a threat to justice everywhere."* Even to his son sleeping so peacefully. "What does it take for people to listen?" he asked himself.

CHAPTER 35

Dr. Bryce Ramsey finished a rousing speech on the need for independent vaccine research at the Health Liberty Conference at San Antonio's Vista Madre Hotel. As he and his wife left the hotel into a rainstorm, they were swarmed by television reporters and cameramen. "How did you falsify the children's medical records?" one reporter yelled.

"You're accused of perpetrating fraud in the 1998 study. Your response?" shouted another.

"I have never falsified anything in my life. I've no idea what you're talking about," Ramsey said. "I've done nothing wrong."

"Lance Reed just released another article claiming that you altered medical records to benefit financially from causing a vaccine scare in England" yelled yet another reporter.

"Nonsense. Sheer nonsense," Ramsey said as he and his wife were pushed and shoved as they tried to get into their cab.

Lance Reed's latest dispatch was well received by the mainstream American media, who immediately pounded away at Ramsey in story after story on television, the Internet, and newspapers. In response, Ramsey appeared on the *Alex Cummings Show* on SNN the next day but was hardly given an opportunity to respond to the host's barrage of questions. At one point, in near total exasperation, he told Cummings and the viewers, "I couldn't have altered results because I wasn't the one who handled that part of the study. There were twelve researchers on this project. I would have had to . . ."

Cummings cut him off and ended the interview with, "Your fraud cost the lives of children. I'm amazed that one man could do so much damage to the vaccine program, to so many children."

The media attacks were merciless and went on for days. A variation of the phrase "Ramsey/vaccines/autism/fraud" was repeated over and over again in every form of media. Ramsey simply retreated from public view because he had no chance of receiving a fair hearing.

E. Gordon Calthorpe enjoyed the hostile Ramsey media coverage on his office's wide screen television while sipping brandy and smoking cigarettes. "This is fabulous, Donna," he told his assistant. "So good of you to pull this together for me. I could watch this for hours."

"Thank you, sir."

Phillip Snyder called in. "You've outdone yourself—Ramsey's getting hammered everywhere."

"Timed perfectly for your Supreme Court's consideration of the *Cornachio* case."

"Supreme Court justices watch television too," Snyder chuckled. "They've got to be noticing this."

"Part of the plan, my friend. This is what we do here at Rollins."

Willoughby was working on files when the other line rang. It was Lance Reed.

"Shouldn't I have received payment by now, dearie?" said Reed coldly.

"I sent it yesterday. You'll get it later today or tomorrow at the latest."

After Reed hung up, Willoughby walked by Calthorpe's office and heard him laugh. She looked in to see Calthorpe enveloped in smoke and watching the portion of the video where Ramsey and his wife tried to get into the cab in the pouring rain while the television crews and reporters blocked their way. One of the cameramen inadvertently hit Mrs. Ramsey with a camera, shoving her to the wet pavement. Ramsey helped his wife up and into the cab.

Calthorpe poured himself more brandy and laughed.

Sensei Akinori Saito sat erect in Dr. Kenji Atsuko's office. As Dr. Atsuko, an older man with gray hair, entered holding a folder, Saito rose. "Please sit, Akinori," the doctor said. He took off his glasses and rubbed his eyes. "I do not have good news, my friend. I have seen this in others exposed at Minamata. I cannot stop this cancer. I can give you medications for pain, but that is all. I am sorry."

"It is what I suspected. The past still reaches out for us," Saito said. "How long do I have?"

"A few months. Perhaps a bit more. I wish this was not so, my friend."

"We accept life on its own terms. I thank you for your honesty, your service, and your friendship."

"I am honored."

The two men rose and bowed to each other. "Sensei, forgive me for asking, but do you have plans for the dojo's future? The art is so important."

"I do, my friend. I have a few more teachings to impart. Thank you."

CHAPTER 36

Tony and Forceski in an unmarked car followed John "Slag" Fusco on his motorcycle around northern Castleton County on a mild September evening. They switched off with Eddie Mendoza and his probation officers who continued the surveillance so Tony and Forceski could get a bite to eat at the Route 9 Diner. Mendoza called Forceski on his cell phone. "What's around Riverview Park in Winston? Fusco just parked his motorcycle and walked into the woods."

"Fusco parked in Riverview Park." Forceski repeated to Tony while chomping on French fries. "Where'd he go after that, Eddie?"

"I don't know, Detective. It's 9:30 p.m., and the freakin' woods are dark."

"Good point." Forceski turned to Tony. "He just walked off into the woods. What do ya think?"

"The guy could walk to anywhere in the town through the woods. We should stop him after he goes back to his chopper. You're not supposed to be in a town park after nightfall."

"Stop 'im on a town ordinance? That's kind of thin."

"It gets fat if we find child porn on him."

Tony and Forceski picked up from Mendoza's team at 10:30 p.m., then parked just past the park boundary. They waited all night for Fusco to return, but he never did.

Mendoza knocked on their car window at 6:45 a.m. "Hey guys. Coffee service from the Castleton County Probation Department."

"Freakin' Slag," Forceski said, bleary-eyed. "He knows we're watchin' him."

"Yeah," Tony said. "But whatever he's doing, he's doing right here in Winston."

Tony picked up Bobby Randazzo at headquarters the following evening and drove him to the dojo to begin his jujitsu training.

"So, is the sensei like some mystical guy?" Randazzo asked.

"Are you already trying to piss me off?"

"I'm just wondering what to expect."

"Do what I do and what you see the other students do. When we walk into the training hall, I'll bow—you bow. It's dojo etiquette. Just stand at attention as I give Sensei Saito your letter of introduction."

"What's in the letter?"

"The letter says 'Mystical Sensei Saito, I respectfully request that you accept this worthless dog into your dojo.' Actually, I talk about your interest in training and that you're a person of good character."

"You say that about me?"

"God forgive but, yes, I do. When Sensei greets you, bow again. He'll give you a uniform. You take your shoes off, get changed, and come out onto the mats. You go to the end of the line and do the exercises that everybody else does. A senior student will teach you how to fall correctly."

"I have to fall correctly?"

"It's critical. You'll see why when tai saibaki starts."

"What's that?"

"It means body movement. It's a set of ten techniques that form the basis of all the learning that follows. You will hear Sensei call out some numbers in Japanese. Just focus on falling correctly."

The two men bowed upon entering the dojo. Tony then bowed before Sensei Saito and handed him a letter of introduction. Saito bowed and accepted the letter. "Welcome, Officer Robert Randazzo."

Randazzo bowed. "Hello, sir."

Saito reached up onto a shelf and took a new judo ghi, the standard uniform, and handed it to the newcomer. "Men's changing area is back to the right. Please remove your shoes and socks." Turning to Tony, he said, "This is the brave but impetuous officer you told me about?"

"This is him, Sensei, in all his glory."

"He seems respectful. Humility, discipline, and routine will help him enormously. Meditation at the end of class will be interesting for him." Saito smiled. "I sense that he has a good heart."

"He does, Sensei."

A few minutes later, Randazzo stood at attention on the mats in his new ghi with a white belt. He went to the end of the line and, as instructed, followed along with the calisthenics. Tony then showed Randazzo the correct falling technique. "Slap the mat with an open hand just before you impact. It disperses the energy into the ground and away from your body." Randazzo tried but couldn't time it correctly. "Like this," Tony said. Randazzo's jaw dropped as he watched Tony throw himself in the air and land on his side, slapping out perfectly.

"Wow! I'd be in physical therapy for six months."

"Train here and it's the bad guy going to PT. Keep falling and slapping."

A few minutes later, Saito said "Mr. Randazzo, this is Miss Susan Miller. She will assist you. It is time to empty your cup."

After bowing to each other, Randazzo flashed his signature smile. "She's pretty, in an intellectual sort of way," he thought. Miller smiled back.

"Teach him the numbers," Saito said.

"Usah, Sensei," Miller began politely. Saito's voice pierced the room. "Eichi!"

Randazzo was tossed in the air, upside down, feet flailing before he slammed into the mat. "Ahhh!" he yelped. Miller helped him to his feet. "Focus on slapping out," Miller whispered.

"I'm focused on how a ninety pound woman just kicked my . . ."

"Ni!" Randazzo flew through the air from a painful wrist grab and slammed into the mat on his side, slapping out correctly.

"That was pretty good," she said smiling.

"San!" This time he was propelled backward and landed hard on his rear. "Holy crap!" he said, staggering to his feet. "I'll have to work on that one."

Sensei walked past Tony and smiled. "He is learning his numbers well."

Tony nodded, then paused. Sensei's eyes seemed uncharacteristically yellow. A few minutes later Tony worked on wrist locks with Susan away from the other students. "Susan," he whispered, "Sensei doesn't look well to me. Something's wrong."

"You noticed his eyes too? I'll ask my parents. They're doctors."

The class ended with meditation. Saito turned to Randazzo. "Officer Randazzo, we welcome you to our dojo and two thousand years of tradition." Everybody applauded. "Have you any questions before we end the session?"

"Um, what does emptying your cup mean?"

"It means to let go of negative thoughts, feelings, and preconceptions. You empty them out so that something new and positive can come into your life."

Tony and Forceski were back in the parking lot in front of Fusco's apartment. A chilly mist hung in the air, signaling the end of summer.

"This is freakin' tedious, bro." Tony yawned.

"I know. We can't sit on this monster, twenty-four/seven. We need a lucky break or we could do this for months."

"It's not like the budget for overtime is endless. The chief wants this guy as bad as we do but he's gotta deal with the bean counters."

Susan Miller's number appeared on Tony's cell phone.

"Hey, Susan."

"Tony, I spoke to my parents about the way Sensei looks. They said his liver must not be working properly. So I spoke to Sensei."

"What did he say?"

"He thanked me and said I shouldn't be concerned."

"He doesn't look well. I'm worried. He has to see a doctor, even if I have to take him myself."

Miller sighed. "He's seen a doctor."

"And?"

"You know the way Sensei talks. He repeated that I shouldn't worry. And I'm to keep working with you on the project. You told him about it?"

"How else would he have known?"

"He said that we honor him with our work."

Fusco's apartment house blurred through the windshield as the mist turned into a cold, hard rain.

CHAPTER 37

October brought a blustery autumnal chill as Tony, Laura, Maria, and Newman met for lunch in Laura's office to review progress on the project. Tony placed a box containing the case folders of all the compensated cases of autism in the middle of the conference table. Laura called it Pandora's Box.

It was the same day that the Supreme Court was hearing oral arguments on the *Cornachio* case. Newman's computer had the Supreme Court website open so the group could hear the case being argued as they worked.

"What do you guys think the Court will do?" Tony asked.

"They're going to back the government's preemption argument," Newman nibbled on a tuna sandwich.

"That's not what Congress intended," Maria said. "The law clearly states that a victim can seek civil redress if they're unhappy with the verdict in Vaccine Injury Compensation Program."

"I fear Herb's right," Laura added. "Many lawyers and legislators now support the VICP as a model for tort reform."

"Does 'tort reform' include concealing past compensated cases from petitioners in a proceeding designed to determine if vaccines cause autism?" Tony said. "I'm not allowed to keep evidence away from the other side in a criminal case."

"And there is discovery in regular civil proceedings too," Newman said. "We weren't allowed access to anything in the Omnibus Proceedings."

"Program's so bad that even a cop and a defense attorney agree it stinks. Imagine if those Supreme Court justices knew what we know," Tony said.

"If they did, they would never block someone's right to have their day in court. That's what is at stake in *Cornachio*." Herb pointed at Tony's box of folders. "Those cases demonstrate that access to civil redress is a critical American freedom. Everyone would know what the real history of vaccine injury was if this were a real court."

"We have to take our findings to Congress," Maria said. "Hopefully, they will act."

"How many cases are in that box?" Newman asked Tony.

"Over fifty."

"That's too many to not notice the pattern." Newman shook his head. "There should never have been an Omnibus Autism Proceedings. They knew the truth all along and ran these hearings to create a false history and conceal the real one. I don't know how these people can live with themselves."

"It's like Watergate," Laura said. "What did the government know and when did they know it?"

"Bangston knew," Tony said, "and he did nothing. He saw the cases roll in. He must've seen the pattern. And he still did nothing."

"And he chose not to notice the news about the autism epidemic?" Laura said. "There's blood on his hands."

"On that committee conference call, he did all the things that someone withholding information does," Tony said, dabbing a napkin on his chin. "He clearly avoided my question."

"Did you really think he'd answer it?" Herb smirked.

"No, but I wanted to see what he would do. He practically did the 'huminah, huminah' Jackie Gleason thing from *The Honeymooners*. The guy knows the truth, and he isn't talking."

"He's done nothing unusual, really." Herb said. "Given human nature, it would have been remarkable for him to have disclosed the truth. Tell you what, though, if he ever did tell the truth, the show is over."

"How so?" Maria asked. "Bangston's just a bureaucrat."

"If he conceded that vaccine injury has resulted in autism and that the government has known this all these years, the whole lie factory comes down. Could you imagine that scene? Sure, there would be denials, finger-pointing, experts blaming each other. Some would still deny it."

"And some would say that it was all still worth it," Laura sipped her tea. "'We saved millions from disease. Some got killed. Some got autism. It was necessary.' That's what they'd say."

"That could be the rationalization for the damage," Maria said. "But people wouldn't sit for that. The vaccine program would be over. No parent will accept that argument and still vaccinate their child."

"And then they'd blame us for disease outbreaks," Newman said soberly.

"This is why we need to get Dr. Z's paper. We need as much proof as possible. We can't allow our fellow citizens to live under a lie," Tony said. "When I was sworn in as a cop, I took an oath to protect the constitution, to protect people."

"Robert Bangston likely took that same oath," Newman said. "Even worse, he also took the Hippocratic oath."

"How did this happen?" Laura asked. "How can people allow this to happen?"

"Given what has happened in my life, I've asked God that same question," Maria said. "Many times good people get caught up in a situation and they lose their way. One lie leads to another lie. Suddenly there's nothing but lies."

"People can be trapped by lies," Tony said. "So much so, that they can no longer see what is real. I've seen that happen to people. You think that's Bangston?"

"He's a conflicted man, Tony. I can tell that he feels burdened."

Everyone looked at Maria as though she were crazy.

"Burdened, my ass," Laura said.

"What makes you say that?" Tony said.

"When Elyse McCormick had a seizure during her hearing, he rendered medical assistance. He did a good job and was compassionate and respectful of Elyse and her family. He was at the proceedings a lot. He would just sit in the back, looking gloomy. That is the behavior of a conflicted human being."

It was almost 11:00 p.m. when Chief Lonnegan got off the phone with Delores Pooles of Lawrence, Massachusetts. Mrs. Pooles related how an MMR vaccine led to her son's seizures and autism in the early 1990s and how she and her attorney struggled to win compensation for him. The government conceded its case, but only after everyone showed up for a fact-finding hearing that was to be held in a conference room of a Ramada Inn. Mrs. Poole's voice dripped sarcasm as she described the scene. "They put a handwritten sign on the conference room door that said 'US Court of Claims.' Not exactly classy."

Lonnegan commiserated with the woman's struggles to get her son into the right kind of school program. "My daughter is going through the same battle with her district, Delores. Our lives are so similar. Trying to care for a special needs child is a humbling experience."

"We've been talkin' for two hours, Chief," she said, "a black woman from a tough town and a white police chief from a New York City suburb. Isn't this something?"

"Amen. I hope we can do as good a job for my granddaughter as you've done for your son."

Marge Riley spent three hours on a telephone call with Carla Cindrich of West Des Moines, Iowa. Cindrich, whose daughter was another case of autism caused by vaccine injury, had become a local disabilities advocate and started a not-for-profit organization to help similar families. "The government lawyers told us that my daughter's case was unique. They said no one else with autism had ever been compensated. Liars! I'm going to talk to Senator Smithson about this."

"You go right ahead, Carla. He should know what's really going on."

"Out here in Iowa, we expect government to be honest. Parker Smithson is already suspicious of these people, I can tell you that."

Raffy hung up the phone and pumped his fists in the air. "YES! YES!"

"What are you so happy about?" his wife asked.

"I just spoke to Jake Bumquist—himself!"

"And that means what exactly, you hairy lunatic?"

"He doesn't have autism anymore, or at least not so bad. Somehow he got better! The kid has a job, a girlfriend. A life! This kid has a life!"

"Fabulous. Now go rake the leaves. It's beginnin' to look like we abandoned this place."

Raffy gave his wife a big hug and kiss. "If this kid can get better, then Ronny can too." He put on his coat and dragged his ten-year-old son away from his video game and out into the yard. Within a few minutes, Ronny was jumping around in a pile of leaves like any other kid playing with his dad on a crisp autumn day.

Russell Sampson saw Senator Parker Smithson's number on his cell phone's display "Hey, Parker."

"Just got a call from my district constituent services people. Apparently some New York–based researchers are looking into Vaccine Court cases. They called one of my supporters and got her all riled up. Know 'bout these people?"

"No, but maybe I should."

"Yeah, amigo. Maybe you should. They're calling families who were quietly compensated for vaccine injuries in back rooms over at the Division of Vaccine Injury Compensation. Guess what they're finding?

"Tell me."

"Autism. *Lots* of autism. I told you this thing was dirty."

CHAPTER 38

"So, you've found government-compensated cases of vaccine-induced brain damage, and these kids also have autism?" said Clyde King, swirling wine in his glass.

"Yes," Maria said. She had invited investigative journalist Clyde King to dinner at the cozy Alchemy Restaurant in Park Slope, Brooklyn, because she knew of his interest in the vaccine-autism issue. The two had met on numerous occasions, and King admitted being smitten by Maria. "This has gone on for years, Clyde. We're now gathering as much supporting documentation as possible to strengthen the findings."

"How many cases?"

"Over fifty," she whispered so that the other patrons in the restaurant couldn't hear. "But we've only called about one hundred and ten people so far."

"What is that? Forty percent?"

"Something like that. We're finding more every week."

"This is outrageous," King said. "I've been assaulted for asking questions about vaccine safety, and this is what's really going on?"

"Keep in mind, there's not supposed to be any because there's no link between vaccines and autism."

"Then how come all of these vaccine-injured children have autism? Maria, why didn't the feds disclose this?"

"I think you know the answer to that, Clyde," she said, stirring her drink.

"So much for transparency in government," he said shaking his head. "I've been doing investigative journalism for twenty years, and it's always the same. Powerful people do something wrong and innocent people pay the price. Then the cover-ups start. How much suffering would've been prevented if people had just told the truth?"

"They protected their policies, not children." Maria's brown eyes glistened in the candlelight. "There wouldn't have been an autism epidemic were it not for this law and the establishment of the Vaccine Court."

"So, this afternoon, a mother will take her newborn to a well-baby visit," King said bitterly, "and she'll be placing her child in harm's way because somebody didn't tell the truth. Cause the reality is kept behind closed doors. I've been called a fear monger and 'anti-vaccine' by people like Phillip Snyder. I've been accused of threatening the vaccine program for pointing out that injecting mercury into infants is unsafe. But it's this kind of behavior that really threatens public confidence in vaccines."

"We need you to write about this."

"Oh, don't you worry. It's a bombshell."

"Honestly, we expect you to," she said, "but we're concerned that they're going to try to shut us down. I think my phone is tapped and Tony, the policeman I told you about, believes that he's under surveillance in his home."

"They're spying on a cop? How did they find out that you were doing this?"

"We think they've known for a while," Maria said. "We sent a Freedom of Information request. They denied it. We're just citizens doing social research. They were going to find out anyway."

"What do you need me to do?"

"I'm going to send you some materials so that you have them if we're shut down. Please promise me that you'll only open the packages if you're contacted by a police chief."

"A police chief?"

"Yes. I'll explain another time. But keep in mind that we can't release anything until we've nailed everything down."

"I'm thinking that you might want to talk to Sara Donovan about this."

"Can you arrange that?

King nodded. "Don't worry, I'll do what you need me to do. But you knew that, didn't you?"

"I'm a good judge of people."

"I think that your son is communicating that he doesn't like this psychiatrist," Anne Colletti said to Veronica Fournier over the phone. "That's why he's acting out. Didn't he see this shrink before the backyard incident last summer?" Anne was preparing a dinner and watching SNN while talking to her friend.

"I guess you're right, but it's so hard to get therapists," Veronica said.

"Can you come to the parents meeting Thursday night? Dr. Tapper is giving a lecture. Then we just talk. You might hear something that helps."

"It's hard to get a baby sitter on short notice."

"Maybe you can drop Evan off here and Tony can watch him. You've got to get out and connect to everybody."

"Isn't that kinda' awkward, Anne? I mean, Evan got Tony shot."

"He's over it. He's taking the guy who shot him to martial arts classes. If he can do that, he can watch Evan and give you a break. "Hang on a minute, Ronnie." Anne turned up the TV volume because SNN was showing a press conference with Senator Russell Sampson and Senator Parker Smithson. Sampson's wife and family were at his side.

New York's Junior Senator Russell Sampson is supporting Democrat Senator Smithson's autism health insurance bill for federal employees. Even with the political polarization in Washington, there is bipartisan support for this autism bill.

Anne's eyes widened. Senator Sampson's youngest child was flapping his hands. She knew the behavior because little Anthony did the same thing. A group of people around Mrs. Sampson and the boy looked as though they were trying to contain the child. Could it be? Did the senator's child have autism?

"Good to meet you, Sara." Tony said. "And thanks for agreeing to meet me."

"I have some free time these days," Sara Donovan said. "I'm sort of on a temporary leave of absence."

"Taking a break for good reasons?" Tony asked as he sat down on the futon.

"The network is reorganizing some things, and it gave me an opportunity to take a bit of time off." Donovan had no intention of telling Tony why she really was on leave. "Cha An is lovely."

"Like I said over the phone, it's a traditional Japanese tea house, simple and light. You forget you're in Manhattan."

"So, Clyde King tells me that you have something interesting."

"You could say that," Tony said. "Some tea? I recommend the Oolong."

"Just so long as it's not coffee. I haven't been too good around coffee lately."

Tony caught the waiter's eye. "Two Oolong, thank you." The waiter bowed and slid the fusuma door closed. "My instructor took me here once. He taught me all about Japanese tea."

"What kind of instructor teaches a man about tea?"

"A tenth degree black belt."

"You better have listened well. I've studied Tae Kwan Do. You?"

"Jujitsu. Guess we have some common interests."

"You didn't invite me here to talk tea, did you?"

"You've covered the autism-vaccine issue." Tony began.

"What does a policeman have to do with vaccines and autism?" she interrupted.

"I've been working with a group of people, lawyers and law enforcement types, looking at the Vaccine Court. We have evidence that the Vaccine Injury Compensation Program has been compensating children for brain damage and . . ."

"They call that encephalopathy. I've studied the Vaccine Court a bit."

"Well, you may want to study it some more. A lot of the kids who've been compensated for encephalopathy also have autism."

"The court ruled there was no connection."

"We've found fifty-five cases of vaccine-induced encephalopathy where the child also has autism. Another one came in today."

"This is unbelievable. How could they issue those rulings from the autism hearings?"

"We ask ourselves that question every day." The waiter entered, served and presented the tea. "*Arigatou gozaimasu.*" The waiter bowed and left, again sliding the fusuma closed.

"You do realize that when the other side figures out what you're doing, they're going to come down on you."

"They've already started," Tony said. "A van has been parked on my corner on many a night. I think they're monitoring my calls. Maybe even conversations in my home."

"Crazy as that sounds, I believe you. These people play dirty. I've seen them go after people professionally."

"You mean like Dr. Ramsey?"

"More than just him," Donovan said with bitterness. She debated whether she should tell Tony about what happened to Dr. Washington, but decided not to. "I have to tell you, Mr. Colletti, that I don't know if I will be allowed to cover this. My network is being steered away from these stories."

"We really need you to cover this."

"But I may not be able to." Donovan kept thinking about the vaccine-injured children in Memphis. "Mr. Colletti . . ."

"Please call me Tony."

"Tony, do you have an affected child?"

"My son was vaccine-injured."

"They'll use that against you. They'll say that you're 'an angry parent' and that you can't be objective. They'll have expert doctors in white coats counter everything that you're saying."

"What does any of that have to do with the government covering up these vaccine injuries?"

"They'll stop at nothing to marginalize you."

"I know. But I still have to try to get the truth out."

"They'll say that you're just a cop."

"I am just a cop."

"I'm sorry," Donovan sipped her tea. "I believe you, and I want to find a way to cover this. But the other side is bottling up the few journalists willing to cover autism and vaccines. I have to be honest with you. I don't have control over what ultimately gets covered."

"Sara, I was hoping that if they shut us down somehow that you could help tell this story. There are other aspects that are also important. I can't tell you about them right now but you wouldn't believe how far back all of this goes."

"I would love to cover this, but I may not be able to."

Tony sensed that she was concealing something painful. "You're in a tough place."

"Frankly, if I push it too much, I can end up blackballed."

"It's an important story."

"Of course it is."

"Then just be prepared to act when you get an opportunity."

"You've really been taught by a tenth degree." She smiled. "The tea is good. And you are not just a cop."

CHAPTER 39

"County PD's license reader has Slag coming into Winston on Route 9 twice a week," Forceski said between gulps of coffee as he stood over Tony's desk.

"The license reader technology is amazing. Someday they won't need cops anymore. This verifies what we learned from following him around—he's doing his thing here," Tony said.

"Kids we know may be the victims," Forceski said. "I gotta bad feeling about this, my friend."

"Me too. I'm having trouble maintaining objectivity. The chief came by yesterday and talked to me about that. Even though he's dealing with all the stress around his granddaughter and autism, he keeps everything around here in focus."

"I got pulled in too," Forceski said. "Say what you will, the guy is a professional. He bleeds blue."

"Ever think about what this place will be like when he retires?"

"I can't. Pain in the ass though he is, I'd run through a wall for him. On a lighter note, hear what's goin' on south of the border?"

"We have 'nough trouble keeping Winston safe."

"Google 'Mexican Flu Terror' and watch the coverage."

It only took a moment for Tony to find the story on the SNN website.

World Health officials are descending upon the Mexican village of Guadalupe Y Calvo, dealing an outbreak of a new type of virulent influenza virus, which has reportedly killed twelve people in and around the small town.

The coverage featured dramatic images of doctors wearing masks tending to sick people in a makeshift field hospital.

The World Health Organization, along with the US and Mexican Centers for Disease Control, have declared the outbreak 'a serious event' and have quarantinexd the town.

An SNN journalist was shown being stopped on a road into the town by Mexican soldiers in biohazard suits.

"You know what they're gonna do?" Forceski said. "They're gonna mandate another vaccine."

"Yeah, but if this thing is really bad, maybe that's reasonable. I mean what're the choices if this thing kills you?"

That afternoon, an Arizona congressman demanded that the US-Mexico border be sealed off. Another representative called for the immediate development of a Mexican flu vaccine.

Congress called Dr. Jennifer Kesslinger, director of the Centers for Disease Control to testify before the Congressional Health Committee the next day. "We may not be able to develop a vaccine in sufficient time to adequately protect the American public," she said. "However, we will move heaven and earth if we have to."

"What can this House do to speed this along?" asked the Health Committee chairman.

"As always, Congressman, it comes down to resources. We have protocols in place to facilitate an expeditious development and production process. Vaccine development comes down to money."

"Director, we have no intention of seeing these images from Mexico on our side of the border."

"This is what the CDC is built for, sir."

Kesslinger walked out of Congress with billions of dollars to parcel out to vaccine manufacturers.

Dr. Randall Cooke interviewed Dr. Phillip Snyder that night in the SNN Studio. "Dr. Snyder, how would you describe the situation inside Mexico?"

"Critical, Randall. There are a lot of sick people. It's heartbreaking."

"How concerned should Americans be?'

"Extremely. This outbreak shows the importance of the CDC's Surveillance Program. This is where the public health community rises to the occasion."

"Is it possible to contain the outbreak?"

"Perhaps, but it's not likely. We really are part of a global community. Disease can spread before governments realize that there is an outbreak. That's why development of a vaccine is now the highest priority."

The next day, a representative of the World Health Organization announced that the Mexican flu virus had been identified as a subtype that was easy to replicate in a laboratory setting. Kesslinger followed quickly with an announcement that Binghampton Pharmaceuticals had been awarded the contract for vaccine development. Production for testing trials would start immediately. Charles Livingston, the CEO of Binghampton, added that he was personally overseeing the work on the Mexican flu vaccine. The FDA declared that the testing trials would be accelerated under emergency protocols designed to respond to pandemics.

While there were reports of Mexican hospitals dealing with victims, no one noticed that the deaths stopped after the first week. Images of scientists in biocontainment suits manipulating petri dishes in laboratories now filled the media.

Once again, a vaccine would save the day. Or so everybody thought.

CHAPTER 40

The black van pulled into its usual location under the pine tree just past the corner of Willow Lane where the Collettis lived. The men inside activated their equipment.

Anne Colletti peeked through her window blinds into the November darkness as the van's headlights turned off. She turned to her husband and nodded. Tony texted Herb Newman—"Case V-163-97 confirmed."

Herb Newman read the words, then turned to Laura Melendez. "Call the desk sergeant, counselor."

Chavez answered Laura's call. "Winston PD."

"My daughter says that she was approached by some men in a dark van with New Jersey plates. They tried to lure my daughter into their van."

"Ma'am, where did the incident occur?"

"Around the corner from the Hudson Elementary School. My daughter's very frightened by these perverts."

"Your name please?"

"I don't want to get involved." She ended the call and handed the phone to Newman.

"Phone worked well for a disposable."

"Sort of a shame to toss it," Newman said.

"You can let go of this one piece of technology, Herb."

"It will be in the garbage, somewhere in New York City later tonight."

Chavez checked the number on the 911 software. It came back "unassigned," meaning it had no identifiable owner. He noted the time of the incident in the computer log and put out the alert. "Suspicious males in a dark van with Jersey plates observed in Hudson School area approaching young children. Report is that they tried to lure children into the van."

Police Officer Robert Randazzo was on patrol in that sector and responded, "Desk, this is car six in sector four. Will investigate."

"Proceed, car six."

Randazzo drove around the quiet Hudson Elementary School then proceeded to Colletti's street as he had planned to. There in the misty rain was the dark van with Jersey plates. "Desk, this is six on entrance to Willow Lane at corner of Lowell. Have located a blue van, Jersey plates, O-M-D-7-6-7. Please run the DALL."

"Running that check in the state computer and sending backup units to assist."

The men in the van were stunned to see police lights suddenly pulsating through the cabin of the vehicle. "Occupants of the van," Randazzo said over the loudspeaker, "place your hands outside of the windows of the vehicle."

"Fred," the thinner of the two said, "we had better do what this jerk says."

"Vincent," the man named Fred replied, "this boy's gonna crap when he hears we're retired federal agents. Lemme go talk to this turkey." He exited the driver's side and turned to find himself face-to-face with Randazzo.

"I didn't say to leave the vehicle!" Randazzo yelled.

"Huh? Hey, listen boy, we're . . ." But before Fred could say anything else, Randazzo grabbed his hand. A perfectly executed kote-gaishi wrist lock sent him crashing into wet leaves on the pavement. "Ahh!! Broke my wrist, you maniac!"

Randazzo cuffed the man. "You're under arrest."

The other man emerged from the passenger side door "Hey!" What the heck do you think you're doing?"

Randazzo, kneeling over his detainee, drew his newly issued Tazer and pointed it at the man. "Stop! Police!"

The man didn't listen and took two steps toward Randazzo. "We are police, you idiot."

Randazzo shot the Tazer, and the man fell to the ground screaming.

The backup car screeched to a halt next to the van. Officer Tommy "Pooch" Puccinelli put his cuffs on the man Randazzo Tazed and then recoiled in disgust. The man had urinated in his pants.

Forceski and the chief showed up about ten minutes later. "Greetings from Winston-on-Hudson, New York, fellas," Lonnegan said. "I'm told you're a couple of retired feds supplementing retirement income with some PI work?"

"You have an overreactive, crazy police officer here, Chief!" yelled the man named Fred.

"Two months ago, he'd a shot you right between the eyes. You should be thankful he's mellowing. Whadya think about the new Tazer technology, Vincent?"

"Tell you what I think," Vincent said. "You small-town jerks can kiss my fat, hairy . . ."

"Watch your tone with me, punk," Lonnegan pushed the back end of a flashlight against the man's chest. "We have a complaint about men in a dark van with Jersey plates trying to pull innocent children into their van. Came in 'bout twenty minutes ago."

"Aw, that's a pile of horse shit, Chief!" Fred complained. "You know we ain't . . ."

"Deviants?" Lonnegan scratched his chin while walking around the men and scanning them with his flashlight. "Why don't you fine, former law enforcement officers tell me who you're doing PI work for?" The men put their heads down. "Not tawkin' tonight, fellas? How do we know you aren't a couple of perverts?"

"We ain't no pedophiles!" Fred said.

"We signed agreements not to disclose who hired us," Vincent added.

Forceski aimed his flashlight into Fred's eyes. "Don't know who they are, anyway," Fred said turning his face away from the light.

"Let me get this straight. You don't know who hired you?" Forceski said through his teeth.

"But you do know who you're surveilling," Lonnegan said.

"You're spying on one of us," Forceski said.

"Detective," Randazzo said. "Pooch and I found a lotta expensive high-end technical equipment in this van. They could be using it for anything, sir."

"Anything?" Forceski said. "Even for recording and photographing children?"

"Saints preserve us," Lonnegan drawled. "Aren't you and Detective Colletti—Detective Anthony Colletti—investigating a case like that?"

"In fact, we are, sir." Forceski said.

"This is bullshit!" The man named Fred exploded. "You ain't got nuthin'!"

"Still think we're small-town jerks?" Lonnegan said. "There's a lot of equipment in that van. We have a complaint that we're investigating, and you guys are suspects."

"You both fit the description of perverts who rolled up on a little girl," Forceski said. "We know what you guys are doin'. You were once one of us. Now you're just disgusting."

"And so gentlemen, we'll be taking your equipment as potential evidence until we have a clearer picture of what really happened here tonight in my sleepy little town," Lonnegan said. "You guys are gonna see the inside of headquarters, and we're going to take your names and addresses and all the other happy horseshit that we do at booking. And then, we'll see if we have enough to make a case. Maybe we do. Maybe we don't. Like apples, Vinny?" The man just shook his head bitterly. "How do you like them apples?"

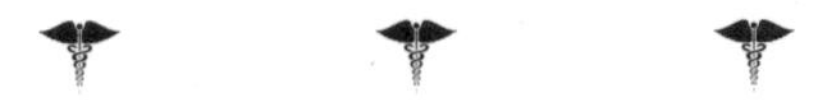

The two men, Fred Hughes of Little Rock, Arkansas, and Vincent McAndrew of Chevy Chase, Maryland, were released later that night.

Although it was determined that they were not pedophiles, they never forgot the hospitality of the Winston PD.

It turned out that the equipment was indeed top-shelf audio surveillance equipment. The men in the van could listen in on every conversation that was going on in Tony Colletti's house, which meant their employers knew an awful lot. They would have been able to know who was participating in the project and who had been phoned. That was bad news.

It was also possible that the other side knew about the plans to get the DPT paper. That was something else that Tony and Herb Newman would have to worry about, since they had booked their flights to Moscow for January.

CHAPTER 41

"Russia is now run by gangsters, Officer Tony," Zvi said. Tony, Zvi, and Newman were again meeting in the Pizza Time section of the Maryland House. "The pharmaceutical companies own the old health ministries and strictly control access to everything. To get my paper out of Moscow and return alive to America, you have to comfortably appear to be men making a business trip. You look too much like a New York cop."

"I can blend in."

"I'm not so sure. You are going to Russia. If you say something wrong, you will die, my friend."

"Take it easy," Tony said. "Let me try some Russian again. 'I request directions to the metro.'"

Zvi guffawed. "You sound like a Klingon. You have no gift for the language. I think that you should stand there and look like a tough guy while Herb Newman does the talking."

"Gotta speak some Russian. Just can't stand there holding my . . ."

"I am quite sure that you cannot," Zvi said firmly. Turning to Newman, "You make the request for the metro."

"Okay," Newman said, clearing his throat. "I request directions to the metro."

"There it is!" Zvi said. "Nearly perfect pronunciation and accent. This man talks. Officer Tony, you stand there and look like tough guy. Russians expect important men to have scary-looking companions with them."

"Really?" Tony asked hopefully.

"Actually, I made that up. I am still worried that you're going to Russia and die."

Maria was working on the first draft of the paper when Tony called. "Hey, kid. The boss has what he needs." That was shorthand for Lonnegan had the media contacts and extra copies of the project materials. If pharma or the government somehow shut down the project, the information would still get to Clyde King, Sara Donovan, and a few others. "So far no blowback from the treatment that the boys in the black van got."

"Good. These steps are still necessary to protect our work. Speaking of that, I'm working on a draft of the paper. Three journals have agreed to accept the paper for peer review."

"That sounds positive, I guess."

"It is. We're looking at publication in the spring.

"Good. Now there's no turning back."

Supervising Probation Officer Eddie Mendoza filed a Violation of Probation and asked for an arrest warrant for Slag Fusco for refusing to take a polygraph exam. Mendoza knew that Fusco would make bail, so he and his officers arrested him late on a Friday afternoon so he would spend the weekend in jail.

"I'm not strapping your lie detector crap on," Fusco said as he sat handcuffed at the Castleton County Probation Department.

"If we can't polygraph you, then we can't work with you in the treatment program," Mendoza replied.

"I don't need your treatment."

"Then we're gonna have issues, Mr. Fusco. And you're gonna have to get used to bracelets."

Senator Russell Sampson and his wife Diana went out for a quiet dinner at their favorite restaurant in Georgetown. There had been a lot of quiet dinners lately because Diana was angry at Russell for supporting the construction of Binghamptom Pharmaceutical's new vaccine factory in Troy, New York.

"Diana, I had to back Lew Miller on the vaccine plant. You know upstate needs the jobs."

"Tell them to make aspirin."

"Not with the damned Mexican flu raging. Look, Jordan is doing better. We should be thankful for that."

Diana could hardly look at her husband. "Only because we have money. Our son can improve because we can take him to the best doctors, the best therapists, and get him the best treatments. What about the people who can't? What about the families who saw this happen to their child and don't know how to get past doctors who deny what's happening?

"What do I do? Call a press conference? Do that, and I'm not a senator for too much longer. Then I can't do anything about this or anything else."

Diana's eyes teared. "Everyone in your office knows about Jordan, Russell. I can tell."

"I know. And Emily said that we needed to have a plan politically for the 'autism thing' because someday soon it was going to come out."

"What did you tell her?"

"I told her we'll say that Senator Sampson's son has autism. And that the senator loves him."

Diana reached out and held her husband's hand.

As the year-end holidays approached, media coverage of the Mexican flu crisis went into overdrive. Cases were reported in the southwestern United States, Central America, and as far away as Japan. The World Health Organization declared that the outbreak had become a pandemic, which caught the attention of Detective Glen Forceski.

"Tony, know what I just noticed about the WHO?"

"I can't notice what you noticed about the WHO before you've told me what you've noticed. Who or what is the WHO?"

"The World Health Organization. They used to define a 'pandemic' as a lot of cases of a fatal disease in several countries."

"Sounds reasonable," Tony looked up from entering case notes in a folder.

"Now the WHO defines 'pandemic' to mean a lot of cases of disease in several countries. Their definition no longer requires significant fatalities in several countries."

"When I hear the word 'pandemic,' I think of piles of bodies and grim scenes. Isn't that what we're seeing in Mexico?"

"I haven't seen a death report in weeks. CDC says that the vaccine trials have begun."

"Where?"

"Who knows? I wonder who the guinea pigs are. Knowing what you know now, would you roll up your sleeve and be a test case?"

The researchers in their white lab coats carrying computer tablets walked through the Immigration Detention Center just south of Tucson. They were escorted by detention center staff to insure their safety. The dry heat of the Sonoran Desert, the cramped conditions, and an overtaxed air-conditioning system made the staff and illegal aliens miserable.

"A flu vaccine for my child?" said a woman in Spanish through the opening of her cell door. She was rocking her infant in her arms while trying to get some benefit from the fan blowing in the far corner of the cell.

"*Si*," the detention officer replied.

"We require her to fill out these forms," the researcher said.

The detention officer relayed the message in Spanish. "She says this is why she had her baby in the States. For the health care."

Within two hours the researchers had more than one hundred infants for the Mexican flu vaccine clinical trials.

The mothers were never told that the vaccine was experimental.

CHAPTER 42

Dr. Washington grinned "You poured hot coffee on Randall Cooke's crotch?"

"He had it coming," Sara Donovan replied. "I was furious. When you told me you lost your job, I snapped."

"Well, it wasn't your fault. Now that I know what all went on, I feel sorry for what you went through."

Sara Donovan returned to work after her leave of absence, to an office two floors away from Randall Cooke. SNN management wasn't happy with her, but Donovan was now a cult hero in the eyes of her co-workers and fellow journalists. While it was understood that she and Seth Millman would not be covering vaccines, SNN did not want the "Randall Cooke Coffee Affair" all over the Internet.

"I still have a job," Donovan said. "What you went through was completely unfair."

"Well, that's life. I'm lookin' to start my own practice. Be a pediatrician who doesn't push vaccines. Somethin' like that."

"Is there a market for those?"

"Hope so. If not, maybe my dad will take me back at his restaurant. My surgical skills might help with the pulled pork."

"You deserve better. You told the truth about what happened. Somehow, we have to come up with a way to cover vaccine safety around here."

Dr. Robert Bangston returned to his Washington office, having danced at his daughter's wedding in San Diego. She was a beautiful bride, and her husband was a strapping young pediatrician. Even his ex-wife had been nice to him. It was the best that he had felt in years.

As he went through the case files on his desk, he noticed that Special Master Gilmore ordered compensation for a child who suffered an "MMR Table Encephalopathy." Bangston read the order and called Department of Justice Attorney Terrence Stone. "Terry, why the hell did you let these comments on the Prisco case into the decision? You let Gilmore use the 'A' word in his compensation order."

"I assume you mean 'autism.'"

"How could you let this through?"

"Look, we don't have the staff to write every order. Petitioners' attorneys get paid too, you know."

"We just conceded that an MMR table injury encephalopathy 'included features of autism.' I leave for two weeks and this slips through? You know what would happen if the anti-vaccine people saw this posted on the website?"

"What's the date of the order?"

"November 29—three weeks ago."

"Then it's already up on the website."

Tony snuck a day off to go Christmas shopping for Anne and the kids. He stopped by headquarters to drop off some updated information packages for Lonnegan and check his email. When he took a look at the Court of Claims website for new vaccine decisions, he saw the Angelo Prisco case and reached for the phone. "Herb, What do you make of this?"

"The case met the program requirements for encephalopathy, and it's reasonable to compensate him."

"But he has autism. I thought they shut that door."

"They did, in a way. But reading this decision, I realize that they still have a problem. Sometimes a case of encephalopathy is going to get compensated when it has, let me read you Gilmore's wording here, "features of autism secondary to brain damage."

"Secondary autism?"

The next morning Clyde King wrote about the Prisco decision on the *Era of Autism* blog. The article was called "Secondary Autism." Dr. Phil Snyder read it and called Bangston. "What the hell are you people thinking about?"

"I took two weeks to go to my daughter's wedding. I wasn't here," Bangston said.

"I want this knucklehead Gilmore removed! We need people who toe the line."

"Phil, the decision is fair. I read the folder in detail. There are cases where this happens and we have to compensate the child."

"Bob, we have *Cornachio* in front of the Supreme Court. They're looking at your stinking Vaccine Court right now. We've spent a fortune to get to this point. Have you considered what this could do to us?"

"What am I supposed to do—stay in my office forever?

"You could stop them from putting this crap on the website."

"No, I can't. The clerk of claims makes those decisions. There are rules about what gets posted."

"Rules, regulations . . . this is why we need a panel of industry experts to decide this stuff."

"The reality is that we get cases like this."

"Do you realize what this autism situation has cost the industry?"

"Phil, I can't change reality."

"Well, then, I'm calling the man who can."

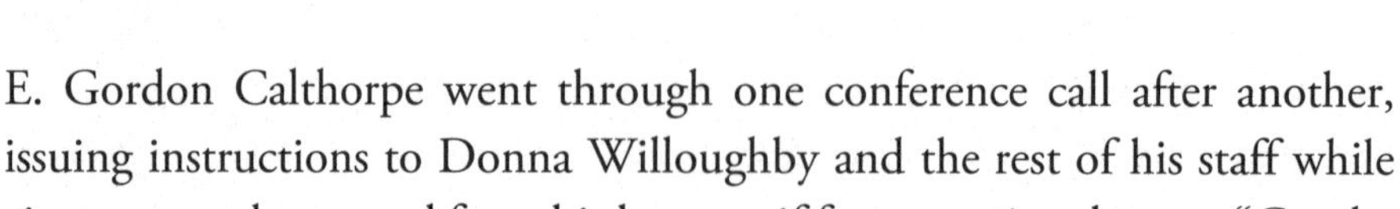

E. Gordon Calthorpe went through one conference call after another, issuing instructions to Donna Willoughby and the rest of his staff while cigarette smoke poured from his lungs as if from a raging dragon. "Get the stories out there. Push the press releases now. I want wall-to-wall coverage on this. It is not every day that the UK's leading medical journal publishes a piece like this."

"Lance Reed on line two, sir," Willoughby said.

"The twits at the journal want more supporting documentation," Reed said.

"We provided materials. What else do they require?"

"Something that shows more definitively that Ramsey created the vaccine scare. Something that connects him to the plot to make money off it."

"Why?"

"Peer-review standards or some such nonsense. You know these upper-class professional folk with their airs."

"Give me the number for Dr. Oliver at the *Journal*. I'll call him myself."

Two days after, the prestigious *United Kingdom Journal of Medicine* published an article by Lance Reed alleging that Dr. Bryce Ramsey started the now infamous "UK vaccine scare" to create a market for an alternative vaccine he intended to market. That such an esteemed journal published an article by a nonmedical professional was extraordinary, but that scarcely seemed to matter. Another anti-Ramsey media frenzy broke out and lasted for days.

Not one mainstream press outlet realized or cared to confirm that Dr. Ramsey had no alternative vaccine to sell. He had been part of a group of researchers looking into a product to help children process vaccines better and perhaps reduce certain side effects. However, the product never got close to development and virtually all of Dr. Ramsey's colleagues abandoned him years ago at the start of the controversy.

The Ramsey narrative knocked the Prisco case coverage off the radar screen. Once again, the federal government had compensated a child for a vaccine injury that included autism, and no one noticed.

"The policeman is an expert in martial arts. Trains regularly," Calthorpe told Nikolai Doshenko, an executive at Xerxes Pharmaceutical's Moscow office.

"Will he really use it or is he a typical, lazy American?"

"Killed a man in New York City years ago," Calthorpe replied into the speakerphone. "He can be dangerous."

"What of the lawyer?"

"All lawyers are dangerous, my friend. I want them followed throughout their stay in your country."

"I've got two men available who do this type of work, Mr. Calthorpe. They are, how do you say, uniquely talented."

"Then we should compensate them as such. Top talent requires top pay."

"That is the beauty of the new Russia. Industrious men get paid well."

"It is a hallmark of a civilized society, my friend. Please advise us in writing of what you require, and it will be taken care of. Good day."

Calthorpe regarded Russians as the white trash of Europe. "Next I'll have to debase myself further and deal with the Irish," he thought. He stared again at photographs of Anthony Colletti and Herbert Newman. Calthorpe was seething over the humiliation his men suffered at the hands of this policeman and his lawyer friends. It didn't bother him that contracted employees got rough treatment; they were well paid and would shut up. But it galled him that Colletti and Newman had moved against him, even though they would never know who he was.

Whatever the policeman and the attorney were planning to do in Moscow, he would handle through Doshenko. If the Russians got brutish, as was their nature, so be it.

He walked into his oak-paneled conference room. Lance Reed sat at the far end of the table, drinking tea and warming himself by the fireplace. "Merry Christmas, Lance."

"Don't really celebrate Christmas. I'm not religious."

"Why am I not surprised?" Calthorpe sat down and reviewed some papers. "Well done over at the *Journal.* I understand that our friend Dr. Snyder is arranging a US speaking tour for you in the spring."

"Spoke to 'im. Seems to be an idiot, really, but I plan to have a grand old time over there."

"By then their pompous Supreme Court should have ruled. Everything that we have done has made it possible for them to come in with the right decision."

"Their 1986 Vaccine Act says exactly the opposite of what their Department of Justice will be arguing. Quite a challenge for you, I'd imagine. Some of these justices take pride in being interpreters of law, not writers of new law."

"This is what people come to us for. We alter the terrain and create the reality that allows decision makers to do the right thing."

"Meaning the right thing for you, my Lordship."

"Meaning the right thing for us, my friend."

Reed slid a folder across the conference table. "I've confirmed that the Prisco case came to the attention of Clyde King due to this woman." Calthorpe opened the folder to a report that included a photograph of Maria Contessa-Guevera. "This is the same woman who attended the autism hearings."

"And who is working on that Vaccine Court paper. Lovely eyes. Interesting. She is associated with our two friends headed to Russia."

"The ones who humiliated your detectives?"

Calthorpe stared coldly at Reed. "Yes, those people. They will be monitored by our industry connections in Moscow."

"Do you know what they are planning?"

"Lance, you're an investigative journalist. Why don't you ask them?"

Reed chuckled and sipped his tea. "And if they cause more mischief?"

Calthorpe exhaled an endless stream of smoke as he snuffed out the cigarette. "Oh, I might just have them killed."

CHAPTER 43

"Welcome to the Vostok Hotel, my friends," said the desk clerk. "We don't get many international visitors in January, so we are happy to see you."

"We are here on business," Newman said in Russian with Tony standing silently by his side.

"We hope that you're not too disappointed by our bout of mild weather," the clerk said in English. "Normally, January is quite bitter."

It was four degrees below zero and snowing like Minnesota on steroids. The cab ride from Sheremetyevo Airport through the morning darkness on slick roads was sheer terror. The awful traffic was amplified by downright violent driving. "We're just happy to have made it your hotel alive," Newman said.

"We Russians approach our driving the same way we approach life—boldness mixed with vodka. Your rooms are ready."

The bellhop put their luggage on a cart and the men followed him to their rooms. The clerk waited till they were on the elevator before calling his contact. "Vitaly, the Americans have arrived."

Newman had received an email that they would meet with Zvi's contact, Dr. Yuri Leonodovich, the next day, so the men rested a while before venturing out for lunch and to see the city. The snow was winding down and Moscow was bustling. Cars buzzed noisily through the streets, and people filled the shops and sidewalks.

"Herb, let's go in this shop and buy something," Tony said.

"Why this one?"

"It's got a big window. I can see if anyone followed us out of the hotel."

"*Dobryi dyen*," Newman said to the shop owner as he looked at some ties. Tony looked out the window from behind a clothes rack.

"Any bad guys?"

"Keep shopping."

"Nice tie. Red Square motif—Saint Basil's and the Kremlin."

"Perfect for a socialist like you. Buy it." A black SUV with tinted windows, the only one driving slowly, cruised past the front of the shop. "There you are," Tony told himself.

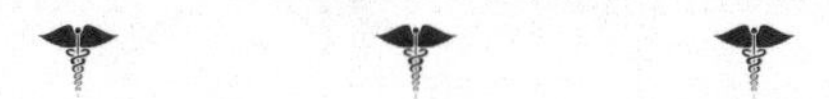

The two men rode the metro to Red Square after deciphering the Cyrillic signage. The metro had the advantage of being underground and out of the weather. It was also more difficult for people to follow. They visited the magnificent Saint Basil's Cathedral and made their way through Red Square to the Kremlin. All the while, Tony tried to determine if anyone was following them.

"I don't think anyone's shadowing us right now," Tony said. "But that doesn't mean that we aren't being watched."

"Aw, you're being paranoid."

"You didn't have the boys in the van in front of your house. I wish we had the paper already and were out of here."

"You're in a historic place," Newman said. "Why not relax a little and enjoy it?" He sat down on a bench and powered up his laptop.

"If you're so enamored with Red Square, why are you playing on your computer?" "Because it can take a photo of us that I can send home. Come on, smile for the camera."

The joy of the moment evaporated as soon as Newman read an email from Maria. The Supreme Court had ruled six to three in favor of the

Secretary of Health and Human Services in the *Cornachio* case. The justices did something that would have been unthinkable a few years earlier: they essentially granted vaccine manufacturers full liability protection against civil suits. Petitioners could no longer opt out of the National Vaccine Injury Compensation Program and sue a pharmaceutical company in a civil court if they didn't like the decision. Civil recourse was preempted. It was now the NVICP or nothing.

"This is what I expected," Newman said.

"What will motivate pharma to make safer vaccines if they can't be sued?"

"The Supreme Court just chained the courthouse doors for anybody who believes a vaccine injured them," Newman said. "Maria's sending me a copy of the decision. She says that the dissenting opinions were strong."

"Our dissenting opinions are always strong," Tony said. "But we never seem to win."

The snow began to fall again in Red Square.

Dr. Phillip Snyder was at an immunology conference at a luxury hotel in the Bahamas when he received a phone call from Jennifer Kesslinger.

"We won, Phil! The Supreme Court ruled in our favor."

"Yeah, baby!" Snyder was so thrilled that he immediately booked a hospitality suite and threw a party. Most of the doctors and researchers had no idea what had sent Snyder into such a tizzy of celebration, but there was free food, champagne, and an open bar so conference attendees poured into the room. After three glasses of the bubbly, Snyder couldn't wait to call Calthorpe. "It's over, you brilliant Limey!"

"Indeed it is. We're supremely victorious, if you'll pardon the pun. I forgive you for waking me in the middle of the night."

"I'm drinking champagne here in the Bahamas, why don't you have a drink?"

"Fine brandy and a good smoke sounds about right."

"Hey," Snyder yelled over the phone, "go easy on the cigarettes. That stuff'll kill ya. I'm dancing with a twenty-something-year-old researcher named—what's your name, kid? Melissa! What a lovely name. Don't tell my wife, Callthorpe baby, but I'm dancing with Melissa somebody!"

"And that stuff will kill you, my friend. But we'll all die someday, so let's all die happy."

Snyder then called Bangston, who was working late, going through files in his office.

"Hey, Bobby!" Snyder yelled. "We won the big one, baby! We're home free."

"So I heard. Are you drunk?"

"I'm working on it, fella! Those lowlife slugs at *Era of Autism* can kiss my . . ." Bangston pulled the phone away from his ear. "We need to get you out of that government job and into some real money. It's over. We won. The industry won. We have the real protection that we need, finally."

"Yes, well, I guess so."

"Why don't you just come down here? The beach looks great when you're drunk. Heck, it looks great if you're not. Come on down!"

"Okay, thanks, Phil, have some fun, and we'll talk soon."

Bangston didn't feel like celebrating. A family had just lost any chance at compensation that could have helped them care for a sick child, and doctors were cheering, drinking champagne, and throwing victory parties. So much for the Hippocratic oath. The Supreme Court had just interpreted a law that assured families the right to civil recourse and decided that it did not say that. He read the dissenting opinion; it was damning because the dissenting justices knew that the majority invented law out of whole cloth.

Snyder and his friends, whoever they were, had done an amazing job. "What did Snyder say?" he thought. "I know a man who can change reality."

Indeed, they had. But Bangston was not Phillip Snyder, and he knew in his gut that this was too much power for any industry to have. The "Big Four" vaccine manufacturers now controlled a marketplace where they could snuff out competition and innovation, set prices, and compel government to mandate their drugs and never be sued for mistakes. They didn't even have to contribute to the Vaccine Injury Compensation Fund that was constantly fed by a tax levied on the consumers of childhood vaccines.

What would pharma do with such uninhibited power?

Bangston looked at the folders on his desk and pondered what he had done with his power. He knew that the Cornachio child, like so many other vaccine-injured children over the past twenty three years, had autism. "What have I become part of?" he wondered.

Senator Russell Sampson walked quietly past the bar at Martin's Tavern in Georgetown and knocked on the door that said "Staff Only." "I know the way," he told the waiter who opened it. Senator Parker Smithson was waiting for him at a small table.

"Hey, Russ," Smithson said. "I'm having Scotch. You?"

"I'm drinking what you're drinking."

Smithson held up two fingers to the server. "So it seems our justices who claim to only interpret law—*never* make new law—opened a whole new line of Supreme Court decision making."

"They read what the act said and ruled that it said the opposite."

"They did indeed, amigo. Justice Romero-Gonzaga took a flamethrower to them. Did ya read her dissent?"

"She's absolutely right. This industry now has zero motivation to ever make a better, safer vaccine."

Their drinks were delivered and Smithson nodded to the server. "And the executive branch is in bed with them. It doesn't even matter which party is hanging out in the White House because both parties are to blame for this bloodbath. Pretty soon now, we're gonna have to do something."

"What? They've won everything."

"That's why the only thing left for them to do is lose everything."

"What do you mean?"

"I may be old and worn, but I know what's settin' up here. History shows that whenever some group gets too much power—a political party, the old robber barons and their monopolies—something always happens to balance the scales. The powerful get too greedy, they overstep reasonable limits, and they screw it all up. You just watch."

CHAPTER 44

"Maria emailed that Dr. Leonodovich located the paper in the archives of the N.F. Gamalei Institute of Poliomyelitis and Virus Encephalitis," Newman said to Tony. "Leonodovich has connections there. We're on for the meeting this afternoon at his office across from Gorky Park." Newman was in Tony's hotel room, nervously watching Tony peer out the window.

"Good," Tony buttoned his shirt collar. "We take two separate cabs. These guys will have to pick one of us to follow. We still have to lose them, somehow."

"I've never done anything like this."

"Me neither. I'm a cop, not James Bond. But look at this traffic—pure chaos. Gotta use the environment to our advantage."

"You think in terms of warfare and tactics. I don't think that way."

"You get the cab driver to cut a hard turn, chuck him money, and then you bolt from the cab. Get lost in the crowd, get on the metro. Whatever it takes, lose them and stay alive. We meet up at—what's the place again?"

"The Old Prospekt Marksa—Sokol Nicheskaya Line at Okhotny Ryad. Write it down."

"Okay. Assuming one of us isn't stopped or killed by these people, we meet up at the Prospect Market."

"It's the Prospekt Marksa—Karl Marx Station, not a market! What do you mean 'stopped or killed'?"

"These people aren't following us just to make a report. You heard Zvi."

"I'm just a lawyer trying to get to the truth about what happened to our kids. I can't believe we could get killed over this."

"People have killed over less." Tony smiled at Newman's ashen face. "Maria told me how you fought in the autism hearings. I know this isn't your kind of warfare, but you're still a fighter. You can do this."

"Okay. But first I want to puke."

The sky was dismal and gray, but the snow had stopped. Vitaly and Viktor sat in their black SUV across the street from the Vostok. The two men were rejects from the Spetsnaz—Russian Special Forces. They were turned out for being undisciplined and overly aggressive, qualities that fit their present line of work.

"Text from the desk clerk—they're coming out," Vitally said.

"There they are," Viktor said. "I say we kill them now."

"Doshenko doesn't want the mess. Killing Americans is never without complications."

"The lawyer got in a cab alone."

"*Chort Vozmi!* They're splitting up. They know we're watching."

"What do we do?"

"Follow the policeman!"

Tony jumped into his cab and turned to see the black SUV following him. "Do you speak English?"

"Little bits, my friend," said the cabbie.

"Head downtown."

"Where is downtown?"

"Central district. Moscow middle."

"I understand."

"Get into heavy traffic."

"This is Moscow, my friend. Traffic, always heavy. Why you want heavy traffic?"

"I'm being followed. I need you to evade the black SUV." The cabbie looked nervously in the rearview mirror and nodded. "I will pay you well."

"You criminal?"

"No. I'm an America policeman trying to stop bad men from hurting children with bad drugs."

"Gangsters?"

"Yes." Tony texted Herb. *"They are on me. Head to Prospect Market."*

"Pay me now," the cabbie said. "I help you. I hate gangsters." Tony handed him a wad of money. "Too much, I not like gangsters."

"It's okay. I need you to drive crazy."

"Driving crazy is in Russian—how you say?—chromosomes. Watch this." The cabbie cut a right turn from the middle lane just as a traffic light turned red, cutting off other cars and triggering a cacophony of honking car horns. "This is how I was born to drive, my American friend."

Tony caught a glimpse of the black SUV swerving to a sudden stop behind cars at the light. "I'll get out here."

"Go, my friend!"

Tony ran into a crowded indoor market and saw a sign for the metro. He moved quickly to the train platform, swiped the metro card, and mixed in with a crowd waiting for the next train, which arrived a moment later. There was no sign of his pursuers.

Finding a seat, he sent Newman a text. "I lost them. But now I'm lost."

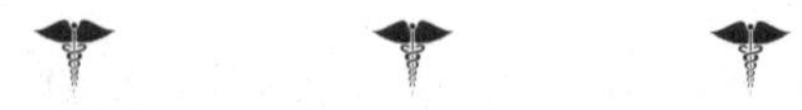

"You lost them both? Idiots!" yelled Nikolai Doshenko over the phone.

"These Americans are not stupid, Nikolai. They know that we are following them, and they split up."

"Whatever they're doing, they are doing it now. And you lost them!"

Tony got off the metro and took another cab to the Old Prospekt Marksa. The bustling station was magnificent, replete with white marble and a mosaic of Karl Marx. He spotted Newman trying to cover his face by reading a newspaper. "You can put the paper down, we're okay. "I got lucky. Cabbie spoke some English and helped me. Drove like a maniac and stranded them in traffic."

"You sure they're gone?"

"For now. Keep in mind that they know where we're staying."

"I'd rather not think about that. The statue of Marx is impressive."

"I liked Groucho better." Tony chuckled.

"Did you ever think that you'd be in the birthplace of Communism with a liberal criminal defense attorney?"

"Hardly. Most guys at Winston PD go to Florida or go skiing in January. I end up in Russia looking for old Soviet research. Ironic."

"What's ironic is that pharma's creating a system that is more 'Soviet' than the old Soviet Union. And that we have to dig up research from the communist era to defeat what I call the vaccine 'corporatocracy.'"

"Ironic indeed," Tony said.

"Svetlana, according to Gamalei Institute policy, I am permitted a copy of the paper," said Dr. Yuri Leonodovich. "I was one of the original authors."

"You know how these corporate types are, doctor," replied the frumpy, middle-aged woman sitting at the archives desk. "They hold onto our old research as though it were gold."

"I don't care about these capitalists. The paper was composed by me and three other men. I am the only one still alive." Dr. Yuri Leonodovich was eighty-two and still a commanding presence. His steel blue eyes glared at the woman.

"The institute bosses say that all of our old research is now owned by Xerxes Pharmaceuticals."

"My paper belongs to the people of Russia." Leonodivich lowered his voice. "Svetlana Sokolova, were it not for me, you would not have this position."

"I know, Doctor. You are a great man. I will give you a copy but the institute managers may ask questions."

"The apparatchiks know where they can find me."

"Go back to the hotel and seize them upon their return," Doshenko ordered.

"But what if we are seen by other guests? You said we shouldn't make a scene. You said no messes."

"You've already made a mess. Whatever they're doing, we must stop them."

Svetlana Sokolova handed Leonodovich the paper. "Thank you, Svetlana. How is your husband these days?"

"Still a drunk." She mumbled.

"Tell him that he must stop drinking and reflect on his life. Good day."

"Good day, Dr. Yuri." Once Leonodovich left, she made the phone call to her supervisor in the front office. "Ivan Krushenko? Sokolova here, with information for you."

"How much will this information cost me?" Krushenko asked wearily.

"I need new boots, Ivan."

"New boots you shall have, but only if the information is useful."

"Dr. Yuri Leonodovich just took an old paper out of the archives."

"Why did you give it to him?"

"He's permitted as an author."

"What is the title of the paper?"

CHAPTER 45

It was snowing again. Worse yet, Tony was worried about Newman. "What's wrong, Herb? You don't look right."

"I think I ate something I shouldn't have."

"You're not going to blow chunks, are you?"

"No, it's—um—my other end . . ."

"Oh, man," Tony said, "let's get the paper from this guy, sneak back to the Vostok, get on a jet, and get outa here." They entered a drab, concrete building that was ugly when new and not aging well. The receptionist buzzed them through the door, and the two men sat in a waiting room that had not seen new furniture since 1975.

Dr. Leonodovich had not yet returned from the archives.

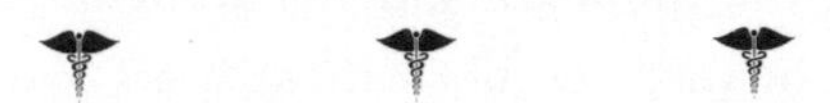

Krushenko returned from lunch and called Nikolai Doshenko. "I don't have time for this now, Krushenko."

"Nikolai, Leonodovich has never embraced the new times. He resents you and the new owners."

"Hold it, I know this man," Doshenko said firmly. "He does not just do things without a purpose. What is the title of the paper?"

Leonodovich entered the waiting room holding his coat and hat. "You would be the gentlemen from America, yes?"

Herb responded in perfect Russian. "Yes, Dr. Leonodovich. We are honored to meet you."

"Almost all the honor has left the world, my friend," he said in English. "Please come into my office."

"This is my assistant, Anthony Colletti."

"*Das vedonya*, Dr. Leonodovich," Tony said.

Leonodovich laughed. "Your Russian is lousy, my friend; you just bid me good-bye."

The office was paneled with oak bookcases packed with books, photographs of Leonodovich with Leonid Breznev and Constantine Chernyenko, and impressive bronze busts of Marx and Lenin on pedestals. It was as though the Cold War had never ended.

"I see that you were a member of the Communist Party," Newman said.

"I still am," Leonodovich said. "However, the Communists failed the country."

"But you're still loyal?"

"Of course, I am Russian. I do not require happy endings to maintain loyalty. Here is the paper." He handed a manila envelope to Newman.

"I thank you, Doctor," Newman said. "I have the money."

"I do not want the money. I did not want money when I decided to get mercury out of vaccines all of those years ago. I did that for our children. Now I do this for yours."

"So, you were the one who . . ."

"The decision was mine," he said sternly. "I was the minister of health."

"What led to your decision?" Newman asked.

"I have read your articles, Comrade Newman. I know you are aware that there is no scientific rationale for injecting this toxin into children. There was no science that supported doing this in the past and there is none now. You know as well as I that using mercury in this fashion amounts to a massive human rights violation. This disdain for the health of children is madness driven by greed."

"Agreed," Newman nodded.

"Any system that treats the people with disdain will fail. The Communists didn't learn that lesson, and they failed. Now your system may be headed down the same path. We shall see. But you should leave, my friends. We may well be under surveillance."

"May I use your restroom?" Newman asked.

"Certainly, I can tell you have a souvenir of what we call 'Lenin's Revenge.'" He escorted Newman to the men's room door.

Before disappearing inside, Newman mouthed, "Thank goodness," to Tony.

"The Americans are taking our research! Yuri Leonodovich is a traitor. Go to his office and get the paper back from them!"

"We will, Nikolai," Vitally shouted over the phone. "Viktor, start the car. Where is that bastard's office?"

"By Gorky. I will text you the street address. Remember that the policeman is an expert in violence!"

"So are we, Nikolai. So are we."

Tony waited nervously for Newman before he emerged from the men's room twenty minutes later. "Let's get out of here." The two put their coats on and hurried out of the building. It was snowing again and getting dark.

"Which way to the metro?" Newman asked.

Tony heard the SUV screeching to a stop behind them. Herb saw it too but didn't comprehend what was happening. "Herb, move! It's them." Two tall men wearing black Russian trooper hats emerged from the vehicle. "Their coats are open so they can get to their guns," Tony explained. One of them made eye contact with Tony and pointed at him.

"Run!" Tony yelled. They took off toward Gorky Park, but it was impossible to move quickly in the snow and ice.

"Vitally! The Americans!" said Viktor, pointing again at Tony and Herb.

"Oh, my God," Newman gasped, "They're going to kill us."

"No, we're going to live. Move!"

"What if they have guns? We don't have guns."

"Keep moving." They were able to get a slight lead as they crossed the street through heavy traffic, but neither man knew where they were going. Tony didn't want to go into Gorky Park. He heard it was large, and he wanted to go where there would be people. These men might not kill them if they were on a sidewalk full of pedestrians. He pondered how to engage them. They had guns, and he didn't. A victim could be shot dead from thirty feet as easily as from point blank range, so it made sense to draw them in close so he could get one of their guns. "Throw Herb to the ground, grab one guy's arm, control the gun, shoot the other man, and then kill the first guy," Tony thought. "Just like in the dojo."

Except this wasn't the dojo. Newman slipped and fell on the sidewalk. "Damn it!" he yelled.

The men were gaining on them.

People were going through a gateway of sorts. Perhaps it was an entrance to a metro station? Tony helped Herb up, and the two ran through the entrance. It was a park with all sorts of odd statues—not a Metro entrance.

"Which way?" Newman asked.

"Here." Tony ran right and started running along a partially shoveled walkway that cut behind some of the statues.

"Lenin and Marx." Newman said.

"Right now they're cover and concealment." They ducked behind a statue with a large bronze base.

"Did we lose them?" Newman asked, breathing heavily.

"I don't know."

"They call this Fallen Heroes Monument Park," Newman shook with equal parts of exhaustion and fear. "What are we going to do?"

"Stay alive. No matter what, stay alive."

A man appeared behind them. "You Americans behind the statue of Stalin! Raise your hands and come out."

Tony suspected that he was trained to some degree as he maintained a distance from them. Tony grabbed Newman and scurried around the monument. They now stood at the feet of Joseph Stalin as they faced another man with a pistol.

"We know who you are. We are prepared to kill you both to get our property back. Give us the paper," the man said.

Tony felt cold metal of the gun against the side of his head and raised his hands.

"I say to you, lawyer, give me the paper. We know your friend is dangerous. Don't make us kill him first."

"Don't make me do it, friend," said the one holding the gun against Tony's head.

"Okay, Okay!" Newman yelled. His eyes darted back and forth.

"Lower your voice, you idiot. Just hand me the paper."

Newman reached into his jacket for the manila envelope, then handed it over. "Here. Now let us go."

"Not yet, friend."

"What else does this killer want," Tony thought, tensing to attack.

"Don't do it," the man with the gun whispered, "you might disarm me, but your friend will die and then you will be shot."

"What else do you want?" Newman asked.

"Give me your computer bag or I will blow your stinking American brains all over Comrade Stalin's feet."

Newman tossed the bag. It landed at the man's feet. He stooped to pick it up, keeping the gun focused on Newman.

"You have what you want," Tony said. "Shoot my friend, and you're both dead."

The man holding the gun on Herb backed away. The other man kicked Tony in the groin, crumpling him to the ground. Then he slapped his gun across Tony's forehead that sent a gush of blood into the snow.

"NO!" Herb yelled.

The man who assaulted Tony also backed away. "Our business with you is over." "Leave Russia within twenty-four hours, or we will come back and kill you both." The men disappeared into the darkness and falling snow.

"Tony, are you all right?" Newman pulled his Red Square motif tie off and used it as a bandage.

"I ever see that punk again," Tony gasped, "I'll snap his neck!"

"Why did he assault you? Damned Philistine! He had what he wanted."

Tony hunched over and vomited in the snow. "They needed me incapacitated so they could exit. I was going to kill them both, and the guy next to me knew it."

"You were?"

"Damn right I was. All this work and it ends with us getting our asses kicked in front of—which one is this?" Tony pointed up at the statue.

"Stalin. We just got robbed by Russian gangsters hired by American corporations in front of a statue of Stalin. Someone disfigured the statue."

"Someone just disfigured me. This sucks!" Tony moaned.

"The irony sucks, I agree."

"No, it's not the irony that sucks! We lost the paper. That's what sucks."

Newman sat in the snow. "But it doesn't really matter."

"What do you mean, it doesn't matter?" Tony spat into the snow. "They got the paper."

"Yeah, they got a copy, but while I was in the bathroom, I scanned it and emailed it to everyone back in the States." Newman kept pressure on Tony's wound. "Then I deleted everything in the computer and activated encryption software that will take weeks to bypass."

"You're saying that we got it anyway?!"

"Yeah," With a handful of snow Newman wiped away more blood from Tony's head. "Mission accomplished."

"You did all this in the bathroom?"

"Well, I'm always multitasking. I figured, get this done. Good thing, huh?"

"Herb Newman, you're brilliant!"

"Thanks. You saved my life."

Tony lay on his back and laughed as snow fell on the statue of the Man of Steel. "Oh God, my head hurts."

Two men waited in Dr. Yuri Leonodovich's office early the next morning at the same time Tony and Newman boarded their flight home. "What can I do for you gentlemen?"

"We have a message for you from our employer," Viktor growled as he and Vitally drew their handguns.

Leonodovich nodded at the guns' silencers. He went behind his desk and stood at attention. "I ask that you reflect on your lives."

"This is not the age of reflection, Dr. Leonodovich," Vitally said coldly.

"Very well then. Give me your message and be done with it."

CHAPTER 46

"I could kill you!" Anne Colletti glared at Tony as he walked through the front door. "Thank God you're alive. What the hell happened?"

"The long and short of it is, we were followed around snowy Moscow by two gangsters who mugged us and took a copy of the paper."

"Your head looks horrible," Anne touched Tony's face. "Enough of this. It has to stop now."

"We still got the paper."

"Screw the paper. I care about you," She hugged her husband. "No more trips to Russia."

"Never again," he said holding her tight. "Those people in Moscow made a big mistake, you know."

"Says the man with stitches on his head."

"They didn't kill me."

"I'm leaving, Robert," Jennifer Kesslinger said cheerfully over the phone.

"Good for you," said Bangston.

"It's hard to make real money in the government. A girl's gotta do what a girl's gotta do. I'll be running the vaccine division over at Binghampton after I take a break."

"I'll miss you."

"You're a bad liar," she chuckled. "I'm just happy I don't have to deal with that drunken Norwegian anymore. Jurgenson's now the next director's headache."

"Where is he?"

"Canary Islands, having sex with a blonde research assistant paid for by our tax dollars. Called last week, drunk as a skunk, threatening to release the Vaccine Safety Research Data Set if he's indicted over the missing money."

"Can he do that?"

"He's bluffing. No one in the industry would give him that."

"Snyder should've gone to someone else for the research. His work was crap and he's not worth the risk."

"But it sold and we won the autism war. Hey, when're you banging out?"

"Oh, I don't know. What does a guy with a background in vaccine injuries do outside of here?"

"Did you forget?" Kesslinger said, "there are no vaccine injuries anymore."

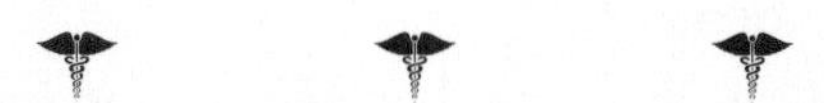

"Now that we have the translation, I see why these Americans wanted the paper," Calthorpe said to Doshenko over the phone.

"My men delivered a strong message. They will not come back to Moscow. And we have destroyed all remaining copies of the research."

"I'm destroying my copy now," Calthorpe watched it burn in his fire place. "And Leonodovich?"

"It seems that he fell victim to the growing crime problem here in Moscow. Tragic end after so many years of service to the state."

"Indeed. Just one more question, my friend . . . what about the other three authors of the paper?"

"Two are long dead. The other disappeared years ago."

"Disappeared to where?"

Bangston took Chief Special Master Carl Mantkewicz out for a farewell lunch at Café Milano in Georgetown.

"I'll spend time with my grandkids," Mantkewicz said. "Get the stink of this program off me."

"Gonna do any legal work?" Bangston asked.

"Eventually," Mantkewicz said, "but just golf, fishing, and grandkids for now. The autism hearings are done and *Cornachio* is in the books, it's time to move on."

Bangston's cell phone rang. It was his daughter. "Excuse me, Carl. Grace?"

"Hi daddy, I've got good news. I'm pregnant!"

"That's wonderful! When's the baby due?"

"End of August. Mom's so happy. You gotta call her."

"I will. I'm thrilled."

"Daddy, one quick thing. Should I get a flu shot? It's recommended, but I know you know the real deal."

Bangston turned white. "Let me get back to you on that. Don't do anything now. Call you later."

"I gathered you're about to become a grandfather," Mantkewicz smiled. "Good for you. Lunch is on me. I can see that you're in shock. You need to get out of here and enjoy your grandchild-to-be. We've both been here too long."

The first half of the Mexican flu vaccine trials in the Southern Tucson Immigration Detention Facility was a disaster. Within twenty-four hours of administration, six of the fifty-five children had seizures.

"We have an obligation to treat these children compassionately," said Warden Joe Walcott in a phone call to his superiors in Washington. "I think that you should tell the CDC people to shut this project down."

"Why should we do that?"

"The female blocks in C Wing are on edge. They talk to each other—particularly about their kids. You do remember what it's like to run a facility like this, don't ya, Randy?"

"Yeah, but you've seen the footage from Mexico. This thing has the whole planet terrified. CDC says the country needs this vaccine, Joe."

"I don't think it needs *this* particular vaccine. I've never seen a vaccine have this result."

"CDC says that the trial is meeting expectations."

"Really? They expected infants to be having seizures that last ten minutes? You should hear their screams. They didn't say we should expect that. All's I heard was some bullshit 'bout fevers and chills."

"They didn't tell us that either."

"Now they're accusing my medical staff of withholding information about the children's medical histories. None of them had histories of seizures."

"I'll make the case to them, but the pressure's comin' from pretty high up."

Within twenty-four hours, three children were dead. And the second group of fifty-five children began receiving vaccines.

CHAPTER 47

"That title sucks," Laura said.

"This is legal scholarship," Maria said. "We can't name the paper 'The Government Screwed Autism Families in the Vaccine Court.'"

"But they did . . ."

"Agreed, but no reputable journal will publish that."

The Saturday morning meeting in Laura's office had already lasted for thirty minutes. Maria and Laura were debating what to name the paper on the Vaccine Injury Compensation Program. Susan Miller took notes while shaking her head at the two attorneys' discussion.

Tony and Herb arrived with their guest, Dr. Zviad Kokochashvili.

"God, Tony," Maria said, "you look like you've been to war."

"I was pistol-whipped, I don't recommend the experience."

"Having a gun stuck in your face is no picnic either," Newman added. "I keep reliving it over and over again."

Susan frowned. "If these men didn't have guns, Tony would've put a hurt on them."

"These men were just the help," Tony said. "The Phil Snyders and Jennifer Kesslingers of the world don't roll in the mud. They pay others to do it."

"Are you all right?" Laura asked.

"It still hurts, but we got the paper. How you think I look?"

"It's an improvement," she said.

"On that note," Newman said, "I would like you to meet Dr. Zviad Kokochashvili, coauthor of "A Comparative Population Analysis of DPT Injuries." The doctor is now an American citizen, but still risks a great deal by working with us. He's a courageous man."

Zvi shook hands with everyone. "It's all of you who are courageous. I should have come forward years ago. This is the least I should do to right a wrong."

"Do you think you were allowed to defect because of your bioweapons research or the vaccine injury paper?" Maria asked.

"I was the youngest coauthor. The others were old guard Russians who died in the nineties. I'm not Russian—I'm Georgian. I believe now that the bioweapons was, how you say, a bonus. They did ask a lot of questions about that program and how it functions but not really about the science. The Americans knew the Soviet science. It was the CDC questioning on the DPT paper that was intense."

Newman powered up his laptop. "The industry had begun to make headway in having the government protect them with the vaccine act. There was significant pressure from parents about the DPT and the problems identified by the National Childhood Encephalopathy Study."

"I know some of the researchers involved in that work," Zvi said. "They admit that autism was a common behavioral consequence from the encephalopathy in that study as well."

Maria began pouring coffee. "So when your paper was discovered . . ."

"It independently confirmed their worst nightmares," Zvi interrupted. "We had a control group that was not vaccinated and none in the control group suffered the array of injuries that the vaccinated group did."

"What sort of vaccine injuries did you identify?" Maria said.

"Death, mental retardation accompanied by severe physical incapacitation, seizures, and what we now understand to be autism."

Tony took a cup from Maria. "Same type of injuries that we're finding in our study. The children with autism are the walking wounded. Many of the families have had children who are completely devastated. Seizures are a continual threat and have killed some."

"Is it your impression that families are fearful of discussing their cases?" Zvi wondered.

"They're afraid that the program will remove their children's funding. DOJ attorneys and special masters put them through the ringer."

Zvi drank some coffee and put his cup down. "So they maintain secrecy through intimidation, like the old Soviets."

"Many are now adults with horrible seizure disorders, and autism is a secondary issue. One mom said her son had ten seizures a day. It's a struggle just to keep him alive. The autism issue is not really that important to her," Tony said.

Newman looked through vaccine injury cases on his computer. "All of these families go through the program alone. It's brutal, takes years. They're left with a devastated child. No one gets any special benefits from declaring 'my child has a vaccine injury.'"

"Twenty years ago, before people recognized an increase in autism, there was no sense of an 'autism community' as we now call it. There were no national conferences." Maria said.

Susan put her notepad down. "That was my family. My parents are in the medical profession and work long hours. Keeping careers going and taking care of my brother has been an enormous challenge."

"You have a brother who's autistic?" Zvi asked.

"Yes. I adore him."

"What's your brother's name?"

"George."

"My son is named George—Georgi," Tears welled in his eyes.

"But you didn't call it autism in your paper, did you?" Laura asked.

"No. We didn't know what autism was. We carefully noted the behaviors—the perseverating, the loss of speech, the hand flapping—and called it a unique behavioral syndrome."

"That's autism, by any other name," Susan said. "That's what we should name our paper. 'Autism by Any Other Name.'"

Maria stirred her coffee. "That's it." Laura nodded in agreement.

"How are you, Dr. Washington? Treating kids or cooking in dad's restaurant?"

"I'm working in a practice down the road a piece in Collierville," Washington said. "I kept burning the chicken, so it was back to medicine."

Sara Donovan was working on a story in her office about a Pentagon weapons program that had gone badly over budget when Dr. Washington called her. "I'm really glad to hear that. You're a good doctor."

"One of the doctors in the practice treats kids with autism at night when the office closes for the day. It's sorta strange. Everyone knows he does it, yet no one talks 'bout it."

"Treating autism is controversial."

"It's supposed to be genetic and all that. But I like the doctor who does this work, and I asked him if I could help out one evening. So guess who came into the office that night with her daughter?"

"Who?"

"Leanna Yearwood," he said. "Daniella Yearwood now has an autism diagnosis."

"The woman I interviewed."

"That's the one. The vaccines I gave that child left her with brain damage and autism."

"God, I'm sorry."

"I don't know what to do about this," Washington said. "Had I not seen this with my own eyes, I might not believe it."

"It's just like what I learned from a cop about the cases in the Vaccine Court."

"There's a Vaccine Court?" Washington said. "I was talking about what you read on blogs and such. Those parents tell similar stories."

"The parents no one will listen to and who I'm not allowed to report on."

"We have to do something, Sara. This isn't right."

⚕ ⚕ ⚕

It took over four hours for the Federal Immigration Detention Service to restore order and regain control at the South Tucson Detention Facility. It was by anyone's recollection the first prison riot caused by a drug research trial gone bad. Warden Walcott negotiated a peaceful end to the hostage situation after female detainees took one of the researchers hostage. Six of the children who received the Mexican flu vaccine died. Eleven others were still suffering severe reactions.

There were only a few news reports of a disturbance at an Immigration Detention Facility in the Sonoran Desert that had been successfully brought under control. Who cared about illegals anyway?

Over the next few weeks, the mothers of the deceased children were quietly deported back to Mexico. The funeral and burial expenses of their children were paid, and the women were given five thousand dollars each.

The CDC issued a press release with Binghampton Pharmaceuticals reporting that the trials for the new Mexican flu vaccine had been a complete success. The vaccine was cleared for production and distribution.

That would have been the end of the story if one of the detention officers had not been Robert McCormick, the father of Elyse McCormick—the case that was turned down by the special masters in the Omnibus Autism Proceedings.

CHAPTER 48

"Check this out, bro," said Detective Glen Forceski reading from a news blog on his office computer. "Department of Justice officials announced a criminal indictment of Dr. Hans Jurgenson. The charge is using grant money from the CDC Credit Union for trips, parties, sports cars, and—you'll love this—female companionship."

Tony laughed. "The feds are always discrete. They call prostitution 'female companionship.' Isn't this the guy who . . . "

". . . who produced the epidemiology that said vaccines don't cause autism. No mention of that, though."

"He took money from the CDC Credit Union. The CDC has its own bank?"

"That struck me as odd too."

Chief Lonnegan walked in. "Hey, guys. You going out or doing paperwork for the rest of the afternoon?"

"We're here for the remainder, Chief," Tony replied. "Need us to do anything?"

"Keep an eye on the place. I'm leaving a little early."

Something was wrong. Lonnegan never left early. "What's going on?" Forceski asked.

Lonnegan leaned against Forceski's desk and took his chief's cap off. "Okay, I guess you'd be the guys I'd tell first anyway. I gotta go to my granddaughter's special ed meeting. My son-in-law walked out on my daughter."

"I'm sorry to hear that," Tony said.

"I guess the guy couldn't handle it all. So I'm steppin' in to help her out. And listen, I'm puttin' my papers in. Be out in a couple of months."

Forceski sat bolt upright. "What?"

"You sure you're ready, Chief?" Tony asked.

"My family needs me. You guys know how overwhelming it all gets with a child with autism. On top of everything, she's in a pitched battle with her school district. You guys look stunned. Didja' think I'd be here forever?"

Tony shook his head. "I guess we did."

"I feel bad, Chief," Forceski said. "I remember you saying that you wanted to travel with your wife when you retired and see what the world's all about."

Lonnegan looked at his cap. "Yeah, well, we've all seen what the world is really all about, haven't we?"

"What's going on?" Tony asked. "Where's Sensei?" As if his day wasn't traumatic enough, Tony arrived at the dojo that evening with Randazzo to find that Susan Miller had opened the doors. Sensei wasn't there.

Susan nodded toward the back room, and Tony followed, leaving Randazzo to change his clothes. "Tony, he has cancer. Sensei is dying. He says that it isn't treatable, and you know that he won't take drugs. I get the sense that he has a couple of months, maybe. He wrote you this note." Susan handed it to Tony.

Sensei Colletti, please instruct the class this evening. I will call you over the weekend.

Still shaken, Tony handed the letter back to Susan, then sat in the oak rocking chair at Sensei's desk.

"What do we do?" Susan asked.

Tony looked at the photographs on Sensei's desk. One showed Saito as a young boy with his father in a small boat on Minimata Bay.

"Tony?"

"We teach the class. Let's get changed and line them up."

"Good news, my friends, 'Autism by Any Other Name' cleared peer review at the *International Journal of Medicine, Law, and Ethics*," Maria said over the conference line to the other team members. "It wasn't easy, but we'll be published in April."

"What do you mean, 'not easy'?" Newman asked.

"Two of the first three peer reviewers returned the paper. They refused to be part of a decision to publish a paper that linked vaccine injury to autism because it damaged public perception of vaccines."

"Isn't that unethical?" Laura wanted to know.

"It is. The editors apologized and went to other reviewers. In the end, those who read it objectively found little to criticize."

Tony chimed in. "Maria, share some of the comments from the final review. Wait till you hear this stuff." He and Maria had discussed the comments earlier in the day.

"Listen to this one. 'This paper is damning. It shows that vaccine injury and the behavioral disorder called autism had been associated since the very beginning of the government's Vaccine Injury Compensation Program. It isn't just the decisions of special masters. It's the dozens and dozens of cases where the government conceded that the child should be compensated for vaccine injury where autism, secondary to brain damage, was a result.'"

"Yes!" Newman exclaimed.

Maria chuckled. "It gets better. One of the reviewers wrote a small comment on the side of one of the pages stating 'It is difficult to envision that those in government reviewing these cases didn't know that autism was so prevalent. Not disclosing this is a shocking ethical failure.'"

⚕ ⚕ ⚕

E. Gordon Calthorpe covered the phone as he coughed. "Nikolai, you mean Zviad Kokochashvili simply disappeared from the Soviet Union in 1985?"

"Apparently so. He took a trip to the mountains and never came back."

"I thought that there was an iron curtain."

"By that time, holes had rusted through, my friend."

"Redouble your efforts. The Americans learned of this paper from somewhere, and you said that there is no record of direct communication between them and Leonodovich."

Donna Willoughby poked her head into Calthorpe's office. "The CEOs are ready to commence the call, sir."

"Excellent! Let's start, shall we?"

On the line were the heads of the "Big Four" pharmaceutical companies.

"Please announce yourselves, gentlemen," Donna said.

"Chuck Livingston, Binghampton Pharmaceuticals."

"Roger Cunningham, CEO, Philbin. Charles, you old pirate, how are you?"

"Making a living. You?"

"Buried in board meetings. You know that dance."

"Joseph Montoya, Xerxes Pharmaceuticals. Hey, guys."

"Brandon Parshavar of Novo Western. Good to talk to all of you."

Calthorpe lit a cigarette. "We're assembled today, gentlemen, to ensure that we maximize the US vaccine market. As you're all aware, the world looks to America."

"At least in medical matters," Livingston said. "And it's time that we removed all the archaic state laws about religious and philosophical exemptions."

"I agree," said Parshavar. "It's not so much about current profitability as much as about the future of our shared market. We all have new vaccines in the pipeline."

"The autism issue has been removed as a threat," said Montoya. "We can now press on to remove the exemptions. State legislatures should be easier to work with now."

"We already spend a small fortune on our political action committee, Women in Public Office," Cunningham said. "WIPO can be ramped up. It's simple; we use the ladies in office to influence the ladies in the living room."

Everyone laughed. Calthorpe smiled as well. Pharma would once again pour millions into Rollins. Having secured billions with absolutely no risk of liability, it was now time to go for some real money. In the next ten years, vaccines of every sort would be rolled out. The sky was the limit.

Calthorpe and Rollins now had a percentage of the sky.

CHAPTER 49

Sipping from a brandy snifter, Calthorpe turned on the recording of the SNN interview of Dr. Phillip Snyder in his office.

"Are vaccine objectors endangering the health of others? Tonight an expert on vaccines speaks out," said SNN Medical Correspondent, Dr. Randall Cooke. In the background was Dr. Phillip Snyder, in a white doctor's coat in an examination room with a mother holding her infant.

"Vaccines are completely safe," Snyder began. *"Industry and government safety standards are so high that I can assure parents with total confidence."*

"What was that mother's concern?" Cooke, also in a doctor's coat, asked.

"She heard rumors on the Internet that vaccines caused autism. I told her the science was in and vaccines had been ruled out. Autism is genetic."

"Was she convinced?"

"She agreed to vaccinate her child in accordance with the schedule set by the experts at the Centers for Disease Control."

"She accepted the word of the experts?"

"Yes. Most parents do. There are only a few individuals who continue to cling to the notion that vaccines are dangerous or cause autism."

Dr. Snyder was then shown testifying at a hearing in the Delaware House of Representatives. *"You recently testified in the Delaware Legislature in support of a bill sponsored by House Member Doris Rogers that seeks to remove that state's religious exemptions to vaccination."*

"Yes. I'm happy to do so in any state considering that kind of bill. Other citizens and other children shouldn't be threatened by families claiming religious exemptions to vaccination. I know of no religion that permits a parent to needlessly risk their child's health. It's criminal, really."

"That's a powerful statement. What do you say to those parents who still refuse?"

"I tell them that science has spoken. Even the Vaccine Court ruled against autism claims. In places where parents refused to vaccinate, children have died. Those deaths rest at the feet of those who are anti-vaccine."

"Is it appropriate for pediatricians to ask families who don't vaccinate to leave their practices?"

"Frankly, yes. I'd never refuse to treat a sick child, but sometimes you have to tell the families to move or get with the program."

Calthorpe smiled. Snyder's friend Cooke at SNN paid off handsomely, he thought while dialing Snyder. As winter ended, the Rollins media machine churned out stories about declining vaccination rates due to "dangerous, irresponsible, anti-vaccine groups who still clung to the notion that vaccines cause autism." Bills restricting religious and other types of vaccine exemptions were now moving through several state legislatures. A bill ending religious and conscientious objections awaited the Georgia governor's signature. "Well done, my good doctor."

"Thanks," Snyder replied. "That should piss off the mutants at the *Era of Autism* blog."

"Indeed. And Randall Cooke's worked out marvelously, hasn't he?"

"Yeah. Good hire. But we shoulda' had Donovan fired."

"Why ignite drama? Let her go cover the gripping phenomena of waste at your Pentagon."

"She'll likely uncover a nefarious conspiracy involving weapons transfers or something. The military will have to deal with her crap."

"Then the military can always hire us."

"We will protect our children from those dangerous individuals in our midst who refuse to vaccinate their children," said Bibb County District

Attorney Norman Newton into a microphone in front of the Macon City Court House. A line of people holding bright yellow documents were waiting to get into the building. "I have issued appearance tickets to those adults who have not complied with the Georgia Public Health Code to vaccinate their children. As you can see, they're reporting to court today. If they show proof of compliance, we'll dismiss the citations without prejudice. We're reasonable people."

"DA Newton," one reporter asked, "Is this just a reelection stunt?"

"Children have died from vaccine-preventable diseases. Dr. Phillip Snyder says so. The man's an expert. And I am not having any dead kids in my county."

Herman Tyler watched the television coverage of Norman Newton's press conference in his office at the Georgia Southern Clinic. "Enough of this," he thought as he stroked his goatee. Within a few days, Tyler had connected with two women who were willing to stand up to Newton. Mary Burdette, a single mother who objected to vaccinating her son due to safety concerns and Phylis Twiggs, who objected to vaccinating her daughter on religious grounds.

Tyler called a press conference in front of the Macon City Court, just as Newton did a few days earlier. A small crowd of supporters stood with Tyler and the women.

"It's time to object to a government that mandates us to place our children in harm's way," Tyler began. "It's time to object to a government that's ignoring our religious beliefs in the name of compliance with a medical procedure. A few days ago, DA Norman Newton appeared on these steps and declared that people, such as myself and the two women you're about to meet, are a threat to our community because we are refusing to vaccinate our children. Even though there's no health emergency, law-abiding citizens were given tickets and directed to appear before a judge. We stand opposed."

Tyler turned the microphone over to Mary Burdette. "I'm a single mom. I work as a cook here in Macon, and I refuse to vaccinate my son.

Show me the independent research that proves these vaccines are safe. Let me evaluate them to determine whether they're good for my child. This is what I have to say about DA Newton's mandate." Burdette ripped her appearance ticket in half.

Phyllis Twiggs spoke next. "I've obeyed every law in Georgia, every day of my life. I'm a Christian woman, and I oppose vaccinating my daughter because I sincerely feel that my faith advises me to do so. You recall that God stopped Abraham from sacrificing his child? I've come to the conclusion that God wants me to remember that." Twiggs tore her ticket.

Tyler returned to the microphone. "My sisters, I am with you." He slowly ripped his citation. "I equate the vaccine program with the Tuskegee experiments. There's no independent science showing that vaccines are safe. The industry that produces them is only marginally regulated and now, due to a recent Supreme Court decision in *Cornachio,* it bears no civil liability. I attended hearings last year in Washington in what some wrongfully call the 'Vaccine Court.' The families involved did not receive justice. Government attorneys defended vaccines and the taxpayers—not the manufacturers—paid the bill. If my child did suffer a vaccine injury, I do not believe that he would receive justice in that forum.

"My sister's child regressed and became sick after vaccination and now has autism. I will not subject my son to such a risk. Norman Newton can put me in jail."

The Macon vaccine objectors became a national story. Images of Tyler tearing his appearance ticket went viral on the Internet, resulting in a swath of coverage about the *Cornachio* decision and the National Vaccine Injury Compensation Program. Was the "Vaccine Court" just? What did the Omnibus Autism Proceedings really mean? One commentator noted that the government's case relied heavily on the research of Hans Jurgenson, who was now a fugitive from justice. Others expressed alarm at pharma's lack of civil liability for vaccines and even voiced support for "The Macon Three." A headline in the *Atlanta Examiner* simply read "Is Herman Tyler Right?"

DA Newton issued a terse press release. "I will enforce the Georgia Health Code. I give Tyler, Twiggs, and Burdette one week to comply or face arrest."

"These people are hurting the program!" Snyder screamed into the phone.

"It's a blip on the radar," Calthorpe responded. "I wouldn't lose sleep over it."

"Equating us with the Tuskegee experiments is beyond the pale."

"Have to say that the ticket-tearing was a good visual. Interesting approach."

"Interesting approach, my ass! I want these people shut down!"

"Phillip, my good fellow," Calthorpe sighed, "my art doesn't work that way. We'll come up with a plan to thoroughly dehumanize these objectors, but it will take a little time."

"These people are coming off as heroic. Make this stop!"

"Rest assured, we shall. We have the resources and the media dances on our strings."

"We haven't come all this way and spent all this money to be taken down by some radical professor!"

"It's looking like we're going to need counsel," Tyler told Maria. "Newton's gonna arrest us."

"Are you sure that you want to do this? You risk losing your law license."

Tyler shifted the receiver to his left ear. "I realize that. But it's time to stand up on this issue. I keep thinking about what happened to my wife and what Mrs. McCormick said to those bureaucrats."

"I'll pull together some lawyers and see what we can do. Herman, if you go to jail, who will take care of your son?"

"My mother. We've talked."

"You're a brave man."

"I'm just a civil rights scholar who needs to remember what he says to his students. Please get me a lawyer."

Maria promptly convened a conference call with a dozen attorneys. Herb Newman joined the call thirty minutes late.

"We're kind of up against it, Herb," Laura said. "We've been kicking it around, and we don't know anybody who's licensed to practice law in Georgia."

"Sure you do, Newman said. "I was a US attorney in Atlanta twenty-something years ago. I've kept my Georgia license active."

"Herb!" Maria cheered. "You're the answer to our prayers!"

"Hold on," Newman said, "I have a family to feed. I can't keep going on road shows like this. I was almost got killed on the last one."

"Come on, Herb!" Laura chuckled. "We'll keep the violence potential down by keeping Colletti in New York."

"There are no attorneys in Georgia?" Newman responded.

"None with your grasp on vaccine safety, research, and law."

" I can't keep doing this stuff."

"I talked to Herman," Maria said quietly. "He needs you."

"You people will get me killed!"

Three days later the deadline for compliance passed, and the Bibb County Sheriff arrested the objectors for child endangerment. Herman Tyler, in a jacket and tie, walked proudly into the Macon City Court in handcuffs in front of a throng of television cameras.

The judge set bail at $5,000 for each defendant. "Professor Tyler, Miss Burdette, Mrs. Twiggs" he added. "The bail I've set is reasonable. Your counsel does not oppose."

Tyler rose "Sir, respectfully, I will not post bail. If you believe that this is the right way for the state to act, then I will have to stay in jail."

Twiggs and Burdette also refused to post bail.

Dr. Ron Washington called Sara Donovan. "Sara, are you seeing this?"

"I am," Sara said, "I want to cover the story, but I still have to get around the blockade."

"It's all over the other networks."

"The other side has people calling and emailing SNN comments that I shouldn't be allowed to cover this because I'm 'anti-vaccine.'"

"What can you do?"

"Wait for an opportunity."

Herb Newman also watched the coverage. "How dare they do this," he seethed as he called Wilson Garrison.

"I was wondering when you'd call," Garrison said. "You goin'?"

"Yeah. My wife wants my head, and I'm going to have to adjourn twelve cases in Manhattan criminal, but I can't sit here and watch this."

"I'll join you as of counsel. I can't practice in Georgia. Try to find a cheap hotel."

Herb Newman threw his suitcase in his car and headed south.

CHAPTER 50

"Amber is my only child and she isn't going to have any children, so our line ends here," Emily Blyfin told Tony. Her daughter suffered horrible seizures within hours of her DPT vaccine in 1990 and now lives in a Minneapolis group home. "My husband died a few years ago. I know that he'd be grateful if you could tell people the truth about what happened to Amber."

Tony's eyes moistened. "I promise, Mrs. Blyfin," he said softly into the receiver.

"Our attorney fought for six years before they finally agreed to compensate Amber. They argued about everything, even the cost of diapers. Bert couldn't understand how people could be so petty, so ruthless. He spoke out against the program, became an activist of sorts. You and he were cut from the same cloth, it seems."

"Thank you."

"Bert took a lot of abuse. They beat him up pretty good."

"We do seem to have a lot in common."

"Why're you doing this, Tony?"

"For my son."

Emily's voice quivered. "Never stop believing in your son's potential. Never stop rejoicing at the blessing that he is to you. I'm glad we talked. But you forgot to ask the question that you really wanted to ask."

"I did?" They had been talking for so long that Tony lost his place on the interview form.

"Yes, you did," Emily said. "Amber suffers from seizures. And my beautiful daughter also has autism."

Tony called Maria at 11:30 p.m. as soon as he hung up. "Emily is amazing. I feel that I was meant to interview her," Tony said. "We have to tell their story."

"Legal scholarship is dry and unemotional. But I'm sure we'll come up with a way to tell the human side."

"We now have seventy-five people compensated by government for vaccine injuries who have autism."

"This will be the final case entered in the data set. The final draft goes to the publisher tomorrow. Good night, Tony."

After she hung up, Maria saw a text message from Donna McCormick.

Maria woke Tony at one in the morning. "They've killed babies and covered it up!"

"Slow down. Tell me what happened."

"The people running the trials on the Mexican flu vaccine used infants born to undocumented women. The testers felt they could exploit the mothers because they weren't citizens. Six children born in the United States suffered seizures and died. Bob McCormick worked there. Told me everything."

"Bob McCormick from the autism hearings?"

"The very same. Their mothers were paid off and sent back to Mexico. Crimes against the weak, suppression of truth, and a dangerous experiment on babies. Then they covered it up and issued a press statement about the trials being successful. They're out of control!"

"Will McCormick talk?"

"Yes. He has documents too."

"We'll need those."

"It's Argentina, all over again. They're disappearing people."

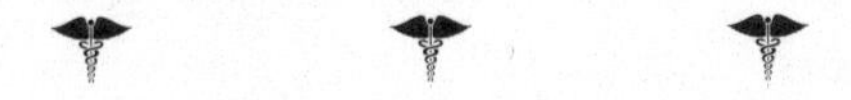

Snyder stormed around his office watching the television coverage of the Macon Three. SNN covered the story with a local reporter who interviewed people on the streets of Macon.

"Why's the government tellin' us what we gotta do with our kids?" one middle-aged white man said. "They should stay outa our family health decisions."

"I think that there are just too many vaccines," an African American man in his thirties said. "I don't see the point."

"Don't see the point?" Snyder screamed at the television. "You're all gonna die!"

"I think pediatricians need to listen to mothers," a mother pushing a baby stroller said. "I had to switch pediatricians until I found one who let me spread my child's vaccines out."

Snyder sneered at the results of a "pop-up poll." Sixty-three percent felt that DA Newton had gone too far, twenty-two percent supported him, and ten percent were undecided. He called Randall Cook at SNN. "Randall, why are you in your office?"

"Huh, what do you mean?"

Snyder twitched with rage. "Why're you in your office when you should be in Bacon!"

"You mean Macon."

"Whatever the name of that stinking backwoods trailer park Southern swamp hole is! Why are you in DC and not there?

"We don't want to legitimize this thing, Phil."

"Your network's affiliate is doing exactly that! Get down there and get this story in line!"

"I'll talk to the execs, but money for travel is tight."

"Tell them we're pulling our advertising to another network. Tell them to try to fill the money hole left by missing erectile dysfunction ads. Tell 'em."

"Come on now. The program may be taking it on the chin, but we can't win every round."

"Wrong! We can never, ever, lose."

Russell Sampson, who watched the same SNN coverage, found the opinions of the people of Macon surprising. Sampson also considered the reactions of people in his office and noted the response to Herman Tyler. He saw his staff, particularly the younger staff and interns, nodding their heads. "Hey, Mark, what do you think about this Professor Tyler?"

"I think that he is a principled man, sir."

"I think Bob's supervisors gave him those documents," Tony said. "The people running the vaccine trial must've pissed the warden off. But he's gonna be attacked by the other side. They'll bring up his claim that vaccines caused Elyse's autism."

Tony and Maria got off the phone with Bob and Donna McCormick late the following night. The story that Bob McCormick told them was disturbing. The good thing was that McCormick took excellent notes. In addition to the names and locations of the women who lost their children, he even had the location of the children's graves in the desert on the US side of the border. He also had "internal" detention center documents that detailed the tragic events.

"I know this man. He's got integrity," Maria said.

"No doubt, but the documents will be critical. What are the odds that this would happen and Bob McCormick would be there? It's an amazing coincidence."

"So was the Abramson case. God wanted us to walk this path."

"We have to go to Sara Donovan with this. We have to get her around the blockade."

Maria put her notepad down. "I think there's something really wrong with the new flu vaccine."

"No kidding."

"You aren't hearing me," she said. "The vaccine shouldn't be that bad. It's killing about five percent of the children. There's no way that that kind of outcome could be acceptable, even to these people."

"I see your point. This is almost insanely reckless."

The results of the trials did in fact cause the researchers real concern. They determined that the experimental adjuvant was too potent. Vaccines require an adjuvant to stimulate the immune system so that the body recognizes the presence of the immunity-building antigen. The levels of the new adjuvant, code name HS-24C, found in the blood of the dead children were too high. Computer simulations determined that the researchers could reduce the amount of HS-24C by seventy-five percent and still produce the desired immune response. This, they reasoned, was good enough to ensure safety. They excluded the cases where the children died as if the horrible events had never happened. The findings they then reported convinced even themselves that the vaccine would be safe. And they were correct. The Mexican flu vaccine that went to market was somewhat safer.

But only somewhat.

CHAPTER 51

"You want me to cover the Macon Three, don't you?" Donovan said into her phone.

"Nope, something else," Tony replied. "We've learned something about the new Mexican flu vaccine. You'll want to see this."

"Look, I still have to run the blockade. Randall Cook's minions are circling like vultures. Internet trolls keep attacking me even though I haven't done a vaccine story in months."

"I'll be in Washington Tuesday morning with Maria. How about some coffee?"

"Maybe it's time to return to coffee. The William Street Coffee House in Alexandria. Tuesday, 8:00 a.m.?"

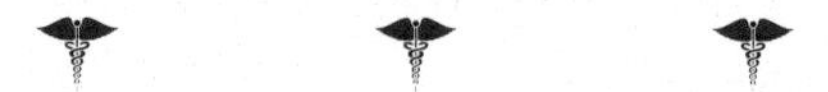

"Hey, Colletti, wanna go on a romantic date to Georgia?" Jack McLeod, the executive director of Fight Back for Autism was sending out word that he had a permit for a rally in front of the Macon City Court for Tuesday afternoon. "Fight Back for Autism is going to Georgia. I need some beef to keep the crowd together. Whaddya say?"

Tony held the phone between his shoulder and chin as he did homework with Sophie. "Thanks for the offer, but I have a prior date in Washington."

"Really? What've you got going on?"

"If I tell you, I'd have to kill you," Tony growled in his best spy-novel imitation.

"Then can you make a detour to Silver Falls Hospital with me?"

"Isn't that where Snyder works? What do *you* have going on?"

"I could tell you, but then I'd have to kill you too."

"I'm spending way too much time in New Jersey." It was ten in the evening, and Tony and McLeod were in a booth at a Turnpike rest stop. "Still beats Moscow."

"Hey, what happened to your forehead?"

"Police work. You know how it goes."

McLeod nodded. "I admire people in your line of work. What's going on?"

"Got some information that I need to get to Sara Donovan. Could be huge."

"Your study?"

Tony put down his cup. "Actually, no. It involves the Mexican flu vaccine. That's all I can say right now."

McLeod stirred his coffee. "Interesting. How's your project going?"

"We're a few weeks from publishing." Tony lowered his voice to a whisper. "We found seventy-five cases."

McLeod pumped his fist in the air. "I knew it! I knew you guys were right."

"Easy. What do you have planned for that gangster Snyder?"

"You're gonna love it!" And when McLeod showed Tony the contents of his car's trunk, they both smiled from ear to ear.

Phil Snyder's cell phone rang as he drove to the office the next morning. It was the hospital security director. "Good morning, Joe. Something wrong?"

"I think that you should use the Spruill Street entrance this morning, Doctor. We have an issue at the main entrance to the staff lot."

"Really? What kind of issue?" As he turned the corner toward the parking lot entrance, Snyder saw for himself. A small crowd of doctors and nurses watched as a huge banner blew gracefully in the breeze just above the garage entrance. It read **"Snyder Is a Pharma Toad—Free the Macon Three!"**

"Tear that thing down!" Snyder screamed into the phone. But he didn't notice the Mid-Atlantic News van driving past him as he pulled in. The crew had already interviewed hospital staff.

"Good morning," Tony slid into a booth across from Sara Donovan. "And why are you grinning like the cat that swallowed the canary? Or are you just happy to see me?"

"Got something here from another network's local that'll warm the cockles of your heart. My producer, Seth, just sent it."

Tony leaned over for a better view of the laptop. "Macon Three Protest Banner at Delaware Hospital"

> *Security staff found an unusual form of protest about the Macon Three vaccine objector controversy this morning. A banner was hung in front of the staff garage entrance. Dr. Phillip Snyder, seen here at a lecture last year in which a journalist was forcibly removed, was the apparent target of the message. Dr. Snyder is regarded as an outspoken critic of the anti-vaccine movement but is often criticized for not disclosing his financial ties to the vaccine industry. Snyder declined comment saying that he was in no way associated with the situation in Macon, Georgia.*

Tony smiled. "Isn't that something!"

"Snyder's a fanatic," Donovan said. "Ever meet him?"

"No. We swim in different tanks. Interesting that vaccine issues are suddenly getting coverage. Even Snyder's conflicts of interest."

"Here, I got you coffee. What happened to your head?"

Tony put a handful of folders on the table. "Little international intrigue. Got pistol-whipped by a couple of gangsters in Moscow a few months back."

Sara laughed then noticed that Tony wasn't laughing. "Are you for real?"

"That's how I got this." Tony took several sheets from a folder. "This paper was written by Dr. Zviad Kokochashvili based on research done by the Soviets in the 1980s. Here's the study in Russian, and here's the independent English translation. This paper is something that vaccine safety advocates have wanted done in the US. It compares health outcomes between Russian children who got the DPT and those who didn't. None of the children in the non-vaccinated group had autism. And many of the vaccinated children did."

"How'd you find this?"

"Dr. Kokochashvili defected to the United States years ago. He has a new identity. He's nervous about releasing the paper, but feels compelled to."

"This all goes that far back?" Sara scanned the paper. "I'd love to interview him."

"I think that he'll allow that . . . eventually. And yes, it seems some in government knew that vaccine injuries included autism."

"And were willing to accept some collateral damage as long as they expanded the vaccine program. Unbelievable."

"The authorities probably deluded themselves into thinking that no one would notice an increase in vaccine injuries. They created the Vaccine Injury Compensation Program, and it's worked well to contain the disaster and remove vaccine injury from public view."

"The Vaccine Court isn't a court. It's a black box."

"The paper we're publishing in a few weeks is the key to that black box."

"Add this story to your project and—wow."

It was Tony's turn to grin. "Now in this folder . . ."

"You have more?"

"The Mexican flu vaccine is not all it's cracked up to be."

Cigarette smoke encircled Calthorpe like a malevolent fog as he stormed around his office. "Nikolai, you mean to say that someone from your own company helped turn Kokochashvili over to the Americans!"

"Apparently so. After weeks of digging through old records we found the name of a retired employee—a Ronald Vincent—who helped him defect."

"Then this Vincent fellow gave you Kokochashvili's new name and location?"

"I dispatched my two specialists to America. They interrogated him at length last night, but he claimed he didn't know the name as the government created the new identity, not us."

Calthorpe slammed his fist on his oak table. "Then re-interrogate him!"

"That is no longer possible. Sadly, he later drowned in his Jacuzzi."

"But Democrats control the Senate," Tony said. "When our paper's published, won't you have enough to hold hearings?"

Senator Parker Smithson listened intently to Tony and Maria. "Maybe, but without the other side, hearings won't get traction. Republicans will just say that I'm anti-business."

"So, you need this to be bipartisan," Tony nodded.

"Yep. Without the other side willing to dance, I'm just handing them an excuse to beat me like a drum." Smithson could see that Tony and Maria were good people. And the research scholar had his complete attention. Maria dressed for maximum impact and looked gorgeous.

Maria smiled. "Senator, how do we get you a Republican dancing partner?"

Smithson sat back in his chair. "None of the Republicans could ever be as lovely a partner as you'd be. There's a scent of Buenos Aires in your accent."

"Help us, Senator. We're just citizens seeking justice. Children are at risk."

"Are you sure that the vaccine program isn't helping more children than it's hurting?"

"There is more that we know. Much more. But we must be careful. People could be hurt."

Smithson rubbed his chin. “I’ve been on Capitol Hill a long time. Survived ’cause I read the cards well. Showing cards too early in the game can be a bad move. I get that.” He put his notepad down. “I’m thinking you should stop by Senator Sampson’s office.”

“But we don’t have an appointment,” Tony said.

“I’ll call Russ. He’ll talk to you. Keep this little call between us.”

Donovan threw the folders on her producer’s desk. “Seth, I got these from Tony Colletti this morning.”

“We’re out of the vaccine business,” Millman said. “I know you like this guy, but we know where this is headed.”

“Seth, read this stuff. I need to go to Tucson, and I need a crew.”

“You know we can’t . . .”

“Just read it.”

Millman called Donovan back within an hour. “Wow!”

“And Maria Contessa-Guevera and Colletti are talking to Parker Smithson right now. He wants to hold hearings, but needs a Republican to step up with him.”

“That won’t be easy. Sara, this scandal is huge—this generation’s Watergate.”

“We have to get around Cook’s people.”

“I’ve taken care of that. I got the powers-that-be to send the pompous bastard to Macon.”

CHAPTER 52

"Randazzo saw Fusco drive through town last night." Tony unzipped his jacket as he entered the office. "We should start surveillance again."

Forceski looked up from his computer. "Chief says we spent a fortune on overtime. Need something more to justify it. Hey, Snyder's at it again. Listen, 'AP Newswire—Japan's Health Ministry reported four deaths from the Mexican flu vaccine.'"

Tony sat down. "Why am I not surprised."

"Ministry Officials suspended the vaccine and are investigating the alleged adverse events. Dr. Phillip Snyder, vaccine industry spokesperson, disagreed with the decision of the Japanese Health Ministry. "The Mexican flu is now pandemic. The Japanese decision is silly."

"Four kids die and this knucklehead calls the Japanese silly?"

The Japanese responded to Snyder's comments with a letter demanding an apology from the United States. The CDC's new director called Snyder after the State Department took the doctor to task. "Hey, pal, who authorized your comment? You know anything about the Japanese?"

Snyder swallowed hard. "Well, no, actually."

"Let me tell you something. They don't do silly. Know what the Japanese minister said to the Secretary? He said we've forgotten that there's a boundary between industry and government. The Secretary had to endure this reprimand because of your insensitivity."

"I'm sorry, Director."

"Some Japanese officials are coming over to study the Vaccine Court program—on my dime. They're interested in it due to the injuries. Maybe this'll smooth the ruffled feathers."

"I'll be happy to call Bob Bangston. I'm sure he'll . . ."

"May I remind you that Bangston doesn't work for you!"

"The people running the trial were callous. It was a horrible situation, horrible. I know these women aren't supposed to be in our country, but their babies died. And the researchers seemed unfazed." Bob McCormick sat across from Sara Donovan as the crew filmed the interview in a Tucson hotel room.

"How so?" Donovan asked.

"I told them that Conchetta Zamora's son died from a seizure last night. You know what the project leader says to me? 'Possible adverse event.' Women grieving on every block, a facility about to go off, and all this cold bastard could say was 'possible adverse event.'"

Later that afternoon Donovan stood over a group of small tombstones in the Sonoran Dessert. "These are the graves of the children who died in vaccine research trials that our government—and Binghampton Pharmaceuticals—claim were a complete success."

"Got it, Sara," said the cameraman.

As Donovan drove south into Mexico, she realized this was the story of her life. Would it ever see the light of day?

"Free the Macon Three!" Free the Macon Three!" Jack McLeod led the rally in front of the Macon City courthouse with a bullhorn. The protestors were getting close to the one hundred foot courthouse boundary that Judge Wetland directed McLeod to observe. Real close.

Inside the building the Macon Three's hearing was about to begin. "ADA Barret is shaking," Newman whispered to Wilson Garrison.

"Looks like a nice kid. Bet they didn't mention this kinda case in law school."

"All rise!" the court officer barked. "Macon City Court's now in session. Honorable William Wetland presiding."

"Free the Macon Three!" could be heard through the window. Judge Wetland pounded the gavel. "Sit yourselves down. We'll endure the noise and administer justice dispassionately. Mr. Barret, what have you?"

"Your Honor," the young lawyer said nervously, "we filed a misdemeanor complaint against Mr. Herman Tyler, Mrs. Phyllis Twiggs, and Miss Mary Burdette alleging that they willfully violated the Public Health Code by failing to have their children immunized. The People charge them with misdemeanor child endangerment."

The judge rubbed his chin. "Mr. Newman, welcome back to Georgia."

"Thank you, Your Honor."

"Shall we read the petitions?"

"We've been served, Your Honor. We waive the readings."

"Very well. How do your clients plead?"

"Not guilty, Your Honor." The three defendants nodded their heads in agreement.

"You are aware that your clients made public statements admitting they have not complied with the immunization requirement."

"Acknowledged, Your Honor. I assure you our clients intended no disrespect for the laws of Georgia. We request a trial before Your Honor to demonstrate their innocence."

"Fine. I'm adjourning 'til next Monday. Remand's continued unless the very reasonable bail is posted. We're adjourned." The gavel's sound competed with the noise from outside. "Free the Macon Three! Free the Macon Three!"

"It's a miracle," Veronica Fournier said joyfully. "Evan says he likes Elvis. All those years without speech. I knew Evan had thoughts and feelings. He just couldn't express them." Anne Colletti watched the teenager work his assistive communication device at the kitchen table, flapping his hands with excitement. *"Elvis rock."* He typed.

Anne's eyes misted. "I'm amazed. Evan, dear, what's your favorite TV show?"

"Gleep."

"He means *Glee*," his mother laughed.

"This machine has done more for Evan than that psychiatrist ever did," Anne said.

"No, like psikiatrust."

"That's interesting," Veronica said. "We don't see him anymore, Evan."

"No like Portnoy. No see Portnoy."

"Why, Evan?" Anne asked.

"He wore a mask and hurt me."

"Randall!" Snyder shouted into his phone and paced around his office.

"Phillip, don't start."

"This is out of control. You guys are turning these people into heroes."

"What do you mean?"

"SNN's local interviewed Clyde King, treated him like some sort of expert."

"King interviewed Tyler in jail. Everyone was talking about it. Front page news."

"That's my point, you idiot!"

"The network is sending me down there. We'll have more balanced reporting soon."

"You'd better get some balance down there. Did ya read some the signs these protestors are holding. 'Herman Tyler, Man of Truth,' 'Vaccines Cause Autism.'"

"I gotta kick out of the one that said 'Jail Snyder Instead.'"

"Get down there!"

"Sara," Seth Millman told her, "get home now."

Sara held her cell phone closer to her ear. "We're an hour from the border. Mexico's freaked out by the drug cartels." The crew drove past another man carrying a rifle. "We're freaked out too."

"We have a window of opportunity. Cook and his girls' softball team are going to Macon for Monday's vaccine trial of the century."

"YES!" she shouted. "We interviewed Connie Zamora. Gut-wrenching."

"We'll do the editing over the weekend—at my house."

"You have studio equipment in your . . ."

"In my basement," he interrupted. "What else would an old studio rat have in his house? We can work it through there and punch it out for Monday's *Nightly News*."

"I could kiss you. You're risking your career, you know."

"So are you."

"We're supposed to. Remember Morrow—telling the truth about smoking, as he smoked? That's supposed to be us." A bullet ricocheted off the hood of the car. "Gotta go."

Clyde King walked through a crowd of protestors in Rosa Parks Park across from the courthouse. Jack McLeod shook his hand. "Hey, Clyde, what do you think?"

"I'm amazed you weren't arrested. These boys don't like Northerners, you know."

McLeod laughed. "You gonna be here Monday?"

"Wouldn't miss it for the world. Right now, I'm going to DC. Snyder's lecturing on the importance of vaccines and bestowing some sort of Good Journalist Award on Lance Reed."

"The Snyder-Reed show—could be wild," McLeod chuckled. "But be careful."

"Tony, please tell me that Evan Fournier is no longer seeing this ghoul." Forceski and Eddie Mendoza sat at the conference table and looked grim.

"Anne spoke to Veronica after the shooting last summer and she cut him loose. But he's still got other patients."

Mendoza looked through Fusco's folder. "Why would Portnoy stop? These guys never do until people like us stop them."

"And believe me, we're stoppin' them, Eddie," Forceski said.

Chief Lonnegan walked in. "What's up? You guys look like you've been hit by lightning."

Forceski folded his arms. "Tell 'em, Tony."

"Chief, Evan Fournier's been learning to communicate on an assistive communication device. Amazing to see this kid connect for the first time. Anne visited him this afternoon, and the topic of his former treating psychiatrist came up. Evan typed this. Anne, ever a cop's wife, hooked up a printer." Tony dropped the printout on the table.

Lonnegan read the document aloud: "No like Portnoy. No see Portnoy. He wore a mask and hurt me." then walked over to the window. "This is the guy who drugged him up so bad last summer?"

Tony nodded. "Portnoy's the guy wearing the mask on the computer disks," Tony said. "That's why Slag Fusco's in Winston all the time."

Lonnegan ran a hand through his hair. "You know, I've seen a lot in my time. Seen people killed by drunk drivers. Found a kid who hung himself in his basement. I still see Johnny Fournier lying lifeless on that blanket. I had to tell his mom."

"Anne got Veronica to dump Portnoy after that incident," Tony reminded him.

"But you know what? Nothing in my career prepared me for what gets unleashed on you when you got a disabled kid to protect. A kid who can't protect himself, who can't even talk. This monster never figured that Evan would communicate what he'd been through. But he figured wrong." Everyone nodded. "Let's go get some justice for this kid."

CHAPTER 53

"This is the best pancake breakfast fund-raiser in all Vermont." Bennington's mayor Hank Peters declared for the benefit of the community's television crew. "Spring's here. Whole town smells like maple syrup."

Reverend Jeffries welcomed congregants and other townspeople into his church's community room. "The Health Department's offering free Mexican flu shots in the coat room. Enjoy your breakfast and support the senior center."

It was early spring in small-town America, and all was well. At least until an elderly man suffered a seizure while carrying pancakes to a lunch table. While an aide cleaned up the spill, Peters comforted the man as the crew filmed. "Call 911!" he shouted.

Across the room a young girl cried out, "I can't move my legs!" The crew continued to film as the girl was surrounded by panicked friends.

An older woman emerged shaking from the coatroom. "My goodness, I feel so dizzy."

"They all just got the flu shot." Reverend Jeffries said.

Peters walked to the coatroom. "Get the doctor out here!" A white-coated man rushed out to attend to the stricken people. The community television station manager poked a microphone into his face. "Doctor, are the vaccines causing this?"

He shoved the microphone aside. "Not now, lady. Vaccines don't do this!"

"We should shut this thing down," Peters said. "No more shots today."

"You've no authority!" the doctor replied. "Only a health official can terminate a . . ."

Peters glared at the doctor. "You seeing what I'm seeing here, fella? This thing's over!"

"My mother!" somebody yelled from the coatroom.

"Only a public health official can . . ."

"Doctor, this is over," Reverend Jeffries interrupted. "There'll be no more immunizations in my church today." And the cameras rolled.

"Donovan waited in the Tucson Airport for her flight to Washington. "Since when does Vermont make news?" she asked herself. Millman had emailed a link to SNN New England. "The Vermont Health Department's Free Mexican Flu Vaccine Program is suddenly the center of controversy. A senior citizen is dead, and several others are in serious condition . . ."

The Mexican flu vaccine had just become a national story. Then she read an email from Dr. Washington: "Sara, This time it happened on camera. They're all going to hell now. We have to stop this insanity. R.W."

Watching the media coverage of the Bennington incident, Zvi wondered what was wrong with this vaccine. He logged into the FDA website and began digging into the reams of documents filed on the study. It was tedious work, and he was denied access to much of the material as he wasn't involved in the approval process. Zvi found a list of the ingredients. The usual suspects were there . . . mercury at 12 mcg and aluminum at 50 mcg. That was expected. Then he came across HS-24-C.

What was *that*?

Clyde King surveyed the Georgetown lecture hall where the lecture sponsored by Every Child Safe for School was about to start. Dr. Phillip Snyder was going to give his usual chat and present Lance Reed with a "Vaccine Hero Journalist Award."

King waved to a friend who was sitting in front. The friend responded by holding up a small video camera. "I'm here for the rematch, guys," he thought. He gave his friend a thumbs-up and took a seat in front along the center aisle to make sure that Snyder, and everyone else, had a good view when he was dragged out. There was no reason to sit mid-row and risk being dragged painfully over chairs and attendees when the goon squad showed up.

Clyde King was, after all, a class act.

Snyder entered to polite applause and immediately blasted the anti-vaccine movement. "The Omnibus Autism Proceedings repudiated the years of damage that Bryce Ramsey's done to the vaccine program. The man who saved the day was investigative journalist, Lance Reed."

Reed took the podium. "I'm honored to be here with all of you to talk about the fraud perpetrated by Bryce Ramsey."

King watched Reed carefully. There was an odd, remote quality about the man. While the audience seemed to agree with Reed, they weren't connecting with him, just smatterings of light applause. The dry twenty-minute commentary left an odd feeling in the room.

Snyder then spoke for another few minutes about the need to reform vaccine exemption laws around the country. "The record of safety that the vaccine industry has established is clear and convincing. It is time to renew confidence in the public health establishment and enforce vaccine mandates."

The first few questions were softballs. Then something remarkable happened. A female pediatrician stood up. "I'm concerned that we bear more responsibility for the public's lack of confidence in vaccines than we're acknowledging here. Frankly, we have put an overly negative spin on legitimate parental concerns. Have any of us considered what our response would be if parents questioned us about other drugs?"

Lance Reed fired back. "Are you saying that you believe Ramsey?"

"I'm talking about the parents of my patients. We should be listening to them." The audience applauded with enthusiasm.

"But those concerns are based upon a deceptive campaign by people with an anti-vaccine agenda," Snyder responded. "It's our job to fix wrong thinking."

Another doctor stood up. "I'm sick of answering endless vaccine safety questions. I can't be spending valuable time dealing with this." Some applauded.

"I have a suggestion that could be helpful," volunteered another member of the audience. "Why don't you invite Ramsey here for a debate, and end this thing once and for all. Scientific consensus is with us. We haven't caused the increase in autism. We just need to make our case."

"I won't take the stage with that charlatan!" Snyder said.

"Debate a criminal?" Reed yelled.

King rose to his feet. "I'm Clyde King. Dr. Snyder, I have a question."

"Oh, it's *you*!" Snyder hissed.

"By now I'm sure that you're aware of the incident in Vermont earlier today where a group of people suffered . . ."

"It wasn't the vaccines," Snyder's palm slammed against the podium. "Vaccines don't cause seizures. Next question."

"I'm sorry, but it's generally agreed that they do," King went on. "Seizures and encephalopathy are acknowledged vaccine injuries. They're on the table of injuries that the National Vaccine Injury Compensation Program uses."

A man seated behind King interrupted. "There's a national compensation program for vaccine injuries? What're you talking about?"

"There is, indeed."

"I want this man removed!" Snyder yelled. "He's anti-vaccine!"

"Dr. Snyder, I am NOT anti-vaccine. I'm a journalist. I've focused on vaccine safety, and I believe that the vaccine program is important."

"You're no journalist," Reed yelled out. "You're just seeking the attention of fawning women."

"I have no idea what you're talking about. And, for the record, I've never lied about my identity when I interview people—as you have.

I've never used deception to get information—as you have. I've always said my name and asked my questions. That's what I'm doing now."

"Security! Security!" Snyder called out, "remove this man. He's disrupting our lecture."

"Dr. Snyder, you were critical of the decision of the Japanese government to suspend the Mexican flu vaccine program. Given today's events, do you feel that the Mexican flu vaccine should be suspended until we have a better understanding of the injuries?"

A man in a blue jacket grabbed King's arm. "Sir, you need to leave."

"I want an answer to my question."

"Sir, you need to leave."

"Drag the rat out!" Reed shouted.

A doctor stood up. "This is outrageous! Why're we removing this man?"

"Throw him out!" someone yelled.

"Let him ask his question!" someone in the back of the room answered. "We're a teaching institution."

"Throw the bloody bastard out!" Reed was absolutely enraged. The audience became hushed as it focused on how frightening Reed was.

"What's wrong with you?" someone called out.

"We're leaving," said a doctor in the front of the hall.

Another security guard grabbed King around the neck and pulled him out of his chair. The audience began to boo, and some left their seats as the guards pulled King up the aisle. When King resisted, they punched and kicked him.

Snyder stood at the podium. "We have to give Mr. Reed his award."

"Please tell me some good news, Nikolai." Sitting alone in his oak-paneled office, Calthorpe held the phone against his ear.

"One document taken by my employees from Mr. Vincent's files mentions a CDC official named Victoria Glazer. However, we've been unable to locate her."

"Find this woman. We need to stop the cycle of negative events."

"I know. Our stock has plummeted and we didn't even manufacture this vaccine. The entire industry is in peril."

"Find this woman, Nikolai." Calthorpe slammed down the receiver and went back to watching the day's events unfold. The Vermont disaster and the assault on the journalist were all over the Internet. "The fall of the vaccine empire has gone viral," he thought ironically.

The SNN *Nightly News* began with the Clyde King story. "Is our public health establishment beyond question?" the anchor said. "You might not think so, but we ask you to look at the following report and ask yourself that question. We take no position on the vaccine-autism controversy debated in this lecture, but the events that unfolded in this Georgetown lecture hall have stunned that university. We warn you that what follows are violent images."

The assault played again before the camera cut to Clyde King, bruised and battered, in a studio chair. "I was just doing my job. Given what happened in Vermont and in Japan, I felt it necessary to ask Dr. Snyder about suspending this vaccine."

Viewers were shown excerpts of the Bennington incident followed by the Georgetown lecture, with Reed unhinged, doctors arguing and walking out, and Snyder looking like a fool.

The images were now all over the planet. It took all of Calthorpe's self-restraint to keep from throwing his laptop against the wall. "You idiots have blown up everything I've won for you."

CHAPTER 54

Randall Cook seethed as he watched the assembled crowd in the park across from the courthouse. He had been dispatched to Macon to finally get balanced reporting on the vaccine objectors, but nothing he encountered made that assignment remotely possible.

Jack McLeod fired up the crowd in advance of an appearance by Macon mayor Sam Sanders. "Today we express ourselves peacefully in support of our fellow freedom seekers in the court across the street."

The crowd cheered. "Free the Macon Three, Free the Macon Three."

"Mayor Sam Sanders wants to speak to you." McLeod passed the bullhorn to the mayor.

"Welcome to Rosa Parks Park, named for a person who also fought for freedom. I support good public health policy. And I also support your right to make your own health choices." The crowd applauded and broke into a chant of "Sammy! Sammy! Sammy!"

"Peaceful civil protest is part of our democracy. Please stop for lunch downtown and visit our wonderful shops and stores."

"Sammy! Sammy! Sammy!"

"Wasn't the mayor of a town like this supposed to be named Buford or something?" Cook sneered at his female producer.

"You should interview him," she replied.

Cook glared at her as his cell phone rang. It was Snyder—again. "Finally get some reasonable coverage of this BS?"

"Not really, Phil. So far everything is pro–Macon Three. Even the mayor came down in support."

"What? An elected official is supporting these . . ."

Thunderous applause and cheering drowned out Snyder's call. Clyde King walked through the crowd, greeted as though he were a rock star. The other networks were filming King greeting protestors, so Cook's crew started as well. All Snyder heard as the call ended was "Clyde King! Clyde King! Clyde King!"

Herb Newman and Wilson Garrison were in a pitched battle with a seasoned assistant district attorney before Judge Wetland.

"Your Honor," Newman pointed at the Georgia Public Health Code sitting on the table in front of Tyler, Twiggs, and Burdette. "There's no need to mandate vaccination. Simply stated, no public health emergency compels it."

"The state has required vaccinations for decades, Your Honor," ADA Campbell said. "It is the expectation that people will comply for the greater good, to protect public health."

"Your Honor," Newman countered, "in *Jacobson v Massachusetts*, the Supreme Court ruled that a state could mandate vaccinations in a time of plague involving an airborne, deadly disease. However, the Court ruled that if a person chose not to vaccinate, the sanction was a $5.00 fine—not criminal charges. *Jacobson* didn't push the mandate to the extent that the People are here."

"Other decisions since *Jacobson* have extended state executive authority to enforce vaccine mandates," Campbell replied. "Mr. Newman's aware of this and . . ."

"None have been tested before the Supreme Court, Your Honor," Newman interrupted. "They're not the law of the land. In fact, decisions since *Jacobson* establish a person's right to bodily autonomy. A person should not be sanctioned for choosing not to take a drug or making that decision for their child."

"Your Honor," Campbell said, "the law is not on trial—the defendants are. The law's the law, and these people broke it."

"The way the People are enforcing the law is the precise issue," Newman argued, "Fine, yes. Crime, no. Mr. Garrison has the Public Health Code in front of him, Your Honor. The preamble is instructive."

Garrison rose and cleared his throat. "The purpose of this act is to respond to public health emergencies . . ."

Clyde King took notes. "This is a debate the country needs to hear," he thought.

Chief Lonnegan's conference room was packed with probation officers, district attorney investigators, and members of the Winston police force. If Slag Fusco kept to his usual pattern, he would drop by the office of psychiatrist Irving Portnoy later that evening.

Forceski began describing the tactical plan. "The warrants are signed. Assuming Slag shows, we're good to go. You have the photos of Portnoy and Fusco in front of you. Target residence is 42 Hudson View Terrace." Forceski showed the home on the chief's wide-screen television via Google Earth. "It's a bang-crash operation—blow in the doors and rush in. Uniforms circle the home and cut off any escape attempt. We aren't taking any crap."

"Teams are me and Mendoza, Colletti and Preston from probation." Tony nodded to Preston. "Multiple teams are needed because the men may be anywhere in separate parts of this old Victorian. Two men on each perp, we don't want people bunching and taking friendly fire if it jumps ugly. It's likely that the arrests will go down in the basement office area. That's in the rear of the house. We got the office layout, but we don't know about the rest of the place. Town building records are a mess."

"The team going through the front door is four strong. Chavez and Pooch, Gomez and Brown from probation. Chavez and Gomez hold floor one and Pooch and Brown head up to floor two. Uniforms take the front porch and yard and fill in as necessary. We'll be on the Winston radio frequency, but use the King's English. Probation people don't use police codes."

"Don't even try to teach them to us," Mendoza chuckled.

"Eddie," Forceski said, "why don't you tell us about Fusco."

"Sure. John 'Slag' Fusco, forty-six, should never have been sentenced to probation, but he got the deal when it became obvious that the victim would be too traumatized to testify against him. Fusco is a violent, sadistic, sociopathic sex offender."

"Great. He's Caligula," Randazzo whispered to Tony.

"Pay attention," Tony whispered back. "Every detail's important."

"Fusco is likely the one who'll resist and may be armed," Mendoza noted." He's going away for a long time. This kind of man, facing that kind of deal, could do anything."

"We don't know Portnoy," Forceski said. "No wife. No kids. Moved down from Ithaca two years ago and set up shop. Believe it or not, he's some big shot on a committee that's revising something called the *DSM-5* for the American Psychiatric Association. I'm betting he's been sexually abusing developmentally disabled children for years."

"There are ritualistic components to his behavior on the videos," Mendoza added. "Guy wears superhero masks. Part of it is to hide his face but part of it is just sick."

"As if sexually abusing defenseless kids wasn't sick enough," Lonnegan interjected.

"So, take nothing for granted," Forceski said. "Everybody wears body armor. Everybody packs backups. This could get ugly, people."

"Real ugly." Tony nodded.

"Oh," Forceski remembered. "Probation takes Fusco. We get the shrink. But cuffs are cuffs—no turf stuff. Randazzo and Molinari will drive the hospital cars with crash bags, packed and ready. If someone gets shot or stabbed, we aren't waiting around bleeding out in this haunted freakin' Victorian. After the house is cleared, Danny and the DA investigators head in with computer forensic equipment."

⚕ ⚕ ⚕

"Hey, Detective," probation officer Preston said. "I got your back tonight."

"Same here. Call me Tony." His cell phone rang as Chavez was bringing in coffee. It was Laura Melendez. "Maria just called. 'Autism by Any Other Name' is up on the journal's website and in print tomorrow. We're published authors, Sluggo."

"That's great. None of this happens without you. You're the best."

"Your mother raised a good kid, Anthony. Talk later."

Tony walked over to Lonnegan and Forceski. "Guys, paper's published. We did it."

"You did it, bro." Forceski said. "Maybe something'll change now."

Lonnegan smiled "Glen's right. "I hope people listen."

"What did Caesar say?" Tony said. "The die is cast."

CHAPTER 55

Donovan and Millman plowed into the SNN production room at 11:00 a.m., prepared to go to war for their story on the Mexican flu vaccine trial. "Got something powerful on the Mexican flu vaccine," Donovan said to Tom Farr, the news division chief. "You'll want to see this."

Farr lifted his earphones to hear Donovan better. "We're cutting to Mayor Peters now. Should be on center screen in ten seconds."

Millman walked gingerly over the wires on the floor of the studio switching room. "The mayor? We've worked all weekend and . . ."

"You know," Farr interrupted, "the chunky mayor from Bennington."

The feed from SNN New England opened up on the main screen to show the mayor behind a podium with the town seal. "On Saturday morning, we held a pancake breakfast fund-raiser for our senior center in the Presbyterian Church hall. As they do every year, the State Health Department offered free flu shots to the community. It was a day none of us will ever forget. One of our beloved neighbors is gone, and several others are still suffering.

"State officials have said all sorts of things over the past coupla' days. Theories ranging from something called hantavirus, Legionnaire's disease, food poisoning, mold toxins, whatever. Last night, a head-shrinker from Montpelier called it a stress-induced psychiatric event. How damn stressful can a pancake breakfast be? This is what we're hearing from those in the know."

"So let's get real. I was there. Minister Jeffries was there. Dozens of sober and respectable Bennington residents were there too. We all saw what happened. Our neighbors were injured by flu vaccines that they received just minutes before. I've asked our town attorney to look into what can be done. I'm told that the families can't sue the drug company, can't sue the Health Department, and can't sue the doctor. They have to sue the Secretary of Health and Human Services, a lady who has lunch with the president of the United States. This just isn't right. I'm outraged and I want a full independent investigation of what happened to my neighbors. I call on Congress to dig into this can of worms and figure out what can be done."

"Whoo-hoo! Go, chunky mayor!" Donovan cheered.

Seth Millman had a smile as big as his face and handed Farr the disk. "Now watch this!"

Senator Parker Smithson was in his office watching coverage of the Macon Three and the Vermont mayor. "Critical mass," he said to himself as he dialed his chief of staff. "Charles, can we reach out to that lawyer who was publishing the paper on the vaccine compensation program?"

"Ah, Maria Contessa-Guevera. She was gorgeous, sir."

"Let's talk to her. She can help us set up panels and such. I have a sense she knows where the bodies are buried." Smithson rocked in his chair. "And, hey, if the mayor of Bennington wants hearings, we'd better damn well have hearings." He hung up and dialed Russell Sampson's cell phone.

"You seeing this, Senator?" Sampson began.

"Yep. It's time."

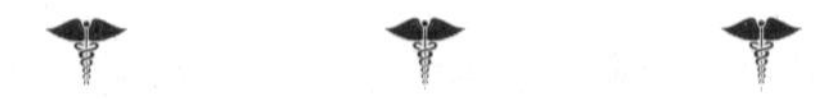

The judge found the Macon Three guilty of child endangerment, then adjourned the case for thirty days for a presentence investigation.

"I'm willing to lower the bail," he told the defendants. "I've no reason to believe that you will evade future proceedings."

Newman looked at the three defendants, who were now holding hands. "Your Honor, may we have a moment to speak with our clients?"

"Certainly."

"People, we support you one hundred percent." Newman nodded grimly. "You've been inside for several days now. Your families need you. Judge Wetland may have found you guilty, but he's a reasonable and honorable man. He knows you're not criminals and you're acting on principle." Newman flashed an encouraging smile.

"We talked," Tyler said, "we understood it could go this way."

"We'll file an appeal to Superior Court," Garrison said.

"Our arguments are ready and Maria's been gathering amicus briefs," Newman added.

"Thank you both so much," Tyler said. "I have asked the ladies to accept release."

"We will stand together through every proceeding," Twiggs said. Burdette nodded in agreement.

Tyler clenched his jaw. "However, I cannot and I'm staying in jail. I got a son to protect. I lost my wife and I have a nephew with autism. He's never received justice. I saw what happened in the autism hearings. This has to stop. Someone has to stand up for my nephew and for your son too, Mr. Newman. Someone has to. So, where I sleep at night is really of no consequence. I say we stand up together, right here."

Newman nodded and rose. "We're ready, Your Honor."

Word of Judge Wetland's decision made its way through the crowd. People lit candles. The chants, "Free the Macon Three," resumed, this time sounding more like gospel hymns. All the TV crews, even Randall Cook's, started filming.

Newman and Garrison crossed the street to a small rise just past the park entrance. Jack McLeod put his arm around Newman's shoulder.

"You gonna make a statement?" Newman nodded, and McLeod handed him the bullhorn.

"May I have your attention?" The crowd grew silent, and the cameras gathered around him. "Our clients want to express their profound appreciation for your support of their principled stand for justice. They also want to express appreciation for the serious consideration that Judge Wetland gave them today although he did find them guilty of child endangerment." Newman held up a hand to silence the smattering of boos. "Further, they acknowledge that the original aspirations of the vaccine program were honorable. However, the Macon Three remain resolute. We're filing an appeal tomorrow morning in the Georgia Superior Court, Fourth Circuit, seeking to have these convictions overturned." The crowd burst into applause, and chants of "Free the Macon Three" resumed.

"Phyllis Twiggs and Mary Burdette have posted bail and will be released shortly. However, Herman Tyler has declined to post bail and asked me to read the following: "Friends, I appreciate your support. I resolved to remain in custody. Last year I lost my wife to a bad drug and I have a nephew who has autism because of a vaccine injury. My nephew serves a type of incarceration that he can never be released from. I cannot be free until justice is delivered to all those injured and until all our children are free from the imposition of drugs we do not choose to take. I stand with him and with all of you. We all stand together, right here. Signed, Herman Tyler."

And the crowd stood together in silence.

CHAPTER 56

Phillip Snyder cursed at the television as he switched between networks—and between bouts of depression and rage. Although it was early afternoon, he was already woozy from whiskey when he connected to Calthorpe in his office.

"Phillip," Calthorpe sighed, "all we can do for now is to try to work our connections until this blows over."

"Is anybody responding to our pitches?"

"Yes, but only to a degree. Most stories still lead with positive references to vaccines. But the larger story is now driven by events on the ground, which we don't have dominion over. So we still end up with reports like the one about Vermont and these objectors."

"Our blogs are now dominated by these people," Snyder moaned. "Hundreds of negative comments an hour. It's like a tidal wave."

"For now, stay away from the media. Go play golf. This will pass. We'll again dominate the field once it does." Calthorpe exhaled smoke. "Remember how things looked very bleak after the Whittaker case? We responded with enormous power and subtlety. Hardly anyone now recalls the affair. We can do it again."

Even as Calthorpe hung up the phone, he knew that his clients were now in desperate shape. Arrogance and greed had pushed them to the edge of disaster. There was no reason to overdramatize the threat of the Mexican flu and pump out an unsafe vaccine. There was no reason to brutalize meddlesome journalists or threaten the small number of people who refused vaccines. But his clients had, and in the blink of an eye, placed everything in peril.

As Russell Sampson watched the press coverage from Macon, the question his wife asked months ago came back to him: "Why did we come to Washington?" And as he looked at the photographs of his children, he realized what his answer ought to have been: "To make the country better for them." He called Diana. "What time can you and the kids get here?"

"I can be there with the girls by 4:00."

"Diana," he said firmly, "I want Jordan here too."

Donovan called Dr. Washington. "Watch our network tonight."

"Might be tough. I'm working in the top-secret autism treatment center," Washington chuckled.

"Find a way. You'll want to see this."

"There's a TV in the waiting room."

"Turn it on. Let all your patients and their families watch too."

Donovan overcame Randall Cook's efforts to scuttle her flu vaccine trial story. The network's law division was pounded with phone calls from pro-vaccine not-for-profits, the American Academy of Pediatrics, and other public health officials imploring SNN not to run it. The legal staff sided with Donovan and Millman because the Vermont and Macon situations changed everything. The flu trial story was going to run.

Then Charles Fontaine and four other lawyers showed up and demanded a meeting.

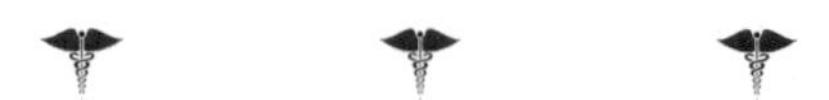

Tony leaned against his desk, checked his gun, and put it back in his shoulder holster. He saw that Forceski was doing the same thing.

He called Anne. "Gonna be late tonight. Looks like we're moving on Portnoy and Fusco."

"Be careful," Anne said. "You have me and the kids. Remember that."

"I love you."

"I love you too."

His family in tow, Senator Russell Sampson entered the conference room and took to the podium. Diana and his daughters formed a supportive ring around Jordan to keep him from running out of the room. Although Jordan was tolerating the room packed with reporters and film crews, Diana knew he couldn't for too long.

"Good afternoon," Sampson began. "I've called this press conference for two reasons. The first is that after consultation with the Senate leadership, I've agreed to co-chair hearings of the HELP Committee with Senator Parker Smithson, my colleague from Iowa." He paused when Jordan suddenly yelled out, jumped up and down, and flapped his arms. "The purpose of the hearings," the senator resumed, "will be to investigate our national vaccine program and the vaccine industry." Sampson paused again as Diana prevented Jordan from leaving the room. "These hearings will be fair and balanced. All of us support the concept of safe and effective vaccines."

Sampson looked around the room. "And now the second reason: last year, my son, Jordan, suffered a seizure after the administration of certain vaccines. He lost the ability to talk, to smile, even to play. He went from being a precocious, affectionate, social child to one who seemed lost. It's obvious to all of you that it's a struggle for Jordan to be here in this busy room with all the cameras and distractions. But he's doing his best, and we are reconnecting with him a little more every day." The photographers clicked photographs of Diana gently comforting the boy.

"Every day is a challenge for us. There will be many more challenging days to come because Jordan has autism. And we love him. We want his life, the good days and the bad days, to serve a greater purpose. My family has always been about service. And so it will be for Jordan Sampson."

Sampson looked around the room. "As you are aware, there has been a raging controversy about whether vaccines cause autism. Though all of you know about this controversy, most of you have been unwilling to cover it. We realize that vaccines are the cornerstone of public health policy. However, many reasonable people have concerns about whether vaccines cause autism and whether vaccines are as safe as they can or could be. As a nation, we've been afraid to talk about this issue openly because we were afraid of where the conversation would lead. Important questions about the health of our children should not be silenced by fear."

Sara Donovan emailed the video of the Sampson press conference to Seth Millman with the heading, "PLAY THIS NOW FOR FONTAINE!" Millman and most of the legal division were in a meeting with Charles Fontaine, who was trying to strong-arm the network's lawyers into cancelling Donovan's piece on the nightly news, now only forty-five minutes away. "I'm advised that we all need to see this, Mr. Fontaine."

Millman started the video on his laptop. Fontaine and his lawyers watched Senator Sampson's press conference in stunned silence. When it ended, Fontaine packed his papers in his briefcase. "Have a good evening, Seth," he said from the door. "See you around."

Zvi called Newman, who was having dinner in the Razorbacks Sport Bar in downtown Macon. With him were McLeod, Garrison, and a group from the demonstration who now referred to themselves as the "Rally Monkeys." Zvi could barely hear Newman shouting over the background noise.

"Herb," Zvi said, "they did something to the adjuvant in the Mexican flu vaccine."

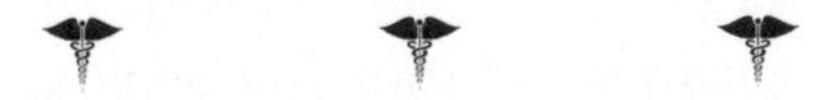

Snyder saw the Sampson press conference and began drinking more whiskey. "Vaccines don't cause autism, idiot!" He yelled at the screen before telephoning Calthorpe.

"Phillip," Calthorpe said once he heard the slurred voice, "please, not now." The line went dead.

Snyder then called Bangston at a bar on New York Avenue. "This senator's going down, Bobby! We're going to wreck this idiot."

"Phil!" Bangston shouted back. "There's gonna be hearings. Did you get that? They're coming after us now. We're in trouble."

"We're . . . we're gonna blow them to pieces!"

"How do you figure that?" Bangston snapped back. The other people in the bar were annoyed, but he was already too drunk to care.

"We have the science, Bob. We've always had the science."

"We do? Really? Have you read our science, Phil? Or did you just read the press releases you put out."

"We have paper after paper!" Snyder insisted, not really listening.

"You've got population studies that show no association. Know why? You excluded people with autism! You paid for a study where a blood draw 'proved' the measles vaccine didn't cause autism. You really read this crap?"

"These people are fringe whackos and nut jobs and . . ."

"And they're holding hearings because your stupid pals got greedy!"

"They have nothing!"

"Yeah?" Bangston swayed on his barstool and felt sick. "And our best study was done by a drunken Viking who's now a fleeing felon. How do you plan to explain that to the United States Senate?"

"Oh," Snyder said triumphantly, "I'm not gonna testify. I'm just an industry spokesman."

Donovan and Millman paced nervously as they watched SNN's *Nightly News* begin with the anchor introducing "the remarkable press conference held by Senator Russell Sampson late this afternoon." The lead-in shot was the South Tucson Detention Center. "Are the Smithson-Sampson hearings necessary? This story from our award-winning investigative journalist, Sara Donovan, strongly suggests so . . ."

"Here we go," Donovan said.

CHAPTER 57

"Feels like I'm back in Iraq," probation officer Preston said to Tony.

Tony slowly turned the police cruiser onto Highview Terrace. "They have haunted Victorians over there?"

"I mean the tension. We did a lot of stuff at night there too."

The men parked their cars in the middle of the street, emergency lights off, doors open, effectively blocking traffic. Preston carried the battering ram for the back door, and Chavez's team brought theirs to the front porch. Winston police and probation officers quietly surrounded the house. Forceski made sure everyone was in place when he clicked the radio. "Ready?"

"Ready." Chavez answered.

"Three, two, one, go," Forceski whispered.

SNN showed Robert McCormick sitting across from Sara Donovan in a hotel room. "Their babies died. And the researchers seemed unfazed."

"How so?"

"I told them that Conchetta Zamora's son died from a seizure last night. You know what the project leader says to me? 'Possible adverse event.' Women grieving on every block, a facility about to go off, and all this cold bastard could say was 'possible adverse event.'"

The footage shifted to Donovan walking in front of a row of detention cells. "A facility administrator, who has requested anonymity, said that he called superiors in Washington to ask them to pressure the CDC to shut the trials down. But the officials insisted the trials continue and that the results were within expectations."

The small tombstones in the dessert were shown as McCormick spoke. "The next day, we took the babies out to the cemetery out in the desert and buried them. I know they took the women back to Mexico, and I heard they gave them some money."

Donovan stood over the graves. "The six children who died were born here. They were Americans." A view of the graveyard in the vast desert filled the screen. "Despite the deaths, the trials were pronounced a success and the Mexican flu vaccine went to market."

Conchetta Zamora walked down a dusty road in the middle of her village. "She doesn't understand why the researchers didn't stop after the first babies died," Donovan said. Zamora's words, translated into English, appeared on the bottom of the screen. "These people felt we were less than human. We thought they were helping our children, but they lied. They are all liars."

The story returned to Donovan in front of the US Capitol. "SNN has requested an interview with Binghampton Pharmaceuticals to discuss the vaccine trials but company officials have declined. Federal, state, and local law enforcement investigations have been launched into the Tucson tragedy. The Senate starts hearings next week on an industry that critics say has lost all sense of accountability."

Blam! Blam! The back door blew in on the second punch, and the four men poured into Portnoy's waiting room. "Police! Search warrant! Police! Everyone down!"

But there was no one there.

The men could hear Chavez and his group go through the upstairs door.

"We go right," Tony said.

"We go left." Both doors off the waiting room were locked. Preston readied the battering ram as Forceski kicked his door down. Tony and Preston shattered theirs and rushed through. Fusco stood behind an examination table, holding a semiautomatic. His eyes darted back and forth between the two officers.

"Police! Put the gun down!" Tony yelled.

Wearing a robe and a mask, Portnoy stood behind his desk, pointing a revolver against his temple.

"Drop the gun!" Forceski shouted.

"Oh, this is freaky," Mendoza said.

Portnoy's hands shook. "You think I'm a monster, don't you? I'm not. I'm a diagnostician."

"Fine." Mendoza said. "Drop the gun."

"I have the power to decide who gets labeled. Watch."

"No!" Forceski yelled.

Portnoy pulled the trigger. Most of his brains erupted out of the other side of his head. His body convulsed as it fell to the floor.

At the sound of the shot, Fusco began shooting. "Die, you bastards!" The officers returned fire, and Fusco's face exploded in a shower of blood. He slumped forward onto the examination table, and then slid to the floor.

Preston had been hit in his chest and his neck, Tony just below the right side of his vest.

Officers ran franticly through the waiting room, guns drawn. Tony dragged Preston through the shattered door, keeping pressure on his neck wound with a blood-soaked paper towel roll. The Kevlar vest stopped the round to the chest, but the other left a horrible wound to the base of Preston's neck.

"NO!" Forceski shouted as he moved to aid the men.

Tony staggered toward the waiting room door, dripping blood. "Get a car! Fusco's dead."

Mendoza took Preston from Tony. "You're hit too!"

Chavez shouted over the radio. "Hospital cars to the backyard! Ten-thirteen! Officers down! Ten-thirteen!"

Sirens wailed as a car careened into the backyard. The men pushed Preston into the backseat. Mendoza jumped in, keeping pressure on the wound. "GO! GO!" he screamed. The vehicle sprayed dirt as it raced back out onto the street, sirens wailing.

"The shrink?" Chavez asked Forceski.

"Creep blew his brains out."

"That's when Fusco shot." Tony fell to his knees. "Oh, God." There was blood all over his lower body, and he was losing consciousness.

Forceski heaved Tony onto his back and ran toward the side of the house. "I got you, bro." Randazzo blasted through a parked car onto the sidewalk as he drove up onto the side lawn. Forceski heaved Tony into the backseat. "GO! GO! GO!"

"I'm not seeing this!" Randazzo yelled. He backed up and smashed into the parked car, cut the wheels, and gunned the engine. In seconds they were flying down Route 9 at eighty miles an hour. Forceski held a white PBA T-shirt against Tony's wound. "Stay awake. Don't black out."

"Gonna be in Valhalla Hospital in no time!" Randazzo shouted into the backseat.

Tony trembled from shock. "Place of the gods."

"Keep talking, Tony," Forceski ripped into the crash bag for clean dressings. "What about the gods?"

"Valhalla. Where you go to be with the gods."

"Not yet, bro. Not tonight."

Tony closed his eyes.

CHAPTER 58

The next morning, a bleary-eyed Phil Snyder was greeted by a media swarm as he walked through his hospital lobby. "Did you see Senator Sampson's press conference?" one reporter asked.

"No comment," Snyder replied.

"Did you see our exposé on the Mexican flu vaccine trials?" Sara Donovan asked.

"No comment."

Donovan followed him through the lobby. "Why are you running for cover? You've always been an industry spokesman."

Snyder glared at her. "Yes, I saw the senator's press conference. I was moved but science doesn't support him."

"Should the flu vaccine be suspended?" a reporter from a local station asked.

"All right, there may be a problem with the Mexican flu vaccine. The industry will study it. We have an excellent safety record."

Donovan stepped between Snyder and the elevator. "There are hundreds of thousands people with autism now when there were hardly any twenty-five years ago. Are you sure vaccines aren't to blame?"

"Those kids have defective genes. Everyone knows it. The senator should know it. That may be hard for him to admit, but those are the facts! There isn't a single shred of published research connecting vaccines to autism. The Vaccine Court ruled no link last year. If there were, the people at HHS who run the Vaccine Court would have acknowledged it. Now let me go to work."

Calthorpe was feeling intense heat. The conference calls were brutal. European and Asian clients who were panicked over "the American situation" refused to order vaccines for their public health programs. It would take years to rebuild those markets. The "Polio Eradication Program" funded by a billionaire American philanthropist had been widely hailed until a few days earlier. But now reports were surfacing that while polio had been eradicated, hundreds of people were left with varying degrees of paralysis. Meddlesome journalists were asking questions that the industry never had to deal with before.

Calthorpe spoke to a Pakistani health official about an emerging story on the side effects of the polio vaccine in India. "My clients are not attempting to poison your children. These are good drugs that prevent disease."

"Then why am I reading reports that adverse reactions to the polio vaccine were swept under the rug?" the official persisted.

Lance Reed was on his second line. Calthorpe gritted his teeth. "Jawad, I will call you back in a few minutes." He picked up the other line. "Yes, Lance."

"I have an idea for a story on Bryce Ramsey that should . . ."

"No," Calthorpe interrupted. "It's no longer realistic to hammer Ramsey and call it a day. The straw man now has an army. People will read your material differently now."

"I have a twist that should knock Ramsey down a peg. Material I still haven't used."

"Lance, other journalists have started to fact-check. I just can't use you right now."

"You have used me, haven't you? You're like all the rest—an upper-class viper!"

"I'll send you money to tide you over. For now, don't write anything!" Calthorpe slammed the phone down as Donna Willoughby poked her head in.

"Sir, the CEOs of Binghampton and Philbin are on three."

"In a minute. I want a moment with that Russian fool." Calthorpe dialed the phone. "Nikolai Doshenko, my old friend. Please tell me you've located Victoria Glazer and that she revealed Kokochashvili's American identity."

"We have redoubled our efforts, and we have some leads. My specialists are en route."

"Tell them not to be sloppy this time."

"Our stock is plummeting. We understand the pressure."

"Then respond to it." He hung up, lit a cigarette, and pressed line three. "Charles. Roger. How are you gentlemen?"

"I'm pissed!" Binghampton's Charles Livingston said. "And who is this Snyder guy anyway?!"

"An industry spokesman," Philbin's Roger Cunningham replied. "He developed a vaccine ten years ago and just kind of grew into the job."

"Well, he threw my company right under the bus, didn't he?" Livingston said.

"What was he supposed to do?" Cunningham responded. "You guys blew it up pretty big here. Pediatrician's offices are ghost towns, and their academy is considering legal action."

"Gentlemen," Calthorpe said. "Let's pause and . . ."

Livingston cut him off. "We agreed to hang together in this sector. It's supposed to be guaranteed income—zero liability."

"Yeah, but you guys got stupid about it, Charles!"

"Gentlemen, please," Calthorpe pleaded.

"*We* got stupid? You pushed so hard in Georgia that you've invented an anti-vaccine Gandhi!"

Calthorpe didn't look as though he was just smoking. He looked on fire.

Dr. Robert Bangston heard Snyder's comments about the Omnibus Autism Proceedings on SNN. He threw his dinner into the garbage and reached for the phone. "Phillip, what in hell possessed you to talk about the compensation program?"

"Reporters accept court decisions. We can hang our hat on those rulings."

"That was a knucklehead move!"

Snyder reached for the bourbon. "Why don't you just relax, okay? You don't have cameras stuck in your face. You don't have nasty posters hung on your garage. You just melt into the woodwork, and people like me have to stand up and take it for the team!"

"*Team*? There never was a team! There was a group of people living fat and happy making huge money together, but that's not a team."

"I've been abused by these anti-vaccine kooks," Snyder moaned. "I did all this for the industry and the public health community."

Bangston snorted. "Public health community? Come on, Phil. You made them money. Lots and lots of money. Where are they now? I won't see any of 'em when I raise my right hand in front of suspicious senators. And here's the topper—I'm the one who has to entertain a bunch of Japanese doctors for the next month all because of those comments you made."

The publication of "Autism by Any Other Name" hardly made a ripple in the media—at first. Few in the press noticed the paper's significance until Sara Donovan ran a story layering findings from the paper over Phillip Snyder's comments made a day earlier.

The middle of the week belonged to "the Vaccine Court paper" and Maria and Laura were all over television, radio, and the Internet.

"Are you saying that the government has been paying out vaccine injury cases for over twenty years and that the compensated children had autism?" Donovan asked.

Maria's eyes sparkled under the studio lights. "Exactly."

"If vaccine injury has nothing to do with autism, then why do all these vaccine-injured children have autism?" Donovan let the question hang in the air. "We're told repeatedly that there's no association between vaccines and autism by our government. And yet, it seems the government was cutting deals."

"These families went through a difficult time proving their cases. They didn't cut deals. They fought and won their cases. The government should have disclosed the presence of all the autism cases."

"But they didn't."

"No, they did not," Maria said firmly.

"Did anyone in the government—the Department of Justice, the Division of Vaccine Injury Compensation under the Department of Health and Human Services, the special masters—ever mention these cases?"

"No. The special masters even mocked the families in their decisions."

Maria's interview was devastating. The news cycle spin was that the government, and particularly a shadowy man named Robert Bangston, had conspired to keep the truth from the country. The press called the scandal "Vaccine-gate" and Robert Bangston's photograph was everywhere.

However, Laura and Maria were unable to enjoy their triumph. Tony Colletti still hung between life and death. The women sat in a hotel bar, staring at their drinks. Laura got off the phone with Lonnegan. "Tony's still in critical condition. This stinks. He'd be dancing all over this hotel if he knew what was happening.

"I just do interviews and pray," Maria said. "That's all I do."

Bangston went into hiding in a hotel room in suburban Virginia. He called attorneys at the Department of Justice because he needed legal help, fast. But they couldn't represent him as they represented the Secretary of Health and Human Services in the compensation program. Then too, some of the lawyers were nervous because they also knew that many of the children compensated for vaccine injury also had autism. It was every man for himself.

Once again, Bangston called Phillip Snyder. "I need a lawyer. I'm in a lot of trouble."

"I'll see what I can do, but I really don't know any who specialize in representing people called before Congress and . . ."

"This isn't like asking for a referral to a good proctologist! No one should know a lawyer who does this cause no one ever figures they're gonna be dragged in front of senators and vilified! I'm supposed to be a backroom bureaucrat. A nobody. Instead, I'm in a world of shit here."

"Take it easy. I'll make some calls."

Bangston downed some bourbon. "Hey Phil, where's that team you were talking about?"

CHAPTER 59

Tony reached for the edge of the ice to pull himself out of the freezing water, but every time he pulled himself out, the ice broke and he fell back in. He lost feeling in his arms and saw the steam of his breath against the stars twinkling in the dark, purple sky. He slid under again. Bubbles migrated peacefully under the ice ceiling as he drifted away from the opening. Then he saw Johnny Fournier's lifeless hand pointing toward the light. Anne cried in his ears. "You can't die. I love you. Your children need you." Tony shook and swam toward the light and again reached out for the edge.

Now Saito stood over him. "It is not your time. Breathe." Tony coughed water out, inhaled, and coughed again. The purple sky faded to blue, then white. His son whispered in his ear. "Freedom, freedom."

Tony opened his eyes and saw Anthony smiling at him. He was surrounded by soft light and had a beautiful, peaceful smile on his face. "Anthony." Tony said in a raspy voice.

"Daddy is awake," Anthony said.

Tony reached out to touch his son's face but found that he was tethered by wires and tubes. Anthony pushed his face up to Tony's and smiled. "Daddy's alive!" Anne and Sophie moved to his bedside. Anne was crying and Sophie was smiling.

"The old man was right," Anne said. "You were not willing to die."

"Sensei came here, didn't he? I need water."

Anne gave Tony ice chips. "You started climbing out of the ditch as soon as he was done with his massage stuff."

"Sensei moved your life energy." Sophie said.

"How do you feel?" Anne stroked his forehead. "I love you."

"Thirsty," Tony said. "Spacey but no pain, really."

"They gave you some stuff to cut the edge off."

Sophie held Tony's hand. "How long have I been out of it?"

"Four long, horrible days."

"How about Preston?"

"He's in tough shape."

"It went down so fast." He swallowed. "I know I killed that guy."

"Dirty rat bastard tried to kill you. I only wish I could shoot him too."

Tony coughed. "You really can't stop, can you?"

Anne gave him another ice chip. "Stop what?"

"Being Sicilian."

Tony awoke later that evening and was startled to see Forceski staring at him. "You scared the crap out of me."

"Thank God you're alive. How you doin'?"

"I got shot in the gut. How do you think I'm doing?"

"You're still you. God listened this time."

"It jumped ugly so fast. Did Portnoy really do himself?"

"Total ghoul right to the end." Forceski shook his head. "We break through and he's standing there with a mask on and a gun at his head. Blew his brains out after saying some wild bullshit about being a diagnostician."

"Fusco heard the shot and opened fire," Tony sighed. "Bastard killed himself and got two good guys shot. Got his buddy Fusco killed too. Nice shrink. Who licenses these people?" Tony swallowed hard against the pain that crept into his body now. "How's Preston?"

"He's going to make it." Tony closed his eyes and exhaled with relief. "Lonnegan's down the hall getting hugs from Eddie and the probation commissioner," Forceski said. "Never seen the chief so uncomfortable in my life."

Tony started to chuckle. "Glen, don't make me laugh right now, it hurts too much."

"It's really good to be talking to you, bro."

Although Zvi called Herb to talk about the modified adjuvant in the Mexican flu vaccine, the men first spoke of their friend who almost died. "He is a brave man," Zvi said. "He reminds me of Red Army soldiers. One minute laughing, the next minute resolute, prepared to die."

"I saw him exactly that way in Moscow. Told me he was going to grab the gun from one man, shoot the other man, and then turn the gun on the first one."

"Those men were killers. The only reason that they didn't kill you was because it was easier not to." Zvi paused. "I grieve for Leonodovich. He deserved better."

"The world owes him a debt."

"He took mercury out of vaccines and was killed for it. The casualties in this war are mounting. It seems that the people at Binghampton modified the flu vaccine adjuvant."

"I spoke to Maria and she says that Sara Donovan will use your documents on the adjuvant and keep your name out of it. But she's doing another big vaccine story before this one. Why do you think they used this experimental substance?"

"Perhaps it was cheaper and gave them some strategic advantage over their fellow cartel members."

"Cartel, indeed," Newman chuckled. "For years I worked with the US Attorney's Office prosecuting drug dealers. I was locking up the wrong ones."

Saito visited Tony the next morning. "You don't look good, Sensei," Tony told him.

"You have looked better yourself. Good to see you are recovering. I need you at the dojo."

"I'll be back. Have to take it slow for a while, but they say that I won't have permanent effects."

"Yes, but you have been through an ordeal. You need rest."

"Thank you, sir. I'm sorry that I had to take another life."

Saito placed a gentle hand on Tony's shoulder. "You were protecting the most vulnerable people in society from evil men. I am honored to be your friend."

Tony swallowed. "I know you worked on me. Thank you for that as well."

"These American doctors, you should have seen them, so worried. 'You're touching my patient!' I told them that I know you for twenty years. And your wife told them to knock it off." Saito laughed. "She is a good woman."

"Don't I know it."

"I removed obstructions so that ki flowed through your body as it should."

"Well, thanks. I wish that more doctors would listen to men like you."

"Perhaps they should." Saito rubbed his chin. "When do you go before the Senate?"

"Next week. I'm going even if I have to take an ambulance there."

"And the doctor from the Vaccine Court, when does he testify?"

"Bangston's after us, I think. Susan says everything is subject to change."

Anne and Laura ate pasta while Tony sipped apple juice—no solid food for at least another day. He wondered how he could be so loved that women would gather around him, eat robust meals, and then laugh about how he was not allowed to have any. "How did I ever get so lucky?"

"You are lucky," Laura said. "Anne makes a great putanesca!"

The television was on, and everybody happily waited for another Sara Donovan segment. She had called Tony earlier to express get-well wishes and to tip him off that a big story was coming.

Sara introduced the story from the front of the Presbyterian Church in Bennington. "Was the Vermont incident an unprecedented, one-in-a-million event? This pediatrician from Memphis, Tennessee, doesn't think so." The piece shifted to Dr. Washington in front of the Memphis Health Clinic. "His name is Dr. Ronald Andrew Washington, and he was involved in a serious incident last August at this community health clinic in downtown Memphis." The story detailed the attitudes of the public health officials and the harsh tone of the CDC investigators and noted that many of the same excuses used in Vermont were rolled out in Memphis as well. "And Dr. Washington, who spoke out, lost his job."

"The authorities call a bad batch of vaccines a 'hot lot,'" Washington told the camera. "We had a number of children suffer seizures. We lost one. The investigators never issued a report explaining what happened. That's troubling. We need a real vaccine safety surveillance system, not one that sweeps problems under the rug." Photographs of officials who refused Donovan's requests for an interview appeared with typical "we are reviewing the incident" quotes.

"And what happened to the victims? We don't know about all of them, but we do want you to meet one." Dr. Washington greeted a mother and her young daughter in his waiting room. "Washington is now working in a pediatric practice devoted to treating children with autism.

Daniella Yearwood, one of the vaccine-injured children from the clinic incident, now has an autism diagnosis."

CHAPTER 60

Calthorpe gritted his teeth as he watched the C-SPAN coverage of big pharma's "Big Four" CEOs sworn in before the Senate Hearings on the Safety of Vaccines (referred to by the media as "Vaccinegate"). He was already furious over footage of the executives landing at Dulles Airport in private jets and taken to Capitol Hill in limousines. The men were being referred to on the Internet as the "Jet-Set CEOs of the vaccine cartel" before even appearing at the committee. His efforts to coordinate them had been an abysmal failure. "They've stopped listening to me," he thought bitterly.

Calthorpe knew that Charles Livingston of Binghampton Pharmaceuticals would be eaten alive. Sara Donovan's piece on the modified adjuvant in the Mexican flu vaccine ran the night before, yet another devastating revelation. How did she obtain those documents?

The senators were tough, even hostile, and Livingston was subjected to murderous questioning. The other three CEOs let Livingston twist in the wind.

"Mr. Livingston," Senator Smithson began, "I assume that you're aware of the SNN exposé on the adjuvant used in your Mexican flu vaccine?"

Livingston nodded. "I wasn't advised regarding the use of this experimental component."

"Really? You made public comments to the effect that you were 'hands-on, all over the Mexican flu vaccine.' You said further, 'Binghampton Pharmaceuticals is leading the way against this dangerous pandemic. I will ensure that we have the safest vaccine ever made.' And then we have the Bennington event."

"Not our finest hour."

Smithson peered over the rim of his glasses. "You're aware that various federal, state, and local law enforcement agencies are investigating this vaccine's research trials. Crimes against children are alleged."

Livingston turned to his attorney who whispered in his ear. "I'm going to invoke my rights as per the Fifth Amendment."

Smithson recognized Senator Russell Sampson. "Mr. Livingston, did Binghamptom compensate the mothers of the children killed . . ."

"Allegedly killed," Livingston broke in.

"Mr. Livingston, do not interrupt me. I will allow you to fully respond. Six American children died. All were given your drug. Someone associated with the trials paid the mothers. Who was it?"

His attorney tapped him on the shoulder and covered the microphone. The two huddled for a moment. "I wish to invoke my rights under the Fifth Amendment."

"Would Binghampton compensate a family for vaccine injury if . . ."

"We don't compensate anyone for vaccine injury. The National Vaccine Injury Compensation Program does that."

"Interesting you mention that. That act doesn't apply to research trials, but your comment is important. You and your fellow CEOs do not pay for vaccine injuries and you don't have any liability for vaccines, do you? So the victims in Bennington and Memphis . . ."

"Alleged victims. There has been no finding of injury. These individuals can bring a petition in the NVICP, a program that has been hailed as a model of tort reform."

"Let's assume there was a finding."

"The 1986 act holds us harmless for vaccine injuries," Livingston explained. "We are not the respondent."

"That's my point. Perhaps if you were the respondent you might be motivated to make safer vaccines. You might even think before experimenting on children."

"We have an outstanding safety record."

"The people of Bennington and Memphis don't agree. The children buried in the desert don't agree. There could be many others who have been . . ."

"We have no civil liability. We aren't paying for anything."

Sampson raised his voice in indignation. "I know that. We taxpayers are. And the families and the victims have to use this marvelous pillar of tort reform and sue the Secretary of Health and Human Services. No other industry in the United States has such protection. Look what you've done with it."

When the questioning later shifted to Hans Jurgenson who was still wanted for stealing CDC money, Smithson pointedly criticized the Norwegian research. "It's so poorly constructed that it's essentially meaningless. And yet, we have emails indicating that Xerxes—your corporation, Mr. Montoya—influenced *The Journal of Childhood Vaccines* to publish this flawed autism research."

"We asked the journal to consider publication."

"Your vaccine division chief points out that Xerxes donates over a million dollars a year to the journal and funds annual conferences and sponsors research. That sounds like pressure to me."

"Well, yes, but the CDC asked us to do so," Montoya answered.

"The CDC gave you their blessing, did they? Who at the CDC?" Montoya looked down. "Who at the CDC asked you to twist arms at the journal?"

His attorney covered the microphone and the two quietly spoke. Montoya was visibly upset and needed a moment to sét himself. "It was the director, Dr. Jennifer Kesslinger."

Senator Sampson then delivered the coup de grâce. "Mr. Montoya, can you cite me independent research that compares health outcomes between children who have been vaccinated and those who have not?"

"We have several studies that when taken together strongly refute the notion that vaccines are causative for autism."

"That wasn't my question. Is there any research that compares health outcomes between children who've been vaccinated and those who have not?"

Montoya paused for a sip of water. "No, there is not."

"Then how do we know that there's no link between vaccine injury and autism?"

Charles Livingston fled Washington in his jet that evening. He read his high-priority emails while having a drink. He first read that the administrator he had appointed to run the Mexican flu vaccine test trial was found dead from a drug overdose in a Denver hotel room. Three emails later, Livingston learned that Binghampton's board of directors had fired him.

The next morning Dr. Ronald Andrew Washington told the committee about the Memphis incident. Some senators challenged Dr. Washington, but only so much. Was it possible that the CDC investigators were just being rigorous? Was it possible that there were alternate explanations for that tragic morning?

Smithson lowered his glasses. "Dr. Washington, do you think that the vaccine that caused Daniella Yearwood's seizures also led to her autism?"

"I do. I once believed that people who felt that vaccines could cause autism were nothing more than conspiracy nuts. I see them differently now. Keep in mind what autism really is and look at the history. Autism isn't a disease. It's a behavioral diagnosis applied to a person who exhibits the behaviors described in the *Diagnostic and Statistical Manual*, the *DSM*, of *Psychiatry*. Autism was unknown seventy years ago." The senators leaned forward. "It occurs in the presence of brain damage, what we call encephalopathy. Seizures early in life are associated with encephalopathy.

People with autism often suffer seizures. Seizures and encephalopathy are on the table of injuries that the NVICP uses. It all adds up."

"All children are vaccinated but they don't all develop autism. Why?" Smithson asked.

"Certain children have genetic predispositions. We know that children with fragile X and tuberous sclerosis develop autism more frequently than the general population. However, many people with these syndromes do not have autism. I think that vaccines may be the trigger—not the only trigger—for people with predispositions that we haven't identified yet. That is why it's so important to study the vaccine-injured people who also have autism. We could learn from them and prevent future injuries. The population we should study is the people compensated by the Vaccine Court. That's what "Autism by Any Other Name" is calling on us to do."

Phillip Snyder had seen enough. He called a press conference at his hospital to respond to the first two days of hearings. "I see that we're going to spend the taxpayers' money to watch senators smacking around CEOs," he began. "How original. These companies have reliably produced the vaccines that have saved millions of lives, but I guess that doesn't matter now. Now it's become fashionable to tear down the entire program because of one bad vaccine and a few radicals spouting nonsense about autism. Are we going to let a paper in a legal journal—not even a scientific journal—scare everyone into believing that the government knew about autism and vaccines years ago and covered it up? Come on, smarten up. People can't keep secrets like that. If it were going on, responsible citizens would have come forward years ago. There is no accepted science that autism has actually increased. It's a genetic disorder. It runs in families. We've known this for years. These senators are pandering to the media."

Snyder then gathered himself and let out a breath. "Why am I so worked up?" The reporters laughed. "And I admit that I am, but I do it for good reason. I'm hearing that vaccination rates are plummeting.

We're going to have disease outbreaks and children will die from vaccine-preventable diseases."

A reporter asked about Dr. Washington.

"The guy has about two years of experience and got fired from his first job. Smithson and Sampson gave him hours to wax poetic about his insights into vaccine safety and whether vaccines cause autism. Is this kid an expert on autism? No. Is he an expert on vaccine injury? No. But he got three hours of Senate face time because Sara Donovan put him on TV."

"Be careful about tearing down that which has kept all of us safe for so long. Any of you know someone suffering from polio?" No one in the press answered. "I thought so. That's because vaccines conquered polio. The country has forgotten that."

Calthorpe watched Snyder's press conference. The guy could be a bit over the top but effective. Snyder wasn't going down without a fight and his press conference helped.

The next day many editorials that Calthorpe's agents had been pushing were published. Some commentators began to ask whether the committee—and the media—had overreacted.

The pro-pharma senators who had been sitting on their hands came out swinging on day three.

CHAPTER 61

"Will the senator from Virginia please refrain from questioning Dr. Wenzel's character," said Senator Smithson.

The congressman in question, Frank Reynolds, pursued the line. "Dr. Wenzel is a proponent of chelation therapy for children with autism. That therapy has been described as dangerous, Mr. Chairman. It goes to his judgment."

Dr. Wenzel took off his glasses and leaned back in his seat. "Chelation therapy has long been recognized as a treatment for heavy metal toxicity. Children with autism fall into that category most likely because of the mercury and aluminum in vaccines."

"Is it not true that an autistic child died from chelation therapy a few years ago?" Reynolds asked.

"Regrettably, the child died because the wrong drug was administered. A medication error caused the death, not this therapy."

"Is it not true that you have spoken at fund-raisers for the discredited Bryce Ramsey?"

"I was proud to do so! Dr. Ramsey has been vilified for speaking the truth."

"But he was formally disciplined and the paper he published has been retracted."

"What was done to him was no different than what was done to Galileo or Semmelweiss," Wenzel pounded his fist. "This is suppression of science!"

Smithson rapped his gavel. "We are in a hearing of the United States Senate. Let us proceed with more civility."

Civility had ended, and the rest of day three was filled with tension and accusations from each side. The war was back on, and the outcome was again in doubt.

Because he knew the nurses would be angry with him for not resting, Tony spoke quietly into the phone. "Pharma came out swinging today, didn't they?"

"They did," Donovan said. "What choice do they have? You gonna testify?"

"Assuming no setbacks, it looks like next Thursday with the other authors. I've earned my shot, pardon the pun."

"Not funny. I was shot at in Mexico. It was terrifying. When I heard what happened to you, I lost it."

"I'm sorry. You going to run the story on Zvi's paper?"

"I want to, but Seth feels that we need Dr. Kokochashvili to come out and back it up in person. It's a bit arcane for most people to wrap their brains around without putting a face to it."

Tony knew Sara was right, but Zvi would have to come out of the shadow, most likely in front of the senators. "When do you want to run the piece?"

"We can get on the *Sunday Night News Magazine*. But we need Dr. Z."

At 12:30 a.m. Tony was running a conference call in secret from his hospital bed. "We promised the guy," Newman insisted. "We can't disclose his identity."

"We can ask him. Sara needs him for this story. It counters everything that Snyder was screaming about the other day."

"I don't think anything could be done to him," Laura said. "He was granted citizenship."

"Suppose the hearings end in a stalemate?" Newman said. "Then pharma goes after him in the same way they went after Ramsey."

"The man needs protection," Maria said. "A guarantee."

"I think it helps him if he ends up testifying," Laura said. "If he testifies in Congress, it makes him legitimate. If anyone comes after him, everyone knows it's retaliation."

"Zvi took his family and fled his homeland," Maria said. "There is a fear that such people have that no one else can really understand."

Zvi arrived at his office early in the morning as usual. He went through his email and reviewed some reports, then decided to visit the online version of his local news. On the screen was a photograph of a face that he hadn't seen in over twenty years. He read the story and broke into a cold sweat.

The photo was of Vicky Glazer, now with a married name of Robinson, the woman from the CDC who interviewed him years ago about his paper. She had been shot dead by two men in the middle of a quiet street near the Emory University campus. According to witnesses, the men fled on foot. The police who went to her home found her husband had been murdered as well.

Leonodovich had been killed. Now Glazer.

Zvi searched the internet for news on individuals who helped him defect. Ronald Vincent had "accidentally drowned in his Jacuzzi" a few weeks earlier.

Leonodovich, Vincent, and now Glazer.

Zvi dialed the phone. "Herb, I need your help."

Zvi returned home that Friday in a torrential thunderstorm. Anya greeted him with panic in her eyes. "The bags are packed. You are late, Zviad."

"Our escorts will be here soon. The girls?"

"They are at my friend's and can stay there for a while. Georgi will stay with Allison. He's almost done packing."

Zvi reached into the cabinet over the refrigerator for the vodka. "You want some?"

"I prefer not to drink right now."

"I strongly prefer the opposite." Zvi drank the vodka straight and walked to the staircase. "Georgi! Come down."

"I'm almost packed," Georgi walked down the stairs. "What's going on Papa?"

"Come and sit. I will tell you." Georgi Petrov was an Adonis. Women loved the young med student for his dark curly hair and deep blue eyes. "Have some vodka."

"Okay, tell me what's happened."

"There is an old Georgian proverb that a man is not a man until he sees his father as he really is."

"Whew!" Georgi said. "This vodka is strong."

"This vodka is for men." Zvi poured his son another drink. "It is time that you saw your father as he really is."

Anya trembled. "Zvi, don't!"

Zvi held out his hand. "Anya, I love you. I love my family. But I also love my country. And it is time to stop being afraid." Zvi looked into his glass. "Georgi, we are not Georgians from Kurdistan. We are Georgians from Georgia, from the Sakartvelebi. I was a microbiologist in the Soviet Union. You don't remember but . . ."

"I do remember. I knew that I shouldn't talk about it."

"I see. You are already a wiser man than I have been." Zvi belted down another glass of vodka and refilled it. "I worked for the communists, making biological weapons. Weapons of mass destruction, as the old president used to say. The Soviets would have used these weapons against this country. They would have done this to preserve an economic system. They were insane. They thought only of power and then more and more power." Zvi put his glass down. "Then one day, I was approached by a man while I attended a conference in Sarajevo. The man worked for a drug company that later became Xerxes Pharmaceuticals. He offered me a way to come to America. And so, with the covert help of these people, you, your mother, and I defected. We met a man in an old Byzantine Church. They called it the Hagia Sofia—the Church of Holy Wisdom," Zvi said ironically. "And he delivered us to America."

"And?"

"I eventually figured out that I was really allowed to come here because I researched an old vaccine that produced some complicated side effects. It left children with autism. I have known this for all these years, and I said nothing out of fear." Zvi looked at his son. "And now it is time to come forward and speak the truth. I am sorry, Anya, but it is time. I should have done this years ago."

"Who would have listened?" she said. "Look what they did to the English doctor."

"That is no excuse. I have friends who have the ear of a senator who has promised that no one can harm us once I testify in front of Congress. We shall see. I have seen government promises before. But it does not matter. My life is forfeit. The people who are protecting these vaccines are no less insane than the old Soviets. It seems that I defected to nowhere." Zvi poured his son another shot of vodka. "And something else. Your name is not Petrov. You are Georgi Andrei Kokochashvili."

"What do I say?"

"I do not know, my son. But now you know who you really are." Zvi started at the sound of a knock at the front door. "Stay here with your mother and be prepared to call the police." Through the side of the curtains, Zvi saw two men standing at his door. Anya shook in fear. Georgi picked up a fireplace poker and stood behind his father. Zvi opened the door just enough to peer out. "Who are you?"

"Dr. Z, my name is Glen Forceski, Winston Police Department."

"And you?" he said to the other man.

"Eddie Mendoza, Castleton County Probation Department."

Zvi turned to Georgi and Anya. "We are safe. Officer Tony sent the probation department. We're going to Washington."

Georgi sat with his girlfriend, Allison, on her couch. They watched his father's interview with Sara Donovan on SNN's *Sunday Night News Magazine*. "What did you think, Allison?"

"It's shocking," she said. "They knew for all these years."

"What did you think of my father?"

"He is complicated and sad, but brave. It was a lot to carry around."

"Yes, it was." Georgi Andrei Kokochashvili had finally seen his father as he really was.

Calthorpe received a phone call from Phillip Snyder just as he was turning in for the night. Calthorpe listened to Snyder vent and quickly realized what had happened. "Phillip, allow me to view the report and I'll get back to you." Calthorpe went online. Sara Donovan had once again scored a devastating torpedo strike below the water line. He dialed Doshenko and woke him up. "Nikolai, it seems that we have found Dr. Kokochashvili."

"We have? Where is he?"

"On SNN with Sara Donovan!" Calthorpe hung up, lit a cigarette, and watched the report again. "It's over," he said aloud.

The Rollins Group had spent millions to secure covert control of media outlets and influence legislators, and even the US Supreme Court. None of that mattered now. The stock values of the "Big Four" were tanking. CEOs were being fired, and now pharma couldn't give their vaccines away.

It was time to take care of himself and Rollins. There was serious exposure for the company because of certain people. Whatever one thought about Snyder, the man was faithful to his beliefs. Whatever the outcome, Snyder was not a concern.

But Lance Reed was another story. The ongoing questions about Reed's journalistic integrity were no longer limited to autism blogs. Calthorpe knew that Reed was not a man of character. Reed was in it for the money and prestige. Both had dried up. Such men are capable of anything. And Reed could tie him to everything. He dialed his phone again. "Nikolai Doshenko, my old friend . . ."

CHAPTER 62

Week two of the hearings the day after Sara Donovan's Russian study bombshell. Media again referred to the hearings as "Vaccine-gate."

Committee staffers were busy preparing a subpoena for Dr. Zviad Kokochashvili. The hearing schedule was being amended, and pro-pharma senators were howling that they were not being allowed to put their witnesses on as easily as the anti-pharma senators. But Smithson and Sampson knew from staff meetings that many pro-vaccine industry witnesses were trying to get out of testifying. No one wanted to be publicly associated with the scandal.

In his orange jumpsuit, Professor Herman Tyler sat in a county jail cafeteria listening to Herb Newman and Wilson Garrison discuss the briefs submitted to the Superior Court. "Word is that Judge Hawkins is an old-school Southern judge," Garrison said.

"In other words," Tyler said, "not a good time to be a black man."

"Who's defying Georgia authorities and is represented by another black man and a Jew," Garrison responded.

Newman looked up from his notepad. "A Jew from New York."

"I could be doing a bullet here." Tyler acknowledged.

"We don't know," Newman said. "Maybe he won't give you a full year if he doesn't overturn the conviction."

"Do you think he might do that?" Tyler asked.

"We're arguing *Jacobsen* all the way. As there's no epidemic of communicable disease, the mandate to vaccinate your children could be interpreted as not applying."

Tyler nodded. "And if he views it that way, then I—along with my codefendants—have not endangered our children."

"But keep in mind that amicus briefs are pouring in from the APA, the AMA, and the Georgia Immunization Alliance," Newman said. "He's receiving considerable pressure."

Tyler looked around the cafeteria. Inmates mopped floors and cleaned tables. "I may have to miss watchin' my son grow for a while. I am not the only man in this jail who's had to ponder that loss." He drank some coffee. "You've both been everything that a man in my situation could ask for. I'm at peace with whatever happens."

Bangston had been to the office twice in the past two weeks. One of his visits was the official "you are on your own" session with the Department of Justice attorneys. The other was a meeting with representatives from the Japanese Health Ministry. Conversations with them contained not one mention of Phillip Snyder and not one reference that the program they had come to study was about to go down in flames. Could they really be considering the NVICP as a model for their country? Bangston knew that the program had failed. And he realized that he had failed.

He should have said something, but it was too late now. In the end, he was just like all the others who knew and didn't want to speak out because of fear. "I even lied to my daughter," he thought bitterly.

Bangston watched the proceedings on television in his hotel room. The remaining pro-pharma senators were not even trying. The last report by Sara Donovan ended any pretense that mainstream medicine clung to about no science connecting vaccines to autism. Bangston never knew about the

Russian paper, although he always wondered why the Russians took mercury out of vaccines so many years ago. Inevitably, he would be asked if he knew about all those cases of vaccine injury that included autism. His attorney, Jeff Biely, spent hours with him and he still couldn't figure out what he was going to say. "I have no idea how to explain my conduct."

"Just don't perjure yourself," Biely said.

"How do I avoid doing that?"

"Can you say, 'Yes, I noticed some cases of autism but not in numbers that raised my concern?' Could that be accurate?"

"I don't know, Jeff." Bangston looked out his hotel window. "How do I say that? It was over forty percent of the cases."

After being sworn in by Senator Smithson, Dr. Zviad Kokochashvili offered a statement about why he decided to speak out. "The work I did all those years ago showed autism to be more common in vaccinated children. Those are the facts. It was time to speak openly."

"Dr. Kokochashvili," Senator Sampson asked, "I notice that the word 'autism' doesn't appear in it. Please explain."

"Yes. No one on our research team had ever seen autism before. We knew that these children manifested odd behaviors—hand flapping, toe walking, limited speech, what people now call autistic behaviors. No one in Russia had seen children who acted this way. So we described the behaviors in detail and called it the 'unique behavioral syndrome.'"

"Doctor," Sampson asked, "what led the Soviet government to look at this?"

"These were children from families that had party connections so part was triggered by the concern of the elites. Also, an army general was angered by the vaccines' effects on soldiers. A lot of the resources of the former Soviet Union went into the military, and the leadership worried that the vaccines had so many adverse reactions in adults. One question led to another, and soon we were looking at injured children."

"But this project was not your main line of work, was it?"

Zvi sipped from his water glass. "No, my main purpose was to work with microbes for use in biological weapons. I am not proud of that, but you must remember, I lived under a dictatorship. I thank God that the weapons were not used."

Zvi testified for four hours. He was so articulate and precise in his testimony that the pro-pharma senators had virtually nowhere to go. However, one took one odd, last shot.

"Dr. Kokasher . . . Dr.Koka Colachacola . . ."

"Dr. Kokochashvili," Zvi said slowly as some of the senators and staff began to chuckle.

"Thank you. Doctor, are you a Communist?"

Zvi smiled. "Senator, I am not now, nor have I ever been, a member of the Communist Party."

The room erupted into laughter and applause.

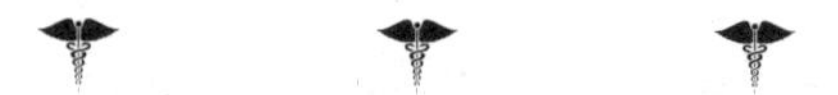

There was a knock on the door of Lance Reed's London apartment. "This had better be my check," he thought. He saw through the peep hole a tall blond man. "Who are you?" Reed asked.

"A messenger."

He opened the door. The man walked in with another man. "What is this?"

"We have a message for you from our employer . . ."

Phil Snyder scowled as he watched the proceedings. These fools were laughing and applauding the destruction of the American public health establishment. Snyder had not been asked to testify. A staffer to one of the pro-pharma senators told him bluntly, "You'll likely do more harm than good."

But Snyder was now hell-bent on getting in front of Congress. These people needed to be set straight, and he was the man to do it since no one else would. He started making phone calls.

Jennifer Kesslinger sat nervously at Gate 28 at Ronald Reagan International Airport. She had to leave the country now, and her flight to the Cayman Islands was already forty-five minutes late. She trembled at SNN's coverage of Hans Jurgenson's arrest in France. Jurgenson would soon be back in the United States to face justice. Kesslinger knew he would reveal things that could send her to prison.

She shook with anxiety as her cell phone rang "Juan," she whispered harshly, "I told you not to call me anymore!"

"There are FBI Agents all over the CDC headquarters. They have evidence vans, and they are pulling out files and . . ."

"No more calls!" Kesslinger hit the End button. A woman across from her looked concerned. She turned away and slugged a quick hit of whiskey from the flask in her pocketbook. She hunched over and lit a cigarette. When she looked up, she saw two men looming over her, displaying badges and FBI ID cards.

"Ms. Kesslinger, we need you to come with us . . . and put the cigarette out. There's no smoking in the airport."

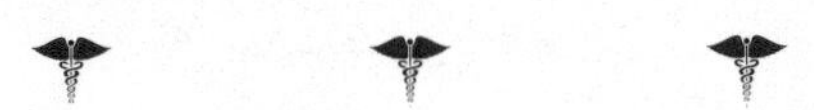

Jack McLeod called Clyde King at 1:00 a.m. in his Macon hotel room. "Clyde, how you doin'?"

"Oh, I'm waking up, thank you. How are you?"

"Celebrating with champagne."

"Why's that?"

"Because the networks are saying that Lance Reed is dead."

"What?!"

"He could create facts from thin air but he couldn't fly through it. He was found in the courtyard of his apartment building. Apparently took a twelve-story tumble." McLeod chuckled. "Cause of death was cement poisoning."

CHAPTER 63

As the authors of "Autism by Any Other Name" were sworn in, Tony looked around the room, breathing deeply to focus his nerves. Sara Donovan was there. Anne sat with all the members of the project family contact team, including the chief. Sensei Saito sat with Susan Miller behind Lonnegan. "He's dying and he came anyway," he whispered to Maria.

Bangston sat alone in his office watching C-SPAN. Anthony Colletti was the man who called him that afternoon on the conference call. That man and his friends had hunted him down.

And now they had gathered for the kill.

Jack McLeod had the crowd going loud and strong in front of the courthouse by 10:00 a.m. "Free the Macon Three! Free the Macon Three!"

Inside the courtroom, Twiggs and Burdette sat at the end of the table, looking tense. Newman and Garrison sat next to Herman Tyler who wore a jacket and tie. "You seem pretty calm," Newman said to Tyler.

"Like I said, I'm at peace."

"I'm glad you are," Garrison said, "because I'm going to be pissed off if we don't prevail. I'm tired of losing vaccine cases."

Senator Hutch leaned into the microphone and asked, "Are you telling me that these families really have children with this autism disorder or are they just brain damaged?"

"They were compensated for encephalopathy, a brain injury, Senator," Laura said. "They also had autism."

"Well, which is it?" Senator Hutch asked.

"Autism is a behavioral disorder," Tony interjected, "so if you have the behaviors that fit the diagnosis of autism in the manual that psychiatrists use, then you have autism. Our findings indicate that vaccine-induced brain damage can often include autism."

"Yes," Maria added. "It should never have been the case that people had to prove that vaccines cause autism. The program should have functioned as designed so the petitioners should only have been required to prove that a vaccine injury occurred. That was supposed to be the burden of proof. When you realize that so many of the children compensated in the past also had autism, you have to wonder why the Omnibus Autism Proceedings happened."

"All we did," Tony said, "was ask the next question. HHS says these children suffered vaccine injuries and were compensated for those injuries. We then asked, 'Does the person also have autism?' The answer came back 'yes' so many times that it's impossible for me to see how those in the program missed this."

Sampson cleared his throat. "Let me ask that exact question. Is it possible that, somehow, those running this program didn't notice?"

"Senator," Laura said, "people began talking about this well over twenty years ago. It's become popular to blame Doctor Ramsey for the controversy, but he was not the one who originated it. We spoke to a small percentage of those compensated, and we still found seventy-five cases of autism. I don't see how the people running the program could have missed the connection in case after case."

⚕ ⚕ ⚕

Tony sat between his wife and Maria and watched as Phillip Snyder was sworn in. Snyder took his seat alone at the table and glared at the senators.

"Thank you for coming before us, Dr. Snyder," Senator Smithson said with no warmth in his tone.

"I wanted to come. Someone has to set the record straight. I have a prepared statement."

"You have five minutes."

Snyder launched into a scathing, fist-pounding diatribe against the hearings and the "anti-vaccine people who've been allowed to attack the cornerstone of public health." He declared that vaccines did not cause autism, genetics did. "There's no real increase in autism, and all of this questioning will lead to vaccine-preventable disease outbreaks. Children will die, and those deaths will be on your head."

"Dr. Snyder," Smithson said. "Will you turn around and look at the faces of the people sitting behind you?"

"I don't understand."

"The honorable gentleman from Iowa makes a good point," Sampson said. "Will you please look at the people in this room."

Snyder turned to find everyone in the room looking at him with contempt. A moaning teenager with autism rocked back and forth in his wheelchair.

"The chair recognizes the gentleman from New York," Smithson said quickly.

"Do you see what we are seeing, Dr. Snyder?" Sampson said.

"What of it?"

"These people have come to Washington in hopes of seeing their government finally do something about what happened to their children."

"And what you feel happened to your child. Isn't that what this is really about?"

The crowd gasped. Smithson tapped the gavel. "Order, Dr. Snyder. Order, people." Smithson glared at the audience. "This is a committee of the United States Senate."

Sampson leaned in. "Dr. Snyder, I know what happened to my son. I saw what happened with my own eyes. My wife saw what happened to my son. I only wish that I spoke out sooner, that I had the courage of the people sitting behind you. The courage to speak out in the face of ridicule . . . "

"There should be ridicule!" Snyder pounded his fist. "There isn't a single shred of evidence that supports . . ."

"The evidence sits behind you, sir! But people like you won't listen."

"We don't have to listen. We have science!"

"Science that is paid for by the industry that profits from it. Science that ignores the observations of parents. Science that refuses to study the children who got sick. Science that refuses to compare the health outcomes between vaccinated and un-vaccinated children. Did you not listen to what the other witnesses have told this committee?"

"We don't have to listen! We know what we know. We've saved millions of lives."

"What about the ones who were injured?"

"What does it matter?"

"Order!" Smithson raised his voice over the boos and groans.

Sampson pointed at Snyder. "You don't care that so many were injured?"

"I don't acknowledge the injuries. There's not a shred of proof! Vaccines don't cause encephalopathy! They don't cause brain damage!"

"Dr. Snyder, our government has compensated people for exactly those injuries. Children died. Others were left completely disabled. They do have brain damage and some even have autism."

"They had bad genes. They would've had autism anyway!"

"Sir!" Smithson shouted. "We shall have order here." Smithson was losing control. People stood, booing Snyder loudly.

"What are you talking about, doctor? People from every walk of life have reported the same thing. They've told the truth."

"I don't care what they said."

"What? How can you say that?" Sampson asked.

"I don't care about the truth!"

There was a collective gasp from the crowd. The senators looked at Snyder in astonishment.

"My God," Smithson whispered.

Snyder looked down at the table, unable to make contact with the senators.

"Mr. Chairman," Sampson said quietly. "I have no further questions."

Smithson looked at the other committee members, then addressed the witness. "Dr. Snyder, you may leave."

Snyder gathered his papers, nodded to the panel, and walked up the center aisle toward the door. The only sound was the moaning of the teenager with autism.

CHAPTER 64

As Bangston watched Snyder's testimony, he cleaned out his desk and piled his personal belongings in a carton. "They don't even fill it," he thought sadly.

His assistant rang his line. "A Mr. Saito, another of the Japanese delegation, is here."

"Please, not now."

"I'm sorry, Dr. Bangston, but he says that you need to talk to him. He's quite insistent. Seems different than the others."

"Sure, whatever. Send the shogun in."

The door opened, and Saito and Susan Miller walked in. Bangston rose to shake hands. "How do you do, doctor, please have a seat."

"I think I should stand," Saito said. "I am not a doctor, but I understand healing."

"Okay. What can I do for you?"

"You can listen."

"Fine, I'll listen. Nothing else to do right now."

"My name is Akinori Saito. My family lived in a small coastal village in Japan called Minamata. I saw my family die horrible deaths from mercury poisoning. The company responsible for this tragedy misled people for years. They made up science. They blamed those who sought answers and made it so that even their fellow villagers would not listen to them."

Bangston didn't know what to do. Was this man crazy? Should he call security?

"This afternoon you will have a choice." Saito stood unsteadily on his feet. "You can continue on your path or you can act to preserve your honor and tell the truth."

Bangston saw the yellow cast of Saito's eyes and that he was shaking. "Please sit."

"I may be weak from illness, but when I speak to a man about his honor, I stand. It is time that someone outside of your group spoke to you."

"What do you know? You don't know me."

"I know what has gone on in this controversy. I have seen this all before."

"You think that I'm like Snyder?" Bangston loosened his collar. "I never asked for any of this."

"That does not matter. What you wanted and what you did in the past does not matter. What matters is what you do today. What matters is your honor."

"You're dying, aren't you?" The answer came from Miller, who nodded grimly while Saito said nothing and remained at attention. "Yet you came here, in this condition to say this to me? To a man you don't even know. Why?"

"I have come to offer you an opportunity to undo horrible suffering."

"You don't even know me! Why would you waste your breath?"

"Hearing the truth spoken will bring healing to many people. Maybe even to you."

Bangston seized on that possibility, as if dark clouds had parted. "I shouldn't be allowed to breathe the same air as you. I lost my honor."

"There is a way that you can get it back."

The bailiff announced, "All rise! Georgia Superior Court is now in session." Clyde King didn't have a good feeling about what was to come. The judge looked that morning like the kind to send a man away for a hundred years and then go to dinner.

Judge Hawkins pounded his gavel. "You may all be seated. I appreciate all of you waiting so patiently into the late morning on this matter. You there." He pointed at Tyler. "You happy with the counsel you've received from your attorneys?"

Tyler rose slowly. "Yes, Your Honor. Matter of fact, I am."

"You ladies feel the same way?"

Twiggs and Burdette rose. "Yes, we do Your Honor," Twiggs said. Burdette nodded.

"You should be. I've reviewed all the briefs and the facts of the case, and I'm fining each of you five dollars for violating the Health Code. However, regarding the child endangerment charges, there is no imminent health emergency in Georgia that causes me to see why the defendants should subject their children to a medical procedure that they feel is unwarranted. There is no compelling reason to inflict the will of the state, no matter how honorably conceived, upon the rights of these people to raise their children as they choose."

Tyler closed his eyes in prayer. Twiggs and Burdette hugged. Garrison looked at Newman, who was dumbstruck. Clyde King wrote notes on his pad so quickly, he was afraid his pen would snap.

The judge continued. "Now, you all should consider that there may be a time when you should vaccinate your children. But absent a health crisis, I think that we should align our response to your behavior, your parental choices, in the way the Supreme Court instructed us to do over one hundred years ago. The criminal charges against the defendants are hereby dismissed. Mr. Tyler is to be released forthwith."

The courtroom erupted in cheers. Newman raised his fists in the air. Garrison fell back into his seat, smiling ear to ear.

"This matter is resolved." The judge pounded the gavel. "We stand adjourned."

The network cameras recorded the crowd celebrating in Rosa Parks Park as the Macon Three and their lawyers emerged from the courthouse.

Wilson Garrison had his arms around Newman's shoulders and pumped his fists in the air. McLeod gave Newman a bear hug. "What do you think, big fella?"

"I don't know," Newman said. "Never thought that I'd see a day like this."

McLeod handed the bullhorn to Herman Tyler. "My friends, we cannot thank all of you enough. Can we get some love for the lawyers?" The crowd cheered Newman and Garrison. "I want to thank Judge Hawkins for seeing the truth when so many were urging him not to." The crowd applauded. "I have something from Dr. Martin Luther King to read to you that captures the spirit of what happened here. 'When evil men plot, good men must plan. When evil men burn and bomb, good men must build and bind. When evil men shout ugly words of hatred, good men must commit themselves to the glories of love. Where evil men would seek to perpetuate an unjust status quo, good men must seek to bring in a real order of justice.' Thank you."

The air was heavy with silence as Robert Bangston entered the hearing room and took his seat at the witness table, accompanied by his attorney. His hand shook as he was sworn in.

"Good afternoon, Dr. Bangston," Senator Smithson said. "Do you have a statement?" Bangston shook his head. "How long have you been director of the Division of Vaccine Injury Compensation?"

"Over twenty years," Bangston whispered.

"Sir," Smithson said, "I cannot hear you. You'll have to speak louder."

"I've been at the Division since day one. Twenty years."

"Please describe your duties to the committee."

"I review the medical records of all the cases, and I advise the Department of Justice and the special masters about whether the case is sufficient to settle without a hearing or to proceed further."

"Now, you are aware of this recently published paper, "Autism by Any Other Name"?

Bangston stared straight ahead. "Sir, did you hear my question?"

"I heard you, Senator," Bangston said. "I'm aware of the paper."

"And, so, I assume that you know that the authors claim to have found all of these cases of autism?"

"Yes, I'm aware that they make that claim."

"Well, do you have a response? Are there in fact a great number of children that our government has compensated for vaccine injury who also have autism?"

Bangston put his head down as if unable to answer. His attorney at his side said, "One moment, Senator," then whispered, "Robert, you have to respond or I'll have to state that you take the Fifth . . . Robert?"

"They're right, Senator."

There was a stirring from the audience. "Dr. Bangston, do you need a moment to speak with your lawyer?" Smithson said.

"No, I will not take the Fifth. I want to breathe again. I just want to breathe again. Their claims are correct. There are many more cases like the ones those people found. Because it's true. Vaccine injuries included autism because the vaccine injuries caused autism. I knew. Other people knew. We all knew, but we said nothing. And we should have . . . I should have."

Russell Sampson looked at Smithson and shook his head, not knowing what to say. "Sir, why didn't you speak out earlier?"

"Because I was afraid. I was afraid of what would happen to me, what would happen to my career. I should have said something. But I worried no one would listen to me or that I would just be fired. I saw how other doctors who spoke out were treated. I saw how no one listened to the families. So, I stopped listening to . . . to my conscience. I started to not believe what was staring at me in file after file. I didn't listen. I failed to listen, and now I am here. God forgive me."

From his seat in the gallery Tony saw Maria talking quietly to herself. "I'm praying," she looked up and said.

"Dr. Bangston," Senator Sampson asked, "what do we do now?"

"I don't know. What happens to me is up to you. I accept whatever happens because I deserve it. But I would like to spend the rest of my days working to treat these people. Just be a doctor again. It's the only honorable thing I can do."

The news of Bangston's testimony reached the crowd in Rosa Parks Park where people had lit candles. Mainstream media outlets reported what many believed would never be said openly: the government had conceded that vaccines caused autism.

The *Era of Autism* blog ran a simple bold headline: We Were Right.

Sara Donovan and her cameraman caught up to Tony and Anne leaving the building. Tony was exhausted, and Anne was practically holding him up. "Tony, do you have anything that you want to say about what Dr. Bangston did?"

"Sara, thank you for what you did. You risked your career. You even risked your life."

"I was doing my job." Donovan put a microphone in Tony's face. "Your comments on Bangston's confession."

"You're interviewing me? I'm just a cop."

"You're not just a cop. Do you think people will listen now?'

"I hope so. The truth is out. That's what I wanted for my son and for other families."

"What about vaccines?"

"What about them?"

"You proved that vaccines cause autism."

"No, I didn't. They're just drugs. Vaccines don't cause autism."

"Really? What does?"

"Not listening does."

Susan Miller sat next to Sensei Saito on the Amtrak train heading back to New York. In and out of sleep, Saito opened his eyes to find Susan holding his hand.

"Sensei," Miller said, "Dr. Bangston told the truth. I got a text from Laura Melendez. He's asked for forgiveness and wants to treat people with autism. It's over. The war is over."

"The man still had honor. He finally listened to his heart." Saito looked at the family seated across from him. A lovely young woman with dark hair rocked her infant son in her arms. "I am so tired, Susan."

"Then sleep. Just sleep."

Saito closed his eyes and drifted off. And he dreamed of the sea.

EPILOGUE

"Dear Sensei Colletti:

I would be honored if you would look after things for me at the dojo after I have joined my ancestors. The rent is paid for the next three years so the dojo is secure with the landlord. I ask only that you teach others as I have taught you. Our ancient art lives through people and so it must be passed on to others. It must be given away.

I do not have much money, but I have decided to leave what I have to your son and Susan's brother so that their lives might be a little better.

I ask that you perform one other duty for me . . ."

Tony Colletti stood in the water of Minamata Bay, holding a cup containing the ashes of Akinori Saito. Minamata was warm and beautiful and the lush landscape was framed perfectly by the deep blue sky. The men from the village wore black suits and ties. The women wore beautiful white kimonos. Anne and Susan wore white kimonos too.

Tony thought of all the wisdom that Saito had given to him and so many others. He recalled their conversation about Minamata and the words Saito said that night came back to him: "The only way to understand suffering and not be defeated by it is through service to others."

Tony realized this was the true lesson of the Autism War—and Minamata.

But there was one last lesson that Saito wanted to impart.

The Shinto priest began a rhythmic chant of prayers that ended with him clapping his hands vigorously together to invoke the spirits of the ancestors. A delightful breeze stirred the trees and rippled across the water. The priest looked at Tony and nodded. It was time to return Saito to the sea.

And so he emptied his cup.

ACKNOWLEDGMENTS

This work could never have been completed without the encouragement of Mary Holland, the guidance of my editor, Steve Price, and the courage of Tony Lyons. I also owe much to the input of Anne Dachel and Teri Arranga.

I would be remiss if I didn't thank my fellow coauthors—Mary Holland, Robert Krakow, and Lisa Colin—of "Unanswered Questions from the Vaccine Injury Compensation Program: A Review of Compensated Cases of Vaccine-Induced Brain Injury" (*Pace Environmental Law Review,* May 10, 2011). I also want to thank all of the people who worked with us on the project that led to the publication—John Gilmore, Lisa Rudley, and so many others. I must acknowledge Ed and Joyce Alger, Debbie Fields, Sue Leteure, and Sarah Bridges for having the courage to speak out.

I've been blessed to work at the Westchester County Probation Department—the best in the business. I hope my respect for our mission shows in this work.

Thank you for all those who have instructed me in the martial arts over the years. This book would never have been possible without your wisdom.